Little Novels of Italy

LITTLE NOVELS OF ITALY

Maurice Hewlett

Ginger Classics

United States
1899

CONTENTS

MADONNA OF THE PEACH~TREE

I

VANNA IS BID FOR

Not easily would you have found a girl more winning in a tender sort than Giovanna Scarpa of Verona at one and twenty, fair-haired and flushed, delicately shaped, tall and pliant, as she then was. She had to suffer her hours of ill report, but passes for near a saint now, in consequence of certain miracles and theophanies done on her account, which it is my business to declare; before those she was considered (if at all) as a girl who would certainly have been married three years ago if dowries had not been of moment in the matter. In a city of maids as pretty as they are modest— which no one will deny Verona to be— there may have been some whose charms in either kind were equal to hers, while their estate was better in accord; but the speculation is idle. Giovanna, flower in the face as she was, fit to be nosegay on any hearth, posy for any man's breast, sprang in a very lowly soil. Like a blossoming reed she shot up to her inches by Adige, and one forgot the muddy bed wondering at the slim grace of the shaft with its crown of yellow atop. Her hair waved about her like a flag; she should have been planted in a castle; instead, Giovanna the stately calm, with her billowing line, staid lips, and candid grey eyes, was to be seen on her knees by the green water most days of the week. Bare-armed, splashed to the neck, bare-headed, out-at-heels, she rinsed and pommelled, wrung and dipped again, laughed, chattered, flung her hair to the wind, her sweat to the water, in line with a dozen other women below the Ponte Navi; and if no one thought any the worse of her, none, unhappily, thought any the better— at least in the way of marriage. It is probable that no one thought of her at all. Giovanna was a beauty and a very good girl; but she was a washerwoman for all that, whose toil fed seven mouths.

Her father was Don Urbano, curate of Santa Toscana across the water. This may very easily sound worse than it is. In Don Urbano's day, though a priest might not marry, he might have a wife— a faithful, diligent companion, that is— to seethe his polenta, air his linen, and rear his children. The Church winked at her, and so continued until the Jesuits came to teach that winking was unbecoming. But when Can Grande II. lorded in Verona the Jesuits did not, and Don Urbano, good, easy man, cared not who winked at his wife. She gave him six

- 1 -

children before she died of the seventh, of whom the eldest was Giovanna, and the others, in an orderly chain diminishing punctually by a year, ran down to Ferrantino, a tattered, shock-headed rascal of more inches than grace. Last of all the good drudge, who had borne these and many other burdens for her master, died also. Don Urbano was never tired of saying how providential it was that she had held off her demise until Giovanna was old enough to take her place. The curate was fat and lazy, very much interested in himself; his stipend barely paid his shot at the "Fiore del Marinajo," under whose green bush he was mostly to be seen. Vanna had to roll up her sleeves, bend her straight young back, and knee the board by the Ponte Navi. I have no doubt it did her good; the work is healthy, the air, the sun, the water-spray kissed her beauty ripe; but she got no husband because she could save no dowry. Everything went to stay the seven crying mouths.

Then, on a day when half her twenty-first year had run after the others, old Baldassare Dardicozzo stayed on the bridge to rest from the burden of his pack— on a breezy March morning when the dust filled his eyes and the wind emptied him of breath. Baldassare had little enough to spare as it was. So he dropped his load in the angle of the bridge, with a smothered "Accidente!" or some such, and leaned to watch the swollen water buffeted crosswise by the gusts, or how the little mills amid-stream dipped as they swam breasting the waves. In so doing he became aware, in quite a peculiar way, of Vanna Scarpa.

Baldassare was old, red-eyed, stiff in the back. Possibly he was rheumatic, certainly he was grumpy. He had a long slit mouth which played him a cruel trick; for by nature it smiled when by nature he was most melancholy. Smile it would and did, however cut-throat he felt: if you wanted to see him grin from ear to ear you would wait till he had had an ill day's market. Then, while sighs, curses, invocations of the saints, or open hints to the devil came roaring from him, that hilarious mouth of his invited you to share delights. You had needs laugh with him, and he, cursing high and low, beamed all over his face. "To make Baldassare laugh" became a stock periphrasis for the supreme degree of tragedy among his neighbours. About this traitor mouth of his he had a dew of scrubby beard, silvered black; he had bushy eyebrows, hands and arms covered with a black pelt: he was a very hairy man. Also he was a very warm man, as everybody knew, with a hoard of florins under the flags of his old-clothes shop in the Via Stella.

Having spat into the water many times, rubbed his hands, mopped his head, and cursed most things under heaven and some in it, Master Baldassare found himself watching the laundresses on the shore. They were the usual shrill, shrewd, and laughing line— the trade seems to induce high mirth— and as such no bait for the old merchant by ordinary; but just now the sun and breeze together made a bright patch of them, set them at a provoking flutter. Baldassare, prickly with dust, found them like their own cool linen hung out to dance itself dry in the wind. Most of all he noticed Vanna, whom he knew well enough, because when she knelt upright she was taller and more wayward than the rest, and because the wind made so plain the pretty figure she had. She was very industrious, but no less full of talk: there seemed so much to say! The pauses were frequent in which she straightened herself from the hips and turned to thrust chin and voice into the debate. You saw then the sharp angle, the fine line of light along that raised chin, the charming turn of the neck, her free young shoulders and shapely head; also you marked her lively tones of *ci* and *si*, and how her shaking finger drove them home. The wind would catch her yellow hair sometimes and wind it across her bosom like a scarf; or it streamed sideways like a long pennon; or being caught by a gust from below, sprayed out like a cloud of litten gold. Vanna always joined in the laugh at her mishap, tossed her tresses back, pinned them up (both hands at the business); and then, with square shoulders and elbows stiff as rods, set to working the dirt out of Don Urbano's surplice. Baldassare brooded, chewing straws. What a clear colour that girl had, to be sure! What a lissom rascal it was! A fine long girl like that should be married; by all accounts she would make a man a good wife. If he were a dozen years the better of four and fifty he might— Then came a shrug, and a "Ma!" to conclude in true Veronese Baldassare's ruminations. Shrug and explosion signalled two stark facts: Baldassare was fifty-four, and Vanna had no portion.

Yet he remained watching on the bridge, his chin buried in his knotty hands, his little eyes blinking under stress of the inner fire he had. So it befell that La Testolina saw him, and said something shrill and saucy to her neighbour. The wind tossed him the tone but not the sense. He saw the joke run crackling down the line, all heads look brightly up. The joke caught fire; he saw the sun-gleam on a dozen perfect sets of teeth. Vanna's head was up with the rest, sooner up and the sooner down. Even from that height the little twinkling beacons from the bridge shot her through. He saw her colour deepen, head droop; she was busy long before the others had wrung their joke dry. "Soul of a cat!" grunted Baldassare between his teeth, "what a rosy baggage it is!" He waited a little longer, then deliberately passed the bridge, rounded the pillar by the steps, and went down to the women like a man who has made up his mind. Lizabetta of the roving eye caught the first hint of his shadow. Her elbow to Nonna's ribs, Nonna's "Pst!" in Nina's ear, spread the news. Vanna's cheeks flew the flag.

"Buon' giorno, Ser Baldassare!" shrilled La Testolina, plump and black-eyed leader of mischief.

"Giorno, giorno, La Testolina," growled the old man.

Vanna, very busy, grew as red as a rose. The others knelt back on their heels; compliments of a homely sort flew about, sped on by flashing teeth. Baldassare's own were black as old channel-posts in the Lagoon, but in tongue-work he gave as sharp as he got. Then a wicked wind blew Vanna's hair like a whip across her throat, fit to strangle her. She had to face the day. Baldassare pondered her straight young back.

"When Vanna's a nun she'll have no more trouble with her hair," quoth La Testolina, matchmaker by race.

"When Vanna's a nun the river will be dry," said Vanna from between her elbows.

"When Vanna's a nun the river, on the contrary, will be in flood." This from Baldassare.

"Hey! what's this?" Caterina cried; and Nonna pinched her arm.

"Adige will go crying that she comes no more to dip her arms," said the old man, with the utmost gravity and a broad grin. The women screamed their delight, slapped their knees, or raised witnessing hands to heaven; La Testolina caught Vanna round the waist and gave her a resounding kiss.

"Compliments, my little Vanna, compliments!" Her voice pealed like a trumpet.

"Vi ringrazio, signore," said Vanna under her breath, and La Testolina held up a tress of her long hair to the light.

"When Vanna's a nun you would bid for that, eh, Baldassare?"

"I will bid for whatever she will sell me," says he, with a blink. Whereupon the matchmaker made no more music. The scent was too hot for that.

Yet for all his adventuring he got little reward; she turned him no more than the round of her cheek. Vanna never stayed her work, and he, ordinarily a silent man, paid no more compliments— yet ceased not to look.

Going up the street at dinner-time, he made his bid. He limped by the tall girl's side without speech from either; but at the door he looked up queerly at her and pinched her ear.

"Go in and feed the youngsters, my chuck," said he; "I know where to meet Don Urbano, and please Madonna you shall feed your own before long."

"Yes, Ser Baldassare," says pretty Vanna in a twitter.

The conference between the high contracting parties was wordy, bristled with the gesticulations of two pair of hands, and was commented on by all the guests in the "Fiore del Marinajo." The girl, said Don Urbano, was the very pride of his eye, prop of his failing years, a little mother to the children. She had had a most pious bringing-up, never missed the Rosary, knew the Little Hours of the Virgin, could do sums with notches in a stick, market like a Jew's housekeeper, sew like a nun, and make a stew against any wife in the *contrada*. Dowry, dowry! What did such a girl as that want with a dowry? She was her own dowry, by Bacchus the Thracian. Look at the shape of her— was that not a dowry? The work she could do, the pair of shoulders, the deep chest, the long legs she had— pick your dowry there, my friends! A young woman of her sort carried her dowry on her back, in her two hands, in her mouth— ah! and in what she could put into yours, by our Lord. Rather, it should be the other way. What, now, was Ser Baldassare prepared to lay out upon such a piece of goods? Baldassare shivered, grinned fearfully, and shook his head many times. Money was money; it was limited; it bore its value in plain figures upon its face: you knew where you were with money. But you could get wives cheaper than ducats, and find them cheaper value, soul of a cat! Besides, what was he? A poor pedlar, by his faith! At this he spread out his arms and dropped them with a flop upon his knees. The priest sat back in his chair and cast appealing looks at the rafters; the company chuckled, nudged each other, guffawed. Baldassare was made to feel that he had over-coloured his case. True, he admitted, he had a roof over his head, shared fortune with the rats in that. But look at the thing reasonably, comrades. Vanna would make another to keep; a girl of her inches must be an eater, body of a dog! Had his reverence thought of that? His reverence made a supreme effort, held up one pudgy forefinger, and with the other marked off two joints of it. "Of mortadella so much," he said; "of polenta so much"— and he shut one fist; "of pasta so much"— and he coupled the two fists; "and of wine, by the soul of the world, not enough to drown a flea! I tell you, Baldassare," he said finally, emboldened by the merchant's growing doubt— "I tell you that you ask of me a treasure which I would not part with for a cardinal's hat. No indeed! Not to be Bishop of Verona, throned and purfled on Can Grande's right hand, will I consent to traffic my Vanna.

Eh, *sangue di Sangue*, because I am a man of the Church must I cease to be a man of bowels, to have a yearning, a tender spot here?" He prodded his cushioned ribs. "Go you, Ser Baldassare Dardicozzo," he cried, rising grandly in his chair— "go you; you have mistaken your man. The father stands up superb in the curate's cassock, and points the door to the chafferer of virgins!"

he tavern-room, on Don Urbano's side to a man, beat the tables with their glasses; Baldassare had to surrender at discretion. The bargain, finally struck, was written out by an obliging notary on the scoring-slate. In the name of the holy and undivided Trinity it was declared to all men living and to be born, that Baldassare Dardicozzo, merchant of Verona, was obliged to pay to the reverend father in God, Urbano, curate of Santa Toscana in the Borgo San Giorgio, the sum of sixty florins Veronese and two barrels of wine of Val Pulicella, under condition that if within thirty days from those presents he did not lead in marriage Giovanna, daughter of the said reverend, he should be bound to pay the sum of one hundred and twenty florins Veronese, and four barrels of wine of Val Pulicella.

The notary executed a monstrous flourish at the bottom— a foliated cross rising out of steps. On the last step he wrote his own name, Bartolo de Thomasinis; and then Baldassare, smiling as he should, but feeling as he should not, stuck his seal upon the swimming wax, and made a cross with the stile like the foundations of a spider's web.

The affair was thus concluded; before the thirty days were up Vanna was taken to church by her father, and taken from it by her new master. Within a week she appeared at the doorway of Baldassare's little shop, very pretty, very sedate, quite the housewife— to sit there sewing and singing to herself from grey dawn to grey dusk.

II

TERTIUM QUID

A year passed, two years passed. Vanna was three and twenty, no more round but no less blooming in face and figure; still a reedy, golden-haired girl. But Baldassare was fifty-seven, and there was no sign of issue. The neighbours, who had nudged each other at one season, whose heads had wagged as their winks flew about, now accepted the sterile mating as of the order of things. Pretty Vanna, mother as she had been to her brothers and sisters, was to be a mother no more. There was talk of May and December. Baldassare was advised to lock up other treasure beside his florins; some, indeed, of the opposite camp gave hints none too honest to the forlorn young wife. The Piazza Sant' Anastasia at the falling-in of the day, for instance. Thus they put it. All girls— and what else was Vanna, a wife in name?— walked there arm in arm. Others walked there also, she must know. By-and-by some pretty lad, an archer, perhaps, from the palace, some roistering blade of a gentleman's lackey, a friar or twinkling monk out for a frolic, came along with an "Eh, la bellina!" and then there was another arm at work. So, for one, whispered La Testolina, dipping a head full of confidence and mystery close to Vanna's as the girl sat working out the summer twilight. The Via Stella was narrow and gloomy. The tall houses nearly met in that close way. Looking up you saw the two jagged edges of the eaves, like great tattered wings spread towards each other. When the green sky of evening deepened to blue, and blue grew violet, these shadowing wings were always in advance, more densely dark. There it was that Vanna worked incessantly, sewing seam after seam, patching, braiding, and fitting the pieces. By no chance at all did a hint of the sun fall about her; yet she always sang softly to herself, always wore her pretty fresh colours, and still showed the gold sheen in her yellow hair. Her hair was put up now, pulled smoothly back over her temples; she spoke in a low, sober, measured voice, and to La Testolina's sly suggestions responded with a little blush, a little shake of the head, and a very little sigh. "Ser Baldassare is good to me," she would say; "would you have me do him a wrong? Last Friday he gave me a silver piece to spend in whatsoever I chose. I bought a little holy-water stoup with a Gesulino upon it, bowered in roses. On Sunday morning he patted my cheek and called me a good girl. To say nothing of the many times he has pinched my ear, all this was very kind, as you must see. With what do you ask me to reward him? Fie!" La Testolina snorted, and shrugged herself away. Vanna went on with her sewing and her little song— —

"Giovanottin, che te ne vai di fuora,
Stattene allegro, e così vo' far io.
Se ti trovassi qualche dama nuova,
L'ha da saper che tua dama son io."

So sang she, innocently enough, whose sweethearting went no farther than her artless lips. There was not a spice of mischief in the girl. What she had told La Testolina had been no more than the truth: Master Baldassare was good to her— better than you would have believed possible in such a crabbed old stub of a man. He was more of a father to her than ever Don Urbano had been to anything save his own belly; but it was incontestable that he was not father to anything else. That alone might have been a grievance for Vanna, but there is no evidence that it was. Baldassare was by nature gruff, by habit close-fisted: like all such men, the more he felt the deeper he hoarded the thought under his ribs. The most he would venture would be a hand on her hair and a grunt when she did well; so sure as she looked up gratefully at him the old man drew off, with puckered brows and jaws working together. He may have been ashamed of his weakness; it is dead certain that no one in Verona, least of all Vanna herself, suspected him of any affection for his young wife. Mostly he was silent; thus she became silent too whenever he was in the house. This was against nature, for by ordinary her little songs bubbled from her like a bird's. But to see him so glum and staring within doors awed her: she set a finger to her lips as she felt the tune on her tongue, and went about her business mute. Baldassare would go abroad, stooping under his pack: she took her seat at the shop-door, threaded her needle, her fingers flew and her fancy with them. The spring of her music was touched, and all the neighbours grew to listen for the gentle cadences she made.

So passed a year, so two years passed. Vanna was twenty-three, looking less, when along there came one morning a tall young friar, a Carmelite, by name Fra Battista, with a pair of brown dove's eyes in his smooth face. These he lifted towards Vanna's with an air so timid and so penetrating, so delicate and hardy at once, that when he was gone it was to leave her with the falter of a verse in her mouth, two hot cheeks, and a quicker heart.

This Fra Battista, by birth a Bergamask, accredited to the convent at Verona by reason of his parts as a preacher, was tall and shapely, like a spoilt pretty boy to look at, leggy, and soft in the palm. His frock set off this petted appearance— it gave you the idea of a pinafore on him.

He did not look manly, was not manly by any means, and yet not so girlish but that you could doubt his sex. His eyes, which, as I say, were soft as a dove's pair, he was not fond of showing; and this gave them the more searching appeal when he did. His mouth, full and fleshy in the lips, had a lovely curve. He kept it very demure, and, when he spoke, spoke softly. This was a young man born to be Lancilotto to some Ginevra or other; and, to do him justice, he had had his share of adventure in that sort at an early age. He had learned more out of Ovid than from the Fathers of Divinity, you may believe. Very popular he was in whatsoever convent he harboured, as a preacher famous all over Lombardy and the March,— in Bergamo, in Brescia, even as far as Mantua he had been heard of. The superior at Verona did his best to spoil him by endearment, flattery, and indulgence; but this was difficult, since he had been spoilt already.

He passed down the Via Stella morning and evening for a week. Morning and evening his eyes encountered Vanna's. The third evening he smiled at her, the fourth morning he saluted her; the fifth evening he stopped and slipped in a gentle word; the first evening of the second week he stopped again, and that night, La Testolina being by, there was quite a little conversation.

La Testolina had black eyes, a trim figure, and a way of wriggling which showed these to advantage. Fra Battista's fame and the possibility of mischief set her flashing; she led the talk and found him apt: it was not difficult to aim every word that it should go through and leave a dart in Vanna's timid breast. The girl was so artless, you could see her quiver, or feel her, at every shot. For instance, was his sanctity very much fatigued by yesterday's sermon? *Eh, la bella predica!* What invocations of the saints, what heart-groping, what reachings after the better parts of women! It was some comfort to know that a woman had a better part at all— by the Saviour! for their handling by men gave no hint of it. Let Fra Beato— ah, pardon, Fra Battista she should have said— send some such arrows into men's hides! See them, for the gross-feeding, surly, spend-all, take-all knaves that they were! One or two she might name if she had a mind— ah! one or two in this very city of Verona, in this very Street of the Star, who— But there! Vanna must go and hear the Frate's next sermon, she must indeed. And if she could take her old curm— Pshutt! What was she saying? How she ran on! She did indeed. Fra Battista, leaning against the lintel, kept his eyelids on the droop, seemed to find his toes of interest. But now and again he would look delicately up, and so sure as he did the brown eyes and the grey seemed to swim towards each other, to melt in a point, swirl in an eddy of the feelings, in which Vanna found herself drowning and found such death sweet. La Testolina still ran on, but now in a monologue. Fra Battista looked and longed, and Vanna looked again and thrilled. It grew quite dark; nothing of each other could they see and little know, until the friar put out his foot and found Vanna's. A tremor, beginning at her heart, ran down to her toes; Battista felt the flutter of it and was assured.

When he left her that night he kissed her cold hand, then La Testolina's, which he found by no means cold, and moved off leisurely towards the Piazza dell' Erbe. Neither woman spoke for a while: La Testolina was picking at her apron, Vanna sat quietly in the dark holding her heart. She was still in a tremble, so ridiculously moved that when her friend kissed her she burst out crying. La Testolina went nodding away; and the end of the episode may be predicted. Not at one but at many sermons of the tall Carmelite did Vanna sit rapt; not for one but for every dusk did he stoop to kiss her hand. All Verona saw her devotion,— all Verona, that is, but one old Veronese. The essence of comedy being that the spectators shall chuckle at actors in a fog, here was a comedy indeed.

III

THE SEED OF DISCORD

When Vanna announced her condition the neighbours looked slyly at each other; when her condition announced Vanna, they chattered; the gossip sank to whispering behind the hand as time went on, and ceased altogether when the baby was born. That was a signal for heads to shake. Some pitied the father, many defended the mother: it did not depend upon your sex; sides were taken freely and voices were shrill when neither was by. Down by the river especially, upon that bleached board below the bridge, *ci* and *si* whistled like the wind in the chimneys, and the hands of testimony were as the aspen leaves when storms are in. Some took one side, some another; but when, in due season, it was seen what inordinate pride Baldassare had in the black-eyed *bambino* there was no question of sides. He had ranked himself with the unforgivable party: the old man was an old fool, a gull whose power of swallow stirred disgust. Vanna had the rights of it, they said; such men were made to be tricked. As for Fra Battista's pulpit, it was thronged about with upturned faces; for those who had not been before went now to judge what they would have done under the circumstances. Having been, there were no two opinions about that. Messer Gabriele Arcangelo, some said, judging by the honey-tongue; San Bastiano, others considered him, who went by his comely proportions; and these gained the day, since his beardless face and friar's frock induced the idea of innocence, which Sebastian's virgin bloom also taught. The quality of his sermons did not grow threadbare under this adventitious criticism: he kept a serene front, lost no authority, nor failed of any unction. There was always a file at his confessional; and at Corpus Christi, when in the pageant he actually figured as Sebastian, his plump round limbs roped to a pine-stock drew tears from all eyes.

Unhappily you have to pay for your successes. There were other preachers in Verona, and other eloquent preachers who, being honest men, had had to depend upon their eloquence. These were the enemy— Franciscans, of course, and Dominicans— who got wind of something amiss, and began to nose for a scandal. What they got gave them something besides eloquence to lean on: there were now other sermons than young Fra Battista's, and the moral his person pointed had a double edge. In fact, where he pointed with his person, the Dominicans pointed with their sharp tongues. The Franciscans, more homely, pointed with their fingers. Fra Battista began to be notorious— a thing widely different from fame; he also began to be uncomfortable, and his superior with him. They talked it over in the cloister, walking up and down together in the cool of the day. "It has an ugly look, my dear," said the provincial; "send the young woman to me."

What of the young woman, meantime? Let me tell the truth: motherhood became her so well that she was brazen from the very beginning. No delicacy, no pretty shame, no shrinking— she gloried in the growing fact. When she was brought to bed she made a quick recovery; she insisted upon a devout churching, an elaborate christening of the doubtful son (whereat, if you will believe me, no other than Fra Battista himself must do the office!); thenceforth she was never seen without her *bimbo*. While she worked it lay at her feet or across her knee like a stout chrysalis; the breast was ever at its service, pillow or fount; when it slept she lifted up a finger or her grave eyes at the very passers-by; her lips moulded a "Hush!" at them lest they should dare disturb her young lord's rest. The saucy jade! Was ever such impudence in the world before? It drew her, too, to old Baldassare in a remarkable way. This the neighbours— busy with sniffing— did not see. She had always had a sense of the sweet root under the rind, always purred at his stray grunts and pats, taking them by instinct for what they were really worth; and now to watch his new delight filled her with gratitude— and more, she felt free to love the man. For one thing, it unlocked his lips and hers. She could sing about the house since Cola had come— they had christened him after good Saint Nicholas— because Master Baldassare was so talkative on his account. The old man sat at home whenever he could, in his shiny armchair, his cup of black wine by his side, and watched Vanna with the baby by the hour together, poring over every downward turn of her pretty head, every pass of her fingers, every little eager striving of the sucking child. There were, indeed, no bounds to his content: to be a father— poor old soul!— seemed to him the most glorious position in the world. Can Grande II. in the judgment-seat, the bishop stalled in his throne, the Holy Father himself in the golden chambers of his castle at Avignon, had nothing to offer Ser Baldassare Dardicozzo, the old-clothes man.

Though the neighbours knew nothing of this inner peace, they could not deny that Monna Vanna, brazen or no, was mightily become by her new dignity or (as you should say) indignity. She was more staid, more majestic; but no less the tall, swaying, crowned girl she had ever been. She was seen, without doubt, for a splendid young woman. The heavy child seemed not to drag her down, nor the slant looks of respectable citizens, her neighbours, to lower her head. She met them with level eyes quite candid, and a smiling mouth to all appearance pure. When she found they would not discuss her riches, she talked of theirs. When she found them over-satisfied with their children, she laughed quietly as one who knew better. This was a thing to take away a woman's breath, that she should grow the more glorious for her shame. Party feeling had been stormy, like crossing tides, between those who held Baldassare for a gull and those who resented Vanna's unruffled brows. But now there was but one party. It was very well to hoodwink an old skinflint; but, by the Mass, not honest to flaunt your methods in the world's face. And since our own dignity is the skin upon which we rely for all our protection, while contempt for our neighbours is but a grease we put upon it for its ease, it was self-defence which brought it about that the party against Vanna grew ominously large, while Baldassare gained quite a host of sympathizers. The girl was now shunned, ostentatiously, carefully shunned. Even La Testolina was shy of her. But, bless you, she saw nothing of it— or cared nothing. She chattered to her grossly deceived husband, went (nominally, you may be sure!) confessing to the grossly deceiving friar, she cooed to her baby, warbled her little songs, looked handsome, carried herself nobly, as if she were the Blessed Virgin herself, no less. This could not be endured: a thousand tongues were ready to shoot at her, and would have shot but for fear of old Baldassare's grim member— reputed forked. While he was in the way, fat-headed fool, there was no moral glow to be won by a timely word. The tongues lay itching; two or three barren women in the Via Stella were hoarding stones.

Then, just about the time when the prior of the Carmelites bid Fra Battista send him the young woman, Baldassare took the road for a round of chaffer which might keep him out of Verona a week. The Via Stella felt, and Fra Battista knew, that the chance had come.

IV

THE HARVEST OF LITTLE EASE

Verona, stormy centre of strife, whose scarred grey face still wears a blush when viewed from the ramp of the Giusti garden, was in those times a place of short and little ease. The swords were never rusty. A warning clang from the belfry, two or three harsh strokes, the tall houses disgorged, the streets packed; Capulet faced Montague, Bevilacqua caught Ridolfi by the throat, and Della Scala sitting in his hall knew that he must do murder if he would live a prince. It seems odd that the suckling of a little shopkeeper should lead to such issues; but so it was. And thus it was.

On the morning of Baldassare's setting-out for the Mantuan road, La Testolina— at that time much and unhealthily in Fra Battista's hire— came breathless to the Via Stella. Craning her quick head round the door-post, she saw Vanna sitting all in cool white (for the weather was at the top of summer), stooped over her baby, happy and calm as always, and fingering her breast that she might give the little tyrant ease of his drink. That baby was a glutton. "Hist, Vanna, hist!" La Testolina whispered; and Vanna looked up at her with a guarded smile, as who should say, "Speak softer, my dear, lest Cola should strangle in his swallow."

But La Testolina's eyes were like pin-points, centring all her alarms.

"You must come to the Carmelites, Vanna. There is a great to-do. The warden of San Francesco has been to the bishop, and the bishop is with Can Grande at this moment. You must come, indeed, at once— *subitissimo!*"

Vanna laughed— the rich quiet laugh of a girl whose affairs are in good train, and all other affairs the scratch of a flea.

"Why, what have I to do with the bishop and Can Grande, La Testolina?" says she. "My master is out, and I must mind the shop. There is baby too."

"By Saints Pan and Silvanus, my girl, it will be the worse for you if you come not," said La Testolina, with a tragic sniff. "Eh, you little fool, don't you know that it is you and your brat have set all Verona by the ears?"

Vanna had never thought of the ears of Verona, and knew not how to think of them now; but she saw that her friend was in a fever of suppressed knowledge. Therefore she shawled her head and her baby in her sea-blue cloak, locked the shop-door, and followed La Testolina.

The sealed gates in the white convent wall were barred and double-locked. A scared brother cocked his eye through the grille to see who was there.

"It is she," hissed La Testolina.

"*Dio mio*, the *causa causans*!" cried he, and let them in through a cranny. "Follow me, mistresses, and God give good ending to this adventure," he prayed, as he slippered up the court.

Vanna, blank and smiling, La Testolina with wandering, fearful eyes, followed.

They found the prior sitting well back in his ebony chair and in meditation, his chin buried in his hand. Behind him (and behind his back his hands) was Fra Corinto the pittanciar, pockmarked, thin, and mortified. He looked the prior's reproach, and was.

"Now, women," said the prior, testily— a fat and flabby old man with a sour mouth— "now, women, which of you is at the bottom of this accursed business? Where is the baby? Let me judge for myself."

La Testolina, protesting her remarkable innocence by every quiver of her head, edged Vanna to the front. Vanna stood up, straight as a candle, and unveiled her bosom.

"Do you want to see my little son, reverend prior?" she said. "Behold him here (*Eccololì*)." She held him out proudly in her arms, as if he were monstrance and she priest.

Now whether it was that motherhood had fired a comely girl with the beautiful seriousness of a woman, so that she was transfigured before him; or whether some chance passage of the crossing lights played tricks with his vision— which it was, or whether it was both, I know not. He saw, or thought he saw, a tall, smiling lady, hooded in blue over white, holding up a child; he saw, or thought for a moment that he saw, the Image of all Mothers displaying the Image of all Sons. His fingers pattered over his scapular. "Eh, my Lady the Virgin! What dost thou here, glorifying this place?" As soon as he had said it he might have known that he was a fool; but Vanna's large grey eyes loomed upon him to swallow him up, her colour of faint rose glowed over him and throbbed. *Vera incessu patuit dea!* "By her presence ye shall judge her," quoth the prior to himself, and hid his eyes.

There was a hush upon all the group in the chamber, during which you could have heard afar off the nasal discords of the brethren in choir droning through an office. No one spoke. The prior's lips moved at his prayers; Fra Corinto looked frowningly before him; La Testolina was fidgety to speak, but dared not; Vanna, her long form like a ripple of moonlight in the dusk, cooed under her voice to the baby; he, unheeding cause of so much strife in high places, held out his pair of puckered hands and crowed to the company. So with their thoughts: the prior thought he had seen the Holy Virgin; Fra Corinto thought the prior an old fool; La Testolina hoped his reverence had not the colic; and Vanna thought of nothing at all.

Fra Corinto it was (looking not for Madonna in a baggage), who, by discreetly coughing, brought his master back to his senses. The prior cleared his throat once or twice, looked at the young woman, and felt quite himself. Ridiculous what tricks a flicker of sunlight will play on the wisest of men!

"Monna Vanna," said he, "I have not brought you here to judge between you and my brother Battista, now at discipline in his cell. The flesh, which he should have tamed, has raised, it appears, a bruised head for one last spite. My brother was bitten, and my brother fell into sin. Whether, as of old, the tempter was the woman, it is sure that, as of old, the eater was a man. I will not condemn you unheard, lest I incur reproach in my turn. But our order is in peril; the enemy is abroad, with Envy, Hatred, and Malice barking on their leashes. What can the poor sheep do but scatter before the wolves? Fra Battista, his penance duly done, must leave Verona; and you, my sister, must do penance, that God be not mocked, nor the Veronese upraised to mock Him."

Of this solemn appeal, Vanna, to all seeming, understood not one word. True, she blushed a little, but that was because a prior was talking to her: her honest grey eyes were quite untroubled, her smile as tender as ever. She spoke as one deprecating temerity— that she should speak at all to so great a man— and by no means any judgment.

"I am only a poor girl, reverend prior," said she, "most ignorant and thick-witted. Pray, what have I and my baby to do with these high matters of Fra Battista's error?"

The prior grew angry. "Tush, my woman," he grunted, "I beg you to drop the artless. It is out of place here. Let me look at the youngster."

"Yes, yes, mistress, let us see the child," said Fra Corinto, who croaked like a nightingale in June.

Vanna moved forward on a light foot. "Willingly, reverend fathers," said she. "He is a fine child, they all say, and reputed the image of his father." A sublime utterance, full of humoursome matter, if it had been a time for humours.

But it was not. La Testolina could not contain her virtuous indignation— for who is so transcendently righteous as your rascal for once in the right?

"Hey, woman!" she cried shrilly, "what grossness is this? Do you think the whole city don't know about you?"

Vanna turned quivering. "And what is it that the whole city knows but does not say, if you please?"

The prior wagged helplessly his hands. Like Pilate, he would have washed off the business if he could. He looked at the two women. Eh, by the Lord! there would be a scene. But the whole thing was too impudent a fraud: there must be an end of it. He caught Fra Corinto's eyes and raised his brows. Fra Corinto was his jackal— here was his cue. He went swiftly to the door, set it open, came back and caught Vanna roughly by the shoulder. He turned her shocked face to the open door, and his dry voice grated horribly upon her ears.

"Out with you, piece!" was what he said; and Vanna reeled.

For a full minute she gaped at him for a meaning; his face taught the force of his words only too well. She sobbed, threw up her high head, bent it, like Jesus, for the cross, and fled.

The old porter leered by his open gates. "He! he! They are all outside," he chuckled— "Magpies and Dusty-hoods, Parvuses, Minors and Minims, Benets, and Austins, every cowl in Verona! Come along, my handsome girl, you must move briskish this day!"

She heard the hoarse muttering of the men, and, a worse poison for good ears, the shrill venom of the women. Out of the gates she blindly went, and all the pack opened their music upon her. Stones flew, but words flew faster and stuck more deep. The mob, as she blundered through the streets, shuffling, gasping, stumbling at her caught gown, dry-eyed, open-mouthed, panting her terror, her bewilderment, her shame and amaze— the mob, I say, dizzied about her like a cloud of wasps; yet they had in them what wasps have not— voices primed by hatred to bay her mad. There was no longer any doubt for her: the pittanciar's word (which had not been "piece") was tossed from pavement to pavement, from balcony to balcony, out at every open door, shot like slops from every leaning casement, and hissed in her ears as it flew. It was a mad race. The Franciscans tucked up their frocks and discarded stones, that they might run and shout the more freely. The Dominicans soon tired: their end was served. The cloistered orders were out of condition; the secular clergy came to weary of what was, after all, but a matter for the mendicants. The common people, however, had the game well in hand. They headed her off the narrow streets, where safety might have been, and kept her to the Lung' Adige. Round the great S the river makes she battled her blind way, trying for nothing, with wits for nothing, without hope, or understanding, or thought. She ran, a hunted woman, straight before her, and at last shook off the last of her pursuers by San Zeno. Stumbling headlong into a little pine-wood beyond the gates, she fell, swooned, and forgot.

It was near dark when she opened her loaded eyes— that is, there was no moon, but a great concourse of stars, which kept the night as a long time of dusk. The baby was awake, too, groping for food and whimpering a little. She sat up to supply him: though in that act her brain swam, it is probable the duty saved her. Fearing to faint again, she dared not allow herself to think; for children must be fed though their mothers are stoned from the gates. Vanna nursed him till he dropped asleep, and sat on with her thoughts and troubles. Happily for her, he had turned these to other roads than the Lung' Adige. She knew that if he was to be fed again she must feed also.

V

THE MIRACLE OF THE PEACH-TREE

Directly you were outside the Porta San Zeno the peach-trees began— acre by acre of bent trunks, whose long branches, tied at the top, took shapes of blown candle-flames: beyond these was an open waste of bents and juniper scrub, which afforded certain eatage for goats.

Here three herd-boys, Luca, Biagio, and Astorre, simple brown-skinned souls, watched their flocks all the summer night, sleeping, waking to play pranks with each other, whining endless doggerel, praying at every scare, and swearing at every reassurance. Simple puppyish folk though they were, Madonna of the Peach-Tree chose them to witness her epiphany.

It was a very still night, of wonderful star-shine, but without a moon. The stars were so thickly spread, so clear and hot, that there was light enough for the lads to see each other's faces, the rough shapes of each other. It was light enough to notice how the square belfry of San Zeno cut a wedge of black into the spangled blue vault. Sheer through the Milky Way it ploughed a broad furrow, which ended in a ragged edge. You would never have seen that if it had not been a clear night.

Still also it was. You heard the cropping of the goats, the jaws' champ when they chewed the crisp leaves; the flicker of the bats' wings. In the marsh, half a mile away, the chorus of frogs, when it swelled up, drowned all nearer noise; but when it broke off suddenly, those others resumed their hold upon the stillness. It was a breathless night of suspense. Anything might happen on such a night.

Luca, Biagio, and Astorre, under the spell of this marvellous night, lay on their stomachs alert for alarms. A heavy-wheeling white owl had come by with a swish, and Biagio had called aloud to Madonna in his agony. Astorre had crossed himself over and over again: this was the Angel of Death cruising abroad on the hunt for goats or goat-herds; but "No, no!" cried Luca, eldest of the three, "the wings are too short, friends. That is a fluffy new soul just let loose. She knows not the way, you see. Let us pray for her. There are devils abroad on such close nights as this."

Pray they did, with a will, "Ave Maria," "O maris Stella," and half the Paternoster, when Biagio burst into a guffaw, and gave Luca a push which sent Astorre down.

"Why, 'tis only a screech-owl, you fools!" he cried, though the sound of his own voice made him falter; "an old mouse-teaser," he went on in a much lower voice. "Who's afraid?"

A black and white cat making a pounce had sent hearts to mouths after this: though they found her out before they had got to "Dominus tecum," she left them all in a quiver. It had been a cat, but it might have been the devil. Then, before the bristles had folded down on their backs, they rose up again, and the hair of their heads became rigid as quills. Over the brow of a little hill, through the peach-trees (which bowed their spiry heads to her as she walked), came quietly a tall white Lady in a dark cloak. Hey! powers of earth and air, but this was not to be doubted! Evenly forward she came, without a footfall, without a rustle or the crackling of a twig, without so much as kneeing her skirt—stood before them so nearly that they saw the pale oval of her face, and said in a voice like a muffled bell, "I am hungry, my friends; have you any meat?" She had a face like the moon, and great round eyes; within her cloak, on the bosom of her white dress, she held a man-child. He, they passed their sacred word, lifted in his mother's arms and turned open-handed towards them. Luca, Biagio, and Astorre, goat-herds all and honest lads, fell on their faces with one accord; with one voice they cried, "Madonna, Madonna, Madonna! pray for us sinners!"

But again the Lady spoke in her gentle tones. "I am very hungry, and my child is hungry. Have you nothing to give me?" So then Luca kicked the prone Biagio, and Biagio's heel nicked Astorre on the shin. But it was Luca, as became the eldest, who got up first, all the same; and as soon as he was on his feet the others followed him. Luca took his cap off, Biagio saw the act and followed it. Astorre, who dared not lift his eyes, and was so busy making crosses on himself that he had no hands to spare, kept his on till Luca nudged Biagio, and Biagio cuffed him soundly, saying, "Uncover, cow-face."

Then Luca on his knees made an offering of cheese and black bread to the Lady. They saw the gleam of her white hand as she stretched it out to take the victual. That hand shone like agate in the dark. They saw her eat, sitting very straight and noble upon a tussock of bents. Astorre whispered to Biagio, Biagio consulted with Luca for a few anxious moments, and communicated again with Astorre. Astorre jumped up and scuttled away into the dark. Presently he came back, bearing something in his two hands. The three shock-heads inspected his burden; there was much whispering, some contention, almost a scuffle. The truth was, that Biagio wanted to take the thing from Astorre, and that Luca would not allow it. Luca was the eldest and wanted to take it himself. Astorre was in tears. "*Cristo amore!*" he blubbered, "you will spill the milk between you. I thought of it all by myself. Let go, Biagio; let go, Luca!" So they whispered and tussled, pulling three different ways. The Lady's voice broke over them like silver rain. "Let him who thought of the kind act give me the milk," she said; so young Astorre on his knees handed her the horn cup, and through the cracks of his fingers watched her drink every drop.

That done, the cup returned with a smile piercingly sweet, the Lady rose. Saints on thrones, how tall she was! "The *bimbo* will thank you for this to-morrow, as I do now," said she. "Goodnight, my friends, and may the good God have mercy upon all souls!" She turned to go the way she had come, but Astorre, covering his eyes with one hand, crept forward on three legs (as you might say) and plucked the hem of her robe up, and kissed it. She stooped to lay a hand upon his head. "Never kiss my robe, Astorre," said she— and how under Heaven did she know his name if she were not *what she was*?— "never kiss my robe, but get up and let me kiss you." Well of Truth! to think of it! Up gets Astorre, shaking like a nun in a fit, and the Lady bent over him and, as sure as you are you, kissed his forehead. Astorre told his village next day as they sat round him in a ring, and he on the wellhead as plain to be seen as this paper, that he felt at that moment as if two rose-leaves had dropped from heaven upon his forehead. Slowly then, very slowly and smoothly (as they report), did the Lady move away towards the peach-trees whence she had come. In the half light there was— for by this it was the hour before dawn— they saw her take a peach from one of the trees. She stayed to eat it. Then she walked over the crest of the orchard and disappeared. As soon as they dared, when the light had come, they looked for her over that same crest, but could see nothing whatever. With pale, serious faces the three youths regarded each other. There was no doubt as to what had happened— a miracle! a miracle!

With one consent then— since this was plainly a Church affair— they ran to their parish priest, Don Gasparo. He got the whole story at last; nothing could shake them; no detail was wanting. Thus it was: the Blessed Virgin, carrying in her arms the Santissimo Bambino Gesù, had come through the peach-trees, asked for and eaten of their food, prayed for them aloud to Messer Domeneddio himself, and kissed Astorre on the forehead. As they were on their knees, she walked away, stopped, took a peach, ate it, walked on, vanished— *ecco!* The curate rubbed his head, and tried another boy. Useless: the story was the same. Third boy, same story. He tucked up his cassock with decision, took his biretta and walking-staff, and said to the three goat-herds:—

"My lads, all this is matter of miracle. I do not deny its truth— God forbid it in a simple man such as I am. But I do certainly ask you to lead me to the scene of your labours."

The boys needed no second asking: off they all set. The curate went over every inch of the ground. Here lay Luca, Biagio, and Astorre; the belfry of San Zeno was in such and such a direction, the peach-trees in such and such. Good: there they were. What next? According to their account, Madonna had come thus and thus. The good curate bundled off to spy for footprints in the orchard. Marvel! there were none. This made him look very grave; for if she made no earthly footprints, she could have no earthly feet. Next he must see by what way she had gone. She left them kneeling here, said they, went towards the peach-garden, stayed by a certain tree (which they pointed out), plucked a peach from the very top of it— this they swore to, though the tree was near fourteen feet high— stood while she ate it, and went over the brow of the rising ground. Here was detail enough, it is to be hoped. The curate nosed it out like a slot-hound; he paced the track himself from the scrub to the peach-tree, and stood under this last gazing to its top, from there to its roots; he shook his head many times, stroked his chin a few: then with a broken cry he made a pounce and picked up— a peach-stone! After this to doubt would have been childish; as a fact he had no more than the boys.

"My children," said he, "we are here face to face with a great mystery. It is plain that Messer Domeneddio hath designs upon this hamlet, of which we, His worms, have no conception. You, my dear sons, He hath chosen to be workers for His purpose, which we cannot be very far wrong in supposing to be the building of an oratory or tabernacle to hold this unspeakable relic. That erection must be our immediate, anxious care. Meantime I will place the relic in the pyx of our Lady's altar, and mark the day in our calendar for perpetual remembrance. I shall not fail to communicate with his holiness the bishop. Who knows what may be the end of this?"

He was as good as his word. A procession was formed in no time— children carrying their rosaries and bunches of flowers, three banners, the whole village with a candle apiece; next Luca, Biagio, and Astorre with larger candles— half a pound weight each at the least; then four men to hold up a canopy, below which came the good curate himself with the relic on a cushion.

It was deposited with great reverence in the place devoted, having been drenched with incense. There was a solemn mass. After which things the curate thought himself at liberty to ruffle into Verona with his news.

VI

THE VISITATION OF THE GOLDEN FISH

When a beast of chase— hart-royal, bear, or wolf— has been bayed and broken up, the least worthy parts are thrown to the curs which always come in at the heels of the pack. So it is with a kingly seat: the best of the meats, after the great officers of the household have feasted, go to the dependants of these; the peelings and guttings, the scum and scour of the broth, are flung farther, to the parasites of the parasites, the ticks on ticks' backs. Round about the Castle of Verona, where Can Grande II. misused the justice which his forefathers had set up, lay the houses of his courtiers; beyond them the lodgings of the grooms; beyond them again, down to the river's brink, were the stews and cabins and unholy dens, whose office was to be lower than the lowest, that there might still be degrees for the gentlemen of gentlemen's gentlemen. And since even cockroaches must drink, in this fungus-bed of misery there flourished a rather infamous tavern by the sale of *vino nostrano*, black and sour, of certain sausages, black also and nameless, speckled with white lumps, and of other wares whom to name were to expose. This was the tavern of the Golden Fish.

On the evening of the day of the Translation of the Peach-stone, this tavern was full to suffocation. Stefano, the purple-faced host, in shirt and breeches, stood dealing the liquor from a tub. Two outlaws lay under the benches, partly for fear of a visit from the watch, partly because, having already fallen there once, they feared to fall there again if they rose. In one hand each held his knife, in the other his empty mug. Two ladies, intimates of theirs, Robaccia and Crucciacorda, sat immediately above them, with petticoats ready to make ambush the moment a staff should rattle at the door; round the table half a dozen shabby rogues bickered over their cards; Picagente, the hairy brigand, lay snoring across the threshold, and his dog on him; on a barrel in a corner a gigantic shepherd in leather, with bandaged legs and a patch over one eye, shut the other eye while he roared a hymn to Bacchus at the top stretch of his lungs. The oil-lamp flickered, flared, and gloomed, half drowned in the fumes of wine. A smell of wicked bodies, foul clothes, drink, and bad language made the air well-nigh solid. The hour was at the stroke of ten; outside the streets seemed asleep.

In the middle of the uproar Stefano the host looked up sharply, listening.

"Stop your devil's ferment, Malabocca!" he thundered at the shepherd; "stop it, or I'll split your crown."

       "Bacco trionfante,
       Amante e spumante,
       Evviva l'ubbriacchezza!"

roared Malabocca, screwing up his eye.

Stefano brought down a mug full of wine upon his pate, which gave him a red baptism.

"Mum, you blockhead, mum!" said his host "There is a stir outside the door I tell you!"

The shepherd grew sober in a moment.

There was a brief scramble in the room— then silence. The ladies' petticoats went farther than they were ever intended to go; Picagente rolled over and over till he reached cover under the table; the cards were hidden, all the players' heads buried in their elbows. Stefano blew out the light. Then they heard distinctly a fluttering knock at the door, timid but continuous.

Feigning a yawn, Stefano growled, "Who's there at this hour?"

The answer came in a woman's voice, saying, "Open, open, in the name of high God." It brought every head into the air again, but hushed every breath.

The shepherd broke the silence with a groan. He brought his hand splashing on to his wet head, then fell to his knees and began to confess his sins.

"My fault, my fault, my exceeding great fault! O Mary! O Jesus! *O nobis peccatoribus!*"

Thus the shepherd, voicing the suspicions of the rest. So he became their prophet as well as their priest. He towered in the room.

"I tell you, comrades, that the hour of our visitation is come. Not Can Grande and his hounds are hunting us this night; not the tumbril, the branding-irons, nor the cart's tail, are for us; but the pains of death, the fire eternal, the untirable worm, the trumpet of the Last Things! Who comes knocking in high God's name? Who saith 'Open'?— I will tell you: it is She who last night lit upon my village and my own sister's son. Eh! bodies of all dogs, what will become of us sinners?" Here the shepherd beat the drum of his breast as a signal before he fell flat on the floor.

From behind his wailful voice the gentle knocking was heard running on. It had never ceased; it was insistent! Crossing himself desperately, Stefano slid back the bolts, then paused, then turned the key, then paused again to breathe hard, his hand upon the latch. He threw his head forward with a gesture of abandonment to what must be, flung wide the door, and dropped upon his two knees.

Against a mild radiance, softer than any lamp could shed, was a tall shrouded woman's figure. They saw the round of her cloaked head, they saw the white stream of her under-robe run from a peak at her bosom in a broadening path to her feet. They saw the pure grey moon of her face, guessed by the dark rings where her eyes should be, watched with quicker awe the slow movement of her arms, lifted their own to what she held up, and to the running under-current of the two sobbing drabs muttered in one voice their remembered adoration.

The tall shepherd rose up by the help of the table, swayed and spoke. No one knew his voice again, hollow as it was like the sea-grumble.

"O Holiest, O Rose, O Stem of Sharon, O Tree of Carmel!" said he. "What wouldest thou with us sinners?"

And the woman at the door said, "My friends, I have no roof to my head; will you take me in? I am hungry; have you no meat for my child and me?"

The host in Stefano jogged the sinner to speak. "Surely, surely, sweet Lady! Surely, surely. I entreat your Graciousness to enter, to step in, to accommodate, to sit down, to be pleased to be easy, to— to— to— " inspiration failed him— "to sit down, in short," was his lame conclusion. His sweat (as he said next day) would have blinded any other man.

Through the backing ranks of the scared company— Robaccia leaning face to the wall, sobbing her heart out; Picagente, the hairy brigand, breathing short and hard; the shepherd, glorified, exalted, bursting with prophecy; two thieves at their prayers and a wanton taking the words from them— through such an assembly the Lady of the Peach-Tree (who else, pray?) walked to the table. A soft grey light from without filled the room; there was no need of a lamp, nor did any eye then on watch fail to see all that followed. Bread and wine were served by Stefano on bent knee; bread and wine (but sparingly) did the Lady eat from cup and platter. That cup, that platter, encased in gold leaves and crusted with turquoise, are to this day in the Treasury. Crutches have been cast before them, hearts innumerable burn about them. When she had finished she sat a little while with her white cheek against her hand, whispering words in an unknown tongue (they said, who knew no baby language) to the child on her lap. He lifted up a little hand, and, "Eh, my son, my son," she said, "wilt thou take of me?" Then she gave him the breast, while not a soul said anything but prayers for half an hour.

When the child slept the Lady folded up her dress, covered him with her cloak, and rose up in their midst.

"Only the poor love the poor," said she, in those low tones which all Verona came to know by heart, "and only they who have little to eat give to them that have less. My little son will bless you for your charity; and I, good friends, will pray my Master to reward you when He comes. *Addio, addio*, be with God."

Then she would have gone and left them crying had not Robaccia, the blowsy wench and good-for-naught, wailed aloud and caught her by the knees.

"Mother, mother, mother!" whimpered this hardy rascal, "bless me a little more than the others, a very little more! I am bad— eh, God, I am vile, enough!— but I will never let thee go save thou kiss me."

You could have heard the roomful of them catch breath together. Crucciacorda, the other woman, laughed horribly; the shepherd made a step forward to drag the slut away. But no! The light seemed to swell and grow towards that point where it threatens to be music, so charged with messages it is— it came undoubtedly from the heart of the Lady through her smile. For smile she did, as sweetly, as tenderly, as a breaking cloud. The sun of her smile was like a clean breath in the stivy den; and, behold, she took Robaccia by the hand and lifted her up, she encircled her with a mothering arm, and drew her close to her own breast. Her lips touched the bad girl's cheek, lingered for a moment there, wistfully withdrew; and Madonna of the Peach-Tree, none staying her now, went out into the dead street, and was seen no more of that company.

The sun at noon looked down upon Verona at peace, upon her citizens at their prayers. Never was such a scene in the stormy little city before. All the bells of all the churches pealed all day— with no lack of arms to pull them. Men and women ran to and fro kissing whom they met, with a "Save you, brother!" "Save you, sister! well met, well met!" The Grey Brethren, the Black Brethren, the White Brethren of Carmel, held hands, and confessed to each other as many sins as they had time to remember. Can Grande went unarmed about his own city, Bevilacqua unbarred his door, Giusti married his mistress, the bishop said his prayers. The cripples at the church doors had no need to whine. As for the tavern of the Golden Fish, it smelt of lavender and musk and bergamot the day through. At one time there were eight litters with their bearers, eleven stallions, trapped and emblazoned, held by eleven grooms in livery, outside its door. The ladies of the litters were in the room upon their knees; the knights of the horses, their great helmets on their backs, knelt in the kennel praying devoutly. The wail of "Dies Iræ" went down the Corso and up again, "Salve Regina" wavered over the sunny spaces of the Brà. In the amphitheatre, after an open-air mass, the Cardinal-Legate solemnly exposed the relics of last night's miracle, and a bodyguard of twenty noble youths, six chaplains, and a Benedictine abbot went to the suburb to escort into the city the curate with the Peach-stone. It was a glorious day, never to be forgotten in the annals of Verona. Charity and the open heart went side by side with compunction and the searching of the heart. Tears were shed and kissed away; kisses induced the fall of gentler tears. It might be stoutly questioned whether Verona held one unshriven soul, one sin unspoken, or one solace unawarded.

It might be reasonably questioned, yet it must be denied. Within the walls of the friars of Mount Carmel were two uneasy spirits. Fra Sulpicio, the fat prior, was extended face downwards before the high altar; Fra Battista, the eloquent preacher, chewed his thumb in his cell. The pittanciar, on the other hand, was of the common mind. He was ambling down the Via Leoni with Brother Patricio of the Capuchins on one arm and Brother Martino of the Dominicans on the other, singing "In Exitu Israel" like a choir-boy. But the prior, who had half believed before, was sobbing his contrition into the pavement, and Fra Battista was losing faith in himself, the only faith he had.

VII

LAST CONSIDERATIONS OF CAN GRANDE II

You are not to suppose that the spectacle of Verona garbed in a gown of innocence, singing hymns and weaving chaplets of lilies, was to go unnoticed by the ruling power. Can Grande II. was lord of Verona, a most atrocious rascal, and one of many; but, like his famous ancestor and namesake, he had a gibing tongue, which was evidence of a scrutiny tolerably cool of the shifts of human nature. Human nature, he had observed, must needs account to itself for itself. If it met with what it did not understand, it was prompt to state the problem in a phrase which it could not explain. The simplicity of the plan was as little to be denied as its convenience was obvious. It was thus that Can Grande II. understood the emotions of Verona; it was thus, indeed, that he himself, confronted with statements and an explanation which did not satisfy him, accounted to himself, like any mother's son of his lieges. He explained their explanation, but only by another inexplicable formula. The energy with which he expounded his own view to those about him betrayed, perhaps, a lurking uneasiness in the burly tyrant.

"Pooh, my good lord," said he to the bishop, who had come full of the day's doings and night's report, "don't you know your own flock better than this? Did you ever hear a man with a broken limb attribute his mishap to other than Domeneddio? However drunk he may have been, however absurdly in a hurry— act of God! If it thunder and lighten of a summer night, if it turn the milk— a judgment! Luckily Monsignore has broad shoulders by all accounts; *per Bacco!*— He had need. Now then, look at this case. A belated woman with a baby stumbles upon a company of shepherds all in the twittering dark. Hearts jump to mouths, flesh creeps, hairs stand tiptoe— Madonna, of course! Whom else could they call her, pray? They don't know the woman: name her they must. Well! Who is there they don't know whose name comes readiest to the tongue? Madonna, of course. Good: *Ecco Madonna!*"

This was very eloquently reasoned, but the bishop shook his head. "It was not a brace of goat-herds last night, Excellency, but a roomful of brigands and their trulls in the Golden Fish. The worst company in Verona, Excellency— the most brazen, the most case-hardened. But the story is the same from their mouths as from the lads'; not a detail is wanting; not one point gives the lie to another. Excellency, I would bow to your wit in any case but this. The affair is inexplicable short of a miracle."

Can Grande knit his black brows; he objected to be crossed, and the more so when he had a sneaking thought that he was rightly crossed.

"I should like to see my Lady this night with my own eyes, bishop," said he.

"Hey, Excellency," cried the other, "there are many devout souls in the same case."

Can Grande pished. "Devout jellyfish," he grunted; and then— "She seems to haunt one quarter, eh?"

"It is so, Excellency, save that yesterday she must have passed through the Porta San Zeno unseen of the guard."

"Have you interrogated the guard?" asked the tyrant, sharply.

"It was done, Highness. Nothing entered between Compline and Prime but a couple of bullock-carts and a cavalcade of merchants from Brescia."

"What was in the bullock-carts, bishop?"

"Birch-bark, Excellency, for the yards."

"H'm!" was all Can Grande had to say to this.

He changed the conversation. "I have had the warden of the Minorites and the provincial of the Dominicans here this morning," he said, "about that accursed business of the rag-picker's wife. It is another example of what I told you just now, that these people attribute what they cannot understand to persons they can only dream about. They put down the whole of your miracles to a special reward for their zeal in hounding down the Carmelite and his mistress. They want the order expelled; I think they would like the house razed and the church washed out with holy water, or Fra Battista's blood— the latter for choice. Now, I cannot pull down religious houses, lord of Verona though I be, because a herd of frightened peasants have gone capering over the city singing, 'Salve festa dies.' I must really do the parties the honour of an interview before I draw the sword. Let me be sure which back I am going to score before I begin to carve. You had better bring the prior and Fra Lancillotto-Battista to me, and if you can collect the young woman and her brat, so much the better."

"Alas! Excellency, I fear the young woman is in pieces," said the bishop. "She has never been heard of since the day of her expulsion."

The advice, however, was good, the judgment good enough; but before it could be followed a stroke more telling than any Can Grande's sword could have made was wrought by Madonna of the Peach-Tree.

On the night of that same day Can Grande was sitting in the palace with two chosen companions, as dare-devil as himself, waiting the hour of an assignation. It was about ten o'clock: at half-past the hour they were to go out cloaked into the streets, bent upon the lifting of a decent burgess's wife from her bed. Hence they were not in the castle, which is near San Zeno, but in the Della Scala Palace, in the very heart of the city. The two accomplices were Baldo Baldinanza, a grey villain, and young Francesco della Rocca Rossa. All three were armed with swords and daggers; the cloaks lay with the masks on the table. A servant came to the door, knocked, and waited. Can Grande, who (to be just) feared no eye upon his goings, shouted him into the room.

"Well, son of a pig," was his greeting, "and what is it now?"

The fellow, whose teeth chattered in his head, announced a veiled lady, very tall, who would not be denied. Baldinanza, grizzled and scarred as he was, took a quick breath and glanced at Rocca Rossa. The younger man was at no pains to conceal his emotions. His face ran the gamut from white to red, from red back again to white. It ended ashen. Neither looked at his master.

"Let her in," said Can Grande; and each noticed how laboriously he spoke.

The servant turned to obey: there in the doorway stood the Lady.

Tall enough she was, her head seemingly about a foot from the cross-beam of the door. She was cloaked from crown to foot; nothing but the oval of her face, colourless white with lips very wan, and a droop to them inexpressibly sad, showed out of the dark column she made. The servant shrank into the passage and stayed there praying; of the three men at the table only one, Can Grande himself, had the spirit left to be courteous. He got up; the other two remained seated, Francesco with his face in his arms.

"Madonna," began the tyrant; but she uncloaked her hand and put a finger to her sad lips.

"I may not stay," she said, in a voice so weary that it drew tears to Baldinanza's wicked old eyes— "I may not stay; but I must warn you, Can Grande, before I go. Walk not in the streets this night, walk not by the Piazza, pass not the arched way; peril lies there. No sword shall help you, nor the royal seat you have,— enter it not. Now I have warned you; let me go."

She put back her lifted hand under her cloak. Can Grande saw the round head of the Babe asleep. For five minutes after her disappearance no one spoke.

Francesco was the first. He groaned, "God have mercy upon me a sinner," between his hands. Then Baldinanza began to swear by all devils in Christendom and Jewry, not blasphemously, but in sheer desperate search for a little courage. Can Grande shook his head like a water-clogged hound, as if to get the ring of that hollow voice out of his ears. The first to rise was the eldest of the three. His eyes were very bright, and you could see the long scar plainly shining on his cheek.

"I am a sinner too," said he, "but this night I will sleep clean." He made to go.

"Do you desert me, comrade?" Can Grande asked.

The old dog turned upon his master.

"Mother of Pity!" he said in a whisper, "you are never going after this?"

"I am going, good sir. What of you?" Baldinanza blinked hard. "I am your servant, Can Grande," he said shortly; "where you go I follow. That is how I read the Book of the Law."

"Well, Checco," the tyrant went on, turning to the youngster still at the table, "what of you?"

Francesco threw up his arms. "Never, Excellency, never!" he groaned in his anguish. "I dare not, I dare not!" He concealed neither his tears, nor his despair, nor his bodily fear.

Can Grande shrugged. "Are you ready, Ubaldo?" he asked.

Baldinanza bowed his head. The two men cloaked and masked themselves, and went out of the palace. The moon shone broad over the Piazza; it was a cold white night. They crossed at the farther corner, went up a few steps, and then were lost in the glooms of the arched way.

They never came out alive. Six hired daggers hacked the life out of them and their hearts from their bodies. To this day the unwholesome place is called for a testimony the "Volto Barbaro," the horrid entry. So died in his sin Can Grande II., a man who feared nothing and won nothing but fear, and Can Signorio his son reigned in his stead. You might trust the cloth-white lackey and the stricken conscience of Francesco della Rocca Rossa to spread the news they had.

VIII

THE REPROACHES

A scared city of blank casements, a city of citizens feverishly asking questions whose answers they knew beforehand, a city of swift feet and hushed voices, was Verona on the morrow of Can Grande's murder. They carried the two torn bodies covered with one sheet to Sant' Anastasia, and laid them there, not in state but just huddled out of sight, while the bishop and his canons sang a requiem, and "Dirige" and "Placebo" went whining about the timbers of the roof. Nobody mourned the man, yet he had his due. His yellow-skinned wife knelt at his feet; Can Signorio, the new tyrant, frozen rigid, armed in mail, knelt at his head. The mercenaries held the nave, the bodyguard the door, archers lounged in the Piazza. All this parade of force was mere superfluity; Verona had no desire to revolt. The Veronese were for rending their hearts and not their rulers that day.

In the afternoon the show of a trial-at-law was made. The depositions of the lackey, of Rocca Rossa, of the finders of the murdered, and the hunters for the murderers, were taken and recorded by the *Podestà* in the presence of the council. After that the six unknown dastards were publicly condemned to death by the civil power from the loggia of the palace, and as publicly excommunicated by the bishop from the steps of the cathedral. It was felt on all hands that on this occasion the bishop had wielded the heavier arm: at least, in the absence of the criminals, he had brought his chances level. But what gave him most weight was that which had made the testimony of Francesco and the lackey overshadow every event of a week full of events— the interposition of Madonna of the Peach-Tree. Not a soul in the city was left to doubt; it might be said that not a soul was left to save, if faith can save you. The churches were packed from dawn to dark, not an altar in a chapel went bare of a mass. There were not enough of them. Altars were set up in the squares, and the street-ends blocked by a kneeling, bowing, weeping, adoring crowd. The bishop spoke the common mind when at Vespers that night he gave notice that he should go forthwith to purge the Carmelite church of the stain upon it, "at the request of my reverend brother the Prior Provincial of the Order." He set out then and there in solemn procession of the whole cathedral chapter. Rank formed on rank behind him till his ordered following trailed across Verona like a host.

Now, although, as it has been said, and truly said, there was no soul in the city who doubted, there was one soul very much in doubt. That was Fra Battista's. The offer of purgation had come in frenzy from the lips of his prior; by its acceptance Fra Battista saw himself driven to one of two courses. He must destroy his reputation for obedience to heavenly commands which it had been rank heresy in him to overlook, or that other reputation he had won, for being a desperate lover, upon which he shrewdly surmised some of his fame depended. He may have been right about that— I am not here to defend him. If he admitted his guilt, he would be unfrocked; he would show like a chanticleer stripped of his hackles before his hens. If he denied it, he could never preach to the women again. Admit it? Be degraded? Eh, that would be a nasty shift! Deny it? Oh, preposterous! The whole day he battled with himself, voice crying against voice, without result. Observe, it was a mere case of expediency: he had no thought to own a fault or repudiate a slander— the fellow had no conscience at all. Expediency, indeed, was his conscience, his attention to it the ladder whereby he hoped to climb to the only heaven he knew. No imagination had he, but very tender senses. Applause— the hushed church, the following eyes, the sobered mouths, a sob in the breath— stood him for glory. He had worked for this, and, by the Lord! he had won it. And now he must lose it. Eh, never, never! Stated thus, he knew the issue of his battle. He knew he could not give up these things— eye-service, lip-service, heart-service— of which he had supped so thirstily. Rather be unfrocked, driven out of the city, reviled, and spit upon, than admit such a shame as that other: to prove himself a vapourer before his slaves, to be pricked like a bulging bladder, slit open like a rotten bag— God of the love of women, never, never in life! The other course, then? He pictured himself, the tall and comely youth, standing up alone before the grim assembly of elders, flinty old men who knew nothing of my Lord Amor, how he rides afield in a rose-coloured garment, throwing a flower and a dart to boy or girl as he goes. He saw a dewy-eyed Battista owning himself Love's priest. The women called him Sebastian for his beauty. A Sebastian he was, *per Dio!* stuck all over with Amor's fiery darts. Like Sebastian, by his persecutors he would be stripped bare; like that martyr's enemies, they would wound his tender flesh; like Sebastian he would endure, casting his eyes upwards; and like Sebastian he would infallibly be wept by the women.

If women will weep for you they will bleed for you; the fount of tears feeds a river as well as betrays a hidden well. Good, then; good, then! He saw a future in all this. From the other spike of the dilemma he saw nothing but his impaling; in this case, if he was impaled, balm at least would be laid upon his wounds. Fra Battista determined to brazen it out before Verona.

They lit the tapers in the sanctuary betimes; and then all the brethren in their hoods sat in choir awaiting the bishop. With him and his clergy should come the reverend prior. Fra Battista was to stand on the rood-step to make his purgation. He would be backed by the light. So much of grace they would do him, that he should face a sea of dark, and be seen but in outline by it.

The bishop's procession, long announced by the indefinable hum a great crowd breeds, swept up the nave with a slippering of countless feet. The bishop in purple, his canons in scarlet, his cross-bearer, his chaplains and singing-men, the bearer of his mitre, his ring on a cushion; after these the archdeacon and his chaplains, the clergy of the city, heads of religious orders, representatives of the civil arm, Can Signorio with the officers of his household; finally, the silent, eager people, edging past each other, whispering, craning their heads to see what there was and what there was not to be seen. So came Verona in a multitude to the great business of Fra Battista and the rag-picker's wife, in reality thrilling with but one thought: Madonna of the Peach-Tree was in the city, for any waking soul to see!

After the penitential psalms, a litany, and the office appointed, the bishop stood with his back to the altar, and spoke *urbi et orbi* from the text, "God, who in divers times and in divers places," etc. I cannot do more than report the sum of his discourse, which was that, as it was plain these late marvels had some root in the hidden ways of men's hearts, so it behoved him as a father to lay all such ways bare. That for himself, if he might speak as a man only, he was conscious of no sin unpurged which the apparitions might condemn, and certainly (alas!) of no graces of his own which they could have been designed to reward. Let each speak for himself. If there was any man in that vast assembly unshriven, let him confess now what his fault was; so that instant prayer might be made to their glorious Visitant for forgiveness by intercession. If, on the other hand, there was some Christian virtue blossoming in secret, let them (brethren) find it speedily out, that thanks might be given for mercies vouchsafed. It was noticed afterwards that the death by butchery of the feudal lord was passed by without a comment. There might have been reason for this in the circumstance that Can Grande II. had been warned of his sin, had nevertheless set out to commit it, and had died in the act, as it had been foretold. To discuss all this in the hearing of Can Signorio, his successor, might have been a task too delicate for the bishop. But I believe that the scent of the miraculous, which was all about him, was too much for him. He could nose out nothing beyond the line which that fragrance seemed to point. All his thoughts, with those of his auditors, were upon Madonna of the Peach-Tree, whom there was nothing, absolutely nothing, to connect with Fra Battista, his doings and undoings. No one detected this, so Can Grande may have been inspired. A great to-do, which no one had the rights of, was followed by mysterious appearances which no one pretended to understand. What more natural than that one mystery should be allowed to explain the other?

The bishop having ended, the prior (who was very nervous) began. There were certainly foxes here and there in the vineyard, wild grapes on the vines as well as grapes. No community was so holy but that, through excess of zeal, over-inflamed by charity, it might nurture upon its bosom a fanged snake. Might he not allude to the detestable and never-enough-to-be-condemned sin of simony which, as they knew only too well, had fattened in the Dominican convent at B— — ? What should he say of that Friar Minor, the famous preacher of S— — , who had been found dead of a surfeit of melons and white wine? Alas! he brought the taint of gluttony— a deadly sin— upon his order! Wonderful, then, would it be in such days as these if the most renowned of all orders and most venerable, that of Mount Carmel, should pass unscathed through the tempting fires! Not only wonderful, but in itself a snare. What a temptation to the sin of pride in the order! What a drawing on of others (too disposed already) to the sin of envy, to uncharitable speaking— ah, and to unlovely dealing! Let sin be owned, therefore, since men were born sinners; but let purgation be done, the wicked member plucked out, etc.

He passed to the sin of Fra Battista— that promising young apostle— handled it soberly yet gingerly, hinted extenuating circumstances— the pride of life, young blood, the snares of women, Satan's favourite sitting-places, etc.— drew a tear or two from his own eyes and floods from La Testolina; and then called Fra Battista to come forth that he might purge himself or be purged by the canon law.

Thus exhorted, Fra Battista, becomingly tonsured, delicately combed, with an aspect most meek and hands at a pretty droop, came demurely out of the friars' door into the full light of the chancel. To the bishop he bowed, to the altar he bent a knee, to his father in religion he bent both, to the hush in the nave he cast a glance of wistful appeal. It was truly aimed. They could see nothing of his face, nothing but the shape of him, yet the women were sure he made a wistful appeal. Many were affected; the anxiety to hear him was intense, the squeezing fearful. An enormous fish-seller from the Lago di Garda, who had come in express, leaned over La Testolina and ground a braized heel into her toes. "*Achi!*" whimpered the little laundress; but "Snakes of Purgatory!" said the other, "what's a toe more or less when Madonna is round the corner with a blessing for us in her maunch?"

In a rapt silence, with no preface at all, Fra Battista made direct confession to all his gods (whether remote or throned within the sanctuary-rail) that he had committed the sin whereof he was accused. A perceptible shiver of sensation swept over the church, although everybody in it was sure, before he had uttered a word, what that word ought to be. Indeed he had never denied it; but not to deny is different from bold affirmation. The prior, whose avowal had also been tacit, looked pained: avowals are painful things. The bishop, more used to avowals, did his best to look shocked; the archdeacon (professionally enough) thought avowal the most indecent part of an indecent business. The Dominicans looked at each other, frankly delighted; the Friars Minor told each other what they had always said. What the people thought can only be guessed, for the nave was in darkness; but when Battista had made an end, a shuddering sigh came from a woman far down the church, and then stopped, hidden in some hasty new movement there which could not be accounted for. There seemed to be a stampede, a sudden rush to the side, the surging of some great unsuspected wave, which broke, as it were, in the midst of the throng, and washed an open space to right and left. Up in the choir, after the first surge of this wave (which made every heart beat), all ears heard the long-drawn following "Ah!"— not fear only, not expectation made real, but rather awe, expectation shown just. It began low and hollow, ran up to a hiss: then the silence was such that the cracking of a man's ankle-bone by the door sounded like a carter's whip to him upon the bishop's throne. In that deathly state the whole body of people remained breathless, waiting what was to ensue.

Out of the dark, stealing (it appeared) from the middle of the nave and floating down the church upon a bodily silence, came a cold voice. Like a wind from the snow-mountains it came in a thin stream, before which Fra Battista shrivelled visibly.

"O thou craven!" it said, "thou wicked man! what sin can be greater than thine? If thou hadst done this thing thou ownest to, it had gone better with thee than now, when thou standest a liar and boaster in a filthy cause. Wilt thou foul thyself, Battista, and think it honour? I tell thee that it was more tolerable for that stoned simple wretch than it shall be for thee; and it were better that men should go unsouled like the dogs, committing offence with their bodies, than souled horribly like thee, thou sinner of the mind, idolater of thine own image! Dost thou yet make slippery the ways of Mount Carmel, Battista? Dost thou yet hang the pearls which are the tears of Mary about thy neck? It shall be in such case that Carmel will be her holy hill no more, and those same pearls turned to leaden bulls to seal thee in Tophet. There is no mercy for the coward, and none for him that serves false gods. Go forth, thou groper after vainglory, kennel with the swine!"

The voice ceased. Fra Battista, who had been rocking under its chill breath, fell with a thud. The bishop adored the altar; the rest— priests, monks, people alike— broke into "Salve Regina," so loud, so wild, the very church seemed to shake. At that time the west doors flung open of themselves, and a roaring wind swept round, disastrous to candles. A quick flicker of blue flame jagged across the nave; the thunder came instant, pealing, crackling, braying ruin, fading at last to a distant grumble; and then the rain. No one got home that night with a dry skin; but it was Madonna who had quenched the doubting of Fra Battista, and washed fragrant the memory of Vanna to whomsoever had loved her once. As her lovers in early days had been many, it follows that they all forgot in the delight of reminiscence any harsh judgments she had received.

IX

THE CROWNING PROOF

The week went its way without further miracle; but Verona had supped full of miracles, and had need to digest. The signs and wonders she had witnessed, as one soul, in the church of the Carmelites had been so astonishing that you will easily understand how all little differences between order and order were forgotten. The root of disturbance— Vanna and her baby, Fra Battista and his luxurious imaginings, Baldassare and his addition— were also forgotten. Baldassare was at Mantua, Vanna had been stoned to death ("martyred" was now the word)— all was well. Fra Battista had been quietly ridded the very next morning: unfrocked, he took the way of the Brenner and the mountains, and Veronese history knows nothing further certainly of him. It is thought he may have got so far as Prague, where at any rate a perfervid preacher called Baptist von Bern was burnt for heresy in the year 1389— a spreader of anabaptistical doctrines he was, Gospels of the Spirit, Philadelphianism, and what not. Everything settled down to routine: Can Signorio to tyranny and coquetting with Visconti of Milan (who finally swallowed him up), the bishop to accommodating the claims of God, the Pope, and his temporal lord, to those of salvation and his stomach; and in like manner did every person in this narrative after his kind.

Then, on a bright morning in early September, old Baldassare came limping up the Ponte Navi with his pack on his back, paused a minute on the bridge, as his habit was, to look down on the busy laundresses by the water, spat twice, and so doing was observed, threw a cracked "Buon' giorno, La Testolina!" over the side, and went on his slow way to the Via Stella.

It was still very early, but not so early that Vanna was not in her shop-door sewing and crooning to the baby on her lap. She heard his step the moment he rounded the bottom corner of the street, blushed prettily from neck to temples, caught up the child, and went out to meet her lord. Standing before him in her cool cotton gown, there was no sun in the dusky place but what her halo of hair made, no warmth but that of her welcoming mouth. Half shyly she stopped, holding up the baby for him to see: it was not for her to make advances, you must understand; but it needed no magic to make one believe that what a man's wife should be to a man that was young Monna Vanna to her rag-picker. Baldassare blinked and tried to look harassed; the next minute he had pinched Vanna's cheek. She put the baby into his wiry old arms— a very right move of hers.

"Eh, *bambinaccio*," he muttered, highly pleased, "it is good to see thee! So thou art come out to meet thy old dad— thou and thy little rogue of a mother? Come, the pair of ye, and see what my pack has in store."

The baby crowed and bubbled, Vanna nested her arm closer in his ribs, and the trio went into the house.

A keen shot from one eye sufficed to assure the old fellow that as well as a little beauty he had a domestic treasure to wife. The house was as fresh as her cheeks, as trim as her shape. "Now the saints be good to this city of Verona," said he, "as to me they have proved not amiss." This was great praise from Baldassare; his generosity gave it point. From his pack came a pair of earrings— wagging, tinkling affairs of silver and coral; next some portentous pins, shining globes like prickly pears; a coral and bells for Master Niccolà, and a *scaldino* of pierced brass for the adornment of the house. "Thank you, Baldassare," said Vanna to her blinking old master; then she kissed him. Before she knew where she was, before she could say, "Già!" he put his arm round her and whispered in her ear. Then she clung to him, sobbing, laughing, breathing quick; and the rest it were profanation to report.

Verona rubbed its eyes as it came out yawning to its daily work. There was the open shop, ever the first in the street; there the padrone; there, by the manger of Bethlehem, were the padrona and the baby, whom they had last seen huddling from their stones. Vanna wore her colours that morning; she was rosy like the dawn, she was smiling, she had very bright eyes. But there was a happy greeting for man or wife who looked her way; and when La Testolina came peeping to behold the discomfiture of Baldassare, Vanna's gay looks found her out, and "Buon' giorno, La Testolina," came more cheerfully from her than it had come from her husband on the bridge. All the little woman could do was to squat upon the threshold at her friend's feet and pretend that she was troubled with spasms.

The crowning proof remains to be told. As La Testolina (who blazed the story abroad) is reported to have said, you might have drummed the guard out with her heart-beats. Vanna, by way of weaning her baby, it seems, was tempting him with gobbets of peach from a wine-glass. She bit a corner from the peach and tendered it in her lips to the youngster on her lap. The baby (a vigorous child) made a snap at it like a trout at a fly, and a gulp so soon as he had it. The peach was hard, the morsel had many corners,— went down bristling, as it were.

Cola had his first stomach-ache, was hurt, was miserable, prepared to howl. At that moment La Testolina happened to look at him: she stared, she gasped, she reeled against the door-post.

"Hey, Mother of Jesus!" she cried; "look at the baby!"

"It was a corner-piece, I'm afraid," said Vanna, with great calmness; "but the natural juices will thaw it."

"No, no, no! It is not that, woman," her friend went on feverishly—"it is not that! Look at his face, look at his face!"

Vanna looked. "Well," she asked, "what of his face?"

The *bambino*, to express his agony, was *grinning from ear to ear*.

This was the last miracle wrought by Madonna of the Peach-Tree.

IPPOLITA IN THE HILLS

I

THE GLORIOUS IPPOLITA

Almighty God, that supreme Architect, Who, alone among crafts-men, knows when to give and when to stay the rein, has chosen the Plain of Emilia to be, as it were, the garden of Italy, a garden set apart betwixt Alp and Apennine to be adorned within a garden; has filled it with every sort of fruit and herb and flowering tree; has watered it abundantly with noble rivers; neither stinted it of deep shade nor re-moved it too far from the timely stroke of the sun; has caused it, finally, to be graced here and enriched there with divers great and grave cities. Man, who has it not in him to be thrifty in so prodigal a midst, has here also thought it lawful to go free. Out of that lake of rustling leaves rise, like the masts of ships crowding a port, church towers, the belfries of pious convents, the domes and turrets of great buildings walled into cities. Among which, prized as they all are and honourably addi-tioned,— Vicenza, Treviso, Mantua, Verona, Ferrara,— there is none more considerable than Padua, root of learning and grey cupolas, cho-sen to be the last resting-place of Antenor, King Priam's brother, and the first of Titus Livy.

It is of Padua that I am now called upon to report certain matters which may seem strange to one who does not know her well: to the others, *verbum satis*. Whether it is their University (too famous, per-haps, for so quiet a place) or the suspiration of their greatest citizen which has kindled their wits; whether that cauldron of brick, the *Santo*, bubbling with silver domes, is the stem or flower of their exaltation; whether their seat at the head of a sun-steeped marsh (at whose mouth is Venice) hath itself unseated them; whether Petrarch set boiling what Saint Antony could not allay; what it was, how it was, who gave them the wrench, I know not— but the fact is that the people of Padua have been as freakish a race as any in Italy; at the mercy of any head but the aggregate's, pack-mules of a notion, galley-slaves of a whim, driven hither and thither in a herd, like those restless leaves (souls once) whose nearer sight first made Dante pitiful. Not that they, for their part, asked for pity or got it. Mostly they paid their tavern bills when the last cup had been drained and the last chorus led. When Ezzelin was master of the revels they paid in blood: that tower of his by the river is dark with it yet. Petrarch from his mountain-vineyard at Arquà tipped them a brighter stave: they broke their hearts for pretty women and had every one the comfort of a swanlike end, since sonnets are a knack. With Antony they flagellated, with Carrara defended walls, with Gattemelata knocked them down. Then Venice took what Padua could never keep; the Euganeans hailed on either side the Lion of Saint Mark; the Arts flourished; Squarcione cut out small-clothes and taught anatomy none the worse; Mantegna dreamed of Julius Cæsar, smouldering while he dreamed; and Ippolita, the stone-mason's daughter, from too much courting fled in breeches to the hills. She, like all the Padovani, paid her score without flinching. It may have been run up without leave asked, but it was run up in her name. The rule in Padua was so; I never heard that she repined. Maybe that she had her money's worth; but of that you will be able to judge as well as I.

Padua is a city set in meadows full of light; it is well spaced, plentifully watered, arcaded, green with gardens. The streets are like cloister-walks; as in Lucca, the plane is the sacred tree, and next to that flag of green on a silver staff, the poplar shows the city blushful in the spring and thrilling all a summer with the memory. It is a place of brick and marble, painted orange, brown, yellow, and warm white, where every cornerstone and every twig is printed sharply on a sky of morning blue.

"Quivi le mura son fatte con arte,
Che parlano, e rispondono a i parlanti."

A tale of Padua should have the edge of a cut gem. So let Ippolita's be told.

In her day— that day when, at sixteen years old or so, the sun briefly lit upon her golden head and showed her for the lovely girl she was— Padua was passing through a time of peace. Novello was dead at last, poor heroic gentleman, Verona was shaken off; Venice was supreme— easy, but unquestionably mistress of the Emilia. There was time to make madrigals, to make eyes, to make love, to imagine portraits. Mantegna was painting giants in the Eremitani and Bellini picking his brains, but not as yet a quarrel. The classics, the ingenuous arts, lovely woman— always interwoven when times are happiest— flourished in that sunny place: it was not really wonderful that Ippolita the stone-cutter's daughter, classically fair, indisputably a beauty, should win all seeing eyes and be the despair of all rhymers. Given the vision to the visionary (and both came in their time), she might be trusted with the rest; for she was remarkable by contrast; there were none like her. The Paduan girls are all charming, and mostly pretty. Ippolita was neither: she was beautiful, and when you came to know her face, lovely. They are brown, she was fair; they are little, she was very tall. They have eyes like a dove's, glossed brown; hers were deeply blue, the colour of the Adriatic when a fleeting cloud spreads a curtain of hyacinth over the sheeted turquoise bed. Beautifully hued in mingled red and white, delicately shaped, pliant, supple, and shy, such as she was (an honest, good girl, Heaven knows!) she might have lived and died in her alley— sweetheart of some half dozen decent fellows, wife of the most masterful, mother of a dozen brats, unnoticed save for her qualities of cheerful drudge and brood-mare; beautiful as a spring leaf till twenty, ripe as a peach on the wall till thirty, keen-faced and wise, mother and grandmother, at forty; and so on— such she might have lived and died, and been none the worse for her reclusion, had she not leaned more than half out of her window in the *Vicolo* one bright April morning of her sixteenth year, to exchange lively banter with a friend below, and been seen by Messer Alessandro del Dardo, who within the cuirass of Sub-Prefect of Padua nourished the heart of an approved Poet; been seen of him for the miracle of young beauty she really was. Chance sparks kindle chance tinder; and so here. I am far from alleging the heart of Messer Alessandro to be dry tow; but I do repeat it, Padua was a freakish cityful, Ippolita lovely exceedingly, amorous poetry in the air.

He, then, passing by, saw her stoop flushed and sparkling from above him; the sun caught her shining hair; a loose white smock revealed so much of her neck as to picture him the snowy rest. Snow and rosebuds— O ye little gods! As he stood in ecstasy she saw him at the end of the lane, and blushing drew back with a finger in her mouth, to thrill and giggle at ease. She saw a great gentleman stare; he saw a rosy goddess stoop and laugh, then blush and hide. *Vitas hinnuleo me similis, Chloe!* Away he went, his heart leaping like a wood-fire, to report to Meleagro de' Martiri and Stazio Orsini, to Donna Euforbia, Donna Clarice, and Donna Simpatica— friends and poets alike— that he had had a most rare vision.

"To me it seems," he said, "that that fair-haired daughter of the Greeks, Madonna Elena, the slim, the rosy-fingered disturber of the repose of cities, hath appeared to distract this our city of Padua. Me at least she hath distraught. Fair friends, sister and brother poets, you shall understand that henceforth I devote myself to this lady and her praise. More, I vow a vow, and call upon you to register it in the Golden Book of the Amorous Gests of Padua, that I will never cut my nails again until I have enthroned her sovereign lady of me, and of you all, and of this our humane Commonwealth. By golden Venus and her son, by Mars armipotent powerless in such toils, and by Vulcan in chains too cunning for his pincers; by Saints Ovid and Sappho, the Chian, the Mantuan, and the Veronese, I swear this oath."

"It is well done, Alessandro," assented the listening company.

That evening in his fellowship, Meleagro and Stazio, cloaked and lurking under the arcades, saw Ippolita walk down the Via Pozzo Depinto arm in arm with two shawled friends, transparently in the ranks of the *popol basso*, but as obviously not of them. Her golden head was bare; also by a head she sailed above them. They followed her by the Via Zitelle, over the Ponte della Morte, further yet, between garden walls topped with lilac, into the Prato della Valle. There the three unconscious girls mingled with the concourse of those who took the air under the still trees. Ippolita, that slim, tall marvel, seemed not to be remarked by any; Alessandro, swooning on his friend's arms, could scarcely believe it.

"Edge up, Alessandro, edge up— accost, accost!" said Meleagro; but—

"Do you think I would profane the *aura* of her by my abhorred presence?" cried the lover. "Ah, God of Love, I would die sooner! I feel, indeed, my Dæmon at work. Let me sit upon this bench— my tablets, ha!" He sat. Finely disordered verse, *rime sciolte*, resulted; but Ippolita was so far unperturbed.

Gradually, however, it came to her notice that she was watched. There was singing under her windows at night; the day brought parties of noble youths into the *Vicolo* scarlet-capped, feathered, slashed, and booted youths; ladies were with them as often as not; garlanded ladies with square-cut bodices showing half their bosoms; flowers came, verses, platters of Urbino, Gubbio, Faenza. She was saluted in the street, followed to the church door, waited for at the coming out from mass. It came, more or less, to this, that whenever she went abroad by ways where the honourable might pass, her going resembled that of the processional Host rather than of a respectable young woman. Her friends were no protection: the girls thought it fun, courted it, found stuff in it for giggling and peering with the eyes into dark corners; the lads of her station shrugged at it, then sulked, and at last fairly fought shy of such a conspicuous mate.

Ippolita herself tried to laugh it off, but failed absurdly. She became plaintive.

"What do these signori mean by their my-ladying?" she cried to Annina, her bosom friend. "Why do they send me these things? Platters! What use are platters to the likes of us, who as often as not have nothing to put on them?"

Annina looked demurely. "It is easy to see what they want of thee, dearest. What does a gentleman always want of a poor girl that takes his fancy?"

Ippolita tossed her high head.

"Eh!" she snapped. "They may fill the house with crockery at that rate. I'm not rubbish!"

She was not; but she wronged her adorers, who neither thought it nor hoped it of her. Messer Alessandro was not growing his nails for that sort of ware; nor could he have treated the Pope with more respect. He had never ventured to speak, though he had never failed to salute her. What he wrote was chiefly in verse, and as Ippolita could not read, it really did not much matter what his letters contained. Meleagro had opened his mouth to pay her a compliment: he won a frightened look out of her blue eyes, a fine blush, and lived upon them for a week. The ladies were bolder. Some of them had walked with her once in the Prato. There was very little to say, except that they loved her and thought her like a goddess. Ippolita was rather scared, laughed nervously, and said, "Chi lo sa?" Donna Euforbia then told her the story of the original Ippolita, the Scythian queen; of King Theseus, and the child born to them in sea-washed Acharnæ. The Paduan Ippolita said "Già!" several times, and asked if her namesake was a good Catholic. Finding she was not, she took no further interest in her fortunes than to suppose her deep in hell for her pains. The ladies asked her to come and be their queen; she said she couldn't leave her father. They offered her jewels for her hair, neck, fingers, wrists, ankles; she laughed, and said that they were not for the likes of her. They spoke of Alessandro, the Poet. She asked if he were any relation to the Signor Sotto-Prefetto. He was that same, said they.

"Dio buono!" cried Ippolita. "Is he the gentleman who wants to undo me?"

They were shocked. "He asks no more than to sit at your feet, Ippolita, and read the secrets of your beautiful eyes. It is your soul he loves; he asks nothing of your body." "They never do, Madonna," said Ippolita; "but I am a poor girl, so please you, who have to look every way at once, as the saying is. Domeneddio is the only Signore I ever heard tell of who could get on with people's souls. Men want more of us than that."

Protests were wasted, and Alessandro, watchful of his nails, went mad in numbers. This it was to be tall out of common, this to lift up in dark-browed Padua a brave golden head; this to carry the bosom of an Oread beneath the smock of a girl in her teens; this, merciful Heaven, to be a vortex when poets are swirling down the stream of Time.

II

MESSER ALESSANDRO THINKS TO CUT HIS NAILS

Not to weary you, it is clear that Ippolita was the fashion. The poets, the courtiers, the painters, of whom in that age of peace Padua was full, were wild about this glowing girl, this sumptuous nymph of the Via Agnus Dei; they were melodiously, caperingly, symphonically wild, according to their bents. She saw herself on plates of faience, where the involutions of a ribbon revealed "Ippolita Bella" to the patient eye; she found herself (or they found her) an inordinate tri-syllable for a canzone, saw her colours of necessity reproduced on her lover's legs and shoulders as colours of election. One by one she could appraise her own possessions, and those they fabled of her. Her hair was Demeter's crown of ripe corn— she knew nothing of the lady, but hoped for the best. Her eyes were dark blue lakes in a field of snow— this she thought very fine. Her lips were the amorous petals of a rose that needs must kiss each other; kissing, they made a folded flower— ah!

> "La virtù della bocca,
> Che sana ciò che tocca,"

sighed the poets. But, bless her good innocence! that sweet mouth had touched nothing more mannish than her father's forehead or the feet of the Crucified. Her cheeks, said they, were apple-blossoms budded, her neck the stem of a chalice, her breast— but I spare your blushes, though they never spared hers. There is a book, "Gli Ornamenti delle Donne," which will tell you what that bastion of a fair girl should be; and what it should be those Paduan lyrists will more than assure you Ippolita's was. Thus passionately they fingered every part, dwelling here, touching there, with no word that was not a caress. What she had not, too, they gave her— the attributes she sowed in them. She was "vagha," since they longed; "lontana," since she kept them at a distance; "nascosa," since they drove her to it; cold, since she dared not be warm.

The painters, not to be behind, expressed what the others hinted. She saw herself, first, as *Daphne* behind a laurel-bush— the artist, kneeling in the open, offered his heart smoking upon a dish; second, as *Luna*, standing in shrouded white on a crescent moon— the artist, as *Endymion*, asleep in a rocky landscape, waiting to be kissed; third, as *Leda*, naked in reeds beside her pair of eggs— the plumed artist near by, ruffling and flapping his wings. Luckily, their allusiveness escaped her; she knew nothing of the diversions of the ancient gods.

But of all the vantage she gave them, none equalled that for which her gossips should have answered, her most commendable name of Ippolita. The verses she received on that theme would have made a *Theseid*, those she had to hear would have kept the rhapsodists for a twelve-month, those she saw the very Sala del Consiglio could not have contained. Ippolita at war with the Athenian, or leading her Amazons afield; Ippolita turning her unmaimed side to an adoring warrior (the painter) and you, or suckling Ippolita (with the artist's strongly marked features) in an ivied ruin with peacocks about it; Ippolita in a colonnade at Athens on the right hand of the king— thus she saw herself daily; thus the old palace walls of Padua, if they could yield up their tinged secrets through the coats of lime, would show her rosy limbs and crowned head. Mantegna has her armoured, with greaves to the knee and spiked cups on her breastplate. Gian Bellini carried her to Venice, to lead Scythians in trousers against Theseus in plate-armour and a blazoned shield. Giorgione set her burning in the shade, trying to cool her golden flank in deep mosses by a well.

All this, and much more, Ippolita endured because she was a good as well as a beautiful girl. Sometimes she wept in a friend's arms, sometimes (really frightened) she sought her parish priest; mostly it was the wonder-working Virgin in Sant' Antonio or, at the greatest stress, the Saint's own black sarcophagus in the lighted chapel, to lay upon it a feverish palm or hot, indignant cheek. By some such aids as these she preserved entire her head, her heart, all her precious store, so that no flattery ever tarnished the clear glass of her mind, no assaults, however fierce, could bruise the root of modesty within her.

Her father, vexed man, at first felt the glory of his daughter, shone by her reflected light, guessed (and had reasonable grounds for guessing) the profit it might be; but lastly, seeing the suitors sought not to marry her, and she would do no less, he grew disgusted with so windy a business, beat her for what was no fault of hers, and bade her be sold or begone. Ippolita, who began her day's processioning with music and flowers, ended it mostly in tears and stripes. There seemed no escape. If she went to draw water at the well the courtiers jostled for her first salutation; if she went to mass in the grey of the morning, so, blinking, did they. The priest who confessed her paid her compliments, the blind beggar at the church door looked at her out of one eye. She was incredibly the fashion; and the women, far from being jealous, were as wild about her as the men. She could have had a Court of Virgins, or gone like Artemis, buskined through the thickets, with a hundred high-girdled nymphs behind her, all for her sake locked in chastity. They also made her presents, which her father sold, until (learning to fear the Greeks, their brothers), she gently forbore them. Whereupon, the honest stone-mason had fresh cause for chastisement of so incalculably calculating a child.

The hunted fair at last came to a point where she must stand or deliver. From three desperate lovers there seemed no sure road. All that was possible she did. She consulted her priest; he patted her cheek. A very old woman of her intimacy advised her to look in the glass; she did, and blushed at her own distressful face. A friar of the order of Saint Francis plumply told her to choose the most solid of her pursuers and make the most of him. "Such roses as yours, my daughter," said he, "should be early to market. You are sixteen now; but remember that by the mercy of Heaven you may live to be six and sixty. That's the time when the pot wants lining. If you have not the experience, pray how are you to direct the young in the way they should go? Yet that is the trade for an old lady whose life has been an easy one. For my part, I regret that the rules of our convent do not allow me to open the gate."

She pouted, and went out into the sun again, to find her way to the Santo barred. The three poets, with three lutes, were singing a madrigal in her honour. They were understood to say that her going was over the tired bodies of lovers, that she went girdled with red hearts, that her breast was cold ivory, and her own heart carved in ice. *Nymph* rhymed with *lymph* and *Ippolita* with *insolita*; the whole, ingenious as it was, was not *ad rem*; and as for the poor subject of it all, her heart (far from being ice) was hot with mutiny. She knew herself for a simpleton— just a poor girl; she knew herself made ridiculous by this parade; could see herself as she was. Her crisping hair was over her ears and knotted behind her neck, without garland or fillet or so much as a brass pin; her green dress, though it was low in the neck, was tightly drawn over her bust; for what were glorious to be shown in a great lady, in her had been an immodesty. When she lifted her skirt out of the gutter you could see some inches of bare leg. Her hands were brown with work, though her neck was like warm marble in the sun. Eh, she knew herself through and through just a low-born wench; and "O Gesù Rè!" her heart cried within her, "why can they not leave me alone!"

The three poets— Stazio Orsini in white and yellow, Alessandro del Dardo in white and green, and Meleagro de' Martiri in a plum-coloured cloak— accompanied her down the Via Pozzo Depinto to her poor house in the quarter of Santa Caterina; she lived in the Vicolo Agnus Dei. To their florid exercises in the language of courts she replied in monosyllables— "Sissignore," "Grazie, Signore," or "Servo suo"; the humble words were as much her daily use as *Padre nostro* or *Ave Maria*. At the door she must have her hand kissed three times in face of the nudging neighbours; and to each salute her honesty prompted a fresh "Grazie, Signore," a curtsy, and a profound blush. Meleagro beat his forehead to see her so lovely and so unapproachable; Orsini bit his lip; but Alessandro, mindful of his nails, and not to be Sub-Prefect for nothing, went away to find the girl's father.

This worthy bowed to the earth before his visitor. In what way could His Excellency be served? By the acceptance, on Matteo's part, of twenty ducats? Benissimo, e tante grazie!

"Matteo," said the Sub-Prefect when this little transfer was accomplished, "your daughter is the most beautiful lady in all this city of Padua."

"She is a choice thing, I own it," said the good Matteo; "and how dear to her old father your honour hath no notion."

"I can very well imagine it," returned Messer Alessandro; "and, indeed, I remember that you are twenty ducats in hand."

"Oh, va bene, va bene!" cried Matteo. "I am your Excellency's humble servant. You shall take her when you like and as you like."

"All will be done scrupulously," Alessandro said with fervour. "We shall crown her Queen of our College of the Muses; she shall be priestess, sacred image, and oracle; and most honourably served."

"Honour of course," said Matteo, "comes into the game. I have played it myself, and know what I am talking about. There was Beppina, that fat Venetian hussy— to see her eat! But she always had her whack. Eh, I have been a blade in my day!"

To this testimony the Sub-Prefect had no comments ready. He returned to the object of his thought.

"We shall in turn contemplate her excellence," he explained, "and derive inspirations in turn. A fine body of devotional rhyme should be the result of this."

"The result," Matteo broke in, "will be a fine one, I warrant your Excellency, if such things as that are in your mind— and call it what you will, she's as healthy as ever her mother was. And *she* had seventeen of 'em, one way with another, before I buried her."

"She shall be crowned with stars, rest upon beds of roses, walk in flowery meadows, hide from the heat in thickets where water is— " Alessandro went lilting on. "We will sing to her all day, and of her all night. The saloon of the Villa Venusta shall depict the story of her glorious arising."

"Pretty, pretty!" cried Matteo, "I see that your honour knows the rules of play. Now when shall the game begin?"

"My honest friend, the litter will be at your door come daybreak," said Alessandro. "Three noble ladies will attend Madonna to bathe and dress her. After that, you shall leave her safely in our keeping."

Matteo bowed. "Excellency, I am your servant. Everything shall be as you wish."

He did not add, though he might well have added, that it was more than himself had dared to hope for.

At time of sunset home he came, but not to beat his beautiful daughter. On the contrary, he made much of her. Fuddled he was, but not drunk. He took her incontinent upon his knee and began to deal in rather liberal innuendo. Divining him darkly, she went to work with such arts as she had to wheedle the worst out of him.

"Carissimo padre,"— so she coaxed him, with hands interwoven about his scrubby face,— "tell me more of this gallantry of young blades."

"Chuck, chuck, chuck," he babbled, oozing wine, "come and feed out of my hand. Bill me, sweeting, and I bill thee. Ho, ho! Two doves on a branch! What, turtle? Wilt thou mope for ever?"

She trembled. "Nay, nay, I'll mope no more, father," says she. "But do thou tell me who my mate is to be."

Slyly he looked at her burning face and slyly kissed it. Then he began to sing—

> "Quell' drudo, Messer Amore,
> Ha scelto un Dardo per cuore!
> Dardo acerbo, ardente,
> Che fa gridare le genti—
> Ohimè! Dolce dolore!"

She had been a fool indeed to miss such a rebus. So the peril was worse than her dread! The lees of twenty ducats shabby in his fist told her how near the peril was.

Going to bed, he folded her in his arms, making her prop while he mumbled comfort.

"It is all for the best, my beauty-bright," he hiccoughed, "all clearly for the best. Messer Alessandro is a lover in ten thousand. I shall be as good as a father-in-law any day of the week. Why, it's 'My honest friend' that he hails me already! That is what a man may call climbing up, I hope, when a poetical roaring blade cuts out your 'servo suo' in that fashion. And he's Sotto-Prefetto, remember. That means all Padua yours for the asking. Sleep sound, my pretty bird, Ippolita bella! After this night you shall sleep by day." So he found, by good luck, his bed, and she a time for tears.

III

THE JEW IN THE VIA DELLA GATTA

If there is not much to be said for the Via della Gatta in these days, there was even less when Ippolita was the reigning toast. It was cloistered (as now), it was cobbled, shabby-white, secret, blind; it echoed silence, was a place for slippering crones, for furtive cats, and the smell of garlic and charcoal fires. Of nights, by the same token, it was not the place to choose for an after-supper walk. The watch used to go through it with swords before and daggers behind. Lanterns were little use save to reveal the cut-throat blackness all about.

Now, on the very night when Matteo was fuddled, Ippolita in tears, Alessandro in a fever, and the more reputable Padovani turning down their beds, the watch came rattling at the Sub-Prefect's door to report a dead Jew in the Via della Gatta. Of all nights in the year, this, the eve of the Glorious Ippolita's home-bringing, to be vexed by a dead Jew! Messer Alessandro was exceedingly annoyed.

"Take your accursèd Jew," he said to the lieutenant, "and stuff him underground. I am busy, I am absorbed in work. When I have leisure I will attend to him. You can dig him up again. And I take this opportunity to tell you, Lieutenant, that your visit is most inopportune. For six months you have brought me nothing of the sort, and to-night, for example, you plump a Jew on my doorstep. Bury your beastly Jew and leave me in peace."

"But, Excellency," stammered the Lieutenant, "your Excellency will see that I have no control over the assassins of Padua. This Jew has not died happily. There is a great hole under his ribs. He is scarcely cold yet."

"That is soon remedied," said Alessandro; "put him in the ground."

"But, Excellency, a murdered Jew, a Jew in holes— "

"The Jews have been damned from the beginning of our dispensation," cried the Sub-Prefect in a rage. "Well, I add my malediction. I say, Damn your Jew!" And he shut the door in the face of the watch.

The Lieutenant was hungry. If his chief could damn the Jews, so could he.

"Corporal," says he, "I am going to supper. Do what you like with the Jew, so long as you put him decently away when you have finished. Good night."

The Corporal conferred with his men. Here was the Jew— what should they do with him? One of the archers suggested a source of profit. He might be shown in the wine-shops at a quattrino a head. Agreed. Off they set.

They showed him at the Codalunga— there were some low-browed hovels there, as was usual about the gates: the Jew did well. Thence they skirted the walls by the Riviera Santa Sofia, tried him at the outer gate of the Carmine, worked their way from tavern to tavern, till they came to the Vicolo Agnus Dei. It was a thousand pities Matteo was drunk in his bed; he had quattrini enough and would not have missed the treat for the world. Ippolita, whimpering in hers, wondered what the buzzing and sliding of shoes in the street below could be about. She had troubles of her own, poor girl, but she could not stand this. Up she got: a single glance out of window was enough. She shuffled on a shift and a petticoat, snatched a shawl, and tiptoed out. Annina, her bosom friend, had no troubles. She was half undressed, but she too slipped a shawl over her head and went peering into the alley. There she met Ippolita, and joined hands. Flaring torches, a swarm of eager black heads, whispers, grunting, the archers' plumed helmets— "Madonna! What's all this?" cried the two girls together in a stew of curiosity. A dead Jew? A murdered Jew? O Gesù! They borrowed a quattrino apiece from a neighbour and were richly rewarded. Ah, the blood, the staring, his grey old fingers! There was a something, if you like, to talk about at the house door; and a something to dream of, per Bacco! I believe the Jew engulfed all her annoyances of the past and all her fret over the immediate future.

When they had done with him, came the question of his interment. It was the small hours, very near the time to relieve guard. The Jew's hosts found themselves out by the Porta Santa Croce— an empty quarter of the town, abounding in gardens.

"Over the wall with him," said the Corporal; "we'll plant him here." It was done. The Jew, who, by the look of him, had earned more money an hour after death than in all the years of his life, was put a foot and a half underground among the pumpkins in a garden of the Via di Vanzo. Padua went to sleep.

IV

IPPOLITA LIFTS UP HER EYES TO THE HILLS

Waking from a late troubled sleep, Ippolita found her little room possessed by three noble ladies— Emilia Malaspina, Euforbia di Ponterotto, and Domenica di Campodarsego— dressed all in saffron and white (her sacred colours, they told her), who announced themselves, with much kneeling and folding of arms over breasts, as her handmaids. "Sagro cuor di Gesù!" thought poor Ippolita, "what a way to undo me!" But aloud she only murmured, "Tante grazie, gentildonne," and got out of bed.

They had prepared for her a scented bath, into which, in her dazed condition, she entered without overmuch persuasion. True, she thought to find her death in so much water, and crossed herself vehemently when first it touched her back; but there might be worse deaths (she supposed) than drowning for a poor girl bought and sold, and not so very long ago a Jew had been baptized in Santa Giustina in water up to his neck. Nothing, however, would induce her to sit down. They dressed her then in silk, tied and garlanded her hair, put a gold chain round her neck, silken shoes on her feet— talking in quick whispers to each other all the time; and so announced with curtsies that she might enter the litter as soon as she would. She was at the disposition of these ladies, was her faltered reply. Emilia waved her hand out of the little window; chords of music sounded from the street; the voices of men and ladies rose upon a madrigal—

"Fior' di Maggio— Soave, pio e saggio— Salve, Ippolita!"— the work of Alessandro's muse upon that night of discord from the Jew. So she went downstairs.

The Vicolo Agnus Dei— a blind alley of low jutting houses over arcades, full of squalor, pink wash, children, and cats— was on this early morning ablaze with colour and music. From wall to wall (and eight feet will measure that) it seemed packed with the nobility. Tousled heads from above looked down curiously on heads elaborately frizzed, on scarlet caps, on plumes, on garlands, on jewelled necks. Poverty and riches touch at their extremes, like houses in the South. The shoulders of the ladies at play were no barer than those of the slatterns who gaped at them playing; but for Ippolita, who had always been a decent girl, let us hope her blushes were a cloak. She felt naked. And the bath, remember, had unnerved her.

What these neighbours of hers may have thought is no concern of ours, since the actors in the play took no concern in it. Twenty pieces of silver had bought an incomparable peg for their conceits. They were rescuing, they said to each other, a lily from the gutter, taking a jewel from a dirty finger, glorifying the glories— a pious act which could not fail of returning honour to those who took honour in doing it. The people! Sacks to be filled with garlic and black wine, liver and blood-puddings— grunting hogs, let them keep their sty. Let them not dare (and in truth it never occurred to them to dare) interfere with the diversions of the great. Yet as the veiled sacrifice went to mount the litter, one brown-eyed rascal from an upper window, holding a towel over her neck, shrilled out in homely patois, "A vederti, 'Polita mia!" and Ippolita turned her lovely head and showed for a moment her shining wet eyes to those who watched. She smiled tenderly at the send-off, but "Addio, Annina, addio!" she said softly, and turned bowing to her bowing gaolers.

As the swaying litter of gold and white went out into the Pozzo Depinto and turned up towards the Pontecorbo Gate; as the music and chanting— "Candida Ippolita, premio d'Amore! Grazia insolita del sommo Fattore!"— died away to a murmurous underflow of sound, perhaps a tongue or two was thrust into a cheek or two, perhaps a bare shoulder shrugged or one shock-head wagged to another. The air was sharp, beds still warm— whose business was it? The street was left to the rats and snuffing dogs again.

But Annina had sparks of fire in her brown eyes, and panted as she tugged at her staylaces. It was not long before she clattered downstairs on her clacking heels, and went to mark the cage they had gilded for her dear Ippolita.

Those hierophants, that Collegio d'Amore (as the new style ran), bearing in their midst the garlanded victim— Goddess at once and Sacrifice— awoke the echoes of the streets without comment. The city gates were open, it is true; in some churches the doors stood wide for the first mass; they passed a priest or so just up, a friar or so, furtive truants from their beds; then, at the edge of the Piazza del Santo, Ippolita peeping through her curtains saw a little company of goatherds, blanketted, brown-legged, shabby rogues, their feet white with country dust, new in from the hills with their flocks. They blinked to see the gay procession; but wistfully, longingly, she looked after them from her cage. They were not so much market-stuff, per Dio! They walked at large over bright hillsides, singing to the sky and the winds. They were not pestered with love or fine buzzing ladies or capering signori, who larded poor girls with compliments, and showed their teeth most when they meant least. Ah, if she could run away! If she could hide with them, lie on the hillsides while the goats cropped about her; lie on her back, her hands a pillow, and sing to the sky and the winds because she was so happy! The thought possessed her; she ached for freedom; felt the water of desire hot in her mouth. The sleepy shepherds huddled in their rags watched her go by; they little knew what a craving the sight of their dusty ease had stirred in a heart whose covering was fine silk and strung pearls. Her wrongs came back upon her like heaped waters of a flood. That shameful bath— ah, Soul of Christ, to strip one naked, and let souse in hot water, like a pig whose bristles must come off! More than songs which she did not understand, more than compliments which made her feel foolish and pictures which made her look so, was this refined indignity. Seethed in water like a dead pig— ah, Madonna! She arrived sulky— if so humble-minded a girl could be sulky; defiant, suspicious, at least.

The place chosen for the new Collegio d'Amore was the Villa Venusta, whose shady garden can still be seen from the Riviera Businello. This garden is full of trees, myrtle, wisteria, lilac, acacia— flowering trees— with a complement of firs and shining laurel to give a setting to so much golden-green and white. It has a canal on two sides, is a deep, leafy place, where nightingales sing day and night; it abounds in grass lawns, flowers, weeping trees, and marble *hermæ*. The villa itself is very stately, a three-storied house in the Venetian style, from whose upper windows you can command a fine stretch of country; below you on either hand the Piazza del Santo, the Prato della Valle, with their enormous churches, pink and grey; beyond these the city walls, the green plain; lastly, the ragged outline of the far distant hills. It has a courtyard with lemon trees, long, dim rooms empty of all but coolness, shuttered against the glare of noon; above, a great saloon coffered in the ceiling, frescoed on the walls, with a dais and a throne; an open loggia full of flowers; above all this again, raftered bedrooms smelling of lavender. A roomy, stately place for those whose lives move easily in such surroundings; for Ippolita, the girl of the people, happy in her dark tenement in the Vicolo, gossip of the upper windows, shy beckoner to the street, burnisher of doorposts at sundown— for Ippolita this windy great house was a prison, neither more nor less.

It was a prison, at least, conducted according to the best rules of gallantry then obtaining. They bowed her up the staircase to the refectory: they sat her down and plied her on their knees with fruit and cups of wine. They led her to the throne room, where, high above them all, she was to sit, and (being crowned) hear them contend in verse and prose for the privilege of her love for the day. It was all arranged. She was to have a favourite every day, man or maid. Favour was to go by merit among her slaves. The theme was always to be her incomparable virtues— her beauty, discretion, wit (poor dumb fish!), her shining chastity, power of binding and loosing by one soft blue ray from her eyes, etc. They displayed her emblems on the walls— the peacock, because her beauty was her pride, her pride her beauty; doves, because they were Aphrodite's birds; rabbits, because the artist understood rabbits; the beaver, that glorious witness of virtue, who makes himself less certainly a beaver that he may be more safely a saint; the beaver, I say, in white on a green field. Other symbols— the lily of her candour, the rose of her glowing cheeks, the crocus of her hair, the pink anemones which were her toes, the almond for her fingers: she saw herself articulated; her fauna, her flora, her moral and physical attributes cried at her from the four walls.

Ippolita sat very scared on her throne, and endured what she could by catching firmly to the knobs of it and blinking her eyes. One by one they came creeping, these silken ladies, these slashed and curled young lords, to kiss her hand. "Dio mio!" thought she. "What is all this about? And are maids courted this way among the great?" She knew very little about it, yet was quite sure they were not. She wondered when Alessandro's business was going to begin. As a matter of fact, it *had* begun. He was now removing several inches of superfluous finger-nail with a sword.

For the first day that same Alessandro del Dardo won her to himself by his descant upon the theme, "How a gentleman may dismember himself without dishonour for a lady's love; and how not."

"Now he has me," thought poor Ippolita, and set her teeth. But he lay at her feet most of the day, and though at night he led her into the garden, if you will believe me, he never even kissed her hand.

"Who is mad?" thought she to herself, staring from her bed into the shadowy angles of the room. "Am I mad? Are these signori all mad? Is this a mad-house? Dio! it soon should be at this rate." She cried herself to sleep at last.

Next day it was Meleagro who won her by a careful consideration of the question, "Whether or no, when a gentleman has served a lady for ten years, and she falls sick of the small-pox, he is *ipso facto* absolved of his vow?" Meleagro decided that he was not, and was accepted by Ippolita, not because she admired his reasoning but because she thought it part of the game.

Next came the turn of Donna Emilia, a very burning poetess, for a Sapphic ode; and so on and so on. After three days Ippolita found herself yawning her head off; the longing for freedom returned, for the open country, the hills, the goatherds. Not for her home in the Vicolo: this everlasting love-making with its aftertaste of stale sugar had turned her sick of Padua. The whole city, to her mind, reeked of bergamot; she guessed a fawning lover at every street corner, a pryer at every window— basta, basta, la città!

No: it was to the hills she lifted up her eyes, to the hills and the swart goatherds free of their mystery. That *riviera* across the canal, where the budding planes made a mist of brown and rose, was a favourite haunt of theirs. There they assembled and milked their goats, thence set out homewards at night. Sitting in the pleached arbours, with two adoring ladies at her feet and a little cluster of youths behind and beside her, she used to peer long and earnestly through the branches to see them collect their flocks and start for the hills at dusk. Lithe, brown, sinewy lads they were! What long legs they had, with what bravery wore their ragged cloaks! One carried a great bulging skin under his arm— bagpipes! She was sure they made good music to each other in the green country places. Very early in the morning she heard them come in; they were known by their bells. She jumped out of her luxurious bed at the first tinkle, and was at the shutter watching for them before ever they rounded the angle of the Ponte della Morte. There they came! colour of dust, with the straggling goats following after in a cloud of it. Her impulse was to fling wide the casement, hold out both her arms, call to them with all her might, "Ha! help, in the name of the Trinity! Take me with you to the green hills. I am weary of life in this place!" Then, knowing she could not, she would hold herself back by main force, stare about her, run back, throw herself on the bed, lie there sobbing wildly, and so be found by her ladies who came to put her in that detestable bath. She was sure her skin was being rotted by so much water; she used to feel her arms and thighs secretly to see if they were palpably more flabby. It stood to reason that the water must soak in— where else could it go to! She thought that she walked like a bladder, supposing a bladder were to take itself legs. The whole affair was clean abominable; but she saw no way out.

The way came.

V

ANNINA AS DEMIURGE

They held a tournament in the courtyard of the villa; quite a concourse thronged the painted lists. Ippolita, a miracle of rose and gold, in a white gauzy robe, her hair crowned with daisies, was Queen of Love and Beauty, fanned by ladies in red. Del Dardo tilted with Vittore Marzipane, Gottardo de' Brancacci with Giacomo Fèo, a young lion from the Romagna. Messer Meleagro very nearly fell off his horse. They were all in gilt armour, their steeds blazoned with peacocks; but there was no dust, for the ground had been wetted with rosewater; no bones were broken and no blood drawn. The gallants of the Quattrocento could not abide what gave the salt to their grandfathers' feasts. They had other ways of deciding issues which appeared satisfactory; and when at the end the conquering champion went down on his two knees before the throne, when Ippolita, with deprecating hands and downcast eyes rose timidly to crown him, the silver trumpets pealed as shatteringly as ever over a blood-fray, and the company cried aloud to the witnessing sky, "Evviva Ippolita bella!" They could have done no more for a sheaf of broken necks.

This was a great day; but at the close of it its glorious Occasion locked herself into her chamber with breathless care, and sat tearful by the window, with crisping hands and heaving bosom, watchful of the happy idlers she could see afar off in the broad green Prato. Under the shimmering trees there walked mothers, whose children dragged at their skirts to make them look; handfasted lovers were there; a lad teased a lass; a girl hunched her shoulder to provoke more teasing. An old priest paused with a finger in his breviary to smile upon a heap of ragged urchins tumbling in the dust. The air breathed benevolence, the peace of afternoon, the end of toil. Round about, so still and easeful after the day's labour, were the white houses, green-shuttered, half hidden in the trees, the minarets, the domes, the coursing swallows: over them the golden haze of afternoon, a sky yellowing at the edge, beams of dusty sunlight coming slantwise, broad pools of shadow; further still, the far purple shoulders of the hills. Ah, those velvet-sided, blue-bathing, bird-haunted, wind-kissed hills!

But what was that? The jangle of little bells— the goatherds were going out of the city! This poor prisoner then, this watched and weary beauty, whispered to herself of her despair. "Oh, Madonna, Madonna, Madonna," she fretted, "let me go!"

As by miracle they announced a visitor: one Annina, a girl of the town. Would her Majesty see her?

Ah, Heaven! but her Majesty would! In came, staring and breathing hard, a brown-eyed girl with a shawl over her head, below it a blue stuff gown, below all a pair of sturdy bare legs. "Corpaccio! that's a lady; that's never my 'Polita," she stammered when she saw the white silk wonder of the room, the jewels in her neck, the chains of gold, the bosom.

"Oh, Annina! Annina! it is, it is your poor Ippolita," panted the beauty, and fell into the red arms of her friend.

"Sakes! dear sakes! Thou'lt spoil thy glory, my lovely dear," cried the other; "but there then, but there then, there's nothing to wail about. Tell me the trouble, tell thy good Nannina!" So she petted her, like a mother her child.

Donna Euforbia stood confused, but dutiful ever. "Has her Majesty any further commands?"

"Grazie, grazie," said her kissing Majesty, "niente!" and so was left alone with all that she held true in Padua.

"Oh, come, Nannina, come and sit with me; come to the window— let us have the air." She led her there. "O lasso!" said she then, and sighed; "how good it is to see thee, child!"

Before the other could let out a "Madonna!" she began her plaint. "They give me no rest, Nannina, no rest at all. Day long, night long, they are at their postures. I am dressed, undressed, put to bed, taken out, fed, watered, like a pet dog. They put me in a bath, they do my hair out every day: to get me up in the morning according to their fancies is an hour and a half's work for three ladies. Figure it!"

"Christian souls!" cried Nannina, "what's the meaning of this? A bath? What, water."

"Full to the brim with water, on the faith of a Catholic. Of course, if this continues I must die."

"Oh, sicuro, sicurissimo!" she agreed. "This is very serious, Ippolita. Eh, let me feel you. Are you ever dry, my poor child?"

"Dry to the touch, Nannina, dry to the touch. But it is within my body I fear it. I must be sodden, dearest."

"Send for a priest, Ippolita, that is the only chance. But, remember, when they have washed you, they put clothes upon you like these. Ah, but it is worth a girl's while to have silk upon her, and these chains, and these pearls. Corpaccio! there is no Madonna in Padua with such stones as these, nor any bishop either, upon my faith!"

Ippolita shook her beautiful head. "They are not worth the price of all that smelling water," she complained. "Try it, Nannina, before you speak. Seriously, I am very unhappy. Let me tell you something."

"Well?"

"No— come nearer. I'll whisper."

The two heads were very close together. Nannina's eyes became a study— attention, suspicion, justified prophecy, hopefulness; then saucerfuls of sheer surprise to smother every other emotion.

"Ma! Impossibile! And they have never— ?"

"Never so much as a finger."

"But what? Are they— ? Don't they— ?"

Ippolita shrugged, pouting. "Chi lo sa? I tell you, Nannina, I shall go mad in this place."

"And why not?" cried the other, with a snort. "You have examples enough about you, my conscience! What is all their singing and stuff about?"

"I think it is about me, Nannina."

"And their disputing?"

"It is about me."

"And the rhymes?"

"They are about me."

"And you have never— ?"

"Never, never, never!"

"What, not in the garden even?"

"No, never, I tell you. Only my hand."

"Your hand— pouf! The nightingales sing there, I suppose."

"All night."

"And there is moonlight?"

"Floods of moonlight."

"Dio! Dio santissimo!" cried Nannina, striking her friend on the knee, "you must be out of this, Ippolita! This is unwholesome: I like not the smell of this. Faugh, fungus! Mawkish! I will see your father this very night."

Ippolita shook her head again. "My father is paid by these signori."

"Then the priest must do it. Father Corrado must do it."

"He dare not."

"A convent— ?"

"No, never! That is worse than this. But— oh, Nannina! if I dared I would do such a thing."

"Well, let me hear. If it can be done it shall be done."

"Ah," sighed Ippolita, with a hand on her heart, "ah, but it cannot be done!"

"Then why speak of it?"

"Because I want so much to do it. Listen."

Then Ippolita, clinging to her friend's neck, whispered her darling thought. The goatherds on the hills! There was freedom— clean, untrammelled freedom! No philandering, for no one would know she was a girl; no ceremony, no grimacing, no stiff clothes; no hair-tiring— she must cut off her hair— no bathing, ah, Heaven! If she might go for a few months, a few weeks, until the hue and cry was over, until the signori had thought of a new game; then she would come back, and her father would be so glad of her that he would not beat her more than she could fairly stand. It was a great scheme; indeed it was the only way. But how to do? How to do?

"I suppose it is a dream of mine," sighed she, knotting her fingers in and out of the gold chains.

Annina said nothing, but frowned a good deal. "I see that you are not safe in Padua," she said in the end. "You are really too handsome, my child. You couldn't show your nose without being known and reported. You must go outside if you are to be in peace."

"But I can't go, Nannina; you know it as well as I do."

"I am not so sure. Do you mean what you say, Ippolita?"

"Ah, Nannina!"

"Then you shall go. It so happens that I know one of those goatherds— a rough lout of a fellow called Petruccio. I could tell him that a youngster had got into trouble in the city and wanted to lie quiet for a week or two. I can do it, Ippolita."

"Oh! And will you, will you?"

"Corpaccio! If you mean business."

"I mean nothing else."

"Then it is done."

They clung together and kissed. Annina was to return the next evening at the same hour.

That night it was remarked on all sides that Ippolita's beauty had never been so disastrous, her eyes so starry bright, her colour so fire-flushed. Messer Alessandro, who loved her like a maniac, went shivering out alone into the moonlit garden to expostulate with Nature. "Thou hast formed, most cruel Mother," cried he, "an image of thy fatal self, whose eyes are sharp swords, and her breath poison of ineffable sweetness; whose consummate shape killeth by mere splendour; to whose tint of bright fire every arm must stretch as moth to flame, and by it be blasted. All this thou hast done, and not yet content, hast set this glory so low that all may reach for it, and yet so remote that none can touch. Burning-pure is my Beloved, at whose approach I faint. What hard miracle is this of thine, Goddess, that all must love and none be found worthy?" Thus we may reflect, as Alessandro beat his resounding forehead, to what a pass poetry may bring a youth, who buys for twenty ducats what twenty thousand cannot give him the use of. Pygmalion made a woman one day, moulding all her gracious curves as his experience taught him. There went his twenty ducats. But not he could warm that image into glowing flesh, however much he sang to it and hymned. That was another's affair. So here.

Annina came on the morrow full of secrecy and other things more equivocal still in appearance. Her burden proved, however, to be a bundle of rags which, she assured Ippolita, represented all that was necessary to the perfect goatherd.

"We will do what we can here, child," said she, "in the way of staining your skin, cutting off your hair, and such like. Then you shall veil and come into the garden with me; but whereas you shall come in as the Madonna of these heathens, you shall leave, per Dio, as Silvestro, who murdered the Jew in the Via della Gatta and has to hide in the hills. Do you remember him, Ippolita?"

"Of course I do," said Ippolita. "Have I killed that Jew, Annina?"

"It is to be understood, my dear. Now come, there is everything to arrange."

There was indeed. Del Dardo would have swooned to see how Annina handled his Unapproachable. Her burnished hair was off with a clip or two of the great shears; a mixture of soot and walnut-juice hid up her roses, and transformed her ivory limbs to the similitude of a tanner's. Ippolita did not know herself. Veiled up close, she crept into the garden with her confidante, and in a bower by the canal completed her transformation. Not Daphne suffered a ruder change. A pair of ragged breeches, swathes of cloth on her legs, an old shirt, a cloak of patched clouts, shapeless hat of felt, sandals for her feet, shod staff for her hand— behold the peerless Ippolita, idol of half Padua, turned into a sheepish overgrown boy in tatters, whose bathing could only have been in sweat, and the scent of his garments the rankness of goats. On the floor in a shining heap lay the silk robes, the chains and jewels, only witness with Annina of what had been done. That same Annina clasped in her arms the tall boy.

"Oh, my dear, my dear!" she said, half sobbing, "if any ill should come of this I shall kill myself."

"No ill will come, Nannina, believe me," replied Ippolita, quite calm. "You are sure they expect me?"

"I see them on the riviera now. Slip into the boat. I will put you across."

On the other bank, Ippolita was received by the herd-boys, all agog to see the champion who had killed the Jew.

"Addio, Silvestro," said Annina, keeping up the play.

"Addio, Nannina," said Silvestro, with a chuckle.

"Are we ready, boys?" Petruccio called out, turning about him. "We must be careful what we're doing."

"Hist, Silvestro," whispered one, with a nudge; "did he bleed much?"

"Cosa terribile— a flood!" Silvestro spread out his hands.

"Cristo! The glory of it!"

"Valentino, I scrag you, my man, if you speak of the Jew till we are out of the Porta San Zuan," growled Petruccio, the leader: "Avanti!" And the drab-coloured crew moved off towards the sunset.

VI

SILVESTRO

The guard at the Porta San Zuan let them go unheeded; one ragamuffin more or less made no odds. The heart of the new-born Silvestro gave a great bound as they cleared the gate, and she saw before her the straight white road with its border of silver stems and the spreading tent-roof of golden green. These stems were so obviously like the pillars of a church that Silvestro ventured to remark as much to her neighbour— a broad-faced, thick fellow, not quite her own height, but twice as big in the girth. His mouth was large, his eyes were small and rather hot. He blinked a good deal, was very sulky, and met her advances with a grunt. "Chi lo sa?" was as far as he would go along with her in the matter of tree-trunks.

It was annoying. Every one had seemed friendly at first. But being free, she could not feel daunted long; and at the second bend of the road the hills sailed into full vision— the solemn hills in a long line of peak and hollow, velvety, dark, and brooding sleep, like a bank of cloud edging the pale sky. The frogs were singing vespers in the ditches, the sharp chorus of the cicalas shrilled on all sides. At the sight of this enormous calm Silvestro forgot rebuffs. For a murderer he was in a very cheerful humour; he began to sing; soon he had all the boys (except that blinker) rapt to attention. Andrea slewed round his bag and pipes and began upon a winding air; they all sang, going at a trot. The goats pricked up their ears; they too began to amble; it became a stampede. The sun went down behind Monte Venda, the bats came flickering out, the great droning cockchafers dropped on the road like splashes of rain. The night found them still far from Abano, but still talking and nearly all friends. Silvestro was hand in hand with Petruccio and another boy, called Mastino because he was heavy-jowled and underhung. Their tongues wagged against each other about nothing at all. Silvestro strengthened his position by hints and shrewd winks, but it was decided that the Jew should be kept for the night fire. That was too choice a morsel to be eaten on the road; that must be rolled on the palate, to get the flavours. It was a pity, certainly, about the pig-eyed boy, who snorted whenever the exploit was mentioned— but "Never mind him," thought Silvestro; "I have all the others."

They passed through Abano; Monte Ortone was ahead, a spur of the great body of the hills.

"There's the hermit's candle," said Petruccio. A twinkling light showed deep in the trees. "There was a most excellent miracle there— the Blessed Virgin in a tree. Two girls saw her and thought she was a kite entangled. But they fetched a priest from Abano, and he knew better. So then they built an oracle or some such place, and paid a hermit to pray there. And now, whoever has ague, or is with child, or hath bandy-legged children, or witch-crossed cows, always goes there; and the hermit cures them. That was money well laid out, I suppose."

"Per Bacco!" cried Andrea, "I'll tell you some more. Did you ever hear of Monna Betta's short leg?"

Petruccio cuffed him well. "A palsy on her leg, and a palsy strike thee," he thundered, "if with thy old women's tales we miss the path! Go drive the goats in, thick-chops, and stay that clapper of thine till they ask for a crow-keeper. Move now, be off!"

"'Tis a hard thing, Petruccio," blubbered Andrea, "if one may not tell the honour of his own land to a stranger."

But Petruccio sent him flying with grit in his ear.

By a brambly path they climbed Monte Ortone— Petruccio first, the others after him, the newcomer as best might be, then musically the goats. That round-faced, blinking boy, whom they called Castracane, was behind Silvestro now, much diverted by her panting efforts to go up without panting what he could rise on with closed mouth and scarcely any sharper whistling at the nose.

"Hey, comrade," said he, grinning, "one sees that the Jew's stair was easier going for thee than Ortone." And he prodded her with his staff.

This was not friendly. Ippolita did her best to humour him. "I go up as well as I can, Castracane," she said. "But do you go first, if you will."

"Nay, nay," he replied, with a chuckle; "I make very good practice in the rear." So saying he caught her ankle in the crook of his staff, and brought her down into the bushes like a running ram.

Silvestro was hurt in his feelings; all the rest laughed; his late-won empire seemed slipping. And it was very strange treatment for the Queen of the Collegio d'Amore, if wholesome. She arrived wet and breathless at the top, feeling moreover that she must by all means make a friend of this ugly fellow.

The fire was made, the pot put on, the pot boiled. Then for a time, though jaws worked like mill-clappers, it was to better purpose than words. But when the last shred of garlic or last gobbet of pork had been fished up, when the wine-skin was flabby, the last crust's memory faded from the toothpick, Petruccio slapped Silvestro on the knee.

"Now, comrade," cried he, "we'll have the Jew for dessert."

"The Jew, the Jew! Now for the Jew!" went the chorus.

Silvestro coloured. "The Jew? Eh, well, I killed him— ecco!"

The flaming logs lit up a ring of tense, pale faces— not one of which, Silvestro saw, would rest content with that. The interrogatories began, a dropping fire of them.

"How did you do it?"

"With my knife, of course."

"Where did you strike?"

"Under the ribs. I took him by his great goat's beard, the old dog, and jerked up his head— so. Then I drove in between his ribs— ping!"

Surely that would do? Not at all.

"The left ribs?"

"Ah!"

"Did he gurgle?"

"Didn't he!"

"Blood choked him— eh?"

"Per Bacco!"

"You stabbed him on the stair?"

"Già!"

"Did he roll down?"

"No, no; he just lay where he fell."

"Why did you kill him?" said Castracane, suddenly— bolt upright.

This was awkward. Silvestro fenced. "Eh, corpo di Bacco, why does one kill the Jews?"

The others at first took the same side. Why, indeed? The question seemed absurd. Did they not crucify young children, and eat them afterwards? Did they not kill Gesù Cristo? Everybody knows that they did; and, as for proof, look at them with a dish of pork. Ugh!

But Castracane blinked his small eyes, and held to it.

"Did you kill him because of Gesù Cristo?" he asked.

Silvestro shrugged. "It was partly that, of course."

"What else?"

Silvestro grew hot— desperate. Why, after all, would one kill a Jew? Something must be urged, something solid.

"There was Annina, you know," said Silvestro, at his wit's end.

"Annina— that girl you were with? What of her?" Castracane licked his lips.

"Well, this Jew, you must understand, was a limber young fellow-"

"Young!" shouted the other. "You told me he had a great grey beard like a goat."

- 66 -

"It wasn't very grey— not so grey as a goat's. Well, he was always following Annina about, making her presents, cadging for favours. Accidente! I couldn't stand it, you must know. So, thinking of Annina, and of Gesù Cristo, and one thing and another, I decided to follow him back to the Via Gatta— and so I did."

Andrea leaned forward, hoarsely whispering (blessed diversion!)—

"Say, Silvestro, what colour was the Jew's blood?"

Silvestro opened wide those blue eyes, which had wrought such havoc among the Paduan nobility.

"Black, Andrea!" he whispered again; "black as pig's blood!"

Andrea crossed himself. "Pio Cristo," he prayed, "let me kill a Jew some day!"

Even then Castracane, the sceptic, was not satisfied. "All I know is," said he, "that I saw a Jew cutting bread at the *Albero Verde* last Martinmas, and he slipped into his own thumb, and came off as red as a dog's tongue. Bah!"

"Damn the Jew," said Petruccio, yawning; "let's go to sleep, boys."

VII

CASTRACANE

She woke early, with the full light of day in her eyes. She felt tired, but not inert, languid and luxurious, rather, and explored to the full the happiness of stretching. Round about her were huddled the drowsy boys; on the slopes of the steep place where she lay she could see the goats browsing on lentisk and juniper, acanthus, bramble, mountain-ash. Misty on the blue plain lay Padua, a sleeping city, white and violet— remote now and in every sense below her and her concerns. The sky was without cloud, very pale still, glowing white at the edge; the sun not yet out of the sea. The freshness of the air fanned her deliciously; larks were climbing the sky singing their prick-song, scores of finches crossed the slopes, dipping from bush to bush. Ippolita clasped her hands behind her head, and looked lazily at all this early glory. The freedom of her heart seemed explicit in that of her limbs. What she could do with her legs, for instance! How she could sprawl at ease! She was just like all the others— as ragged, as dirty, at least; and soon she would be as brown. Dio buono, the splendid life of a goatherd!

Then she found that Castracane was watching her out of one wicked eye. He had rolled over on to his belly, his face lay sideways on his hands; one eye was shrewdly on her. She considered him, rather scared, out of the corner of hers. Decidedly he was a sulky boy— you might say an enemy. As unconcernedly as she could she got up, stretched herself with elaborate ease, and strolled off along the edge of the hill. Castracane followed her; she affected not to know it; but her heart began to quicken, and when he was close beside her she found that she had to look at him.

"Good morning, Castracane," says Silvestro.

He grunted. "Look here, Silvestro," he began, "about that Jew— "

The accursed Jew, who, so far from denying the resurrection of the dead, seemed a standing proof of it! Was she never to have done with the Jew?

"Well, what about him?"

"Did you kill him or not? That's what about him."

"I told you last night."

"Yes, but I don't believe it."

"What!"

"I don't believe it. Now then?"

Silvestro looked about for help: they were out of sight of the others, and there lay Padua, slumbrous in the plain. It seemed as if Castracane meant quarrelling. Well, what must be, must be.

"I don't care whether you believe it or not. Now then?" The blue eyes were steady enough on the black by this time.

"Look here," said Castracane after a pause, "I'll fight you if you like. That'll settle it."

Silvestro laughed nervously. "Why should we fight, Castracane? Besides, we have no knives. How can we fight?"

"Like this," said the other between his teeth. His left arm whipped out, like a lizard's tongue, and Silvestro lay flat on his back among the cistus flowers, seeing ink and scarlet clouds.

"Stick a Jew indeed!" cried Castracane. "Stick a grandmother! Why, you're as soft as cheese!"

Silvestro's shoulders told a tale. He had turned on his face, but his shoulders were enough. Lord, Lord, look at that! Scorn in his conqueror gave way to amazement, amazement to disgust, disgust to contempt. Last came pity. Who'd have thought such a leggy lad such a green one? He was crying like a girl. Castracane had no malice in him: he was sorry for those sobbing shoulders. He stooped over the wreck he had made, and tried to put it together again.

"Come, Silvestro," he said gruffly, "I never meant to hurt you."

The wet face was up in a moment— red and wet and angry.

"It's not that! It's not that! I never killed the Jew— there! But I was a stranger, and I tried to be friendly, and you hated me. I hate being hated. Why should you hate me? What have I done?"

This was too subtle for the youth. "The trouble was," he said, "that I hit you in the right place. That's the knock-out blow, that one. Morte di Ercole, and down you went! Well, I'm sorry; will that do?"

"Yes, yes— I want no more. Let us be friends, Castracane."

"Benissimo."

He helped his late enemy up; they kissed each other, then sat together on the grass— admirable friends.

"So you didn't kill the Jew?" Castracane began. "I knew it! But what did you do to run away?"

"Ah, you mustn't ask. Indeed, I can't tell you. It was rather bad."

Castracane looked keenly at his new friend. "Was it a girl?" he said.

Silvestro blushed. "Yes, it was a girl."

"Ah, ah! Then I say no more. I like girls myself. But they get you into trouble quicker than anything. You would rather not tell me any more— quite sure?"

"No, I can't indeed. Let's talk of something else. How old are you?"

"Seventeen."

"I'm not sixteen yet. Is Castracane your real name?"

Castracane looked pleased.

"I'm glad you asked. No; they call me that among ourselves, because of a little knack I have; but my name is Pilade."

"That's a very nice name," said Silvestro.

"I believe you— it's a splendid name. There's no better. It's the name of a Roman— Emperor of Rome and Sultan of Padua he was— who killed a giant called Oreste, having first caused him to become a Christian."

"But why did he kill him when he had made a Christian of him?" asked Silvestro, greatly interested; "or why did he make him a Christian, if he was going to kill him?"

"Pouf! What questions!" cried Castracane. "He made him a Christian because he was a good Catholic himself, and killed him for being a giant, of course. Or take it this way. If he hadn't been a Christian, how could he have made a good death? He couldn't, naturally. So the Emperor christened him first and killed him afterwards— ecco! It's always done like that, they tell me."

"I see it now," said Silvestro; "it was very fine. I like your name of Pilade best. I shall always call you that, if you will let me."

"Call me what you like," says Pilade. "Let's go and wake the others. I'm as hungry as the devil with all this talking."

The result of this was that Silvestro became Pilade's foot-boy, his slave. The lout was in clover; nothing could have suited him so well. No more goats to herd in the heat of the day— Silvestro would do it; no share of foraging for him; no more milk to carry into the valley; no more fires to make up; nor strays to follow; nor kids to carry to new pastures— Silvestro would do it. The luxurious rascal lay out the daylight stretched on his back with his hat over his eyes; he woke only for his meals. He would not be at the pains even to swathe his own legs or strap his own sandals. Silvestro, bathed in sweat, his fair skin burnt and blistered, his delicate hands and smooth legs scratched by brambles, his slender neck bowed beneath the weights he carried on shoulders stretched to cracking point— Silvestro worked from dawn to dusk, rejoicing in the thankless office. Thankless it was, since Master Pilade took no sort of notice; yet Silvestro gave thanks. Pilade allowed the other to stoop to his shoe-ties, to wind the swathes about his sturdy calves, to carry his very cloak and staff, while he slouched along with hands deep in breeches pockets, and his hat pulled down to his nose.

Silvestro would proudly have carried him, too, had that been possible. Most unmanly of Silvestro, all this; but the rogue he petted was too snug to consider it. At the falling-in of night, having his belly full of meat and drink (which Silvestro had prepared and served him with), he might, if the mood took him, pull out his reed pipe.

"Silvestro," he might say, "you have been useful to-day; perhaps I'll play you something."

And the beautiful Silvestro (tanned counterpart of the Glorious Ippolita) would hang upon the melancholy noise, and observe with adoring interest every twitch and distension of the fat-cheeked hero; and at the end sigh his content, saying—

"Ah, thank you, Pilade; you have been very kind to me."

"The truth is," Pilade would allow, "I am a good-natured devil if you take me the right way. I'll tell you what, Silvestro; you have pleased me to-day. You may sleep at my feet if you like: it will keep them warm, to begin with, and you'll be near me, don't you see?"

"Thank you, thank you, dear Pilade," cried the enraptured Silvestro.

The world is a very odd one, and it is most true that the man who is for taming hearts should pursue, ostensibly, any other calling. Not that Pilade had that in view. He only sought to be comfortable, good lad.

VIII

RESURRECTION OF THE JEW

This idyllic state of things might have lasted no one knows how long, with Ippolita-Silvestro finding joy in unreasonable service, and Pilade both ease and reason. Where either partner was so admirably suited it might have been interesting to see what would have happened: whether Ippolita would have betrayed herself or Pilade found her out. She was over head and ears in love, but he was vastly well served; and there is nothing like content for drugging the wits.

Things, however, fell out otherwise. The Jew, to begin with, fell out of the grave to which he had been hastily recommended, and most insecurely at that. He made himself felt in a variety of ways, was discovered by the gardener in the Via di Vanzo, and stuck into a gutter in the Via Man di Ferro. He was discovered again by some one who had either less to do among Christians or more among Jews than the generality in Padua; and this time he was carried to the Guard House. Being reported (reporting himself, indeed) to the watch, he was reported on to the Capitano, by him to the Prefect. The Prefect put the Sub-Prefect, who had met him before, upon the look-out.

"The Most Serene Republic," said that authority, "cannot have unburied Jews adrift in the city without finding out why the cemetery does not hold them and why the gutter does. Inquire, Alessandro mio, inquire! There was a wound in the man's ribs big enough for a nest of rats."

Alessandro bowed, but raised his fine eyebrows. He was at that hour most happily unhappy over the late disappearance of his Glorious Lady. The peerless beauty of Padua, the incomparable Ippolita, was gone. His business was to devise dirges, monodies, laments, *descortz* in the Provençal manner; to cry "Heigho!" and "Well-a-day!" not "Ban!" or "Out, haro!" To have these high frenzies, these straining states of the soul, disturbed by the unclaimed remains of a resolving Jew, was a cruel test. Yet, he reflected within himself, if his piercing love survived this inquiry, it was founded on rock. And, indeed, Alessandro believed that his heart was slowly turning to stone. He felt a curious chill there when he got up in the morning, a dead weight, a mass to lift with every choked beat. Perhaps the Jew would end what Ippolita had begun. If so, well. But, ah, Ippolita, Ippolita bella, Ippolita crudel! Ah, ohimè!

Habit set him to work. He instructed his officers, he visited the gates, questioned, took notes, inspected the gutter in the Via Man di Ferro, even inspected the Jew. He went to the Via della Gatta, to the fatal staircase; he bullied two or three landlords of two or three low taverns; went to the stews, to the Ghetto; talked very loud, flourished his sword, drove his men this way and that— in fine, did everything that becomes a young official of spirit. The result of his labours was that the Jew got posthumous fame out of all proportion to his merits. The city fairly hummed with him; nobody talked of anything but the dead Jew.

The goatherds, coming in by the Porta San Zuan a day later, were shrewdly scrutinised by the Guard. They were numbered off, their names taken; they were pulled about and flustered, asked questions, contradicted before they had time to answer, and then called prevaricators because they said nothing; they were, in fact, brought to that state of breathless hurry in which a boy will say anything you choose. This, as everybody knows, is the only way of getting at the truth.

"There were more of you fellows the other night," said the Corporal of the Guard. "Where are the rest of you? Come now, out with it; no lies here!"

Petruccio, who had some sense, shammed to have none; but Andrea, less happy, was a real fool. At this invitation he looked wise.

"Castracane is not here— true, but it wasn't Castracane," he muttered, and found his neck in a vice.

"Who was it then, son of a pig? Who was it?"

"Mercy, mercy, my lord! I will tell the truth!" he whined as he twisted.

"Gesù morto! Tell anything else and I cut thy liver out, hound!" swore the man who held him.

"Ah, Dio! I will! I will! It was Silvestro who killed the Jew!"

"You shall come with me to the Signor Sotto-Prefetto," said his holder. "There's a ducat for me in this affair." The poor little company were driven into the gatehouse and there pent; but Andrea went off between two archers to be examined at greater length by Messer Alessandro, and to give blubbering confirmation of the fact. All the unfortunate particulars wrung out of Silvestro on his first night of Monte Ortone— the stab under the ribs, the Jew's beard, his black blood, etc., etc.— were now screwed out of Andrea and went to prove his story.

"By the twenty-four ears of the Twelve Apostles," swore the Corporal, "we've got him at last, Messere."

The Sub-Prefect felt that he must act upon this news. So much insistence had been laid upon the affair by his chief, he dared not send his lieutenant: he must go himself. This is what comes of neglecting new-killed Jews! he might have thought. He little knew what was to come of it.

Two mounted men, Andrea with a rope round his neck, himself very splendidly booted and cuirassed, made up a sufficient cavalcade to fetch home one snivelling goatherd. It was four by the time they were off, seven before they were at Abano, eight when they reached the foot of Monte Ortone and faced the deep chestnut woods in which that precipice dips his flanks. But though it was getting dusk there were eyes sharp enough on the top of the mountain to watch for what sharp ears had heard— a most unaccustomed sound in those leafy solitudes— trotting horses and jingling steel. Castracane from the summit saw it all; and what is more, guessed at once what Andrea in a halter meant.

IX

PYLADES FINDS HIS ORESTES

"Silvestro," he called softly, without moving from his ambush or turning his eyes from those he watched, "Silvestro, come here!"

The obedient stripling came eagerly, and knelt as close to his master as he dared— just so as to touch him.

"Eccomi, Pilade," says he.

"Get back over the brow as fast as you can," said his friend, "and hide in the cave. Wait there till I come. Go now; do as I bid you."

Silvestro went at once.

Castracane squared his jaw and waited. Every now and then he muttered to himself, with lazy lifted eyebrows. It was too much trouble to shrug. "Poor little devil— it would be a shame! And I knocked him down for nothing. And he loves me, per Bacco! Certainly, I have never been loved before— by a man, I mean— except by my big old mother out yonder, and she is a woman. She'll be sorry— she's old— eh, she's horribly old! Accursed, most rotten ass, Andrea! The whole story out of him— and a lie at that. Cospetto! I can't let the poor lad swing. And I did knock him down— and he cried like a girl; but not because I grassed him. By my soul, I'll do it— there, then!" Then he mortised his chin in his brown hands and blinked while he waited.

He had not so very long; but you might have given him an hour, it would have made no difference to Castracane then. The guard came reeking to the brow of the hill; Andrea, haltered, was with them. Alessandro, mopping his head and cursing the flies, came last.

"Look yonder, Marco," said one. The other said "Ha!" and pounced upon his treasure. He had him by the ear and was pricking him with his sabre in the fleshy parts.

"Easy, friend," said Castracane; "I'm not running away."

He went like a sheep to the Sub-Prefect. Andrea watched him twittering.

"What is your name, fellow?" said that heated officer.

Andrea's eyes yearned for his mate's. Castracane gave him a terrible look.

"Silvestro is my name, Signore," says he; and Andrea knew his game.

"We have found our bird, I think," said Alessandro, turning to his men.

"Yes, Excellency, this is the lad we want. There was another of them— Castracane they call him."

"Ah, yes. Where is Castracane, fellow?"

"He is over Venda. Gone to Noventa, to his mother," replied Castracane.

"Well, we don't want him so far as I know. Now, attend to me. You are suspected of that business in the Via della Gatta."

Castracane shrugged. "Chi lo sa?" says he.

"We shall see about that. Meantime, what have you to urge?"

Castracane scratched his head. "What would you have me say, Messere? I am a poor lad. You are many, and I am one."

Alessandro turned to his archers. "Bring him down to the hermitage," he said. "I am going to eat something. Tie him up and wait for me there. You can let the other go. This is the lad, fast enough. Avanti!"

So the shackles were taken off Andrea's raw wrists, and transferred to Castracane's; the neck halter was shifted; Castracane was bond, Andrea free. Then Messer Alessandro went down the hill to what supper the hermit could afford.

In about half an hour Silvestro, who had been fidgeting in the cave, came out, restless to have stayed so long beyond sight or hearing of his Pilade. His reception by Andrea was shocking. The gaping boy sprang forward with his arms out.

"Ha! Here is a terrible affair," he wailed.

"Our Castracane is taken, and for your fault; he will be hanged, and for you! Make your supper of it, you Jew-jerker. What sacrifice, Dio mio! There has been nothing like it, I suppose, since Giulio Cesare kissed Brutus, or Judas Gesù Cristo. You kissed him this morning; you know you did! You always do, you blush-faced sneak! And for that kiss he has taken your sins upon him, and is to be hanged. Fie, Judas, fie! Oh, Madonna Maria, the terrible affair!"

So ending as he began, he danced about the hill-top, wringing his hands.

But Silvestro, very pale, came quickly up, and laid hold of him.

"Tell me all, Andrea," says he; "for I know nothing except that I love Castracane and will save him. Who has taken him?"

"It is a lord— the Sotto-Prefetto— the hook-nosed gentleman with thin eyebrows; him they call Messer Alessandro. Castracane is tied like a netted calf— his hands behind him, and them to his neck. What's the good of his strength? He is as strong as the town bull; but if he writhes his hands he strangles, and if he thrusts his neck he chokes. Ecco!"

Silvestro was staring down into the valley. "Where is Messer Alessandro, Andrea? Tell me quickly, for I can save Castracane."

"He is eating with the hermit in the wood. But what can you do?"

"You stay here," said Silvestro with decision; "that's what you can do. I'll go down."

The sound of breaking through undergrowth was followed by rapping at the hermit's door.

"What do you want, boy?" said the pious man to the ragged figure in the dark.

"Messer Alessandro, my reverend— Messer Alessandro at once."

"Are you come about the Jew? He will bear no more. He is eating. He tells me he knows more about the Jew than he does about our holy religion— which is a dangerous state of things, except that he is sick to death of him."

"It is not about the Jew, father," said Silvestro, out of breath. "Tell him it is about— Ippolita."

"Va bene," said the hermit. "Stay where you are."

Messer Alessandro dropped his tools with a clatter, wiped his mouth, beat his breast, and began to walk up and down the cell.

"Send him in, hermit, send him in! Forty ducats if he has any news, ten ducats in any case for bringing my thoughts from Jews on earth to Ippolita in Paradise. Despatch, despatch, send me the goatherd."

The pale apparition of a fair-haired boy, timid in rags, cloaked in rusty black, with bandaged legs, and his old felt hat crushed against his breast, stood in the doorway.

"Oh, boy!" cried Alessandro, gesticulating with one hand, "may you be my Hermes, my swiftfoot messenger. Tell me what you know of the divine Ippolita."

"I know where she is, Signor Sotto-Prefetto," says Silvestro huskily.

"Tell me, by Venus and all her doves!"

For answer the blushing boy looked appealingly at Alessandro, with eyes so deeply, limpidly, searchingly blue, with lips so tenderly parted, with a smile fluttering so timidly, and limbs so drooping under their disguise, yet so quickly transformed from frightened lad's to bashful beauty's, that—

"Saints of the Heavenly Court— ah, God of Love!" cried Alessandro; and the Sub-Prefect fell upon his knees before the goatherd.

Later you might have seen that same goatherd enthroned in the hermit's armchair, his hands locked in his lap, his legs modestly disposed, his head gracefully bowed, a blush on his burnt cheeks, his long lashes casting a shade, his breath coming and going with a pretty haste— and at his feet a splendid gentleman, booted and cuirassed, who poured out voluble assurances of eternal respect, of love undying, of the sovranty of Venus Urania, and the communion of beautiful minds.

"I will see you again; yes, I will certainly see you again, since you so desire it," said Silvestro, after a good deal of this. "And I will give you what you ask, if it is in my power. But you must trust me so far: you must go away from here, and wait till I send word. I shall owe you every gratitude, every reward I can give you. Now, however, you must let me go; and I must take with me the goatherd, who is as innocent of the Jew's death as I am."

"Ah, I will do all that you wish," sighed Alessandro. "Sacred lady, I will do it. But surely you will have pity upon a humble slave who has served you long and faithfully, and now is putting himself in peril for your pleasure. Pay me my poor fee, lady. Enrich me boundlessly with what costs you so little."

So he urged, until—

"Well," says Silvestro, "I will do it. Rise up, Messere; take what you will."

Messer Alessandro shut his eyes, and slowly rose to his feet. Having kissed the goatherd's hand, he very delicately kissed the goatherd's proffered cheek. "I am paid immeasurably, most holy one," he said. "Lead now; I will do what you desire."

Out sped Silvestro into the wood, the Sub-Prefect bareheaded behind him. In a glade not far from the hermitage sat the two archers. The horses were tethered to one tree, Castracane to another. Seeing their chief, the men sprang to attention; their astonishment at what followed was no greater than Castracane's. Silvestro (that timid slave), now as bold as brass, walked straight to him, the Sub-Prefect tiptoeing behind.

"Loose him, Signore," says Silvestro.

The Sub-Prefect with a knife cut his bonds. "Your will is done."

"Thank you, Signor Alessandro: God be with you. Come, Pilade."

Silvestro took Castracane by the hand, but not before the gentleman had kissed his own with profound respect. Then Silvestro led his friend away through the trees, and the Sub-Prefect was understood to say—

"We have been on the wrong scent, men. Mount. To the city— Avanti!"

"What's all this? Whither now?" stammered Castracane.

Silvestro squeezed his hand. "Oh, dearest, let us go to the cave— let us go to the cave on the hill!"

Castracane felt his friend trembling. Trembling is infectious; he began to tremble too.

"Yes, yes, we will go to our cave," he agreed in a quick whisper.

X

CYMON FINDS HIS IPHIGENIA

They struggled upwards through the bushwood and starry flowers. It was a scented night, the air heavy with the burden of midsummer. The fireflies spread a jewelled web before their faces, great white moths flapped and droned about them. On they pushed, their hands locked through all hazards of brake or briar: neither would let go for a whole world, but Silvestro was always in front, leading Castracane for this once. One knew the way as well as another; but Silvestro led it. They rounded the hill-top.

"Here we are at last," said Silvestro. "Let us sit here, and look at the splendour of the night. Oh, Pilade! Oh, dear friend! How couldst thou do so much for me?"

"What else could I do?" said he gruffly. "You never killed the pig-Jew."

"Nor did you, Pilade. Tell me why you gave yourself up."

"Because you didn't do it, of course."

"But you didn't do it either?"

"Well, but I knocked you down."

"Did you do it because of that; or because— because you like me?"

Pilade grunted. "Suppose I did?"

Silvestro sighed, and leaned his head on his friend's shoulder.

"O wondrous night!" said he, whispering. "Look, the stars are like moons."

It was certainly a wonderful night— a night of enormous silence, of great steady stars, of gold-dusted air, of a sky like a purple dome encrusted with jewelled lights. The two boys sat together, blinking at so much speechless glory. Castracane's arm was round his fellow's shoulder; that fellow's lips parted, and his breath came soft and eager— yet too quickly for ease. It was certainly a night of wonder.

Castracane's arm slipped down to Silvestro's waist; Silvestro sighed, and snuggled into the haven it made.

"O holy night!" said he. "Now might miracles happen, and we be by."

"Ah," said Castracane, "the miracle of choice would be an angel with a basket of bread and cheese— or a beautiful maiden to come and lie in one's arms."

Silvestro thrilled. Castracane gave a responsive squeeze, and went on.

"I am not too sure, you must know, that one has not happened already. To see you lead that signore by the nose! You came swimming among the tree-stems like an angel. You might have knocked me down with a feather. And how he kissed your hand! Miracles! Why, if you had been the maiden I dream about, he couldn't have been more respectful. If you want miracles, for example!"

"I do want them, Pilade. I want them very much." Silvestro sighed again, and leaned his cheek till it touched his friend's.

A shock transfused Castracane; he was caught by the starry influences. Suddenly he turned his mouth towards that blushing flower, and kissed Silvestro. Silvestro thrilled but lay close.

"Buon' Dio, ecco miracolo!" said Castracane hoarsely, and kissed again.

Again his nestling companion gave no sign but a quiver.

Castracane surveyed the stars. "A miracle has certainly happened," he said. "I feel very queer. My head swims, fingers and toes tingle; I seem to have hot lead in my legs. It may be that I am empty. I think it is a miracle; but as yet I see no angel."

Some quicker thrill of what he held made him look at Silvestro. At the same moment Silvestro slowly turned his head, and looked at him. What each saw in the other's face beyond a white moon-shape, what shining of truth in the eye, what expectancy, what revelation in the lips, I know not. Two pair of lips, at least, met and stayed together.

"O Dio!"

"Oh, Pilade! Oh, carissimo!" She abandoned herself to joy.

"*You* are the angel, the miracle! You are— "

"No, no, I am not an angel; but oh, I love you, dearly!"

"Ah, la Madonna!"

"I am Ippolita! I love you!"

"You love me? You are mine then— come."

"Andrea," said Castracane next morning, "I think the others will be back before noon. You must wait here till they come. I am going to take Silvestro over La Venda to see my mother, and confess to our curate. It is good for the soul."

"Silvestro looks well this morning," said Andrea, with his mouth full of bread. "What a colour of dawn! What shining eyes! He would make a proper Madonna for a Mystery— eh?"

"He would," said Castracane laconically; "a most proper Madonna. With a *Bambino* on his lap— eh, Silvestro."

Silvestro blushed; Castracane pinched his cheek, which made matters worse.

They took the road together through the deep hedges of the valley. Monte Venda rose before them, dark with woods. Castracane's arm was round Silvestro's waist: every twenty yards they stopped.

"To think of it!" cried Castracane, on one of these breathless halts. "You to be like any one of us— breeched, clouted, swathed— and a lovely lass within your shirt— Madonna!"

"Do you think me lovely?" asked Ippolita devoutly. "I have heard that till I have been sick to death of it; but from you I shall never be tired of knowing it."

"Blessed Angel!"

"Oh, Pilade, my love!"

They loitered on.

"You see that I am not what you thought me," said Ippolita, with an arch look. "You thought I had killed a Jew."

"Never, per Bacco!" cried Castracane. "That I'll swear to."

"You thought I was a boy, even last night, dearest."

But that he denied. "Santissimo! Did I treat you like a boy, I ask you?"

"You knocked me down once, Pilade."

"Every honest man knocks his wife down once," said Pilade gravely.

"And then you kissed me."

"I can kiss you again," said Pilade; and did.

I repeat, Padua is a freakish city. The Sub-Prefect writes madrigals in vain. Castracane, the goatherd, sends Silvestro sprawling, and wins the golden Ippolita for a willing bride. What are we to make of it? *Deus nobis hæc otia fecit.*

THE DUCHESS OF NONA

"L'Anima semplicetta, che sa nulla,
Salvo che, mossa da lieto fattore,
Volentier torna a ciò che la trastulla."
— *Purg.* xvi. 88.

I

BOCCA BACIATA

"Not unprosperous is your Erasmus in England," wrote that man of wiles to one Faustus, a poet; and then— "To touch upon one among many delights, there are girls in this land divinely fair— soft, easy, and more wooing than any of your Muses. Moreover, they have a custom which cannot be too much honoured. Wheresoever you go a-visiting, the girls all kiss you. With kisses you come in, with kisses depart; returning, they kiss you again. Cometh one to you, the kisses fly between; doth she go away, with kisses you are torn asunder; meeting in any place, kisses abound. Go where you will, it is all kisses. Indeed, my Faustus, had you but once tasted of lips so fragrant and so soft, not for a time only, but to your end of days, you would choose to be a pilgrim in this England." By no means the only stranger to be charmed by our welcoming girls was Erasmus. Amilcare Passavente, of a darker blood, found such kisses sweet: those of one at least he vowed to call his own. What he made of them, what they of him, what other diverting matter appertains to the kisser and the kissed, you shall understand who care to read.

Mary was her name in our Lord, Lovel that of her father in the flesh, a respectable wharfinger of Bankside. Molly, Mawkin, Moll Lovel, "Long Moll Lovel," and other things similar she was to her kinsfolk and acquaintance, who had seen her handsome body outstrip her simple mind. Good girl that she was, she carried her looks as easily as a packet of groceries about the muddy ways of Wapping, went to church, went to market, gossiped out the dusk at the garden gate, or on the old wharf, after the 'prentices had gone, linked herself waist to waist with maiden friends. Up river or down, she trafficked in a wherry, and took the waterman's tender glances as part receipt for his hire. In a word, this winsome, rosy creature, grown hardy in a kind soil, adventured herself at ease among them that might have been her poets, adorers, or raveners, nor thought to be cheapened by the liberty she employed. She was rather shy with strangers, conscious of her height, awkward under observation, blushing to know she blushed; but simple as the day, pleased with flattery, pleased with other trifles,— trinkets, snatched kisses, notes slipped into the prayer-book, etc. She told her mother everything before she went to bed, sat on her father's knee when she was too old and much too tall for it, dreamed of lovers, hid trembling when they came, had palpitations, never told a fib or refused a sweet-meat; she was, in fact, just the honest, red-cheeked, pretty, shy simple-ton of a lass you will meet by the round dozen in our country, who grows into the plump wife of Master Church-warden-in-broadcloth, bears a half-score children, gets flushed after midday dinner, and would sooner miss church than the postman any day in the year. Such was Molly Lovel at nineteen, honestly handsome and honestly a fool, whom in Bankside they knew as Long-legged Moll.

To Amilcare Passavente, the young merchant-adventurer from Leg-horn, ravished as he was by the spell of her cool lips, she became at once "La divina Maria," or shorter, "La Diva"; and in a very light space of time, when his acquaintance with her and hers with his tongue had ripened, she had quite a nosegay of names: Madonna Collebianca (my Lady Whitethroat), Donna Fiordispina, La Bella Rosseggiante, were three among three dozen flowers of speech, picked from a highly scented garden of such for her adorning. Amilcare translated them in his hoarse, eager voice, helped on by his hands (which were rapid) and his beseeching eyes (which had the flattery of deference), not only to Molly apart, but to all or any of her acquaintance who could listen with-out giggling. Molly pressed her bosom; her friends, as they loitered home, said in each other's ears, "Blessed Lord, what will become of Gregory Drax?" Gregory Drax was the broad-girthed young master of a trading-smack which coasted between London and Berwick, and was even at that hour in Kirkley Roads, standing off Yarmouth.

All a summer this endured, but went no further while Amilcare, new to the blunt ways of the English, was unable to stomach their cropped speech any better than their sour beer. Those who heard his florid par-aphrase took it gravely, yet held by their "Moll Lovel." They wished that Gregory Drax might have a fair wind home; they wondered what Master Lovel was about; trusted that the black-eyed rascal (whose speech was too glib, surely, to be honest) would not make a fool of the girl. He very soon showed them that, whatever else he did, he intended to make a woman of her. Let them hold, said he (for once expressing his contempt), to their "Molly Lovel"— the name was the Shadow. He would hold, as at that moment he was very devoutly holding, Molly

herself— aha! the blessed Substance. And when the young Molly let
herself go whither her soft desires had long since fled; when she felt
the heart of Amilcare jumping against hers, his cheek, his lips, his soft
syllabling, her own breathless replies— then at last Amilcare, quite enraptured, finding everything about her wonder and delight, made shift
to catch up some waft of her very tongue, closer savour of her very
home, and called her on high his adorable, his unending, his altogether
soul-devastating, destroying mistress, "Madonna Mollavella." Good
Master Lovel the wharfinger neither knew his daughter nor his father's
name in this long-drawn compound of liquids; he was troubled, very
doubtful, anxious for Gregory Drax; but all Lombardy and the Emilian
March came to know it in time. Amilcare rode down opposition. Eloquence! Were ever such cries to great Heaven, such invitations to
Olympus, slappings of the forehead, punchings of ribs, in Wapping before? Molly in tears on her mother's breast, Amilcare on his knees, the
neighbours at the door: Master Lovel, good man, abominated such
scenes. Father Pounce married them at St. Saviour's in Southwark;
money abounded, the dowry passed from hand to hand. On a gusty
November morning there sailed out of the London river the
barque *Santa Fina* of Leghorn, having on board Amilcare Passavente
and Donna Maria his wife, bound (as all believed) for that port, and
thence by long roads to their country of adoption— not Pisa, nor
Lucca, nor any place Tuscan; but Nona in the March of Emilia. No;
Erasmus was not the only traveller whirled about by English kisses, nor
Molly Lovel the only simple witch in turn bewitched.

II

AMILCARE: COMMERCE AND THE AFFECTIONS

Molly was a handsome fool: let there be no doubt about that. There was no romance in her, though sentiment enough. She lacked the historic sense; and if she thought of Rome at all, supposed it a collocation of warehouses, jetties, and a church or two— an unfamiliar Wapping upon a river with a long name. Her sensations on the voyage were those of sea-sickness, on the golden-hazy Campagna those of home-sickness unaffected. Affectation of any sort was far from her. If she was happy she showed her white teeth, if wretched she either pouted or cried; if she liked you there were kisses, if she distrusted you she grew red. But she distrusted no one. Why should she? Since every act of hers was, in seeming, a caress of personal intention, every one loved her. As for her husband, when he was not sacramentally engaged, he mutely raved to the stars, protesting by his dimmed eyes, moving lips, and strained-out arms how every breath she took was to him also an inspiration. Her frankness, the truth lucent in her eyes, her abounding receptivity,— for she believed everything she was told and objected to nothing,— her sweet long body, the tired grace with which she carried her lovely head, her tender, stroking ways, the evenness of her temper (which only that of her teeth could surpass),— all this threatened to make of Amilcare a poet or a saint, something totally disparate to his immediate proposals. His nature saved him for the game which his nature had taught him.

In that great game he had to play Molly (though he loved her dearly) must be, he saw, his prime counter. Coming to England to negotiate bills of exchange, he had Molly thrown in. She would do more for him than rose-nobles. He ecstatised over his adorable capture; but saw no reason in that why he should not lay it out to advantage. It would not cheapen in the chaffer; on the contrary, give him the usufruct for a few years, and he would be not only the happiest but the most considerable of men. Triumphant Bacchus! (so he mused to himself) what had he not gained? A year's pay for his men, the confidence of the "Signori" of Nona, the acclamations of the Piazza and the Council Chamber at once— and Molly Lovel. Hey! that was best of all. For her sake, and by her means, he would be Capitano del Popolo. What else? That would do for a beginning. If Molly could turn his head, she could turn other heads, he supposed. A turned head meant a disponable body, a bending back, an obsequious knee, even a carcase at a quick hand's discretion; votes in Council, delirium in the Piazza, *Te Deum* in the Church.

Amilcare knew his countrymen: he that knows them half as well will have no trouble in conceiving how these trade-calculations can consist with a great deal of true love. And what was Amilcare's trade? His trade was politics, the stock whereof was the people of Nona, the shifty, chattering, light-weight spawn of one of those little burnt-brick and white cities of the Lombard Plain— set deep in trees, domed, belfried, full of gardens and fountains and public places— which owed their independence to being too near a pair of rival states to be worth either's conquering. There were some score of these strewn over Southern Emilia and Romagna in those days, and the time was almost at hand, and with it the man, to sweep them all into one common net of wretchedness. But Amilcare had no clear thought of that. For the moment Nona was as peaceful as Forlì, or Rimini, or Pesaro, or Faenza, thanks to him and his "Centaurs"— that famous band of free riders he had levied from the Tuscan hills. Very much at his mercy, safe under the eye of his trusted Secretary, awaiting his return, he fully intended that peace to continue when she fell huddling to him. It would, indeed, be his care; for it was a maxim of Italian politics that no man willingly stirs after dinner.

The situation was still pretty delicate; he had done little more than win foothold. In the late struggles with Parma he had intrigued with great address; sold himself and his Centaurs to Farnese, brought that thick-necked hero up to the very walls of Nona, then (in the nick of time) resold himself at double the price to the city he was besieging, and routed his yesterday's master by an attack in flank just as the Nonesi were carrying the trenches in front. In the excitement of that wonderful hour— Farnese in full flight, himself borne on men's shoulders round the Piazza, thanksgiving in the cathedral, clouds of incense, clashing bells, wine running in the Fontana delle Grazie— he had for a moment been tempted to believe the times ripe for a proclamation: "Amilcar, Dei Gratia, Nonarum Dux," etc. He had his treble wages in his pocket, the hearts of the whole city throbbing at his feet. He was a young man: tempted he certainly was. But Grifone (the Secretary) touched his elbow and showed a straightened lip. He would not risk it. He contented himself with a footing, the Palazzo Bagnacavallo rent-free, and the title of "Gonfalonerius Populorum Libertatis," which looked passably well about a broad seal. "Pater Patriae," "Nonarum Dux," the control of the bread-tax,— all should be added to him in time, if only the Borgia could be fed elsewhere. At the thought of that hearty eater stalled in the Vatican, he felt that he might indeed thank God for his lovely Molly. With her for decoy even that game-bird might be lured. Lying on the poop of the *Santa Fina*, his dark eyes questing over her face, her hands among his curls, he seemed to Molly the wonder of the world. So of her world he was; but he meant to be that of his own— a very different world.

He was a lithe, various creature, this Amilcare Passavente, his own paradox. Quick as a bird of prey he was, and at times as inert; dark as night, eagle-faced, flat-browed, stiff and small in the head, clean-featured, with decisive lips. A very fluent speaker, hoarse in voice, but cunning in the vibrations he could lend it, he was in action as light and fierce as a flame; at rest as massive as a block of stone, impervious to threats or prayers or tears. Women loved him easily, men followed him blindly, and both for the same reason— that they believed him ruthless to all but themselves. Ruthless, indeed, he had been, and was to all and sundry. Molly was the one apparent exception, and in her eyes he was perfect. For her immediate comfort this may have been true of him. He was a brave lover.

He taught her to falter endearments in his own tongue: he was *carino, caro amico, anima mia, sovrano del mio cuor*, and many other things yet more intimate. In return he gave her a homage which was not without a certain depth because it was done with foresight. He taught her to be his slave by professing himself hers, and so touching her generosity as well as her humility. At all this she was very apt. There was a fund of deep affection in the girl, the makings of an excellent wife, a devoted mother— far more stuff than should go to serve as toy for a man's idle hours. Also she was very demonstrative, by no means averse (quite the contrary, indeed) to demonstrations on his part. She loved to walk belted by his arm, loved to put her head on his shoulder, or have her chin lifted that eyes or lips might be kissed. These favours, which his nation was accustomed to keep at home, she wore without self-consciousness abroad. It enchanted Amilcare, not only as a thing beautiful in itself, but as a clear source of profit in his schemes. He pictured the havoc she would work in a hall full of the signori— keen men all— when she sailed through the rooms offering her lips to whoso would greet them "English fashion." Why, the whole city would be her slave— eh, and more than the city! Bentivoglio of Bologna, Il Moro of Milan, Ordelaffi, Manfredi, Farnese, the Borgia, the Gonzaga, D'Este of Ferrara, Riario, Montefeltro, Orsini— by the Saint of Padua, he would face them each with his beautiful wife; charm them, turn their heads, and then— *ping*! Let the neatest wrist win the odd trick. Very pleasant schemes of witchery and silent murder did he make as the *Santa Fina* drove him through the dark blue waters on his honeymoon, and at last brought him up to point out to his adoring instrument a low golden shore, a darker line of purple shadow beyond, and in the midst a white tower which gleamed like snow. "Civitavecchia, my queen among ladies! Rome beyond it; beyond that Nona— Nona and glorious life for thee and me!" he cried, as he waved her towards these splendid things.

But Molly snuggled closer to him and sighed.

He, very sensitive to alien moods, was conscious of the jar. "You are sad, beloved?" he asked her softly. "You are thinking of your own land?"

"No, no, dearest; not that now. I was thinking only— but it is foolishness of a fool," said Molly, hiding her face.

"You cannot be a fool, blessed one, since you are not so much as human as I see you now," he whispered, holding her close. "You are a rosy god at this moment, my treasure. You are all colour of dawn, auroral, colour of tender fires. Tell me your thought, my holy one."

She whispered it back. "It was— that you will be full of business at Nona, Amilcare. You will have no time to love your poor Molly."

The rogue was fishing for protestations, and got them.

"Love you!" he cried. "Ah, tell me how long I have to live, and I will tell you the hours of my love, O my soul!"

"But you will be abroad, a-horseback, with your captains, in the tents— "

"Why, yes, that must be so," he owned. "But I shall love you the more for that, Molletta."

She pretended to pout, fidgeted in his arm, arched her neck.

"But how shall I know it, Amilcare, if I am not there?"

"By what I do to you when I return, dearest love," cried he; and thereafter, speaking by signs, was better understood.

III

MARKET COVERT

They made Rome a day or two after that little tender and exchange of vows, having disembarked amid a crowd of clamorous Amilcares in rags— she could see some dear trait of him in each; trailed across the bleached marches (with the Sabine Hills like a blue hem beyond); caught the sun at Cervetri, and entered the dusty town by the Porta Cavalleggieri on one of those beaten white noons when the shadows look to be cut out of ebony, and the wicked old walls forbidden to keep still. The very dust seems alive, quivering and restless under heat. St. Peter's church, smothered in rush mats, was a-building, the marble blocks had the vivid force of lightning; two or three heretic friars were being hailed by the Ponte Sant' Angelo to a burning in the Vatican; Molly was almost blind, had a headache, a back-ache, and a heart-ache. Amilcare, who had fallen in with a party of lancers by the way, had ridden for a league or two in vehement converse with their lieutenant. To him there seemed more to say than ever to her. She felt hurt and wanted to cry.

At their inn they learned the news— that is, Amilcare learned it, for Molly was languishing upon a bed, forgotten and mercifully forgetting. Pretty news it was. Don Cesare, it appeared, had stabbed the Duke of Gandia, his brother, three nights ago, and thrown him into the Tiber. The body had only been fished out yesterday; it had nine wounds in it, including one in the throat big enough to put your fist in. It was a sieve, not a body: perforated! His Holiness? Ah, he could be heard even here, howling in the Vatican, like a bitch in an empty house. Don Cesare was in hiding, reported at Foligno. To-morrow there was to be a Holy Conclave— all the Cardinals. God knew what Alexander had or had not in his mind, the conscience-stricken old dog. It was known what he had not in his house, at least. Vannozza had been thrice refused admission; so also La Bella Lucrezia. Think of it!

This was very grave news to Amilcare's private ear. Cesare was his deadly enemy, the one man he honestly feared; the one man, consequently, he wanted to meet. He was still brooding over it when the broad-backed butcher they call Il Drudo slammed him on the back.

"Fortune is with you, Passavente— the slut! She gives you time to breathe. The Borgia had a sinking of the stomach; he hankered after a filling of Lombard sausage a little while since. Gandia cut in, and Cesare cut in, *per Bacco*! But mark my words, Amilcare, the appetite will return. You will have the Duke in your March before many days. There-fore my advice to you is— Avoid Foligno; fortify Nona."

Amilcare looked his man in the face. "And my advice to myself, Galeotto, is— Seek Foligno, and so fortify Nona. *Addio.*" He went out like a man who has found his way.

"Now, what the devil did the fellow mean by that?" cried Il Drudo, with his thick fingers out.

"Devilry expresses it," said a sly secretary in black.

Molly in dreams, soft as a child and glossy with sleep, looked too beautiful for a disturbing hand to dare anything that night. It would have been the act of a brute, not Amilcare's act. In small things he was all gentleness. He crept into bed like a cat, fearful of waking her, and next morning contrived, by a fit of coughing, to waken her no more than half. The rest he did by methods equally adroit, until by impercep-tible degrees she learned that Rome might give no ease to her feet. He had her in the saddle and all the baggage-mules away an hour after the sun.

Arrived at Foligno, he found that his great enemy was at sanctuary in the Convent of Olivet, biting his nails in a red fume there. Hidden behind spires of cypress, Olivet stood outside the walls, a sun-dyed white building deep under brown eaves. Cesare, it was reported, was quite alone with his moods, now consumed by fidgety remorse for what he might have lost in his brother's blood, now confident and inclined to blusterous hilarity, now shuddering under an obsession of nerves. In any guise he was dangerous, but worst of all when the black fit of sus-picion was upon him. So he now seemed; for being told who waited upon him, he refused point-blank to see anybody. Amilcare, at the door, heard his "Vattene, vattene! Non seccami!" ("Out, out! Don't pester me!") rocking down the dim passages of the house; and Molly, whom this sudden new expedition had bereft of what wit she had, turned pale to hear the roaring beast.

"Ah, love, love, love, let us run away! I like not this empty place," whimpered the girl, holding her husband's arm; but he gently removed her hand, kissed it, and held it.

"Courage, dear one; I shall be by thy side. Much depends upon this adventure," he urged in fervent whispers, knowing how much to a tit-tle.

To the monk who came out, distended with Cesare's explosives, he addressed himself in a vernacular too fluid for Molly to catch up.

"I pray you, reverend brother, recommend me yet once more to the feet of his Resplendency, saying that not I alone supplicate his favours.

Add that I have with me, to present, my most beautiful wife, that she may assure him with her own lips how very much she is his slave."

The pantomime of piteous beseeching hands, of eyebrows exquisitely arched, told more than his words. They showed to a hair's breadth how far he expected, how far was prepared, to tempt his customer. No pedlar before a doorful of girls' sidelong heads could more deftly have marketed his wares. The monk, too, sidled his head; he pursed his mouth, furrowed with a finger in his dewlap, tried to appraise the wares. But to allow this would have been to forestall the market.

"Ah, for love of the saints, go, my brother!" he was entreated, with gentle persistence; and so worked upon, he waddled away.

Amilcare let fall a hearty sigh, and considered Molly with anxiety. He had not dared to say a word to her of what her entertainer was, or what her part should be. Premeditation might throw her out of balance, conscious art might exhibit her a scheming courtesan; just in her artlessness lay all her magic. No, no; he trusted her. She was still adorably English— witness her on the ship! He could see how she would do, how the sight would ravish him, lover as he was; for the rest, he must trust to his early calculations. Yes! he was ready to stake everything upon this move. The Borgia would be at her feet: so at his feet also. Oh, wise, wise Amilcare!

"His Eminence the Duke will receive your Lordship," said the returning monk, and turned once more to lead the way.

"My saint, my lamb, my meek burnished dove!" breathed Amilcare in a glow, and pressed her to his heart behind the frate's broad back.

Cesare, magnificently tawny in black velvet, was in a window, raking with a white hand at his beard, a prey evidently to cross-tides of fever. When his visitors were announced he looked sharply round; but Molly was hooded, her face deep in the shade. Of Passavente he had not the slightest concern. That hero was prostrate, bowing and chattering, and explaining with his hands.

Molly stayed twittering by the door, wonderful because she saw her King of Men cringing like a footboy before a shorter than himself. True, it was case of a duke; but she had not known such dealings in Wapping. There men doffed caps to my Lord or his Grace; they gave and took their due, but did not writhe on the floor. And then this particular duke's blockish inattention to what her lord was saying filled her with concern. There he leaned, and there he looked out of window at the twinkling acacias, and there he picked his beard. Amilcare's tact must have deserted him, since he could let this simple slave turn critic. But the part, in any case, was difficult. Presently the Duke threw him a hasty phrase, a sort of *pish, man*! which cut him off in the midst of a period, and walked towards Molly in the doorway. Amilcare flew before on tenterhooks. Cesare came graciously on— it was curious to see how his face had cleared. Molly dropped a curtsy, covering herself closer with a hand at the hood's tie. Cesare showed his teeth, held out both his hands. Passavente, with a displaying air full of alacrity and deference, unveiled his wife, and she went forward to greet his Grace.

She had been uncovered as by a dealer, but even so thrilled to feel his touch upon her shoulders, and showed herself blushing with the emotion, lovelier for love. Cesare was really startled to see how vividly beautiful she was; but, with more command of himself than the other trafficker, was careful not to show it. He smiled yet more sunnily; his words were some pleasant, friendly compliment. Molly, guessing it so, came nearer, took his open hands, and put up her face for his kiss. Cæsar Borgia took a deep breath before he accepted of the rest. Then he did kiss her, twice. He was ridiculously pleased, very much in confusion for a little while. Since he could say nothing and she had nothing to say, the pair of them stood hand-clasped, smiling, dim-eyed and red in the face, like two glad children— Amilcare, anxious mothering hen, clucking about them. The Duke, having recovered himself, murmured some courtesy, and led his captive to a seat in the window. His half-dozen English words and her six Italian, his readiness, her simplicity, put matters on a friendly footing: very soon Molly was chattering like a school-girl. Cesare was enchanted; he recovered his gaiety, forgot his bloody hands, his anxieties, schemes, fret at inaction. He ordered a meal to be served at once, kept Molly close to his side, heaped her plate, pledged her in wine. He went so far as to forget all common precautions and eat whatsoever was put before him.

Be sure Amilcare missed nothing. He saw all, perhaps more than all: he was used to deal with men. Thought he to himself, "Hey! If this was my house of Nona, *amico*, and the time six months hence, you would sleep where you supped." But Cesare had no thought of Amilcare until the end. Then he clapped him on the shoulder.

"My Passavente," he cried, "you have gone far on your pearl-fishing and dived deeper than most of us, but by our hope of salvation you have found a jewel of price! And ah, Madonna," he said, with his burning eyes on the girl, "you have brought the sun into Italy. You shall be called *Principessa della Pace*, who heal all sorrow and strife by the light of your face."

"I humbly thank your Grace," said Molly, very grateful; but Amilcare dropped upon one knee.

"Splendour," says he, "deign to visit our poor house in Nona, if you would learn what willing service is."

"My friend, be sure of me," said the Borgia, and meant it. "Do you bid me come, Princess?" His looks ate her up.

Molly hung her head. "I shall in all things serve your Grace," said she, with a curtsy. She kissed him again, and then Amilcare took her away.

The Borgia wrote sonnets that night.

"Mollavella, pearl of ladies," whispered her ardent husband, when they were on the North Road and in the thick of the violet Roman night, "never have I felt such joy in you as this day." He looked up at the massed company of the stars. "Fiery in all that galaxy, yonder I see my own star!" he cried in a transport. "Behold, it points us dead to the North. O Star, lit by a star! 'Tis you have set it burning clear, my glorious Princess."

"Dearest heart, I shall die of love," sighed swooning Molly, out of herself at such praise. "But indeed I have done little enough for you as yet."

"More than you think, or can dream," he answered, and spoke truly; for the girl saw nothing in their late visit but a civility done to a great lord.

"If the Duke comes to Nona, Amilcare, I will try to put him at his ease," she said after a little.

"Try, try, dear soul; it is all that I wish."

"He seemed not so to me when first we went to him, Amilcare."

Amilcare shrugged. "Eh, per la Madonna— !" he began, as who should say, "Being known for his brother's butcher, how should he be?" But he stayed in time. "He has many enemies," he added quietly.

IV

MARKET OVERT

Nona, little city of domes and belfries and square loggias, all in a cluster behind brown walls; with gates of Roman masonry, stolid Lombard church, a piazza of colonnades and restless poplar trees; of a splayed fountain where the Three Graces, back to back, spurt water from their breasts of bronze— Nona, in our time, is not to be discerned from the railway, although you may see its ranked mulberry-trees and fields of maize, and guess its pleasant seat in the plain well enough. It is about the size of Parma, a cheerful, leisurely place, abounding in shade and deep doorways and *cafés*, having some thirty churches (mostly baroque), a fine Palazzo della Ragione in the principal square, and the remains of a cathedral of the ninth century glooming behind a monstrous façade of the seventeenth, all whitewash, cornucopias, and sprawling Apostles. Thus it seems now to the strayed traveller who, breaking his journey at Castel Bolognese, simmers for four hours in an omnibus along with priests, flies, fleas, and old women. The *cortège* from Papal territory saw a vastly different city of it when it approached the gates in the early spring of 1494. The young leafage shimmered like a veil of golden gauze, the poplar buds were pink and brown, the chestnuts had all their candles afire; larks by dozens were abroad in the clear sky. Below the old Rocca del Capitan Vecchio— a grizzled and blind block of masonry on a spur of limestone, which held not a few of Ezzelin's secrets— two miles from Nona, stood a company of boys and girls in white garments, their laps full of flowers. Their shrill song of welcome hailed the riders, and to the same hopeful music they went on. The towers were all standing in those days, the battlements intact; at every gate stood a guard. The Cathedral of the Santi Apostoli had no Apostles; its great front was a cube of unfinished brick; but colonnades ran in all the streets, row after row of beautifully ordered arches; over them were jutting cornices enriched with dancing children, sea monsters, tritons, dolphins, nymphs blowing conches, Nereus, Thetis, and all their sleek familiars, moulded in red clay. The fountain shone, the displayed Graces jetted their crystal store; from every window hung carpets, on every tower a gonfalon, from every church belfry came the riot of bells. The people were massed at the gates, at the windows, on roofs and loggias and balconies— a motley of orange and blue, crimson and green. Soldiers lined the ways, priests with banners were on the steps of their churches. "Evviva, Amilcare!

Evviva, Madonna Inglese!" ran like a river of sound from the gates about the streets, until, in the Piazza Grande, where the Signoria waited in the solemn estate of brocade and ermine, the volume of it had the throbbing roll of breakers on a cliff. Thud upon thud came "Evviva!" each with a shock which made pale Molly catch her breath; more than once or twice her eyes swam, and she felt herself wag helpless in the saddle. But Amilcare, snuffing wine, was in his glory, idol of a crowd he despised and meant to rule. Proud he looked and very greatly a ruler, firm-lipped, with a high head, and a flush on his dark cheeks.

At the steps of the Palazzo della Ragione he halted, cap in hand. The trumpeters shrilled for silence, the Secretary of the Republic read a Latin speech; everybody applauded what nobody understood. Amilcare, at the end of it, swung off his horse and ran up the steps. He embraced the orator, embraced the signori one after another; greetings flashed about, tears, laughter, clappings on the back. But he kept his head throughout: it was seen that he wished to present his wife. Present her! Enthusiasm grew frenzied; he had to battle his way down the steps to regain her side. He lifted her lightly down; hand in hand they went up the steps again. Molly excelled herself, was the wonder of the whole city. How she curtsied to their lordships— what a figure she had for that grace— how tall, how supple, and how slim! When she gave her rosy cheek to each in turn, there was a kind of caught sob audible in the crowd. The simplicity of the act brought tears to tender eyes: men laughed or looked haggard, according as the trouble took them; women, more at home with tears, clung to each other as they cried. A marvel all believed her— an angel clean from heaven; the kiss of peace, *la bocca della Carità*! A young Dominican became inspired; he showed the whites of his eyes, he spumed at the lips, began to mutter, with gurglings in the throat. At last his words broke strangling from him— "O mouth of singular favour! O lips of heavenly dew!" he stuttered, with a finger on high seesawing to the rhythm: "O starry eyes conversant with the aspect of angels!" He dropped down plump in a fit, barely heard at the palace door; but all the square surged with his cry— "O mouth of singular favour! O starry eyes! Evviva Madonna!"

Men and women all told, Molly must have been forty times kissed. Twice forty times would not have sufficed for the candidates who jostled, strained, and prayed between the soldiers' pikes below the steps. It would be difficult to say which sex her pretty artlessness pleased the more: she made the women cry, the old men prophesy, the young men dream dreams. Certainly, there was nobody who thought ill of her for a performance so glaringly counter to Italian ways, whose men kiss each other while they keep their women at home. The thing was so transparent, done in such pure good faith, there was no room for judgment in it. She went among that people as, in these days, a child still might go. To those bullet-headed captains, grim and shaven close; to those painted great ladies, whose bare necks looked the more naked for their jewels; to those cruddled, be-robed old men; to the dapper sons of them; to their stiff-laced daughters— Molly went blushing, smiling, shy, and glad, and to each she gave her fresh cheek and the balm of her English lips. O mouth of singular favour! O starry eyes! She bereft them of compliments by her speechless welcome, overcame policy by having none, led captivity captive. Amilcare might hover behind her with plots, a delighted and forgotten shade: Molly Lovel of Bankside was Duchess of Nona, and might have been Queen of Italy, if all Italy had stood in the Piazza Grande. She was throned at a banquet, escorted home by the Signoria bareheaded; she was serenaded all night by relays of citizens, by straining poets, by all kinds of music. She had not a wink of sleep till morning, nor the faintest idea what it was all about.

There was no withstanding the popular voice; the Nonesi went mad to be a Duchy, with Molly for Duchess. Amilcare might be thrown in. They besieged the Bagnacavallo *Cortile*; they wrote sonnets and madrigals, and sang them day in, day out. Amilcare, acting with admirable discretion, kept very much to himself; he sent his beautiful wife on to the balcony twice a day to be saluted, and (more sparingly) let her work for him among the higher sort with her lips, her blushes, and her friendly grey eyes. He was humble in the Council, sober beneath the heaped-up honours of the popular voice, stern only with his mercenaries. A fortnight of this swept him to the top of his hopes. A deputation, with a laurel crown and the title of *Dux* in a casket, waited upon him. He had expected it for a week, and carefully dragooned his Molly.

"I must refuse the thing," he told her, "for your dear sake, my angel. The fatigues, the affairs of a Ruler of State are incredible. I will never let you bear them. The signori may pluck their beards out by the roots. I am resolved." Molly wept to hear him.

When the great morning came— a luminous April day of showers and warm wind— he was as good as his word. Molly, shining with pride in him (herself wearing the day's "uncertain glory"), saw him fold his arms in face of the pompous line of men his seniors, compress his mouth, shake his cropped head. The deputation was much taken aback, the crowd drove hither and thither; she saw head turned to head, guessed at wounds which certainly any one there was incapable of feeling. She, however, felt them, rose up from her chair, laid a hand upon her lord's arm: they saw her plead with him. Oh, lovely sight! with her they too began to plead: "Pietà di Nona, Signore! Pietà di noi, Madonna!" She was their graceful choragus; or rather, she, like some slim daughter of the Greeks— Iphigenia or another— voiced the protagonist's part; and they wailed after her, a chorus of elders. Finally, she knelt to him, wound her arms about his hips, put up her entreating face. The comedy was played out. Amilcare showed himself shaken; he stooped to her, lifted her in his arms, embraced her. "O mouth of singular favour!" etc. The convocation broke up in sobs, psalmody, and kisses on the cheek. Amilcare and his wife were led to the broad window and out on to the loggia. There stood Molly in all the glow of her happy toil, quick-breathing, enraptured, laughing and afire. The crown was on her head, by her side her sceptred lord; and below the people cheered and howled. "Udite, citt adini, il vostro Capitano!" cried the heralds. "Duca! duca! Evviva Amilcare, Duca!" cried the throng. Then Amilcare pointed to the crowned girl. "Evviva la Madonna di Nona!" he brayed like a tube of brass. So as Madonna di Nona they knew her to the end. Amilcare was crowned with his laurel wreath in the Santi Apostoli; *Te Deum* was sung. Nona started on her new career— benevolent despotism tempered by a girl's kisses.

V

GRIFONE— AMATEUR OF SENSE

Grifone must now be lifted into the piece, Grifone the grey-eyed, self-contained little Secretary, whose brain seemed quicksilver, whose acts those of a deliberate cat, whose inches were few, whose years only tender. One of Amilcare's rare acts of unpremeditated humanity had been to snatch him, a naked urchin of nine, from Barga, when (after a night surprise) he was raining fire and sword and the pains of hell upon that serried stronghold of the hills.

"Eh, Signore, Signore!" had whined the half-famished imp, padding by the condottiere's stirrup.

"Va via, vattene al diavolo!" a musketeer growled at him, and tried to club him down.

Amilcare looked, as one might idly glance at a shrew-mouse in the path. He saw a brown body pitifully lean, a shock black head, a pair of piercing grey eyes. Further, he saw that the child had not on a stitch of clothing, and that he was splashed to the knees with drying blood.

"What now, Baby?" he asked.

"Lift me into the saddle, Signore," said the boy, with a propitiating grin; "I am getting my feet wet."

The little dog had a humorous twist to his eyebrow, and it was true enough that the kennels were running red.

"Whose blood is that on your legs, my lad?" Passavente stayed his charger.

Grifone shrugged. "Misericordia! Who knows? My father's perhaps; my mother's more certainly, since my father ran away. My mother would have run too, but she had no time. Eh, take me up, Signore! I cannot swim."

Amilcare swung him up by the hand, so saved his life. Next day Grifone saved his.

They burnt a monastery in the plain and ransacked a chestful of correspondence.

"Death of Christ!" swore Passavente, "I can't read this Latin. Go and fetch me a monk and a rope."

The monk, a plausible rogue, began to read: little Grifone stood by the table. At a certain point he broke into the recital with an emphatic word: "Liar!"

"What the deuce does this mean?" fumed Amilcare in a rage.

"The monk is deceiving your Lordship," said Grifone; "the sense is the opposite of what he reports."

It seemed that the boy knew Latin— at any rate enough to hang a few monks. Hanged the poor devils were, and after that very much was made of Grifone. Amilcare took him through all his campaigns, had him well taught, gave confidence for confidence, and found by the time he was at Nona, making his "Gran Tradimento" of Farnese, that he could not get on without him. The accepted remedy for such a state of the case was to kill the youth at once. Amilcare did not do that, and at first was able to bless himself for his second forbearance. Grifone was privy to all his master's hopes and safeguards; Grifone wrought upon the Signoria, cajoled the clergy, bamboozled the *popolani*, descended even to the ragamuffins in the gutters, and taught them how to shout "Duca! Duca!" when his master went proudly a-horseback, or to scribble his effigy in great chalk circles on the city walls. Though it may be true that Molly's graces brought Amilcare the crown of Nona, it must be added that neither Molly nor her Duke could have got in at all if Grifone had not been there to oil the hinges of the gates.

He had the soft purring ways of a cat, the tact of a Jesuit, the penetration of a money-lender, the sensibility of a musical amateur, and the morals of a maid-of-honour. He had extraordinary command over himself; he seemed able to do everything, and wishful to win nothing. There never was a young man (as a matter of fact) who wanted so much or asked so little. It was the very boundlessness of his desires which reined him in. The appetite of the Cæsars would not have represented his, all the gratification they could have commanded would have been for him but a whet. If he had a weak side it was his own astuteness: he could not always see how unutterably foolish a man might be if he were let alone. Another foible he had— intellectual appreciation of beauty pushed to fainting-point. His senses were so straitly tied to his brains that to pluck at one was to thrill the other. Made on a small scale, he was pretty rather than handsome, had quiet watchful eyes, a smiling mouth, very little hands and feet. He seldom dressed out of black velvet, and if he wanted a man assassinated had the thing done at so many removes that it was always entered "private quarrel" or "love affair" in the reports of the City Watch. He generally chose friars for business of the sort, because they could be about at night without suspicion, and their hanging sleeves gave them such a pull. For cup or fruit work he found ladies the only possible agents. No one in Nona would dream of taking wine from a man; and as for presents of figs, Grifone was maturely of opinion that the last and present Pontiffs had exhausted that pretty artifice. Finally, you can easily understand how useful Duke Amilcare found a demure lad of this kind in the matter of moulding his new State.

When his master brought him a mistress he gave her great attention. Like all clever fellows, he was at first disposed to set down her simplicity to her credit; but after watching her for some time, he decided that here was actually a soul clear as glass— thing of inestimable value in a country where lying was an axiom of politics— and his respect for her quickened into something more. If she had been only beautiful she would never have attracted him as she did. There were plenty of women in Italy handsome enough for his needs (the flower of whose amours were mostly for the mind); but simpletons were rarer. This tall wistful girl told the truth— but told it incredibly! Think of this. Shortly after the coronation, Bentivoglio, the chalk-faced tyrant of Bologna, came with an army on his way to Forlì. He had an old grudge against Nona. Finding himself within a league of its walls, his men lusty and well-fed, his artillery in great train, Nona (as he judged it) in ferment— he blockaded the place, and in due time summoned it to surrender. Amilcare laughed at him, told his wife (in secret) that he would attack on the morrow, and went to the Council. While he was there came a new summons from Bentivoglio, a messenger with a white flag. Word was sent to the Duke; the Duke could not be found. "Oh," said one, "seek Madonna for answer." This was done.

"Tell the Lord of Bologna," says Molly, "that we attack to-morrow."

The man bowed himself away. You should have seen Amilcare's face when this was reported to him; he rated his lovely Molly like a fish-fag. Then he had an interview with Grifone; told him the whole story.

Grifone stared. "Ebbene, Monsignore," said he, "your Grace will do well to attack."

"Attack, man? when the fellow knows we are coming! Are you mad?"

"Not so, my lord," replied the Secretary. "Bentivoglio does not know you are coming. What he knows is that you have *said* you are coming."

Well, at last Amilcare saw what Grifone had seen from the first, the mad results which might be won by a truth-telling Duchess. The Nonesi did attack. Bentivoglio, of course, not expecting them, was scattered over the maize fields, and never collected his force again until his own territory was reached. That was why he could not help the Lady of Forlì. "Per Bacco," said Grifone to himself, "truth in Italy is soused in the mud at the well's bottom; in England it seems to lie in a pan.

This pretty creature is as shallow as a crystal cup, where you may study Truth, like a blue jewel, in an inch of water." He went about thoughtfully the rest of that day. This new-discovered quality of Molly's was a thing very beautiful in his eyes. The conclusion he came to was that he was about to fall in love with the lady. "And that, after all," was his comment, "might not be a bad thing, if (as is probable) it become necessary to make her my consort." Then he went happily to sleep.

Grifone's proposals to himself were still very simple. Shortly, they were to get a throne for his master in order that he might the more easily acquire one for himself. "My legs," he said frankly, "are too short to get up without a footstool." Amilcare was to have been the footstool. But then Molly came into play. At first she seemed to make the simple thing simpler. Amilcare was a strong man, but stiff. Grifone was sure he would bungle in his handling of Molly; this truth-telling beauty, this flawless jewel in a cup, would baffle him; he would neither see it the fine nor the delicate tool it was. He worked best with a bludgeon which, as it did brute's work, might be brutishly handled. So far well— he might trust Amilcare to wreck himself. Unfortunately, it seemed only too likely he might involve Molly in the mess. That danger was looming; already he set her to decoy-work which the girl herself (Grifone could see) did not relish. The ladies of Nona were gay and free— too free. Molly recoiled visibly, more than once. The men were worse. Incredible as it seemed to Grifone, they actually ravaged this tender honeysuckle spray to drench themselves with the scent. Molly, beautifully patient, courteous, meek as she was, cast a scared, paling face about the assembly now and again: some of the talk, too, cut her very deep. Grifone was already too much interested in her to stomach this. He decided to make discreet love to his Duchess by a way of his own. The Nonesi (gluttons!) abused her favours; he would refuse them. He would fast where Nona feasted, and be the only unkissed guest at her receptions.

VI

GRIFONE ENTERS THE MARKET

The first opportunity he had he took. The Palazzo Bagnacavallo was thrown open to all worthy citizens, the rooms (since no one in those courting days was held unworthy) were crowded. Ladies, soldiers, churchmen, humanists in brocade, poets in velvet, a Cardinal, a cross-eyed Greek who had forsaken usury at Trebizond for moral philosophy at Nona; Madonna Diamante, too receptive wife of the Count of Cornuto; Madonna Smeralda, her discreet friend; Madonna Saphira; Madonna Rubina; frizzed young nobles in parti-coloured hose; humble abbates, uncured and incurable; a monk crowned with laurel for a sonnet; and a Knight of the Holy Ghost in retirement;— these were some of the company among whom Duchess Molly was paraded by her discerning lord, to carry her smiles of welcome and her pretty ways. Grifone, grave, attentive, in black, was there, be sure, waiting his turn. It came, and with it Molly, blushing and overwrought, new from the very kindly salutations of the Greek. To Grifone she proffered a greeting which was no less kind because her heart was troubled. Her well of trust in mankind was not yet dry. Grifone took her hand and bent over it; it was as much as he did to brush it with his lips. Molly wondered at him.

"You should be Messer Grifone, my Lord's secretary," she said, faltering.

"Alas, I have that misfortune," replied the youth, with averted eyes.

"Why, I know you very well," said Molly, "but see now that I have offended you. What is my injury, Signore? What have I done?"

"Madonna," said Grifone (but so low that no other could hear him), "believe me that the offence is none of your wilful making. It is, however, irremediable. Nothing but misfortune could overcome such misfortune as mine; and that I pray Heaven to keep far from you."

"Alack! good Grifone, what sayings are these for a day that should be happy?" urged the warm-hearted girl, with eyes ready to fill.

"Madonna, let me endure the thought of them alone, I entreat your Grace."

"Never, while I live, Grifone. You make me most unhappy. Will you not kiss me?"

"Never, while I live, Madonna, if I am to live honest."

Molly went white and red, and stood hesitating, uncertain whether to cry or be angry. Either might have been a vent for her distress, which was real. Commanding herself with pains—

"I will require you to speak with me after supper," she said, after a pause for the struggle.

Grifone bowed his head and backed away from her. She, being boundless in capacity for the affections of her kind, spent the interval with an aching heart.

Directly supper was done she hunted for the Secretary. The affair had by now throbbed itself into a question of her physical ease. Her heartstrings were at a dangerous stretch, she quivering at the point of tears. Master Grifone, for his part, had taken very good care that the Duke of Nona should be occupied, and himself not hard to find. Molly came upon him in a gallery of arras; caught him crouching there with his face hidden in his hands. She went to him at once, full of the trouble he showed her, sat by him, put her arm round his neck, and tried to draw his head up. Grifone turned her a white, miserable face.

"Ah!" he said, husky with reproach, "ah! you have come with the ardours of an angel leaping in you; yet no cruelty could in truth be sharper."

"Cruel? Cruel? Oh, Grifone, nobody has ever said this of me before!" whimpered poor Molly. She was swirling in wilder water than she knew.

"The cruelty is unconscious, yet none the less bitter for that," he complained; and then, all at once, he turned fiercely to rend her. "What! When I throb for your footfall, or when I lean swooning to the wall for the scent of your hair as you pass; when I urge against your chamber door that I may feed upon the sound of your breath, or hunt for broken bread under your table that I may grow drunk on what your fingers have touched! When I go raving at night, weeping by day, with a knife in my heart, tears that scald my eyes! When with these pains to endure, these perils to skirt, heights to fly, you will speak, touch me, breathe upon me, tempt me to greet you with kissing of the lips— ah, heaven and hell! it is over-much. I would be an honest man, look you. I have a master to serve, I bid you remember. It is true enough that I love you out of all measure; there is no sin in that which I cannot help; but misery there is, by our Saviour. The sin is gaping all about me, itching here, aching there, gnawing and groping without cease, or stint, or allay. Yes, yes, I know this is true— God help me! I love you deplorably; but I will not touch you. You are the ever-blessed thing to me; but I will make you the ever-abhorred thing, *anathema maranatha*. I love you, I worship you, I adore you; you are my saint, my church, my altar, my soul's peculiar food; you shall be my devil, his hell, his cauldron, my venomous offence. And all this you shall be that I may love you yet more, yet incomprehensibly more, and (withal) live honest. I will hate you because I adore you. Ah! and I will prove whether by hating you most of all I cannot drown myself in love." He threw himself out of her reach, and rocked with hidden face.

Here was pretty hearing for a pretty bride. Molly, with heaving bosom, stood abashed and dumb, and troubled profoundly. Not only had she never tried to stem so fierce a torrent of love, nor ever shuddered under such dry heat in men's words— she had never yet dreamed of so much passion in men created. And glorious passion, too, it seemed, so stern and repressed— a passion which hugged a fetter, a splendid misery of denial. Of course she had nothing to say; she never had anything to say; yet she longed to say or do something. Her interest in all these fine things was painful, if delicious; and it never occurred to her for a moment that it could be a sin to listen where it was evidently such a virtue to declare. She was conscious of no disloyalty to Amilcare in so listening, in being so troubled, in displaying her trouble so unaffectedly. Poor, poor, good Grifone! So very noble, so white and miserable; Heaven knows she would have satisfied him if she could. With her, to feel was to touch (if I may so put it); quite instinctively she stretched out her arms to draw him home; the good fool would have kissed his tears away if he had had any, giving him for comfort what he had screamed upon as a torment. But that was a talent denied to Grifone: he could not cry. All the same, she was at the point to kiss him, when he once more prevented her— this time without violence.

"Ah, my lady, my lady," he said, with a smile whimsically sad, "have a little pity on a torturing wretch!"

Molly now covered her face and freely sobbed. The scene was heartrending, and Grifone judged that he might give the finishing stroke. He stood over her where she was flung (the poor humble soul), and laid his fingers lightly on her silken shoulder.

"Love makes a good reader of a man," he said slowly, drawling his words. "Long ago I discerned the clear stream of truth which is the issue of your love. Henceforward there is a secret pact between us two, a secret wholly honourable, since I have only told it that you might be won over not to dare me too far. Being honourable, you (who are the fountain of honour) will keep it. We go our two ways, we look not on each other, we greet not, neither speak what either knows. Chance will throw us much together; yet this law we will punctually observe. To me the hour will say— 'Guard thee, Grifone, thy sweet enemy draws near.' To you— 'Now goodness be thy guide, Molly, lest thou art a cause of stumbling to thy brother.' So let it always be."

He left her then, knowing very well that he had sworn the good girl to faith inviolable, and given her the subject of perennial thought.

And so he had. Molly kept his secret, honoured it, honoured him. She came by tortuous ways of her hoodblind heart to glory and exult in both; nor had she the wit to discern how or by what stealthy degrees the pain and longing she pitied in him grew to be more pitiable in herself. She watched him wonderfully in those crowded days of court life which followed, and when she was blinded by her tears, held him as a martyr who, for her sake, lay quivering under the knife. It shows the length of her road, that she was never aware how much more in her sight he was than Amilcare, the man of her election. Amilcare, it is true, was greatly occupied: one cannot be a duke for nothing. Not home affairs only (though discontent was never far off) called him from home: the times were full of the shock of alarms; thrones toppled; there were rumours of moving hosts beyond the Alps. Cesare, the flame-coloured Borgia, was still meditating his kingdom in Romagna; already the Lady of Forlì was flogging her sulky lieges into some sort of action for her defence. Now, Nona lay dead in the Borgia's way, and unless the Borgia could be hoodwinked again as he had been hoodwinked before, Nona need not cease to be a Duchy, but Amilcare would cease to be a Duke. No wonder the man was a lacklove just now. He intended to play Molly for his great stake; meantime he must be more of a duke than he was, recognised as such by other powers, by dukes firmly rooted, by grudging republics, or tyrants in thin veils.

And while he was consolidating his throne— ruffling here, fawning there— Grifone was always before Molly's eye; always plucking at her poor heartstrings; always holding up his grave patience, his bleeding, his most eloquent refusals, for her wonder. Wonder, indeed, she did, and much more than that. The thought sat upon her like a brooding evil spirit, frayed her nerves to waste. He used to move her so much by this policy of negation that she found herself panting as she sat among her women; or when from her throned seat at table she saw his pale profile burn like a silver coin in the dusk, the pain of her heart's beating well-nigh made her suffocate. Her troubles came to be day-long; he haunted her by night. When she began to ask the Virgin Mary how long she could endure, it was the signal to herself that she could endure no more. She sent for him then, and implored him brokenly— sobbing, kneeling before him— that he would leave her. Grifone bowed his head.

Next day Amilcare (or some other) told her that the Secretary was to be absent for some months arranging alliances abroad. He went without seeing her or bidding any farewells. She was prostrate for three or four days, could hardly drag herself to church, or away from it when she had once gained its cool sanctuary aisles. After that she got better and more her old self. The relief was as delicious as the grief had been; she was really happy. Then she found that she was beginning to dread his return. This was exactly what he had desired: he was a most astute young man.

VII

A PEDLAR'S ROUND

Grifone's tour of negotiation lasted very nearly six months—
months of comparative ease for Molly, neglected by husband and shadowing lover alike. During this time the latter visited every important
court in Italy, except Naples, whither he cared not, and Parma, whither
he dared not venture— the object of his journey being, of course, to
secure his master's acknowledgment by a better title than the throats of
a marketed crowd. It would be as interesting as it was surprising to see
the little craftsman at work, the ingenuity with which he plied his handful of tools, the proud patience with which he endured snub after snub,
his bland passivity and extraordinary rebound. First of all, he went to
Rome, ever the pivot of danger to an Italian diplomat. Molly's portrait,
done in his best manner by Dosso of Ferrara, was presented to Duke
Cæsar of Valentinois.

In this, the lady with loose hair and a still looser robe (spangled with
stars it was, and slipped off one white shoulder) was sitting in a green
wilderness feeding lions with *confetti*. On a cedar near by, were several
parrots and a pale owl, and from a low-swinging branch a great speckled snake stooped downward to embrace Molly's waist in a dry fold,
and with his head writhed forward to lick her chin. It was a pleasing
piece; Don Cesare was ravished. The seed planted in him at Foligno
germinated, produced a bud, before long a triumphant flower. Not only
would he come to Nona, and that soon, but the Holy Father sent the
Golden Rose to "his dearest daughter in Jesus Christ, Maria, by the
same grace Duchess of Nona." O mouth of singular favour!

With the scent of this rare blossom, Grifone went off to tickle the
nostrils of the North. But he must not delay us. Bologna he dared to
visit: thither the ducal pair must needs go anon. Milan received him to
some purpose; Venice received him to none at all. Barbarigo was not
Doge for nothing. Ferrara was busy with thoughts of piety, the whole
court barefoot, howling "Fac me plagis" between the garden walls. In
other places he cried his wares, and reached Nona again in the heats of
July.

He found his lovely mistress in a shaking fever, languid under the
breathless heat of the plain, yet never at rest. He found her large-eyed
and bodeful, horribly nervous of him. She had been longing to see him,
yet every day made vehement prayer that she might never look on him
again. When she knew that he was indeed in the palace, she shut herself

into her chamber with a crucifix, and spent the whole day at the window peeping from behind a curtain. Grifone saw the shape of her in it, saw her hand at the selvage.

"Courage, Grifone, mio caro," he assured himself; "she is afraid of thee." He resumed his state of armed respect, Molly her tossing nights and pacing days. Affairs were something awry within the Duchy, yet Grifone assured his Lord they were likely to be much more awry out of it. Madonna Duchessa must certainly be shown about— otherwise, an avalanche. Preparations were pushed on. By October the Duke and Duchess, with a great train set out— actually for Bologna, but nominally for Milanese territory. Lodovico, of that great principality, would have been mortally affronted if he believed Bentivoglio to have been considered first. Therefore the visit to Bologna was to be a dead secret, performed by the principals almost unattended. Meantime Grifone (who loved mystification) prepared litters with a dummy Duke and Duchess to go under escort to Borgo San Donnino. He and his wagging escort duly entered that city: excuses to the Podestà secured him a covered passage to the palace. Once there, unfortunately, the populace clamoured for a view, insisted upon their Graces' appearance. Grifone had to set his dolls at a window. There they stared, embraced, while three Ciceronian orations were delivered from the piazza, and all the merchant-guilds marched round it with banners and torches. Next morning he got them off safely by some stroke of good luck; but his joke got wind in time, came round to Cesare Borgia's ears, and at last was repeated against Nona. For no other reason could this absurd incident claim your ears.

At Bologna, also, all had gone well with the real adventurers— up to a certain point Bentivoglio the tyrant (whose name is surely the grimmest of his pleasantries) having seen the lovely Molly, was disposed to forgive her that disastrous veracity which (you remember) had prevented him before. He was so favourably impressed that Amilcare (who never missed a chance) left him alone with her for two hours in the garden after supper. At the end of that time Molly came to him, stumbling over her dress in her haste, flushed and in tears. They must leave Bologna at once, she declared; she would die else, or never look her husband in the face. The man had insulted her, was horrible, most wicked. Amilcare, her dear lord, must go and avenge her, etc., etc.

Here was a pother. What could be done? Grifone, of course, had he been there, would have drawn his master's sword for him, dragged him out of the room, and sent him back in half an hour's time with a bloody testimony of nothing on the blade. Molly would have been pacified, Bentivoglio snug abed, the sword none the worse for a little pig's blood. But Grifone was at Borgo jigging his dolls and listening to Cicero, and Amilcare lost his head. He pooh-poohed the whole affair; Molly grew pale, stopped crying. Amilcare began to feel himself— come, come, she was reasonable after all. He condescended to explain the fine uses of Italian statecraft, the wife's part, the husband's part. He was most explicit; Molly grew white, ended by fainting. Amilcare carried her to bed; she refused to sleep with him. He raged; she cared nothing. She was wild with terror, shame, discovery of her lover's worth, and of her love's. He had to beg her pardon on his knees, made an enemy of Bentivoglio, a fool of himself, and left next morning in a tearing passion.

Grifone, who met his master at Cremona, lost no time in seeing that something had gone counter, and very little in finding out what it was.

"Leave it to me, my good lord," he said comfortably; "I will explain it to Madonna in another way."

Before they went to bed he had a little guarded talk with his Duchess, half excusation of his absence which might have aggravated her alarms, half condemnation of Amilcare; the whole, consequently, a veiled eulogy of himself.

Molly was very quiet at first, subdued and miserable, but sincerely grateful. To express this, she fell into her natural way, a way of little timid tendernesses, little touchings of the arm, urgings of the cheek. Grifone received them rigidly; she was reduced to tears. Thereupon he kissed her ardently, twice, and fled. She remained a long while in the dark, breathless, limp, awed, and absurdly happy. Next morning he was as distant as the Alps and quite as frosty. At dusk they reached Milan.

Whatever Duke Ludovic (titular of Bari, actual of Milan) may have intended to ensue, he gave them a proper reception. Cardinal Ascanio himself came to the city gate with clergy and the Council; cavalry, a parti-coloured array, pennoned and feathered, escorted them to the castle. There, on the steps within the great courtyard, the Moor himself, sumptuous in silver brocade, and Donna Beatrice his wife; there his tired sister, Duchess Bona, and her by no means tired daughter, Bianca Maria of the green eyes, stood panoplied to await them. Trumpets announced the greetings that passed; yet another fanfare the greetings that were to come when within the hall, at the foot of the broad staircase, they found and kissed the hands of the anxious little Duke Galeazzo Gian and his pretty wife— pair of doomed children, even then in the cold shadow of their fate.

Half-hearted, fainting Molly went through her little part with the accustomed success. Her pretty English-Italian, her English lips, again her eager hands, so anxious to search friends out, found their sure way to one at least. Bianca Maria, affianced of the Roman King, delighted to kiss and be kissed, announced herself the shy girl's lover. Pleasure broke over her face, broke the glaze of her bottomless eyes with a gleam like the sun's when in still water it betrays deep green paths of light.

She was an enigmatic rogue, so clever that to most she seemed of unplumbed stupidity. Those blank green eyes of hers, that waxen face, that scarlet impenetrable mouth, her even gait and look of ruminating, look of a dolt— who knew Bianca Maria? Not Maximilian the mild-mannered King; not Duke Ludovic (that creased traitor) who schemed her marriage; not altogether Lionardo, who painted half her portrait and taught her much of his wisdom; certainly not poor Molly of Nona. All Milanese were her lovers, and here was another heart, Molly's, to wit, laid open and soothed by the little witch's quick hand-stroke. Bianca Maria had all her secrets with all her love in the first hour of their embracery.

The two girls sat clasped in one chair in that pretty time of dressing when half is undone and half's to do. Molly, feeling a fool but loving to have it so, sat in the lap of the younger, who mothered her.

After many days Lionardo, who forgot nothing and never her whom he thus happened on, glorified her as the Virgin Mary on the knees of Saint Anne. The indefinite smile, the innocent consciousness, the tender maiden ways! Wife, mother, handmaid of high God, he thought of her as of Molly in *apotheosis*; dutiful for love's sake, yet incurably a child, made for the petting place.

"Grifone the Secretary is your lover, my Molly," said Bianca Maria the wise.

Molly admitted the sobering truth, and the other pinched her lip.

"Take care of him, my dear. He is more perilous than that stiff husband you now have. The husband is a trading fool. He uses you as a carrot to induce donkeys. The other is more curious, and has no use for donkeys. He will use you otherwise."

"Why, how will he use me then?" said open-eyed Molly. She was vaguely ill at ease; but the other shammed stupid. All she could be brought to add was—

"I will take care of you if I can. You will never do here, nor should ever have come— a lamb among our Lombard wolves. Had you no English lover, to kill Amilcare and prevent it?"

Molly thought of Gregory Drax, who had been upon the North seas at the time. Gregory Drax used to lean over the garden gate chewing straws. This he did by the hour together, to the perfect satisfaction of himself and understanding of the neighbours. Molly could not think that it would have led to the slaying of Amilcare.

"What was he like, this Gregorio?" asked Bianca Maria, suddenly alert when she had got his name smoothly.

Molly did her best— ruddy, blue-eyed, always blushing and laughing, fair-haired, very long arms. He was a *marinajo*.

"He sounds to be so," said Bianca Maria. Then she clapped her hands and summoned Lionardo.

The great man had no sooner appeared (noiselessly in the doorway, the inscrutable grey-beard) than she kissed her friend and bade her go with her women to the appointed quarters of the Nonesi. Lionardo gravely saluted her as she went rosy out. He had seen the Virgin in the lap of Saint Anne and cared no more for the poor original.

"Dear Lionardo," said the girl in the chair to the most learned man of her day, "you shall do me the favour to write a letter in Latin to a certain English lord, Messer Gregorio Dras, *Marinajo*, Londra."

"Principessa," said the great man, "I am ready. Recite your letter."

"To her very singular good lord," the letter began— the only one, so far as I know, written by the Empress Bianca Maria to England; certainly the only one she ever wrote to Wapping. The conceit of it was as follows: That the lovely Lady Molly was at Nona on the confines of Emilia and Romagna, wife of a man who would shortly be murdered in order that she might become the mate of the assassin; that a very great lord, son of the Holy Father, was intending for those parts, and would probably take the same means to secure himself the position of her third husband. The writer proposed that the Lord Gregorius, whose virtue and celerity of judgment were well known throughout Italy, should journey out to Nona with all reasonable despatch and repossess himself of the lady. "Thus your lordship," it concluded, "may happily become fourth husband of a lady, whose charms are of a sort so noble and perdurable that they are unlikely to suffer from the arduous duties their excellence involves. Yet such haste as is compatible with your worshipful degree in the realm of England may be recommended. From Milan, etc., in the year of our thankful Redemption 1494."

"How shall we send our letter speediest, my Merlin?" His enchantress laid her emerald spell over him— O incomparable witch! Such sorcery exalted him always. He lifted her question upon one of his towering flights.

"The wings of birds, if we could use them, were admirable for the purpose, Princess," he replied. "But, for the moment, the difficulty of instructing such messengers is insuperable. And not only so, but it is probable that the Lord Gregorio, seeing such an envoy to his hand, might put a bolt into it, and itself into the pot, without interrogatories delivered or answers made. So messenger and message would alike be boiled. Another way occurs to me, which arises out of this consideration. We stand, each bather of us, in a lake of air. A lake? Rather, an illimitable ocean of it spread over land and sea, in which the very mountain-tops do blink. Should not, then, the pulsing of our thought, as it rings outward from us, be discernible in the ripples about the Lord Gregorio's ears? Obviously it should. But the reading of such ripples would be a nice matter; and again we lack means, and again the time, to instruct his lordship. Once more— "

"Ah, you dream your subtleties, and my letter gets cold," said Bianca Maria, pouting. "You are now just as you sit watchfully when you should be painting my picture."

"It is then that I am painting my hardest, Princess Saint Anne," he returned. "But leave with me your letter. It shall go in a man's bosom to-morrow morning."

High affairs of State are not settled in a week, nor dukes so apt at billing as a pair of girls. Duke Ludovic would not declare himself to every adventurer; Duke Amilcare was too patently adventurous to disclose all his hand. Then came Grifone, with a game of his own. Blind each of one eye, they set to dealing their cards for beggar-my-neighbour.

Now Ludovic feared one man in all Italy, and so did Amilcare. That was the one man in all Italy whom Grifone respected, on whom he thought he could honestly rely. Thought he to himself, "Can their Serenities be leagued against this man in my service? Can they not, by our risen Lord?" He fancied that they might.

To this end he proposed to his master, very shortly, the assassination of Borgia by means of the lovely Molly. Let her, at a private banquet, inveigle him to drink a cup.

"Suggest this to the Duke of Bari," he said. "I think your lordship will not be disappointed. Substantial pledges must be exacted, of course; he must tread in deep enough to leave a footmark or two visible 'twixt Milan and Nona."

Amilcare thought well of this advice and followed it. Ludovic, incredulous at first and breathless, took a fortnight to ponder. He consulted Cardinal Ascanio, consulted his astrologers, took the test of the opening Virgil. His eye lighted upon the portentous words: "Tantæ molis erat Romanam condere gentem." Who would have twittered after those? He sought his guest and told him roundly that if the thing went well he would send an envoy to the court at Nona, and support the new Duchy with moral force.

Amilcare did not believe him, naturally, nor did he greatly care for moral forces. He stipulated for an envoy at once, an invitation for himself and his wife to Bianca Maria's wedding, and for a loan of twenty thousand ducats in specie.

Ludovic boggled horribly at this; but they accorded at last. The envoy was to go then and there, the invitation should be sent when the Borgia had agreed to visit Nona, and the money when he was within a day's ride of that city. Reduced to cipher-writing, this treaty was placed below the visible Host on the high altar of Sant' Eustorgio; the allies received the Communion, and after another week's festivities the Duke and Duchess of Nona went home.

At parting, the two girls clung together.

"We shall never meet again, child," cried the chosen Empress. "I am sure of it."

Molly kissed her. "Are we not to come to your marriage, dear Bianca?"

"My marriage?" cried the other. "You will as likely see me there as that shadow of a name which will be my bridegroom. You will see my simulacrum, a plastered effigy of me. I shall be stiff with gold-dust and diamonds; a doll marrying a doll's bed-gown. Why should I be there if his ever-august Majesty is represented by a puff of silly breath? Pray, never look for Bianca Maria in the Queen of the Romans. The Queen of the Romans is a doll, windy ruler of the name of a people; Bianca Maria Sforza, daughter of thieves, has been your friend, as you will see. She has provided for your third husband an honest man. Now kiss me for the last time and, by Heaven, go quickly, or I shall keep you here for my soul's health."

The fierce little hungry creature threw her arms round Molly's neck and kissed her like a lover.

Molly was melted into tears. "Oh, Bianca, you bewilder, you terrify me! What is this of husbands and your soul?"

"Ah, my soul!" cried she. "Do you think so highly of it as to suppose it will survive this marriage, or so lightly as not to care? My soul, poor child, is in the case with your lovely body. It is the tied bird of all these fowlers."

"Alas, alas! But I cannot understand," Molly wailed; but the other caught her the closer.

"That you do not understand, Carina, is your salvation. It proves you immortal. Now go. No! kiss me, kiss me!"

They were parted at last; and though they did meet again, they kissed no more.

VIII

PRIVATE TREATY

To a most elaborately penned invitation the Borgia responded by half a dozen words scrawled by his secretary. He would be in the March at such and such a time, and would spend such and such a day in Nona.

He had heard from Amilcare; he replied to Molly. The insult was glaring, even to her.

"Is this tolerable, my lord?" said the meek beauty, incensed at last.

Amilcare shrugged. "It may not have to be borne very long," said he. "For my part I am accustomed to reckon a gift by its use to me, not by the sacking round about it." He was now beyond his wife's depth: she neither followed nor tried to follow him.

In these days she saw but little of her lord, and could have wished it less. He, who in action was as cheerful a soul as you could wish to serve, was harassed by the long expectances of diplomacy, and in the routine work of governing most grim. The Nonesi had come to hate him a good deal, but to fear him more. Expenses were incalculable, the taxes grew; there were riots. Savage snaps of speech in the Council did harm; imprisonments followed, then some unaccountable sudden deaths. High and low alike, none knew where the blow might fall, but all flinched at it.

In these distresses Molly served him well, for she at least was universally loved. If the Duke had a man stabbed, the Duchess took such sweet consolation to the widow that none could murmur long. To watch her warm tears flow was in itself a solace; to feel her arms, to win her kissing mouth, quickened those doubtful poor souls.

Furtively also, Grifone was on her side; a neat phrase here and there made her position plain to the most infidel in the city. It is true that while he helped her there he tortured her otherwise inexpressibly. He hardly ever left her now, and her heart bled to see him go in fear of her; she prayed night and day that he might have strength to shake off this biting, cruel love. It never entered her head that she could console him by perfidy to a perfidious husband; it had entered Grifone's head a hundred times, but he always put it out. He could afford to wait for what, after all, he only valued as a concession to vulgar opinion. In thought she had been his for a year; and in the mind he lived most deliciously. It was, no doubt, his full intent to make her his in all the grossness of the fact, but not until he had got rid of Amilcare, or induced Amilcare to get rid of himself. This was what the stiffnecked

Condottiere was now doing as fast as his best enemies could have wished. His people hated him so bitterly that he would certainly have worn mail— had not Molly been his mail. They spared him because they loved her, and believed that he still had her heart. "Amilcar, uxoris gratia, Dux," was now the fact. Grifone could have destroyed belief and him together by a lift of the eyebrow; but he wanted more than that, so waited on.

The little fellow was really extraordinary. Luxurious as he was to the root, and effeminate; hating as he did cold water, cold food, the cold shoulder; one and all of these shuddering things he had schooled himself to bear without a blink. He grew even to take a stern pleasure in the bitterness they cost him, as he turned them to his uses and reckoned up his balance at the bank. Amilcare snarled at him, cut his words out of his mouth, struck him, kicked him once like a yard-dog. Grifone added it all to his store.

But as the day for Duke Cesare's visit drew near, Molly began to be much again in her husband's thoughts— how far she would go in this maturer time. She had charmed the man once before, at Foligno; she had charmed everybody. But then she had been charmed herself. Subsequently she had charmed Bentivoglio, not so happily but that she endangered her own spell. That was the present trouble, for hitherto her charm had lain precisely in herself, in the little everyday acts which were her own nature. Bentivoglio had reasonably wanted more: so would Borgia want very much more. Could Molly be brought, not to surrender all he wanted, but to make him want? Amilcare, growing tense between his difficulties, felt that explanations must be given and received, felt also that they must come from himself— in fact, Grifone had declined them— and felt that he was not strong in such work. Direction he could give, but not explanation. However, he must try.

On a vivid morning of early summer, when the lemon-trees in the *cortile* looked as if they had been cut out of metal, and the planes and very poplars were unwinking in the thick blue air, Amilcare came into his wife's room. She had not expected him; he found her lying dishevelled and unbusked, with all her glossy hair tumbled loose. Very much a maiden still, notwithstanding her year and a half of troublous marriage, she jumped up directly she saw him, and, blushful, covered her neck. Amilcare, finding her and the act adorable together, took her in his arms and kissed her; then he led her back by the hand to the window-cushions and made her sit upon his knee. He began to play with her hair.

"What a silken mesh, my Molly! What a snare for a man in this lovely cloud! How fragrant of roses! Ah, most beautiful wife, you could lead all Italy by a strand of this miraculous hair."

She was pleased with his praises, touched and grateful; she kissed him for them. So they grew more friendly than they had been ever since the Bentivoglio had shocked her modesty and faith in him at once. Amilcare rattled on; love-talk comes easily to the Italian tongue, whose very vocables are caresses.

Gradually he drew in and in to the Borgia, centre of all his spinning thought.

"There is a lover of yours, for instance!" he said, comically aghast; and Molly laughed.

"Why, Amilcare, you make all the world to be my lover, all the world to look at me through your eyes. Believe it, they see me truer than you do. I am a very simple person."

Amilcare began to count upon his fingers, one hand meeting the other round Molly's caught waist.

"The Borgia, the Count of Cavalcalupo, Oreste Colonna, Negroponte, three Bishops at Sesto, Bianca Maria, Cardinal Ascanio Sforza, Ordelaffi, Benti— — "

She stopped him there with a hand on his mouth. "Pah, the horrible man!"

Amilcare gaily struggled for vent, and— "voglio!" he concluded the word. "You may not relish the trophy, my wife; but him you undoubtedly charmed. And now Don Cesare is coming. Him also it will be as needful as easy to please."

Molly turned in her husband's arms to consider him. Something in his tone (rather than the words he had used) struck bodefully upon her. Amilcare was kissing her hair and would not give over: she cast down her eyes unsatisfied.

"I hope I may always please my lord's friends," she said in a low voice.

Amilcare settled himself yet more luxuriously in his cushions, and looked at the ceiling.

"You must charm him, my soul," he said intensely; "you must charm him. I am in his hands, in his way; he has sought my ruin and I believe still seeks it. Twice he has tried to poison me, once to have me stabbed; if he tries again he will succeed. Nothing can turn Don Cesare from his path but a woman. Therefore, you must charm him, ravish his eyes. You know very well how to do that."

Molly stared, grew red, began to stammer. "But how can I— ? Oh, Amilcare, what do you ask of me?"

Then he looked at her, severely but without malice. She noticed for the first time the cold-steel hue in his eyes, the complete absence of friendliness— a tinge which his men knew very well, and other men's men even better.

"I ask of you, my Molly, that the man be put at his ease," he said deliberately (happy in ordering at last); "more, that his direction be turned. He must be made high-hearted, full of glorious hope, not counting cost, keen in pursuit. He must blow off the cobwebs of his doubt; rather, these must shred from him as he flies in chase. I cannot afford his distrust. I can do nothing without you. Light of Heaven! am I asking too much? Or do you suppose that my safety with the Borgia is not yours also?" He shrugged his intolerable indignation and threw back his head. Thus he avoided to look at his wife.

She still sat upon his knee, but like an alien, bolt upright, reasoning out her misery with wide tearless eyes, and a hand to press her bosom down. Shocks were no more for her— she had learned too much; but these things seemed like hard fingers on a familiar wound, which opened the old sore and set it aching. The part he now put to her had only to be named to be shown for horrible; was yet too horrible to be named; yet had to be named.

"You ask of me to charm your enemy," she said in a still, fascinated voice (as if she were forced by a spell to speak obscenity): "to beguile your enemy— to make him— make him— seek me? Him, the man who tried to murder you? Charm him? Charm him? Lead him to pursue?"

She could hardly drag the words out of her, but Lord! what a fool she was. At least, Amilcare thought so. The plainest duty, the easiest; this childish woman's game! He jumped up, quivering with nerves on edge, and the sympathy between the pair lacked even touch. Molly found her feet, stood brooding before him, all her hair about her lowered face.

To see her thus, a mute, a block, maddened Amilcare. He clenched his fists. "Yes, Madam"— his words bit the air— "you shall charm this enemy of mine, if you please; this assassin, this ravener of other men's goods. You shall charm him in the way you best know— you and your nation. Bentivoglio I excused you: he was not worth your pains. Borgia I shall not excuse you. I showed you to him with this only view; I asked him here, I speak to you now, with this only view. You are adorable in every part, if you choose to be. Italy has no woman like you, so winning, so much the sumptuous child: such tall buds shoot only in the North.

To it, then! Charm him as you charmed me. Teach him— *Santo Dio!*— teach him to die for a smile. At least afford him the smile or the provocation of it: the rest shall be my affair. Soul of Christ! am I to miss this astounding opportunity? Never in the world. I bid you by all you hold sacred to do your duty. Am I plain enough?"

He was. She had grown as grey as a cloth, could say nothing, only motion with her dry lips. But she bent her head to him, and stretched out her hands in token of obedience to law.

"Good," said Amilcare; "my wife understands me." And he went out then and there to his Council. His conviction of her submissiveness (and of other things about her to modify it) may be gauged by the fact that he never saw her again (except ceremonially) until a certain moment after the dinner with Borgia.

Grifone saw her all the more for that. What he saw satisfied him that she was in terrible trouble. She slunk about, to his view, as if beaten down by shame. He had seen young girls in that strait very often, when the first step had been taken, the first flush faded from the venture, the first after-knowledge come. They always went as though they were watched. More than that, he discerned that she was nearly broken for want of a counsellor: he caught her long gaze fixed upon him sometimes. She seemed to be peering through him, spoke to herself (he thought) as she sat vacantly upon her throne, or at table among the quick wits, with all her spying ladies to fence her in. If any one addressed the word to her she flushed suddenly and began to catch after her breath. He could see how shortly that breath came, and how it seemed to hurt her. If she answered at all, it was stupidly and beside the purpose; then she would look conscious of her dulness, grow uncomfortably red, be at the point to cry. All this, while it could not but gratify him, made him a little sorry too.

One night, at a very brilliant assembly given by the notorious Donna Smeralda Buonaccorso, he saw her standing forlorn on the terrace, like a lonely rock in the sea— the most beautiful woman in Nona and the most splendidly attired, absolutely alone in all that chattering, grimacing crowd. The Duchess of Nona! This consideration alone moved him to real pity— for to be great and unfortunate has a freakish way of touching your heart— it moved him quietly towards her, to whisper in her ear—

"Madonna"— (and Heaven! how she started), "Madonna, what you need now is the courage of your race. But courage, I well know, comes only by confidence, and confidence is what I can give you. Trust for trust; will you hear me?"

But she looked piteously at him, as if she had been found out, and put her hands to her ears.

"I dare not hear you! I dare not! How can you speak to me when I have never asked— never thought? Ah, leave me, Grifone. I have not heard you yet: ask me not— but go!"

It was she that went, that hurried from him, stumbling in her haste, like a hunted thing. He could see no more of her that night, so with a shrug turned to his quiet amusement. There were women there pleasant enough. It was true that he wanted but one woman superlatively; but it was eminently Grifone's maxim that, failing that which you need, you should take that which you can get.

The last stage in the education of Molly, Amilcare found must positively be left to the Secretary.

On the night before Duke Cesare's arrival, when every other preparation had been made, Grifone came into his master's room, late. He said nothing, nor got any greeting; but he placed a little phial on the table, and waited. Amilcare looked at it, did not touch it. It was a very small phial, half full of a clear liquid.

"You prepared it yourself, Grifone?"

Grifone nodded pleasantly.

"Then I may rest assured— ?"

"You may, my lord."

"I will ask you to make all arrangements, Grifone. When the time comes you will take the cup to Madonna Duchessa, with a hint of so much as may be necessary to provide against mischances. Will this be done?"

"Punctually and surely, Excellence." The Secretary retired with his bottle.

Amilcare sat on with a tight smile which neither waxed nor waned, but seemed frozen on his face. He may thus have sat for two or three hours, his eyes fixed on a point at the table's edge. That point, whatever it was, a speck of dust, may be, seemed to grow and grow till it was monstrous and a burden intolerable to endure. Amilcare, with an effort, stretched out his hand and cuffed at it. He knocked a book off the table by this means, then started, then swore at himself. Twice after this he spoke, smiling all the while. "Is it now indeed?" he asked, raising one eyebrow; "is it now indeed?" Then he got up, stretched himself noisily, and lay down as he was on the sofa, to sleep in a moment.

Molly lay with a young maid of hers that night and never had a wink.

IX

THE LAST BIDDING

That golden Duke of Valentinois had a pompous reception from his august ally at Nona. Amilcare, riding like Castor, at one with his horse, went out at the head of his court to meet him. The Centaurs lined the way with a hedge of steel. Hat in hand, the Duke of Nona rode back with his guest to the garlanded gates. There, a fluttered choir, all virgins and all white, strewed flowers; from that point to the Piazza Grande one song came leaping on the heels of another. On the steps of the Duomo were the clergy in brocade, a mitred bishop half smothered under his cope in their midst. The two Dukes dismounted, and hand in hand entered the church; the organ pealed; the choir burst out with the chant, *Ecce, Rex tuus venit*; and then (seeing Cesare had once been a Cardinal), *Ecce Sacerdos magnus*. The smoke of incense went rolling to the roof, *Te Deum* spired between the rifts; an Archbishop intoned the Mass of the Holy Ghost. Cesare, in white satin, golden-headed, red-gold in the beard, cloaked and collared with the Golden Fleece, knelt in the middle of the dome; beside him the hawk-faced Amilcare, splendid in silver armour, knelt also— but stiffly; whereas the Borgia (graceful in all that he did) drooped easily forward on his *prie-dieu,* like the Archangel Gabriel who brought the great tidings to Madonna Maria. Amilcare, at that rate, was like Michael, his more trenchant colleague, that "bird of God."

The Bishop, who knew perfectly well why the Duke had come to Nona, and why Nona's Duke wanted him there, preached a sermon which the saving Italian virtue of urbanity prevented from being either monstrous or ridiculous. Before the altar the two lords kissed each other. One of them had tried and the other was about to try murder as a political expedient; but that was no reason why good manners should not prevail. Decent ceremony was always a virtue of the race.

Half an hour before dinner Grifone (who had not been to church) stood before his mistress, who had not been suffered to go. He had a flagon in his hands, of silver gilt, like the calyx of a great flower whose stem was sheathed in the clustered wings of angels, whose base was their feet. He held it in both hands as if it were a chalice.

Molly, beaten out and white, looked at it dully, but did not seem to see it.

"Madonna mia," said the youth, "this is the loving-cup which I am to hand to you after dinner, and which you are to hand to Duke Cesare."

He hardly heard her answer, but judged by the shaping of her lips that it was, "Well, Grifone?"

"Duke Cesare will ask you to sip of it first, Madonna."

His looks were piercing; yet she was too far gone to be disturbed by such as those. She even smiled faintly at his emphasis.

"Well, Grifone?" she asked again, in that same dry whisper. "How shall that be harm to him if I do it?"

Grifone blew out his lips. "Harm, *per Dio*! None at all, but common prudence on his part. No harm to him, lady; but to you obeying him, destruction, death!"

Molly stared. Her breath came hollow from her mouth.

"Death, Grifone?" she faltered, and then pored over his face again. He nodded his words into her.

"Death, Madonnina."

The girl tottered to her feet— had to balance like a rope-dancer to keep upon them.

"But then— but then— O Saviour!"

She threw her arms up. He thought she would fall, so put one of his round her waist. He felt her heart knocking like a drum, pressed her closer, drew her in and kissed her, with a coaxing word or two. She tried to collect herself— alas! her wits were scattered wide. Her head drooped to his shoulder.

After that there began the most pitiful business. She was pleading with him in a whining, wheedling, silly voice, which would have broken down an Englishman. Grifone himself was pricked. It was like a child, frightened into slyness, coaxing its mother.

"Dear Grifone, dear Grifone! You will not hand me the cup. Oh, please, please, please!"

Grifone kissed her. "Why, what can I do?" he said. "My lord has ordered it so, dear one."

She took no notice of his familiarities; indeed, the tone they lent his voice may have soothed the poor affectionate wretch. But she only wrung her hands at his news.

"No, no, no! 'Tis impossible! No, no, he could never do it!"

"I can repeat his words," said the inexorable Grifone; "he said— "

Then she sprang away from him as if he had whipped her, and crouched in a corner, at bay. She began to rave, seemingly in a high delirium, pointed at him, wagged her arm at him, mowing the air.

"Never repeat them, never repeat them. I shall die if you do!"

Grifone set down his cup, ran forward and embraced her. "My lovely lady, my adorable Molly!" he murmured, in a passion of admiration for her transformed, unearthly beauty.

She noticed nothing of him or his doings, lay lax in his arms. She stared, gulping down horror; she looked like some shocked Addolorata come upon the body of her dead Son. And so, perhaps (since all good women mother their lovers or lords), she was face to face with her dead. Tears came to blot out her misery; she could not stay their fall. They anointed also the burning cheeks of young Grifone, and drove him outside himself with love. He kissed her softly again, with reverence, and whispered—

"Courage, sweet lady; I shall be with you. I have it all in hand. The end for you and me shall be happiness undreamed of yet. The Duke comes in a quarter of an hour." Then he left her alone.

"The affair will go by clockwork," he assured himself. "Neither fast nor slow, but by clockwork." He had an ingenious mind, and loved mechanics.

X

WITH ALL FAULTS

At the coming out from church the two Dukes (mentally at least) separated; their paths coincided, but not their thoughts, nor their behaviour. By common consent, as it appeared, Amilcare at once resumed the obsequious, Cesare the overbearing part. Amilcare talked profusively, smirked, grimaced, pranced by the other's side, writhed his hands, in copious explanation of nothing at all. Cesare shrugged. The amount of disdain an Italian can throw into a pair of dull eyes or an irritable shoulder, the amount of it another will take without swallowing, can still be studied whenever a young lieutenant of the line sits down to breakfast in a tavern, and the waiter slaves for his penny fee. Yet, depend upon it, the cringer has balanced to a nicety the sweets and sours of boot-blacking against the *buona mano*; the rest is pure commerce. So now, the deliberate insolence of the flushed Borgia towards his host was a thing to be dumb at; yet Passavente redoubled his volubility.

Going up the steps of the Palazzo Bagnacavallo, the guest plumply told his entertainer to bring out the woman and go to the devil with his cackling. Amilcare laughed all over his face at the best joke in the world, and bowed to the earth. Thus humoured they went in to dinner.

Molly, in fold over fold of silk gauze which let every lovely limb be seen as glorified in a rosy mist, met them in the ante-room, and thenceforth the Borgia had eyes for nothing but the beauty of her. The moment he saw her, he drew, as once before, a sharp breath; she greeted him in her fashion; he was moved to a fit of trembling.

From that time forth Amilcare was as though he were not. The Roman waited for no invitation and disregarded those he got. Would his Grace be pleased to dine? His Grace went on pouring out his talk to the wonderful rose-coloured lady. Amilcare, patient to excess, watched. Presently Cesare said, "Madama, shall we go to dinner?" and to dinner they went, Amilcare rubbing his hands behind them.

They found the table prepared— a very low one; divans to sit upon; none but Grifone, pale and respectful, in the little painted chamber.

All this had been carefully provided. The Duke's suite dined in another wing of the palace; the choir of minstrels, who held the passage between them, had mail under their cassocks, and two-edged swords made for thrusting. They were fifty strong. Every page-in-waiting in the hall and long cool passages was a "Centaur" armed to the teeth.

Don Cesare, it seems, had walked into a steel trap at last. Do you wonder that Amilcare could afford a supple back?

But as the delicate meats succeeded each other— each duly tasted by Grifone before a morsel went to plate— there was one, in the surge of her terrors, struck dumb with what was, rather, wonder. The magnificent Cesare went his road over the feelings of his host; the host bowed and waved his hands. Why should he not? Never one word of answer, never a gleam of attention did he win from the Roman. Why should he care? His wife was doing her duty, his enemy was webbed: what else could matter? The Italian shrug goes deeper than the shoulders; sometimes it strokes the heart of a man. The very indignities heaped upon the adventurer made his revenge the sweeter nursling.

But Molly, the tall English girl, burning in her shameful robe, saw it vastly otherwise. That a man could bend so low! That she should ever have loved a man with such a stooping back! To think of that made (for the moment) every other degradation light. Her part as yet was one of sufferance: to look handsome, languid with the excess of her burden of beauty; to smile slowly, to keep her eyes on her lap. Pure passivity all this, under which the miserable soul could torture in secret. As she often had a back-ache, it was easy to wilt among her cushions; as she was always mute before flattery, to smile was as simple as to frown and meant no more; as she was ashamed of herself and her husband, she could hardly hope to lift her honest eyes, or temper her furious blushing.

It would be untrue to say that the Borgia's eager under-current of love-language stirred her not at all. Even to her the man's fame made his homage a tribute; something it was, beyond doubt, to be courted by the greatest prince in Italy. And he had not touched her yet. Amilcare, whose desperate grinning made his jaws ache, noticed so much as he watched her, fidgeting in his place. His nails were for ever at his teeth: when the fruit should come in he was to slip out, and Grifone to crown the work. Meanwhile, the flagrant unconcern for his whereabouts shown by the victim might have stung a blind worm to bite, or excused any treachery. Amilcare had no rage at all and felt the need of no excuse. All his anxiety was that Cesare should enmesh himself deep enough; and then— ! The thought of what should happen then set his head singing a song as mad as Judith's.

The still Grifone stood behind his mistress and saw Cesare's golden head sink near and yet nearer to her shoulder. He watched his arm over the back of her seat, and how his other hand crept towards the lady's idle pair. The room held those four, and them not long. In his time Amilcare muttered some excuse and tiptoed out.

Cesare was saying, "Ah, give me love— love only— else I must die!"

Molly answered nothing with her lips, but in her bosom prayed ceaselessly for pity.

"Love me, pledge me with your lips, let me drink of you, O my soul!" sighed the Duke.

"Ecco, Madonna," said Grifone, and handed her the cup.

"The chalice of love!" cried Cesare, straining towards the white girl. "Drink to me, my heart, and I will drink from thee!"

Molly still held the cup, though the liquor curved brimming at the lip. Her eyes were sightless, her head shaking with palsy.

"Drink, drink, my soul!"

"Yes, my lord, yes, yes; I must drink very deep," she said, and raised the cup.

"Pshutt!" said Grifone.

She turned like a caught beast, wild and blanched with horror. She rose suddenly, swaying on her feet, entangled one of them in her long robe and stumbled forward to stay herself by the table. She looked like some spurred Bacchante, lurching over the board with the great flagon a-nod in her hand. Cesare made to catch her in his arms, and reached for the cup; but then she screamed with all her might and threw the accursed thing crash upon the pavement.

"Treachery! Treachery!" Molly shrieked; and again, "Treachery! O God, he has made me a devil!" She threw her head up, herself tumbled back upon the cushions; knew nothing of Grifone's "Go, go, go, my lord; the house is quick with murder!" and when she opened her eyes at last saw Amilcare standing grim and grey before her.

Who can say what shall best reveal a man, whether love or hate or fear? Or how to know which of these three passions stripped her this Amilcare naked? Naked he was now, and she found that she had never known him. The colour of his face was that of old white wax; his mouth seemed stretched to cracking point, neither turned up at the corners nor down, but a bleak slit jagged across his face. He fastened her with his hard eyes, which seemed smaller than usual, and had a scared look, as if he was positively disconcerted at what he read as they glimmered over his wife. In one of his hands (never still) he had a long knife, very lean in the blade.

"Ah, what do you want of me more, Amilcare?" It was Molly spoke first, in a whisper.

He croaked his reply. "I am going to kill you."

"Oh! oh! You are going to kill me, my lord?"

"You have sold me to my enemy. He is your lover."

"No, no! I have no lover, Amilcare; I have never had a lover."

"Liar!" he thundered. "If he had not been your lover you would not have spared his life. There can be no other reason. I am not a fool."

To Grifone that was just what he appeared. To her some ray of her own soul's honest logic showed at the last.

"Amilcare!" she cried out, on her knees, "Amilcare, listen, I pray you. I have done you no wrong; I implore you not to hurt me; I have done you honour. It was because I loved *you* that I saved his life. I speak the truth, my lord, I speak the truth."

"I have never thought you to speak otherwise; but I have been wrong, it appears. The excuse is monstrous. I am going to kill you."

The miserable girl turned him a pinched face. She searched for any shred of what she had known in him, but all the deadly mask of him she saw told her nothing. She began to be witless again, to wring her hands, to whimper and whine.

Amilcare looked fixedly at her, every muscle in his face rigid as stone. So, as he ruminated, some whisp of his racing thought caught light from his inner rage, flared blood-bright before him, and convulsing him drove him to his work.

"Gross trull!" He sprang at her with his knife in the air. Molly shrieked for mercy; and before he could be on her Grifone whipped out his dagger and stabbed his master under the stabbing arm.

Amilcare jerked in mid-career, constricted and turned half. But the blow had gone too deep and too true. He fell horribly, and Molly knew no more.

XI

FROM AN AMATEUR'S CABINET

Grifone received his swooning lady into his arms and held her there to his great content, triumphing in her beauty and successful capture. Truly the adventure had gone by clockwork: he might say (he thought) that there was not one step in it but had been schemed to an eighth of an inch; and when you have to bring temperamental differences into account, the chances of Italian politics, the influence of climate, the panic alarms of a ridden mob— and still succeed, why, then you may lawfully be happy. Happy he was, but Molly was tall and he a light-weight. Moreover, he wanted to wipe his blade and be off. He judged it prudent, therefore, to bring her to herself again, and so did by sousing her liberally with cold water.

Molly, as soon as she could see, was aware of him kneeling by her side and of his arms about her. Before she had done gasping he began to kiss her.

"My heart of hearts, my lovely soul, my lady Moll! Mine altogether by the act of my arm!" were some of his fiery words.

There were others yet more explicit, which left no doubt of his passion, nor any ray of doubt of his intentions. Grifone took everything for granted, as he had from the beginning.

"My charmer," he said, "I have saved you from ignominious death; but I have saved myself also from a death by no means agreeable to me. It was impossible that our love could have held us much longer at a distance from each other, impossible that we could have still suffered a third person to usurp our privileges. If that stabbed stabber under the table had not misunderstood you so grotesquely— the gross-witted hog!— he would have lived, and I died of jealousy. A far from pleasant death, you will allow; worse in that it would have involved your own. For I should have had to kill you too, my dearest joy: so much would have been owing to my self-respect. Things, you see, could not have turned out more fortunately; the fellow trapped himself. We may be happy— we will be wildly happy— you shall see!"

It may be doubted whether Molly heard anything of this exposition; she may well have missed one or two steps in a carefully reasoned argument. Hers was that state of absorbent lassitude when the words and acts put to you sink into the floating mass of your weakness. The late shocking grief hovers felt about you: a buzz of talk, a rain of caresses, hold the spectre off, and so are serviceable— but no more. The cold cheek, the clay-cold lips, the long, lax limbs of the poor doll were at his service. She saw nothing through her dim eyes, made no motion with her lips, sobbed rather than breathed, endured tearlessly rather than lived awake her misery. Misery is not the word: she had been sent down to hell and had come back dumb to earth, neither knowing why such torment was hers, nor thinking how to fly a second questioning. Had she been capable of a wish, a prayer, or of begging a favour, who can doubt what it would have been? Death, oh, death!

Grifone's face was so near to hers, that not to kiss her would have been an affectation; but when he began to make plans, he released her, sat up, and spoke as though he were discussing theory.

"There is very much to do, my love," said he, "but I think I see my way clear. It is instant flight, to begin with, for one of the household may be here any moment, or Don Cesare return. Such an one would have but to open the window and cry, 'Treason, ho!' to secure our being torn to pieces— not for any love the Nonesi bear that carrion; but because not one of them could resist the chance of kicking his benefactors. It is reasonable, after all. Instant flight, my dear, if you please. But whither? you will ask. Luckily I can take you to a pretty safe place, of which I have the key and *custode's* goodwill in my pocket. You know the Rocca del Capitan Vecchio outside the Latin Gate? We go there for our terrestrial paradise. Shawl your lovely head, therefore, stoop your glorious shoulders, and obey me exactly."

He got up as he made an end of speech, drew her gently to her feet, and showed her how to muffle herself in the hood of a man's cloak. He bound the rest of the garment about her waist with his belt, pinned up her skirt and petticoat as high as her knees, and gave her his own stockings and shoes. Then he helped himself to his dead master's pair, to his sword and velvet gown; and—

"Now," he said, "we may start by the privy garden."

He led the way. It was a golden afternoon of late summer; the shadows were lengthening as the air grew tired and cool, all the place was full of that vast peace in which a day of strenuous heat sinks to rest. The faint breeze in the myrtles was like a sleeper's sigh:—

"Majoresque cadunt altis de montibus umbræ— " murmured Grifone to himself, as he slipped among the cypresses over the grass. Molly followed him with faltering knees, nearly spent. As always, she was at the mercy of a clear head, never masterless when a man was near her. Morally, nervously, she seemed to be dead; so she followed her new lord as meekly as she had followed her old— that one to Nona across the seas, this one by gloomy, pent ways through the stale-smelling streets of the city to the Rocca del Capitan Vecchio.

Meekly enough she went, yet not so far nor so meekly but that she gave Grifone a genuine surprise. It seems that the air, the exercise, precautions, what-not, had cried back her escaped wits: certain it is that, once in the storm-bitten old fortress, she thanked her leader and rescuer with a tremulous sweetness all her own, and then— by Heaven and Earth!— urged him gently to go back, "lest her honour should be breathed upon."

Her honour! Grifone, the romancer, turned sick with amazement. He was dumbfounded, could not believe his ears, nor yet his eyes; that there before him should stand that drooping, flagged, pitiful beauty, always at his discretion, now wholly at his mercy within nine-foot walls, and talk to him with wet eyes and pleading lips of the Cardinal Virtues.

As soon as he could collect himself he put this before her in a whirl of words.

Santo Dio! Timidity, prejudice, after what had passed! In what possible way or by what possible quibble of a priest could anything stay them now from the harvest of a sown love— two years' sowing, by the Redeemer, two years' torture; and now— a solid square fortress on a naked rock, deemed impregnable by anything but black treachery! Let him make assurance incredibly secure: say the word, and he would go and silence the old *custode* for ever. It was done in a moment— what more could he do?

So he prayed; but Molly was a rock at last. She ignored everything but the fact that she could never survive the night if he stayed in the fortress-tower. Such, she assured him, was the fixed habit of her extraordinary race. She made no pretence of mourning her dead husband; indeed, her horror of him set her shuddering at his mere name; nor did she affect to deny that she loved Grifone. It made no difference. She was luminously mild, used her hands like a Madonna in a picture, was more lovely and winning in the motions of her little head, the wistful deeps and darks of her eyes, the pathetic curve of her mouth, than any Madonna short of Leonardo's. Grifone threw up his arms; such a pass confounded him; he had no tools to pick this sort of lock. Oh, but the thing was impossible! Two years' longing, the husband dead— why, they might marry, even, if she would. Perhaps that was what she needed? If so, he would risk his life in the city again to find a priest. But, think of it, formalities at this hour!

Molly smiled and blushed; she was sorry for her friend and would have consoled him if she could; but the thing was so obvious. Did not Grifone see?

Grifone did not see; he tore his hair, he threatened, prayed, raved, commanded, coaxed, swore by God and the Devil, clung to her knees— useless!

"Dear friend," she said, and stroked his hot hair, "you have served me well. Never serve me now so ill."

She beat him. From that moment, when love was dead, he began to hate her. She was safe from what she feared. Everything he might have waived but that, a clean blow at his own conceit. The end was near.

Their colloquy, so frenzied on his part, so staid and generous at once on hers, was barely over before the hum of many voices crept upon them, a slow, murmurous advance, out of which, as the hordes drew near, one or two sharp cries— "Seek, seek!" "Death to the traitor!"— threw up like the hastier wave-crests in a racing tide. Again they heard (and now more clearly), "Evviva Madonna! La Madonna di Nona!" and then (more ominous than all) a cry for Cesare Borgia: "Chiesa! Chiesa!"

At this last Grifone, who had been biting his fingers shrewdly, wrung a nail apart till the blood came. His was the desperate caught face of a stoat in a trap.

"What is this crying without?" said Molly in a hush.

"Pest! I must find out," said Grifone.

He climbed to a high window and looked down into the moonlight. "The Nonesi in force. Cesare Borgia and the troops. Hist! He is going to speak to them; they are holding him up." He strained to listen— and it seems that he heard.

"Citizens," said the Borgia, in fact, "I pledge you my sacred word that the Duchess shall be delivered to you whole and in honour. She shall be in the Palace within an hour. The Secretary who has her there, who stabbed his master and (as I learn from Milan) hatched all the plot, must be left to me. Madonna Maria saved my life at the peril of her own. She has no more devoted servant than I am. Trust me to prove it."

"Chiesa! Chiesa! Madonna! Heed the Duke!" cried the mob. And then, "Let the Duke go up and win us our lady."

"That he shall never do," said Grifone, and came down from the window.

Molly, seeing the cunning in his eyes, backed to the wall.

Time does not serve, and pity forbids, that I should dwell upon this misery. What she may have wailed, what he withstood who loved her once, I have no care to set down at large. He strangled her with cruel, vivacious hands, and then (since time had pressed, and all his passion not been pent in one wicked place) fell to kissing the flouted clay. Getting up from this tribute, he was faced by Cesare Borgia and his men; by Cesare who, used to such stratagems as this of late, had had the whole story out of Ludovic at Milan, and forestalled Nona by buying up the troop of "Centaurs" before ever he entered the city. Thus had Amilcare been sold by his own purchase, and thus Grifone griped in his own springe. Cesare found him, I say, and Grifone knew in the first crossing of their eyes that his hour had come.

He bore it without a wink, and lucky he might think it that for Cesare also the time was short. He was sooner dead than he dared to hope, and died cursing the name of Borgia. But that was a seasoned name.

"The populace is on fire, Highness," reported a breathed captain. "It clamours for the Duchess of Nona. We can hardly hold them much longer, strong as we are. We must show her, though I perceive that her Excellency has fainted."

"She is dead, man," said Cesare shortly, wiping his pair of daggers.

"It is a pity, Highness. *Ma——!*" He shrugged the end to his period.

Cesare looked at the girl and shrugged in his turn.

"Luckily it is dark. We must play them that trick they played on Borgo San Domino. She must be put in a litter, and at the palace see to it that the lights are behind her before ever you set her up in the window. Do what you can for us, Ercole."

They worked their best to compose that pitiful dead. She had suffered much, and showed it. Her wide eyes were horrible. And there was little time for more than to order her dress and neck-jewels, and to smooth out her brown hair.

"H'm," said Cesare, "you have made little of it; but at a distance it may serve our turn until the troops arrive. Is the litter below? Good. *Avanti!*"

The church bells rang all night, and all night the Piazza Grande was alive, a flickering field of torches and passing and repassing throngs. "Evviva Madonna! Hail, Duchess of Nona!" were the cries they gave. And above, at an arched window, haloed by candle-light, the staring lady of the land, stiffened and relaxed, played out the last functions of her generous body, in return for the people's acclamation.

Bianca Maria, Queen of the Romans by virtue of proxy and the Sacrament, spurred into the city of Nona next noon at the head of a plumed escort. There, at the fatal window, she saw the whole truth in a flash.

"*O lasso!* Her third husband was her last, I see," she said, and bit her lip to sting the tears back.

"Majesty," said Cesare, hat in hand at her stirrup, "it is not quite so. Grifone was not quick enough for the other fellow. Messer Death is actually her second husband."

"Now I have something for which to thank our Lord God," said Bianca Maria. "Let her be decently buried, but not here."

It was, however, explained that for reasons of policy the Duchess of Nona must share tombs with the Duke. Serviceable in death as in life, there where she was marketed lies her fragrant dust; fragrant now, I hope, since all the passion is out.

I almost despair of winning your applause for poor Molly Lovel, yet will add this finally in her justification. Women are most loved when they are lovely, most lovely when they are meek. This is not to say that they will be worthily loved or loyally: there are two sides to a bargain. Yet this one thing more: they are neither meek nor lovely unless they love. And since Molly Lovel, on my showing, was both in a superlative degree, it follows that she must have loved much. She was ill repaid while she lived; let now that measure be meted her which was accorded another Molly whose surname was Magdalene.

MESSER CINO AND THE LIVE COAL

I

It is not generally known that the learned Aristotle once spent the night in a basket dangled midway betwixt attic and basement of a castle; nor that, having suffered himself to be saddled for the business, he went on all-fours, ambling round the terrace-walk with a lady on his back, a lady who, it is said, plied the whip with more heartiness than humanity. But there seems no doubt of the fact. The name of the lady (she was Countess of Cyprus), the time of the escapade, which was upon the sage's return from India in the train of the triumphant Alexander— these and many other particulars are at hand. The story does not lack of detail, though it is noteworthy that Petrarch, in his "Trionfo d'Amore," decently veils the victim in a periphrasis. "Quell' el gran Greco"— there is the great Grecian, says he, and leaves you to choose between the Stagyrite, Philip of Macedon, and Theseus. The painters, however, have had no mercy upon him. I remember him in a pageant at Siena, in a straw hat, with his mouth full of grass; the lady rides him in the mannish way. In pictures he is always doting, humbled to the dust or cradled in his basket, when he is not showing his paces on the lawn. By all accounts it was a bad case of green-sickness, as such late cases are. You are to understand that he refused all nourishment, took delight in no manner of books, could not be stayed by the nicest problems of Physical Science— such as whether the beaver does indeed catch fish with his tail, the truth concerning the eyesight of the lynxes of Bœotia, or what gave the partridge such a reputation for heedless gallantry. But it would be unprofitable to inquire into all this; Aristotle was not the first enamoured sage in history, nor was he the last. And where he bowed his laborious front it was to be hoped that Messer Cino of Pistoja might do the like. It is of him that I am to speak. The story is of Selvaggia Vergiolesi, the beautiful romp, and of Messer Guittoncino de' Sigibuldi, that most eminent jurist, familiarly known as Cino da Pistoja in the affectionate phrasing of his native town.

Love-making was the mode in his day (which was also Dante's), but Master Cino had been all for the Civil Law. The Digest, the Pandects, the Institutes of Gaius and what not, had given him a bent back before his time, so that he walked among the Pistolese beauties with his eyes on the ground and his hands knotted behind his decent robe. Love might have made him fatter, yet he throve upon his arid food; he sat in an important chair in his University; he had lectured at Bologna (hive of sucking Archdeacons), at Siena, at Perugia. Should he prosper, he looked to Florence for his next jump. As little as he could contrive was he for Pope or Emperor, Black or White, Farinata or Cerchi; banishment came that road. His friend Dante was footsore with exile, halfway over Apennine by this time; Cino knew that for him also the treading was very delicate. Constitutionally he was Ghibelline with his friend Dante, and such politics went well in Pistoja for the moment. But who could tell? The next turn of the wheel might bring the Pope round; Pistoja might go Black (as indeed she did in more senses than one), and pray where would be his Assessorship of Civil Causes, where his solemn chair, where his title to doffing of caps and a chief seat at feasts? Cino, meditating these things over his morning sop and wine, rubbed his chin sore and determined to take a wife. His family was respectable, but Ghibelline; his means were happy; his abilities known to others as well as to himself. Good! He would marry a sober Guelphish virgin, and establish a position to face both the windy quarters. It was when his negotiations to this end had reached maturity, when the contract for his espousals with the honourable lady, Monna Margherita degli Ughi, had actually been signed, that Messer Cino of Pistoja was late for his class, got cold feet, and turned poet.

II

It was a strange hour when Love leaped the heart of Cino, that staid jurisconsult, to send him reeling up the sunny side of the piazza heedless of his friends or his enemies. To his dying day he could not have told you how it came upon him. Being a man of slow utterance and of a mind necessarily bent towards the concrete, all he could confess to himself throughout the terrible business was, that there had been a cataclysm. He remembered the coldness of his feet; cold feet in mid April— something like a cataclysm! As he turned it over and over in his mind a lady recurred with the persistence of a refrain in a ballad; and words, quite unaccustomed words, tripped over his tongue to meet her. What a lovely vision she had made!— "Una donzella non con uman' volto (a gentle lady not of human look)." Well, what next? Ah, something about "Amor, che ha la mia virtù tolto (Love that has reft me of my manly will)." Then should come *amore*, and of course *cuore*, and *disiò*, and *anch' io*! This was very new; it was also very strange what a fascination he found in his phrenetic exercises. Rhyme, now: he had called it often enough a jingle of endings; it were more true to say that it was a jingle of mendings, for it certainly soothed him. He was making a goddess in his own image; poetry— Santa Cecilia! he was a poet, like his friend Dante, like that supercilious young tomb-walker Guido Cavalcanti. A poet he undoubtedly became; and if his feet were cold his heart was on fire.

What happened was this, so far as I am informed. At the north angle of the church of San Giovanni fuori Civitas there is a narrow lane, so dark that at very noon no sunlight comes in but upon blue bars of dust slant-wise overhead. This lay upon Cino's daily beat from his lodgings to the Podestà;[1] and here it was that he met Selvaggia Vergiolesi.

She was one of three young girls walking hand in hand up the alley on their way from early mass, the tallest where all were tall, and, as it seemed to him when he dreamed of it, astonishingly beautiful. Though they were very young, they were ladies of rank; their heads were high and crowned, their gowns of figured brocade; they had chains round their necks, and each a jewel on her forehead; by chains also swung their little mass-books in silver covers. Cino knew them well enough by sight. Their names were Selvaggia di Filippo Vergiolesi, Guglielmotta Aspramonte, Nicoletta della Torre. So at least he had always believed; but now, but now! A beam of gold dust shot down upon the central head. This was Aglaia, fairest of the three Graces; and the other two were Euphrosyne and Thaleia, her handmaids. Thus it struck Cino, heart and head, at this sublime moment of his drab-coloured life.

Selvaggia's hair was brown, gold-shot of its own virtue. In and out of it was threaded a fine gold chain; behind, it was of course plaited in a long twist, plaited and bound up in cloth of gold till it looked as hard as a bull's tail. Her dress was all of formal brocade, green and white, to her feet. It was cut square at the neck; and from that square her throat, dazzlingly white, shot up as stiff as a stalk which should find in her face its delicate flower. She was not very rosy, save about the lips; her eyes were grey, inclined to be green, the lashes black. As for her shape, sumptuous as her dress was, stiff and straight and severe, I ask you to believe that she had grace to fill it with life, to move at ease in it, to press it into soft and rounded lines. Her linked companions also were beauties of their day— that sleek and sleepy Nicoletta, that ruddy Guglielmotta; but they seemed to cower in their rigid clothes, and they were as nothing to Cino.

The lane was so narrow that only three could pass abreast; it was abreast these three were coming, as Cino saw. On a sudden his heart began to knock at his ribs; that was when the light fell aslant upon the maid. He could no more have taken his eyes off Selvaggia than he could have climbed up the dusty wall to avoid her. Lo, here is one stronger than I! At the next moment the three young rogues were about him, their knitted hands a fence,— but the eyes of Selvaggia! Terrible twin-fires, he thought, such as men light in the desert to scare the beasts away while they sleep, or (as he afterwards improved it for his need) like the flaming sword of the Archangel, which declared and yet forbade Eden to Adam and his wife.

Selvaggia, in truth, though she had fourteen years behind her, was a romp when no one was looking. There were three brothers at home, but no mother; she was half a boy for all her straight gown. To embarrass this demure professor, to presume upon her sex while discarding it, was a great joke after a tediously droned mass at San Jacopo. Nicoletta would have made room, even the hardier Guglielmotta drew back; but the wicked Selvaggia pinched their fingers so that they could not escape. All this time Messer Cino had his eyes rooted in Selvaggia's, reading her as if she were a portent. She endured very well what she took to be the vacancy of confusion in a shy recluse.

"Well, Messer Cino, what will you do?" said she, bubbling with mischief.

"Oh, Madonna, can you ask?" he replied, and clasped his hands.

"But you see that I do ask."

"I would stop here all the day if I might," said Messer Cino, with a look by no means vacant. Whereupon she let him through that minute and ran away blushing. More than once or twice she encountered him there, but she never tried to pen him back again.

Little Monna Selvaggia learned that you cannot always put out the fire which you have kindled. The fire set blazing by those lit green swords of hers was in the heart of an Assessor of Civil Causes, a brazier with only too good a draught. For love in love-learned Tuscany was then a roaring wind; it came rhythmically and set the glowing mass beating like the sestett of a sonnet. One lived in numbers in those days; numbers always came. You sonnetteered upon the battlefield, in the pulpit, on the Bench, at the Bar. Throughout the moil of his day's work at the Podestà those clinging long words, in themselves inspiration, *disìo, piacere, vaghezza, gentilezza, diletto, affetto,* beautiful twins that go ever embraced, wailed in poor Cino's ears, and insensibly shaped themselves coherent. He thought they were like mirrors, so placed that each gave a look of Selvaggia. Before the end of the day he had the whole of her in a sonnet which, if it were as good as it was comfortable, should needs (he thought) be excellent. The thrill which marked achievement sent the blood to his head; this time he gloried in cold feet. He wrote his sonnet out fair upon vellum in a hand no scribe at the Papal Court could have bettered, rolled it, tied it with green and white silk (her colours, colours of the hawthorn hedge!), and went out into the streets at the falling-in of the day to deliver it.

The Palazzo Vergiolesi lay over by the church of San Francesco al Prato, just where the Via San Prospero debouches into that green place. Like all Tuscan palaces it was more fortress than house, a dark square box of masonry with a machicollated lid; and separate from it, but appurtenant, had a most grim tower with a slit or two halfway up for all its windows. Here, under the great escutcheon of the Vergiolesi, Cino delivered his missive. The porter took it with a bow so gracious that the poet was bold to ask whether the Lady Selvaggia was actually within.

"Yes, surely, Messere," said the man, "and moreover in the kitchen with the cookmaids. For there is a cake-making on hand, and she is never far away from that business."

Cino was ravished by this instance of divine humiliation; so might Apollo have bowed in the house of Admetus, so Israel have kept sheep for Rachel's sake. He walked away in most exalted mood, his feet no longer cold. This was a great day for him, when he could see a new heaven and a new earth.

"Now I too have been in Arcady!" he thought to himself, with tears in his eyes. "I will send a copy of my sonnet to Dante Alighieri by a sure hand. He should be at Bologna by this." And he did.

Madonna Selvaggia, her sleeves rolled up, a great bib all about her pretty person, and her mouth in a fine mess of sugar and crumbs, received her tribute sitting on the long kitchen-table. It should have touched, it might have tickled, but it simply confused her. The maids peeped over her shoulder as she read, in ecstasy that Madonna should have a lover and a poet of her own. Selvaggia filched another handful of sugar and crumbs, and twiddled her sonnet while she wondered what on earth she should do with it. Her fine brows met each other over the puzzle, so clearly case for a confidence. Gianbattista, her youngest brother, was her bosom friend; but he was away, she knew, riding to Pisa with their father. Next to him ranked Nicoletta; she would be at mass to-morrow— that would do. Meantime the cook produced a most triumphal cake hot and hot, and the transports of poor Messer Cino were forgotten.

Dante's reply to his copy was so characteristic that I must anticipate a little to speak of it. He confined himself almost entirely to technicalities, strongly objecting to the sestett with its three rhymes in the middle, upon which Cino had prided himself in no small degree. The only thing he seemed to care for was the tenth line, "A dolce morte sotto dolce inganno," which you may render, if you like, "To a sweet death under so sweet deceit"; but he said there were too many "o's" in it. "As to the subject of your poem," he wrote in a postscript, "love is a thing of so terrible a nature that not lightly is it to be entered, since it cannot be lightly left; and, seeing the latter affair is much out of a man's power, he should be wary with the former, wherein at present he would appear to have some discretion, though not very much." This was chilly comfort; but by the time it reached him Cino was beyond the assault of chills.

Equally interesting should it be to record the conversation of Monna Selvaggia with her discreet friend Nicoletta; yet I cannot record everything. Nicoletta had a lover of her own, a most proper poet, who had got far beyond the mere accidence of the science where Cino was fumbling now; you might say that he was at theory. Nicoletta, moreover, was sixteen years old, a marriageable age, an age indeed at which not to have a lover would have been a disgrace. She had had sonnets and *canzoni* addressed to her since she was twelve; but then she had two elder sisters and only one brother— a monk! This made a vast difference. The upshot was that when Cino met the two ladies at the charmed spot of yesterday's encounter he uncovered before them and stood with folded hands, as if at his prayers. Consequently he missed the very pretty air of consciousness with which Selvaggia passed him by, the heightened colour of her, the lowered eyes and restless fingers, Also he missed Nicoletta's demure shot askance, demure but critical, as became an expert. A sonnet and a bunch of red anemones went to the Palazzo Vergiolesi that evening; thenceforth it rained sonnets till poor little Selvaggia ran near losing her five wits. It rained sonnets, I say, until the Cancellieri brought out the black Guelphs in a swarm. Then it rained blood, and the Vergiolesi fled one cloudy night to Pitecchio, their stronghold in the Apennine. For Messer Cino, it behoved him also to advise seriously about his position. To sonnetteer is very well, but a lover, to say nothing of a jurisconsult, must live; he cannot have his throat cut if there is a way out.

There was a very simple way out, which he took. He went down to Lucca in the plain and married his Margherita degli Ughi. With her Guelph connections he felt himself safer. He bestowed his wife in the keeping of her people for the time, bought himself a horse, and rode up to Pitecchio among the green maize, the olive-yards, and sprouting vines to claim asylum from Filippo, and to see once more the beautiful young Selvaggia.

FOOTNOTE:

[1] So the Pistolesi described at once their government and the seat of it.

III

There is hardly a sonnet, there are certainly neither *ballate, canzoni*, nor *capitoli* which do not contain some reference to Monna Selvaggia's fine eyes, and always to the same tune. They scorch him, they beacon him, they flash out upon him in the dark, so that he falls prone as Saul (who got up with a new name and an honourable addition); they are lodestones, swords, lamps, torches, fires, fixed and ambulatory stars, the sun, the moon, candles. They hold lurking a thief to prey upon the vitals of Cino; they are traitors, cruel lances; they kill him by stabbing day after day. You can picture the high-spirited young lady from his book— her noble bearing, her proud head, her unflinching regard, again the sparks in her grey-green eyes, and so on. He plays upon her *forte nome*, her dreadful name of Selvaggia; so she comes to be Ferezza itself. "Tanto è altiera," he says, so haughtily she goes that love sets him shaking; but, kind or cruel, it is all one to the enamoured Master Cino; for even if she "un pochettin sorride (light him a little smile)," it melts him as sun melts snow. In any case, therefore, he must go, like Dante's cranes, trailing his woes. It appears that she had very little mercy upon him; for all that in one place he records that she was "of all sweet sport and solace amorous," in many more than one he complains of her bringing him to "death and derision," of her being in a royal rage with her poet. At last he cries out for Pity to become incarnate and vest his lady in her own robe. It may be that he loved his misery; he is always on the point of dying, but, like the swan, he was careful to set it to music first. Selvaggia, in fact, laughed at him (he turned once to call her a Jew for that) egged on as she was by her brother and her own vivacious habit. She had no Nicoletta at Pitecchio, no mother anywhere, and a scheming father too busy to be anything but shrugging towards poets. She accepted his rhymes (she would probably have been scared if they ceased), his services, his lowered looks, his bent knee; and then she tripped away with an arm round Gianbattista's neck to laugh at all these praiseworthy attentions. As for Cino, Selvaggia was become his religion, and his rhyming her reasonable service. His goddess may have been as thirsty as the Scythian Artemis; may be that she asked blood and stripes of her devotees. All this may well be; for, by the Lord, did she not have them?

Ridolfo and Ugolino Vergiolesi, the two elder brothers of Selvaggia, had stayed behind in Pistoja to share the fighting in the streets. They had plenty of it, given and received. Ridolfo had his head cut open, Ugolino went near to losing his sword arm; but in spite of these heroic sufferances the detested Cancellieri became masters of the city, and the chequer-board flag floated over the Podestà. Pistoja was now no place for a Ghibelline. So the two young men rode up to the hill-fortress, battered, but in high spirits. Selvaggia flew down the cypress-walk to meet them; they were brought in like wounded heroes. That was a bad day's work for Messer Cino the amorist; Apollo and the Muses limped in rags, and Mars was the only God worth thinking about, except on Sundays.

Ridolfo, with his broken head-piece, was a bluff youth, broad-shouldered, square-jawed, a great eater, grimly silent for the most part. Ugolino had a trenchant humour of the Italian sort. What this may be is best exampled by our harlequinades, in which very much of Boccaccio's bent still survives. You must have a man drubbed if you want to laugh, and do your rogueries with a pleasant grin if you are inclined to heroism. Ridolfo, reading Selvaggia's sheaf of rhymes that night, was for running Master Cino through the body, jurist or no jurist; but Ugolino saw his way to a jest of the most excellent quality, and prevailed. He was much struck by the poet's preoccupation with his sister's eyes.

"Candles, are they," he chuckled, "torches, fires, suns, moons, and stars? You seem to have scorched this rhymester, Vaggia."

"He has frequently told me so, indeed," said Selvaggia.

"It reminds me of Messer San Giovanni Vangelista," Ugolino continued, "who was made to sing rarely by the touching of a hot cinder."

Selvaggia snatched the scrolls out of her brother's hand. "Nay, nay, but wait," she cried, with a gulp of laughter; "I have done that to Messer Cino, or can if I choose." She turned over the delicate pen-work in a hurry. "Here," she said eagerly, "read this!"

Ugolino scampered through a couple of quatrains. "There's nothing out of common here," said he.

"Go on, go on," said the girl, and nudged him to attend.

Ugolino read the settett:—

> "'His book is but the vesture of her spirit;
> So too thy poet, that feels the living coal
> Flame on his lips and leap to song, shall know,
> To whom the glory, whose the unending merit;
> Nor faltering shall his utterance be, nor slow
> The mute confession of his inmost soul.'"

Reading, he became absorbed in this fantastic, but not unhandsome piece; even Selvaggia pondered it with wide eyes and lips half parted. It was certainly very wonderful that a man could say such things, she thought. Were they true? Could they be true of any one in the world—

even of Beatrice Portinari, that wonderful dead lady? She had never, she remembered, shown this particular sonnet to Nicoletta. What would Nicoletta have said? Pooh, what nonsense it was, what arrant nonsense in a man who could carry a sword, if he chose, and kill his enemies, or, better still, with his head outwit them— that he should turn to pens and ink and to fogging a poor girl! So Selvaggia, not so Ugolino. He got up and whispered to the scowling Ridolfo; Ridolfo nodded, and the pair of them went off presently together.

Oblique looks on Cino were the immediate outcome. He knew the young men disliked him, but cared little for that so long as they left him free to his devotions. A brisk little passage, a rally of words, with a bite in some of them, should have warned him; but no, the stage he had reached was out of range of the longest shots.

Said Ugolino at supper: "Messer Giurisconsulto, will you have a red pepper?"

"Thank you, Messere," replied Cino, "it is over hot for my tongue."

The huge Ridolfo threw his head back to laugh. "Does a burnt man dread the fire, or is he only to be fired one way? Why, man alive, my sister has set a flaming coal to your lips, and I am told you burst out singing instead of singeing."

Cino coloured at this lunge; yet his respect for the lady of his mind was such that he could not evade it.

"You take the language of metaphor, Messere," said he, rather stiffly, "to serve your occasions. You are of course within your rights. However, I will beg leave to be excused the red pepper of Messer Ugolino."

"You prefer coals?" cried Ugolino, starting up. "Good! you shall have them."

That was all; but the malign smile upon the dark youth's face gave a ring to the words, and an omen.

Late that night Cino was in his chamber writing a *ballata*. His little oil-lamp was by his side; the words flowed freely from his pen; tears hot and honest were in his eyes as he felt rather than thought his exquisite griefs. Despised and rejected of men was he— and why? For the love of a beautiful lady. Eh, Mother of God, but that was worth the pain! She had barely lifted her eyes upon him all that day, and while her brothers gibed had been at no concern to keep straight her scornful lip. Patience, he was learning his craft! The words flowed like blood from a vein.

> "Love struck me in the side,
> And from the wound my soul took wing and flew

To Heaven, and all my pride
Fell, and I knew
There was no balm could stay that wound so wide."

At this moment came a rapping at his door. He went to open it, dreaming no harm. There stood Ridolfo and Ugolino with swords in their right hands; in his left Ugolino carried a brazier.

"Gentlemen," said Cino, "what is the meaning of this? Will you break in upon the repose of your father's guest? And do you come armed against an unarmed man?"

The pair of them, however, came into the room, and Ridolfo locked the door behind him. "Look you, Cino," said he, "our father's guests are not our guests, for our way is to choose our own. There is a vast difference between us, and it lies in this, that you and the like of you are word-mongers, phrasers, heart-strokers; whereas we, Master Cino, are, in Scripture language, doers of the word, rounding our phrases with iron, and putting in full-stops with the point when they are needed. And we do not stroke girls' hearts, Cino, but as often as not break men's heads."

Cino, for all his dismay, could not forbear a glance at the speaker's own damaged pate. "And, after all, Messer Ridolfo, in that you do but as you are done by, and who will blame you?"

"Hark'ee, Master Giurista," broke in Ugolino, "we have come to prove some of these fine words of yours. It will be well for you to answer questions instead of bandying them. Now did you, or did you not report that my sister Selvaggia touched your lips with a coal and set you off singing?"

Cino, with folded arms, bent his head in assent: "I have said it, Messere."

"Good! Now, such singing, though it is not to her taste, might be very much to ours. In fact we have come to hear it, and that you might be robbed of all excuse, we have brought the key with us. Brother, pray blow up the brazier."

Ridolfo, with his great cheeks like bladders, blew the coals to a white heat. "Now then," he said, grinning to Ugolino, "now then, the concert may begin."

Cino, who by this time had seen what was in the wind, saw also what his course must be. Whatever happened he could not allow a poet to be made ridiculous. It was ridiculous to struggle with two armed men, and unseemly; but suffering was never ridiculous. Patience, therefore! He anticipated the burly Ridolfo, who, having done his bellows-work, was now about to pin his victim from behind.

"Pray do not give yourself the pain to hold me, Messere," said he; "I am not the man to deny you your amusement. Do what you will, I shall not budge from here."

He stood where he was with his arms crossed, and he kept his word. The red cinder hissed upon his lips; he shut his eyes, he ground his teeth together, the sweat beaded his forehead and glistened in his hair. Once he reeled over, and would have fallen if Ridolfo had not been there to catch him; but he did not sing the tune they had expected, and presently they let him alone. So much for Italian humour, which, you will see, does not lack flavour. It was only the insensate obtuseness of the gull which prevented Ugolino dying of laughter. Ridolfo was annoyed.

"Give me cold iron to play with another time," he growled; "I am sick of your monkey-tricks." This hurt Ugolino a good deal, for it made him feel a fool.

Will it be believed that the infatuate Master Cino spent the rest of the night in a rapture of poetry? It was not voiced poetry, could never have been written down; rather, it was a torrent of feeling upon which he floated out to heaven, in which he bathed. It thrilled through every fibre of his body till he felt the wings of his soul fluttering madly to be free. This was the very ecstasy of love, to suffer the extreme torment for the beloved! Ah, he was smitten deep enough at last; if poetry were to be won through bloody sweat, the pains of the rack, the crawling anguish of the fire, was not poetry his own? Yes, indeed; what Dante had gained through exile and the death of Monna Beatrice was his for another price, the price of his own blood. He forgot the physical agony of his scorched mouth, forgot the insult, forgot everything but this ineffable achievement, this desperate essay, this triumph, this anointing. Cino, Cino, martyr for Love! Hail, Cino, crowned with thy pain! He could have held up his bleeding heart and worshipped it. Surely this was the greatest hour of his life.

Before he left Pitecchio, and that was before the dawn came upon it, he wrote this letter to his mistress.

"To his unending Lady, the image of all lovely delight, the Lady Selvaggia, Cino the poet, martyr for love, wisheth health and honour with kissing of feet. Madonna, if sin it be to lift over high the eyes, I have sinned very grievously; and if to have great joy be assurance of forgiveness, then am I twice absolved. Such bliss as I have had in the contemplation of your excellence cometh not to many men, yet that which hath befallen me this night (concerning which your honourable brothers shall inform you if you ask them)— this indeed is to be blessed of love so high, so rarely, that it were hard to believe myself the recipient, but for certain bodily testimony which, I doubt not, I shall carry about me to my last hour. I leave this house within a little while and go to the hermitage of Santa Marcella Pistoiese, there to pray Almighty God to make me worthy of my dignities and to contemplate the divine image of you wherewith my heart is sealed. So fare you well!— The most abject of your slaves,

"CINO."

His reason for giving the name of his new refuge was an honourable one, and would appeal to a duellist. His flight, though necessary, should be robbed of all appearance of flight; if they wanted him they could find him. Other results it had— results which he could never have anticipated, and which to have foreseen would have made him choose any other form of disgrace. But this was out of the question; nothing known to Cino or his philosophy could have told him the future of his conduct. He placed his letter in an infallible place and left Pitecchio just as the western sky was throbbing with warm light.

For the present I leave him on his way.

IV

The third act of the comedy should open on Selvaggia in her bed reading the letter. Beautiful as she may have looked, flushed and loose-haired at that time, it is better to leave her alone with her puzzle, and choose rather the hour of her enlightenment. Ridolfo and Ugolino were booted and spurred, their hooded hawks were on their wrists when she got speech of them. They were not very willing witnesses in a cause which now seemed to tell against themselves. Selvaggia's cheeks burned as with poor Cino's live coal when she could piece together all the shameful truth; tears brimmed at her eyes, and these too were scalding hot. Selvaggia, you must understand, was a very good girl, her only sin being none of her accomplishment; she was a child who looked like a young woman. Certainly she could not help that, though all the practice of her race were against her. She had never sought love, never felt to need it, nor cared to harbour it when it came. Love knocked at her heart, asking an entry; her heart was not an inn, she thought, let the wayfarer go on. But the knocking had continued till her ears had grown to be soothed by the gentle sound; and now it had stopped for ever, and, Pitiful Mother, for what good reason? Oh, the thing was horrible, shameful, unutterable! She was crying with rage; but as that spent itself a great warm flood of genuine sorrow tided over her, floated her away: she cried as though her heart was breaking; and now she cried for pity, and at last she cried for very love. A pale ethereal Cino, finger on lip, rose before her; a halo burned about his head; he seemed a saint, he should be hers! Ugolino and Ridolfo, helpless and ashamed before her outburst, went out bickering to their sport; and Selvaggia, wild as her name, untaught, with none to tutor her, dared her utmost— dared, poor girl, beyond her strength.

Late in the afternoon of that day Cino, in the oratory of his hermitage, getting what comfort he could out of an angular Madonna frescoed there, heard a light step brush the threshold. The sun, already far gone in the west, cast on the white wall a shadow whose sight set his head spinning. He turned hastily round. There at the door stood Selvaggia in a crimson cloak; for the rest, a picture of the Tragic Muse, so woebegone, so white, so ringed with dark she was.

Cino, on his feet, muttered a prayer to himself. He covered his scarred mouth, but not before the girl had caught sight of it. She set to wringing her hands, and began a low wailing cry.

"Ah, terrible— ah, terrible! That I should have done it to one who was always so gentle with me and so patient! Oh, Cino"— and she held out her hands towards him— "oh, Cino, will you not forgive me? Will you not? I, only, did it; it was through me that they knew what you had said. Shameful girl that I am!" She covered her face and stood sobbing before him. But confronted with this toppled Madonna, Cino was speechless, wholly unprepared by jurisprudence or the less exact science of love for such a pass. As he knew himself, he could have written eloquently and done justice to the piercing theme; but love, as he and his fellows understood it, had no spoken language. I do not see, however, that Selvaggia is to be blamed for being ignorant of this.

Yet he had to say something, since there stood the weeping girl, all abandoned to her trouble. "I beseech you, Madonna," he was beginning, when she suddenly bared her face, her woe, and her beauty to his astonished eyes, looking passionately at him in a way which even he could not misinterpret.

"Cino," she said brokenly, "I am a wilful girl, but not wicked, ah, no! not hard-hearted. I think I did not understand you; I heard, but would not hear; it was wantonness, not evil in me, Cino. You have never wearied of telling me your devotion; is it too late to be thankful? Now I am come to tell you what I should have said long before, that I am grateful, proud of such love, that I receive it if still I may, that— that"— her voice fell to a thrilled whisper— "that I love you, Cino." Ah, but she had no more courage; she hid her blushes in her hands and felt that now she should by rights sink into the earth.

Judge you, who know the theory of the matter, if this were terrible hearing for Messer Cino. Terrible? It was unprecedented hearing; it was a thing which, so far as he knew, had never happened to a lover before. That love should go smooth, the lady smile, the lady love, the lady woo? Monstrous! The lady was never kind. Where was anguish? Where martyrdom? Where poetry and sore eyes? Yet stay, was not such a thing in itself a torment, to be cut off your martyrdom?

Cino gasped for breath. "You love me, Madonna?" he said. "You love me?"

Selvaggia nodded her head in her hands; she felt that she was blushing all over her body.

Cino, at this new stab, struck his forehead a resounding smack. "This is terrible indeed!" he cried out in his distress; whereupon Selvaggia forgot to be ashamed any more, she was so taken by surprise.

"What do you mean, Cino?" she began to falter. "I don't understand you."

Cino plunged into the icy pool of explanation, and splashed there at large. "I mean, I mean"— he waved his hands in the air— "it is most difficult to explain. We must apprehend Love aright— if we can. He is a grim and dreadful lord, it appears, working out the salvation of the souls of poets, and other men, by great sufferings. There is no other way, as the books teach us. Such love is always towards ladies; the suffering is from them, the love for them. They deal the darts, and receive the more devotion. It is not to be otherwise— could not be— there can be no poetry without pain; and how can there be pain if the lady loves the poet? Ah, no, it is impossible! Anciently, very long ago, in the times of Troy, maybe, it was different. I know not what to say; I had never expected, never looked, nor even asked— ah, Madonna," he suddenly cried, and found himself upon his knees, "what am I to say to you for this speech of yours?"

Selvaggia, white enough now, froze hard. "Do you mean," she said slowly, in words that fell one by one, like cuts from a deliberate whip, "do you mean that you do not love me, Messer Cino, after all?"

"You are a light to my eyes and a lantern to my feet," Cino murmured: but she did not seem to hear.

"Do you mean," she went on, "that you are not prepared to be— to be my— my betrothed?"

It was done: now let the heavens fall! She could not ask the man to marry her, but it came to the same thing; she had practically committed that unpardonable sin; she had approached love to wedlock, a mystery to a bargain, the rapt converse of souls in heaven to a wrangle over the heeltaps in a tavern parlour. She was a heretic whom any Court of Love must excommunicate. The thing was so serious that it brought Cino to his feet, severe, formal, an Assessor of Civil Causes. He spread out his hands as if to wave aside words he should never have heard. He had found his tongue, for he was now contemplating the Abstract.

"Be very sure, most sacred Lady," said he, "that no bodily torment could drive me to such sacrilege as your noble humility leads you to contemplate. No indeed! Wretchedly unworthy as I am to live in the light of your eyes, I am not yet fallen so far. There are yet seeds of grace within me— of your planting, Madonna, of your planting!" She paid no heed to his compliments; her eyes were fixed. On he hurried. "So far, indeed, as those worldly concerns go, whereof you hint, I am provided for. My wife is at Lucca in her father's house— but of such things it is not fitting we should speak. Rather we should reason together of the high philosophy of love, which— "

But Selvaggia was gone before he could invite her on such a lofty flight; the wife at Lucca sent her fleeting down the mossy slopes like a hare. It was too dark for men to see her face when she tiptoed into

Pitecchio and slipped up to her chamber. Safe at last there, she shivered and drowsed the night away; but waking or sleeping she did not cease her dreary moan.

Cino, after a night of consternation, could endure the hermitage no more; the problem, he was free to confess, beat him. Next day, therefore, he took horse and rode over the mountains to Bologna, intent upon finding Dante there; but Dante had gone to Verona with half of his "Inferno" in his saddlebag. Thither Cino pursued and there found him in the church of St. Helen, disputing with the doctors upon the Question of the Land and the Water. What passed between the great poet and the less I cannot certainly report, nor is it material. I think that the tinge of philosophy set here and there in Cino's verses, to say nothing of a couplet or two which give more than a hint of the "Vita Nova," may safely be ascribed to that time. I know at least that he did not cease to love his beautiful and wild Selvaggia, so far as he understood that delicate state of the soul which she, perverse child, had so signally misapprehended. The truth may well be that he was tolerably happy at Verona, able to contemplate at his ease the divine image of his lady without any interference from the disturbing original. He was, it is said, meditating an ambitious work, the history of the Roman Polity from Numa to Justinian, an epic in five and twenty books, wherein Selvaggia would have played a fine part, that of the Genius of Natural Law. The scheme might have ripened but for one small circumstance; this was the death of Selvaggia.

That healthy, laughing girl, Genius of Nature or not, paid the penalty of her incurable childishness by catching a malaria, whereof she died, as it is said, in a high delirium of some eight hours. So it seems that she was really unteachable, for first she had spoiled Cino's martyrdom, and next, by the same token, robbed the world of an epic in twenty-five books. Cino heard of it some time afterwards, and in due season was shown her tomb at Monte della Sambuca high on the Apennine, a grey stone solitary in a grey waste of shale. There he pondered the science of which, while she was so strangely ignorant, he had now become an adept; there, or thereabouts, he composed the most beautiful of all his rhymes, the *canzone* which may stand for an elegy of the Lady Selvaggia.

> "Ay me, alas! the beautiful bright hair,— "

Ay me, indeed! And thus he ends:

> "Ay me, sharp Death! till what I ask is done
> And my whole life is ended utterly,—
> Answer,— must I weep on

Even thus, and never cease to moan *ay me*?"[2]

He might well ask. It should be accorded him that he was worthy of the occasion: the poem is very fine. But I think the good man did well enough after this; I know that if he was sad he was most melodiously sad. He throve; he became a professor; his wife bore him five children. His native city has done him what honour she could, ousted his surname in favour of her own, set up a pompous monument in the Cathedral Church (where little Selvaggia heard her dull mass), and dubbed him once and for all, *L'amoroso Messer Cino da Pistoja*. That should suffice him. As for the young Selvaggia, I suppose her bones are dust of the Apennine.

FOOTNOTE:

[2] The translation is Rossetti's.

THE JUDGMENT OF BORSO

"Unde proverbii loco etiamnunc usurpatur, præteriisse Borsii tempora."— *Este Chronicle.*

I

THE ADVENTURERS

It is happily as unnecessary as it would be unwise to inquire into the ancestry of Bellaroba, a meek-eyed girl of Venice, with whom I have here some concern. Her mother was La Fragiletta, of the Old Ghetto, and her father may have been of the Council of Ten, or possibly a Doge. No one could deny it, for no one knew his name. It is certain that his daughter was not christened as she was called, equally certain that the nickname fitted her. *Bella roba*, a pretty thing, she always had been for her mother's many friends; *bella roba* in truth she looked, as La Fragiletta fastened her dark red dress, stuck a bunch of carnations in the bosom of it, and pulled up the laces round her slim neck, on a certain May morning in or about the year 1469. "The shape you are, child," said that industrious woman, "I can do nothing for you in Venice. It is as timid as a nun's. Ferrara is the place of all the world for you. I look forward to your speedy establishment in a city where a girl may be like a flagstaff and yet not thought amiss."

Bellaroba looked humbly at herself in the glass; though she could see that she was pretty, it was not to be denied that she was thin. Ah, no; she did not take after her mother. Here she sighed to remember that her bosom friend, Olimpia Castaneve, took after hers only too well, and was to accompany her fortune-hunting in Ferrara for precisely opposite reasons. Was this fair? she wondered. She, Bellaroba, was to go because she was of a piece with the Ferrarese; Olimpia, because she could furnish a provoking contrast. She was an affectionate, docile creature, this shrinking Bellaroba, absurdly young, absurdly your servant; but tears smarted in her eyes as she stood adorned for sacrifice— in her tight crimson dress, lace at her neck and wrists, a jewel on her forehead, a chain in her hair, and a cold block of lead dragging at her heart. She had never denied any one anything, and certainly not her mother. Her tears glistened as she blinked, her lip was shaky; she was kissed a good-bye none the less, and went down the steps to join Olimpia huddled in the gondola.

"Good-bye, my child," cried Madam Fragiletta from the doorway. "Be wise; remember what I have told you. Never see a priest the wrong side of the grille, and obey Monna Nanna in everything. I shall have a mass for you at San Zan to-morrow, and another on your birthday, which I shall never forget."

The morning was misty and sharp, Madam Fragiletta was very much undressed, and loved her bed. She waved her hand gallantly to Bellaroba, who still stood up wistful in the gondola; she did not wait for it to shoot the bridge or round the square corner of the *rio*, but turned shrugging to the house. There was no reasonable probability that these two would ever meet again. Short outlooks govern La Fragiletta's trade, and Providence, it seems, has little to do with it.

Olimpia Castaneve, the muffled brooder in the poop, was cold, cross, and still. Bellaroba snivelled, but she was scornful under her cloak, and no word passed between the pair until they were in the great blunt-nosed barge, heading against a crisping tide for Chioggia. Then, as the sun shot through the mist and revealed the lagoon, one broad sheet of silver and blue, the shawls were opened, limbs went luxuriously at the stretch; you could see and hear chatter the couple of adventurers if you cared. Bellaroba you have seen already— very gentle, very simple, very unformed without and within. She had pretty ways, coaxing and appealing ways. When she asked a question it was with lifted eyebrows and a head on one side. She would take your hand without art, and let you hold it without afterthought. It was the easiest thing in the world to kiss her, for she suffered it gladly and quite innocently; it came as naturally as to a cat to rub his cheek on your chair or swinging foot. Yet the girl was as modest as a Clare. If you had presumed on your licence to make love to her, it would not have been her scorn (for she had none), but her distress that would have set you back in your place. God knows what La Fragiletta might have taught her. It is certain she was all unlettered in love up to that hour. Bellaroba was not only modest by instinct, but that better thing, innocent by preoccupation.

In all this she was a dead contrast to her handsome friend Olimpia Castaneve, who was really a beauty of the true Venetian mould. As sleek and sumptuous as a cat, as splendidly coloured as a sunburnt nectarine, crowned with a mass of red-gold hair, as stupid as she was sly, and as rich as she was spendthrift, the lovely Olimpia had been sent adventuring to the bees of Ferrara, not as lacking honey for Venice, but as being too great a treasure for her mother's house. Her mother was La Farfalla— a swollen butterfly in these days— and frankly said that she could not afford such a daughter. Olimpia had no instructions; in fact, needed none. She went cheerfully out to what Monna Nanna and the Blessed Virgin should prepare for her, without kisses (which she garnered against the lean years) and without reserves. She neither condemned her mother nor approved. Perhaps she had not the wit; assuredly she lacked the energy. She was remarkably handsome in her hot Venetian way, richly coloured, brown-eyed, crimson-lipped, bosomed like a goddess and shaped like a Caryatid. She half closed her eyes, half opened her lips, smiled and drowsed and waited. You would have thought her melting with love; she was ciphering a price, but being slow at figures, she hid herself (spiderwise) in a golden mesh. Olimpia was nearly always complaisant, had no reticences, no conscience, few brains. She was luxury itself, fond of the fire, fond of her bed, fond of her dinner. Admittedly self-absorbed, she was accustomed to say that she knew far too much about love to fall into it. It was a reflection as serious as she could make it; but Love is very apt to take such sayings amiss. Olimpia out of love might make men miserable; in it, what might she not do? I am about to tell you.

At Chioggia they were to await a shipload of merchants and pack-mules expected from Ancona; but the wind proved counter when their barge had weathered Malamocco, and that which dis-served them befriended the northering freight. They found the train of beasts awaiting them, saddled and loaded, restless to be off. Chioggia to Ferrara, by the road they would go, is a handsome fifty miles.

In that company, as they neared, they observed a calm-eyed youth with a delicate, girlish face, and wonderful shock of light gold hair all about it. He stood alone on the mole, one knee bent, a hand to his hip, and soberly surveyed the group on the barge. He made a charming little picture there— seemed indeed posed for some such thing; he was charmingly pretty himself, but for all that, he had a tragic touch upon him, a droop of the lip, or the eyelid, perhaps. One could hardly say, yet never miss it. Even Olimpia noticed the shadow across him. As they touched— "Look, look, Bellaroba," she whispered, and nudged her friend— "that boy! Did you ever see such a lovely child?"

Bellaroba drew a long breath. "I think he is as lovely as an angel," she replied, her eyes fascinated. And her saying was equally true. He was such a demure boy-angel, bright-haired, long and shapely in the limb, as the painters and carvers loved to set in Madonna's court, careful about her throne, or below the dais fiddling, or strumming lutes to charm away her listlessness. Moreover, Angioletto was the name he went by, though he had been christened Dominick. And he came from Borgo San Sepolcro— far cry from windy Chioggia— a place among the brown Tuscan hills, just where they melt into Umbria; and he was by trade a minstrel, and going to Ferrara. Of so much, with many bows, he informed the two girls, being questioned by Olimpia. But he looked at Bellaroba as he spoke, and she listened the harder and looked the longer of the two.

Everything about him seemed to her altogether gracious, from the silky floss of his gold hair to his proper legs, sheathed in scarlet to the thighs. He was as soft and daintily coloured as a girl, had long curved lashes to his grey eyes, a pathetic droop to his lip, the bloom as of a peach on his cheeks. But you could never mistake him for a girl. His eyes had a critical blink, he looked to have the discretion of a man. A fop he might be; he had a wiry mind. A fop, in fact, he was. He had a little scarlet cap on his head, scarlet stockings, peaked scarlet shoes: for the rest he was in green cloth with a blue leather belt about his waist. He had fine lace ruffles at his wrists, a fine line of white at his throat, and in his ears (if you could have seen them) gold rings. Just the pampered young minion of any Tuscan court, a precocious wrappage of wit, good manners, and sensibility, he looked what he spoke, the exquisite Florentine, to these broad-vowelled Venetian lasses; did not smile, but seemed never out of temper; and was certainly not timid. Self-possessed, reticent he was; but not timid. That was proved.

When the cavalcade was on the point to start, Angioletto stepped forward and took Bellaroba by the hand.

"Little lady," says he to his blushing captive, "I have a mule for the road which I am assured is a steady pacer. Will you be my pillion?"

"Oh, yes, Messere," said Bellaroba in a twitter, and dropped him a curtsy of her best.

"Excellent!" he cried gaily. "I can see that we are to be friends." So she was led away.

He helped her on to the mule in no time, showed her how she must hold him round the middle, how closely and how constantly; he explained how little there was to fear, for all that such a manner of going was as venturesome to her as a steamer would have seemed to Ulysses, that great captain. It was then that Olimpia (watching all this) proved Angioletto not timid, for she saw him conclude his precepts to her friend by kissing her cheek in the easiest manner. "H'm," thought the wise Olimpia, "I pray that Bellaroba may be careful."

She herself accepted the services and part of the horse of a lean Ravennese, a Captain of Lances— two yards of sinew and brown leather— who told her that his name was Mosca, and his heart bleeding at her feet. Olimpia smiled beautifully upon him, but was careful; took a share of the courser, but gave in return nothing more than a hand on its master's belt. He wanted much more, and showed it. Olimpia, far from coy, hinted an exchange. She needed her bearings; did this apparent hero know Ferrara? The Mosca snorted, threw back his head at the word. Ferrara? cried he, did he know it! Saints and Angels, who could know it better? "Ferrara?" he went on to shout, appealing to gods and men, "the gayest court in all Italy— the cleanest air, the most laughing women, the— pest! It is a place of holy days and feasts— all music, loving, and delight! But you will see, my dear; I will see that you see." Olimpia must know more exactly than this, and so she told the Mosca. He could deny her nothing; so as they rode between the grey swamps of the lagoon, he poured out his understanding in his own fashion. His oaths made her gasp, but the facts atoned for that. By the bones of God, but he served a great lord of that city— Guarino Guarini by name, whose blade was the longest, the oftenest out, and the cleanest cutter, as himself was the lightest heart, and most trenchant carver of men in Borso's fief. The good captain carried his loyalty to the edge of his simplicity, and left it there for Olimpia to handle. "By the cheeks of the Virgin, my dear, I know what I know. My young master has an eye which, whether it say 'Come' or 'Go,' needs not say it twice. He is as fine and limber as a leopard on the King of England's shield, of a nature so frank and loving that I suppose there is hardly a lady in Ferrara could not testify to it— unless she were bound to the service of his Magnificence the Duke. Why! Yourself might make a shift to be my little friend, and never repent it, mind you— no, no, I may be battered, my dear, but I am seasoned; I have great experience: you would not repent, and shall not, by the Face on the Handkerchief! But happen you see my master, happen he wear his brocade of white and gold— it is all peacocks' eyes, my seraphic heart, in gold and blue upon snowy white— happen again he look, 'Come' at you— why, off you trot as a hound to the platter, and I speed you thither with open heart. Thus walks his world, Guarino Guarini, my noble master."

Olimpia had a colour, and flew it now most becomingly in her cheeks. It was a wholesome, healthy, happy colour, born of her growing excitement; the Captain highly approved of it. She thus earned more information. Guarino Guarini, it appeared, though not of the reigning family, was very near the throne. He had married one of the d'Este ladies, Madama Lionella, legitimised daughter of Duke Borso, and was now ignoring the fact to his own and her entire satisfaction. Upon the Countess's score, Captain Mosca had not very much to say. "A greathearted lady, amorous, generous, a great lover," he allowed; "a pretty taste for music and singing she has, is a friend of poets and such like. The antechamber is full of them; and there they are— on promotion, you understand. But though she has a wonderful free spirit, she is no beauty, you must know. Her mouth is too big, and her eyes are too small. It is a kissing mouth, as we say, my dear, and a speaking eye— and there you have Madama Lionella, who loves minstrels."

"Tell me," said Olimpia here, "who is that pretty gentleman with my friend? Is he not a minstrel?"

The Captain turned in his saddle and, when he had observed, snorted his disdain.

"That sprout, my deary?" said he. "Some such dapper little chamber-fellow, I'll warrant you. A lap-dog, a lady's toy, with a piping voice and an eye for mischief. Yes, he'll be for climbing by Madama Lionella's back-stair. He has the make of it— just the doll she loves to dandle." Which was all the Captain had to say for Angioletto.

Little as it was, it was more than Angioletto had to say for Mosca. He was, indeed, serenely indifferent to the lean brown man. From the moment of their setting out, he and Bellaroba had wagged tongues in concert, and before they had made a dozen miles each knew the other's story to the roots. Angioletto's was no great matter. The Capuchins at Borgo had taught him his rudiments, his voice had taken him into the choir, his manners into the sacristy. He had been Boy-Bishop twice, had become a favourite of the Warden's, learnt Latin, smelt at Greek, scribbled verses. Then, one Corpus Christi, he got his chance. There was to be a Pageant— "Triumph," he called it— a Triumph of Love and a Triumph of Chastity, wherein by the good offices of his friend the Warden he was chosen for the part of Love. It was to be assumed that he pleased, for Chastity (who was a great lady of the place) took him into her service; and there he stayed until, as he explained, she married again. She had been a widow, it seems, when she took part in the Triumphs.

Bellaroba was much interested.

"Was the lady kind to you, Angioletto?"

"Oh, very kind."

"But you had to go, you say?"

"Yes. It was judged better."

"But I don't quite see. If she was kind I wonder why you judged it better to go, or why she did."

"It did not rest wholly with us," said Angioletto.

Bellaroba did not pursue the subject. But after a short pause—

"And are you now from her house?" she asked.

Angioletto shook his head. "That was a very long time ago," said he; "two years at least. I am eighteen, you must know. When I left the Marchioness she gave me a handsome present. It sufficed to take me to Perugia— to the University there; it afforded me two years' study in the liberal arts, and my outfit for this present venture into the bargain."

"And do you know what you will do at Ferrara, Angioletto?"

"Yes, quite well."

"What will you do?"

"I will marry you, Bellaroba," the boy replied, as he turned suddenly, put his arms about her and took a long kiss.

Bellaroba, in a bath of love, made him free of her lips. For a while the mule had to do his pacing alone.

"Oh, Angioletto, Angioletto," whispered the girl, with a hidden face, "I have never been happy like this before."

"You will never be unhappy again, dearest, for I shall be with you."

For the time there was no more talk, since the broken murmurs of their joy and wonder cannot be so described. The billing of two doves on an elm was not more artless than their converse on the mule's back.

The girl brought prose in again, as became a daughter of Venice. What had led Angioletto to Ferrara?

"The Blessed Virgin," he promptly replied, and she sighed a happy acquiescence in so pious a retort.

"But what else?"

For answer Angioletto drew a silk-bound letter from his breast. "This epistle," he said, "promises me employment and fame almost as certainly as you promise me bliss. It is from a Cardinal of my acquaintance to a noble lady of Ferrara, by name Lionella, daughter of Duke Borso himself, and wife to one Messer Guarino Guarini, a very great lord. The lady is patroness of all poets and minstrels. Consider our fortunes made, my joy."

"They must be made since you believe it, Angioletto," said Bellaroba with faith. "I have never seen any one like you, so beautiful and so wise at once."

The compliment provoked kisses. Angioletto embraced her again; again conversation became ejaculatory, and again the mule tripped over the reins. He learned before the day was out to allow for this new hindrance to his way; he tripped no more. The lovers continued their rapt intercourse all that May-day journey through the rice-fields, until at Rovigo (half hidden in a mist of green) they halted for the night.

II

ARMS AND THE MANNIKIN

The hubbub of the inn-yard, where shouting merchants wrestled for porters, and donkeys brayed them down, the narrowed eyes of Olimpia, the sardonic grin of the gaunt Mosca, brought our lovers back into the real world. They faced their foes together with insensible meeting and holding of young hands. Angioletto did his best not to feel a detected schoolboy, and did succeed in meeting the Captain's terrific looks. Bellaroba made no attempt at heroism. Her blush was a thing to be seen.

"Bellaroba, come with me, my child," said Olimpia severely; but Angioletto kept her hand.

Captain Mosca fiddled at his sword-hilt.

"Would you like spitted lark for supper, Madonna?" he asked with meaning.

Olimpia burst into a shrill laugh, and Angioletto, who had the pluck of a little gamecock, turned to his partner in guilt.

"And you, Madonnetta," he said sweetly, "what do you say to *boars head* larded?"

Bellaroba giggled in spite of herself— for she was terribly frightened— but again Olimpia, the grand indifferent, pealed her delight. The Captain glared round about him over a tossing sea of bales and asses' ears; getting small joy of that, he scowled portentously at the little minstrel and took a stride forward.

"Look you, sprigling," said he, "you have to do with a man of deeds; a man, by Saint Hercules, of steel."

Angioletto was fired, cheek and eye. He never faltered.

"I wish I had to do with a man of sense," he said.

"If you do not drop that lady's hand, my lad— " growled the Mosca.

"What then, sir?"

"Then," the Captain roared, "by the ante-chambers of Paradise; she shall cling to carrion!"

Bellaroba with a little cry fell to her knees; Olimpia bit her finger; Angioletto shrugged.

"You have better lungs than manners, Captain," he said quietly. "These ladies of ours are fatigued with travel and tired of fasting. Moreover, I apprehend a bale of carpets on my back at every moment. We will, so please you, sup. If you and the lady whom you escort will do me the honour of sharing my table we can arrange other matters at our leisure. I have always understood that encounters before ladies are make-believe; but your experience should inform you how far that is true. By leave, Signor Capitano."

Whereupon he lifts up the praying Bellaroba, kisses her forehead, and hands her into the inn as bold as a Viscount. One or two tongues were in one or two cheeks; one hand at least clapped him on the shoulder for a "little assassin"— a compliment: the honours were his to that present. Olimpia followed after him, very much impressed with the thought that the sooner she could exchange Mosca for Mosca's master the better for her. In the rear of the procession stalked that gaping hero swearing rapidly under his breath to keep himself in some sort of countenance.

Angioletto's assurance, and with it his luck, held out the evening. Not otherwise could he have cleared himself of the mess. He fairly froze Mosca by the coolness of his assumptions.

"I will fight you as soon as you choose, and with your own weapons, after supper," said he, "but it is only fair to warn you that you will be killed."

"How so, by the King of Glory!" cried the Captain.

"The wagging finger of Fate, sir," replied Angioletto readily, "and the conjunctions of the stars. My horoscope was taken at Foligno with the utmost exactitude. Mars himself, for reasons of his own, seems to have presided over my begetting. More than that, though I have not the least desire to take your life— should not, indeed, know what to do with it— it will be impossible for me to avoid it. I am really very sorry. Your case is just on a parallel with that of the younger Altopasso who, on this very day a year ago, insisted upon fighting with me. It is true that I do not pretend to love or even to approve of you, Captain; I consider that your legs have outgrown your brains. But for all that, I should be sorry to think that for want of a little ordinary politeness, or for shanks out of due measure, an honest man had lost his life. However, I fear the affair has gone too far."

The Captain grew purple and green by turns. The room of full tables was all agog. He let out an oath which I omit.

"The affair has not gone so far as this blade shall go, turkey-poult," he thundered.

"Make yourself quite easy on that point, my good sir," said Angioletto, cracking a walnut; "your sword shall fly the length of the room. I have a pass that is irresistible. You cannot fight planets, Captain."

"I have never tried yet, by our Lord," the Captain admitted, "but no one has dared to doubt my valour, and, planet or no planet, I'll run you through."

Angioletto smiled at another walnut. "I find the conceit admirable," said he, "yet you will perish so sure as this city is Rovigo and a titular fief of my mistress's master."

"A straw for your mistress, little egg," cried the suffocating Captain.

"I will give it to Countess Lionella as your dying gift, Signor Capitano."

The name smacked him in the face; he shook his head like a worried bull, or as a dog shakes water from his pelt. Olimpia, too, was interested, and for the first time. With face fixed between her hands, she leaned both elbows on the table, watching.

"Is the Countess Lionella your mistress?" she asked. Angioletto made her a bow; the company applauded a popular name. Olimpia turned a glance upon her Captain, which said as plainly as she could have spoken, "Finish him for your master's sake." But it had no meaning for the champion, who possibly knew more about his master than he had been minded to declare.

Angioletto tapped the ground with his toe. "Come, Master Captain," he said, "before your blood cools."

"Have no fear, bantam," said a jolly Dominican in his ear, "that toad's blood was never hot." It certainly looked like it. The Captain scratched his head.

"Look ye now, youngster," he said at last, "I serve his worship Count Guarino Guarini, who is the husband of Madama Lionella; and lucky for you that service is. Otherwise, by the truly splintered Cross, it had gone hard with you this night."

"Oh, brava, brava!" cheered the dining-room, and then hooted the Captain to his bench.

Angioletto put up his little hanger with a curt nod in his enemy's direction. "For the Countess's sake I spare you to the Count, Captain Mosca; though what precisely your value may be to his Excellency I do not at present understand."

Thereupon he turned to his poor Bellaroba, took her in his arms before them all, kissed her eyes dry of tears, and ended by drawing a rueful smile from her lips. The dining-room found him admirable throughout; but Olimpia got up, yawning.

"Come, child, it is time for bed," she declared, "I suppose even this entertainment must have a term." There was no gainsaying it. The lovers were torn apart by the moral force of Olimpia's attendance; but not until it was demonstrated that, though good-night is a word of two syllables, it needs four lips, and is therefore capable of infinite extension.

"Well, my child, I hope you are satisfied with this little day's work," said Olimpia, half undressed.

For answer, Bellaroba, upon her friend's neck, dissolved in a flood of happy tears.

III

HOW THEY CAME TO FERRARA

That was a fair sight which greeted the travellers at the close of the next day— the towers of Ferrara rising stately out of a green thicket. The lovers trilled their happiness to each other: surely nothing but pleasure and a smooth life could come out of so treeful a place!

"In our Venice, you must know," said Bellaroba, "we set great store by green boughs, having so few of them. We think that harshness and clamour may hunt the canals, but that birds can sing in gardens of a world really joyful. What a cloud of green trees— look, look how near the sky comes to them! Oh, my Angioletto, we are going to be so happy!" And the young girl laid her hot cheek on her lover's shoulder.

He, though her premises were undeniable, had his doubts. Her words set him wondering what was to be the end of this light-hearted adventure.

"My dear," said he, "if trees get in a man's way of villainy or incommode his pleasures he will cut them down, depend upon it."

"Well, silly boy," she cried, and gave him a peck of a kiss, "and does not that prove what I say, that there are no villainies in Ferrara? For, see, the trees are as thick as a forest." She made him laugh again before many paces. His ringing tones caught the ears of Captain Mosca, and set that great man scowling.

"If I don't get a crumb down that yapping gullet, call me not Mosca," he grumbled.

"Speak a little louder, Signor Capitano," said his pillion.

"Your pardon, Madonna Olimpia," he answered, "but I believe I was breathing a prayer on account of the little love-boy yonder."

Olimpia laughed. "I love him as much as you do, I dare swear," said she; "but he may be very useful. Remember that I am but a poor gentlewoman with my fortune to make."

"Give me the making of it, my angel," cried the Captain, crushing his heart with his fist. "You shall have the most crowded *cortile* in Ferrara. May I give you a humble bit of advice?"

"Certainly you may."

"It will be this, then, that you hold off from Monna Nanna and keep yourself very much to yourself. Between us we can arrange a pretty future. I know Monna Nanna better than becomes me. Believe me, the acquaintance would become you still less. But with such talents as I have— and they are all yours— I can arrange for you a most proper dwelling-place which shall cost little and bring much in."

"But we cannot live there alone, Captain."

"Hey! I am beforehand. I parry with the head, my duchess," cried the delighted Mosca. "I have thought of all that. There is an old lady of my friendship in the city, by name Donna Matura. She is something decayed in estate o' these days, has fewer crusts than teeth, poor soul, but has mingled with the highest. She will be all that you could wish, and you more than she could hope for. Think of it, lady, think of it."

"I will," said Olimpia, who had already done so. There is no doubt that she and the Mosca understood each other.

They were now riding up the long lime-tree avenue which leads to the Sea-Gate of Ferrara; soon they entered Ferrara itself, that city of warm red brick, of broad eaves, of laughter, and, as it were, a fairy-tale, bowered in rustling green. The streets ran wide between garden walls and the massy fronts of great square houses; they were full of a traffic which seemed that of a prosperous people bent upon pleasure. Happy ladies rode by with hawks or leashed dogs, or crowns of flowers. Cavaliers, in white and yellow, ribboned, slashed, curled, and feathered, went in and out of the throng to keep an assignation, or to break one. The priests joked with the women, the very urchins coaxed for kisses. Every street corner had its lovers' tryst, never a garden walk without its loitering pair, never a lady came out of a church door but there stood a devout adorer to beg a touch of holy water from her finger-tip.

"How happy this people is," cried Bellaroba, flushed and sparkling, to her little lord. "Everybody loves everybody else."

"My dear, we have nothing to do with their loves; we are going to be married," replied Angioletto, looking straight before him.

"Yes, Angioletto," said she, as meek as a mouse.

Olimpia, who was not thinking of marriage, was highly entertained. There was a press of grooms and led horses, richly caparisoned, outside the open doors of a new and very spacious palace. Round about them crowded people of a meaner sort, and beggars not a few; but a lane was kept to the gateway by soldiers in red and yellow, who bore upon their breasts a quartered coat of eagles and lilies.

"Hist!" said Mosca, pulling up his horse. "This is the fine new palace of the Duke, which he calls his Schifanoia. He is evidently expected in from his hawking. The greatest falconer you ever knew, my life! I do assure you."

"That may very well be," said Olimpia, "for I have never known one at all."

"You shall know this one before I die, and another who is my most noble master," cried Mosca, "or I am your kennel-dog for nothing."

"Let us wait a little and see this hawking Duke of yours," Olimpia said, with a gentle pressure of her arms about the Captain's middle.

"Blood of blood," sighed the Mosca, "I am as wax in the candle of you, my soul."

Olimpia pulled down her hood. Her patience was rewarded in no long time by the sound of an approaching cavalcade; presently she saw the nodding plumes of riders and their beasts at the end of the street. Knights, squires, and ladies rode with their reigning prince: he himself with two young men, magnificently dressed, came in advance of the troop, and at a great pace.

Olimpia judged her time well. At the moment Duke Borso drew rein to turn into his gates she threw back her hood and looked him full in the face, as if to dower him with all the splendour of her beauty. The sly, humorous face of the old fox twitched as his eyes caught the girl's. He looked a prude with a touch of freakishness in him; his pursed mouth seemed always to be strangling a smile, the issue of the strife always in doubt. Now, for instance, though Olimpia said to herself that she was satisfied, she could never have denied that he disapproved of her, while nobody could have maintained it. Borso had shot upon her a piercing glance the minute in which he had turned his horse; Mosca had had the benefit of another; then he had acknowledged in military fashion the waving caps and kerchiefs at the gates and had passed into the courtyard.

"Oh, you may be satisfied, my soul," said the Mosca. "Borso will never forget us now: it is not his way. But look, look!" Another pair of eyes was at work, belonging to a very handsome, ruddy youth who had been at the Duke's left hand. Olimpia needed no nudge from the Captain to tell her who this noble rider might be. Guarino Guarini for a florin! And so it was.

"Yes," said Mosca, "that is my most intrepid master. The flaxen lad in silver brocade, who was on the other side, is Teofilo Calcagnini, of whom I know little more than that he is Duke Borso's shadow. You shall hardly see them apart. The other, my charmer, the other is our man. Leave me to deal with him. Come now to the inn. To-morrow you shall have your hired house, and the next day company for it more to your taste than lean old Mosca."

"I shall never forget you, my Captain," said the really grateful Olimpia; and said truer than she knew. "Come," she added, "we should seek out Bellaroba and her little sweetheart. There must be an end of that pretty gentleman, my friend."

"By the majesty of King Solomon, there shall be an end," Mosca swore, and pricked his horse.

Angioletto and his lady-love had been better exercised than to think of dukes. They had thought of religion.

They passed by the Schifanoia at a sober walk, regardless of the crowd.

"My heart," Angioletto said, "there is here what I suppose to be the most famous shrine in Romagna. I mean that of the Madonna degli Greci, a pompous image from Byzantium, which proceeded undoubtedly from the *bottega* of Saint Luke. If that Signore had been as indifferent a painter as he was great Saint (which is surely impossible), we should do well to visit his Madonna. Her holiness is past dispute; there are very few miracles which she could not perform if she chose. As well as burning a candle apiece before her face, we could lay our prayers and new love at her feet. Beyond question she will hear and bring us good luck. What do you think?"

"I think as you think, Angioletto," said Bellaroba, and held him closer.

"Let us go then. I know the way very well."

So they went to the tune which the young lad sang under his breath, and before long came to a piazza, not very broad, but flagged all over and set about with stately brick buildings, having on the left the stone front of a great church, tier upon tier of arches interlaced. The door of it was guarded by two stone lions, and above the porch was the figure of a buxom lady with a smile half saucy, half benevolent, to whom Angioletto doffed his cap.

"They call her Donna Ferrara," he explained. "This is the Duomo. Let us go in."

They dismounted; a lame boy held the mule; they entered the church.

It was very large, very dark, and nearly empty. Angioletto put his arm round Bellaroba's waist, and they began to pace the aisle in confidential talk.

"Where are you going to live in this place, Bellaroba?" he asked her.

"I don't know. Olimpia knows. There was a Monna Nanna we were to live with, I think. But Olimpia will decide. I must do as she wishes."

"But why?"

"She is older than I am— two years. Besides I always have. And my mother commanded it."

"Your last appears to me the only reason worth a thought. Do you not want to know what I think of it, Bellaroba?" He bent his head towards her. Her answer, the flutter of a quick little kiss, pleased him. "Well, I will tell you," said he. "I think we should be married at once— this very minute. I do indeed."

"Oh!" said Bellaroba, blushing beautifully.

"I can see that you are pleased at this, my dear," Angioletto said, looking at her. They were head for head level, these children. "But what would Olimpia say?"

Bellaroba paused for strength to tell the painful truth.

"She would say 'Fiddlesticks,' Angioletto."

Angioletto frowned. "Ah! what is to be done?" he asked.

Bellaroba looked down, plucked at her skirt, saw Angioletto's hand peeping round her waist. It seemed difficult to say, and yet what she did say was very simple: "We have not asked Olimpia, you know."

"No," Angioletto answered; "we have had no time yet. But we will, of course."

"Oh, of course," said she, who kept her eyes hidden, and spoke very low. "Oh, of course. But— "

"Well, dearest?"

"Could we not— would it not be wiser— of course you know best, Angioletto!— might we not ask her— afterwards?"

Angioletto kissed her.

"You are as wise as you are lovely, my little wife. Come, let us find the Madonna degli Greci." And he led her away by the hand.

They found her in the north transept, in a little fenced chapel all starry with tapers and gleaming gold and silver hearts. As it was the eve of Pentecost she was uncovered; they could see her dark outline with its wrought metal ring about the head. Half-way down was another metal ring; Bambino's head should be in there.

Both the hand-fasted pilgrims fell to their knees: Bellaroba crossed herself, and then hid her face with her left hand, Angioletto with his right. After a silence, about the space of two Hail Mary's, the youth looked resolutely up at Madonna, and began to speak to her.

"Holy and most glorious Virgin, Mother of God," said he, "we, thy children, have sought thee first in this famous city of Ferrara, because we are sure that thou wilt love us even more than we love each other, and wilt be glad to share our secret. We are going to marry each other at this moment, Madonna, and thou shalt be the priest. There can be none better, since thou hadst in thy womb for many months the great Priest of all Christians, our sublime Redeemer. Now, behold, Madonna, how I wed this my wife, Bellaroba. With this ring, which was given me by a very great lady," and he took a ring from his breast, "I wed my wife, placing it upon her finger in the name of the Father, and of the Son, and of the Holy Ghost. I do not endow her with my worldly goods, for thou knowest I have none. I do not worship her with my body at this moment, but in the meantime I worship her unfeignedly with my mind, just as I worship thee with my soul. It appears, therefore, that I have wedded her enough. It is useless, most sacred Lady, to ask her whether she will honour and obey me, because of course she will, seeing that she loves me with all her good heart. Such as we are— very young, quite poor, but much thy servants— thou knowest whether thou canst be happy in this mating. I believe that thou canst. Now, therefore, since she is mine, she shall say with me three *Aves* and a *Paternoster*, likewise the *Credo*, or so much of it as she can remember. And, O Madonna, trust me to cherish her, and do thou intercede for us. *Per Christum Dominum nostrum—* AMEN."

"Bellaroba, my wife, look at me," he said, and the girl looked up wondering. He took her happy face between his hands, and kissed her two eyes, her forehead, and her mouth. Then they said the appointed prayers, and rose to their feet to return; nor did they forget the candles, but purchased them at the door of an old lady, who had a basketful to sell.

Coming out of the church into the sun again, they encountered the scrutiny of Olimpia. Captain Mosca, slapping his booted leg, was holding the horse.

"Where have you two children been?" said Olimpia. "Mischief in a corner, eh? You have missed the sight of Duke Borso and a gilded company."

"We have been saying our prayers to Madonna of the Greeks," said Bellaroba meekly.

"There are red flames in your cheeks, child, and a ring on your finger. Did you find those in the church?"

"Madonna gave them to me, Olimpia."

"So, so, so! Do you begin by robbing a shrine, pray?"

"Ah, Madama Olimpia," said Angioletto, "we have only taken from the shrine what is our due."

Not the least of the minstrel's parts was that of speaking as though he had something weighty in reserve. Olimpia, though by nature dull, was also sly. She had a suspicion about Angioletto now; but a quick-shifting glance from one to the other of the pair before her revealed nothing but serenity in the boy, and little but soft happiness in the girl.

She opened her lips to speak, snapped them to again, and turned to the Captain and affairs more urgent than the love-making of babies. It was the hour of supper; the question was of a lodging. Captain Mosca knew an inn— the "Golden Sword"— where decent entertainment could be had for the night. As no one could deny what nobody knew anything about, it was decided. They sought and found the "Golden Sword," and put up with it, and in it. The supper party was, at least, merry, for Angioletto led it. He sang, he joked, made love, spent money, was wise, unwise, heedless, heedful. He charmed a grin at last into the very Captain's long face. That warrior, indeed, went so far as to drink his health in wine of Verona. He and his Olimpia— unhesitatingly his in the gaiety of the moment— drank it out of the same glass. "Love and Ferrara!" cried Captain Mosca, with a foot on the table. "Love in Ferrara," said Angioletto, and stroked Bellaroba's hair. So everything was very friendly and full of hope. At a late hour, and for excellent reasons, Olimpia kissed Bellaroba good-night, was herself kissed by Angioletto, and withdrew. Captain Mosca prayed vehemently for further and better acquaintance with his friend "the divine poet," and his pretty mistress. So went Bellaroba's marriage supper.

IV

"WHY COME YE NAT TO COURTE?"

"Le donne e i cavalier, gli affanni e gli agi,
Che ne invogliava araore e cortesia."

The little house— discreet affair of eaves modest as drooped eyelids, of latticed windows, of wistaria before and a bower of willows behind— was found and furnished out of the girls' store and the Captain's credit. Donna Matura, a brown old woman, hideous, toothless, and inclined to swooning, was installed as duenna. She was, indeed, owner of the house and furniture, for which Olimpia paid and the Captain promised to pay; but that did not appear until much later. There was a great charm, not without a certain deal of luxury, in the place. Of course there was a garden— a bright green nest of flowering trees and shrubs; in the middle was a grass-plat; in that, again, a bronze fountain, which had the form of three naked boys back to back, and an inscription to the effect that it had been set up by a certain Galeotto Moro, in the days of Marquess Lionel, "in honour of Saints Peter and Paul and of the Virgin Deipara," upon some special occasion of family thanksgiving. The weeping willows— themselves fountains of green— sprayed over a stone seat. The place bore signs of an honourable past; it was falling now gently to a comely decay; but it answered every purpose. All promised well. So much Captain Mosca was given to understand; yet it was hinted that his promises were not complete. "My life and soul," cried he on his knees in the garden, "the little affair is a matter of three minutes." It proved to be a matter of more than three months and was then accomplished in another way and with other results than had been looked for. Thus it was.

When Angioletto had been assured of the nesting of his mate, he dressed himself point-device and went to Court to deliver his credentials. He found the lady upon whom so much depended, at the Schifanoia. Madama Lionella d'Este, wife of the Count Guarino Guarini, was a fresh-coloured, lusty young woman of three and twenty, not at all in love with her husband, but very much in love with love. The Captain of Lances had said truly when he shrugged her off as no beauty. Large-limbed she was, the shape of a boy, with a long mouth and small eyes, full-lipped, big in foot and hand. Yet she was a very merry soul, frank if not free in her speech and gesture, and though liable to bursts of angry temper, for the most part as innocent of malice as a tiger cub.

If you remember her an Este, you will forgive her much, excuse her everything, and rather like her.

Angioletto, who found her sitting on the grass among her ladies, advanced with great ceremony and many bows. Madama did not get up; no one did; so Angioletto had to step gingerly into a ring of roguish women to deliver his letter. Lionella scampered through it, reddening with pleasure; she beckoned him with smiles to sit beside her.

"We are making rose-garlands to adorn our pretty heads," she said, laughing. "Come and sit by me, Angioletto, and sing to us. Who knows but what, if you are good, we shall not crown you with one of them?"

It was a great merit of Angioletto's that he always took things and men (especially women) as he found them. Such as they were he could be for the time. He was by no means waxen; elastic rather. Down he plumped, accordingly, cross-legged by his new mistress, and warbled a canzone to the viola which enchanted the lady.

"More, more, more!" she cried, clapping her hands. "Oh, boy, I could have you a prince for less than that! What a throstle-pipe you have!"

It was, as he afterwards found out, of her habit to be for ever at extremes; but just now, not knowing how to take her, he sang on all the better for her praise; and he had her next wriggling in an ecstasy over a trifle he made up on the spur of the moment— a snatch wherein roses and a girl's face (Bellaroba's, be sure) took turns to be dominant. At the end of this pretty piece the Countess Lionella fairly took his own face between her hands, crumpled his lips into a bud and kissed them full. Angioletto coloured, though no one else did. It was evidently quite harmless, and afterwards he was ashamed of his shame.

As it was, a diversion of a different order broke in upon the next song which, so soon as he had picked up his nerve, he adventured. One of the Maids of Honour looked quickly over her shoulder, and "Hist, Madama! The Duke!" she said, with wide eyes and a blush.

The song ceased, the whole company, Lionella included, scrambled to their feet. Duke Borso, his portly body swaying like a carriage on springs, his hands behind him, and attended by a tall young man, very splendid and very blonde, came across the grass towards them. Angioletto could not decide whether to think him rogue or prude. His puckered face twitched, his eyes twitched, his pursed-up lips worked together; it was again as if he were struggling with a laugh. He wore his tall square cap well off his forehead, and looked what he really was— a strong man tired, but not yet tired out, of kindness. The benevolence seemed inborn, seemed fighting through every seam of the pompous face. "Madonna! his generous motions work him into creases, as if he were volcanic soil," thought Angioletto. Watching him narrowly as he came, he decided that this was a master to be loved if not admired, respected but not feared. "I should get the worst of a bout with him," thought he; "but I had rather it were with him than with Apollo." That title was just, as the reflection shrewd. Teofilo Calcagnini would have made a terrible tutor to Master Phaëton.

Duke Borso bowed shortly to the standing maids, and favoured Angioletto with a keen eye before he set a hand on his daughter's shoulder. She looked a pleased welcome as he began to stroke her hair. "Ah, they love the man," thought Angioletto; "good!"

"Why, chick," said Duke Borso, "you are like a cage of singing-birds scared by the cat."

"Your Grace shall judge whether we are too scared to sing," replied his laughing daughter. "Come," she added, turning to Angioletto, "tune your viol and pipe to it again, my little poet."

The Duke made a wry mouth. "Hey, I have no ear for music, my dear," said he.

Angioletto was ready for him. "If your Magnificence will permit," he said, "I will take care not to offend his honourable ear. I will say my piece, with no more music than will serve to tie word to word. May it be so, Magnificence? Have I liberty, Madam?" He bowed, smiling, from one to the other of the great people.

He was a very courtly and charming little person, this Tuscan youth. Above all he had a ready address. So bright and strong, and yet so deferential did he look, pleading his cause among them, Lionella could have kissed him again for nothing more than his dexterity.

"Ah, you shall do whatever you like, Angioletto!" she cried.

Borso's eyes twinkled, and he primmed his lips. "I do not go so far as Madama, Master Angioletto, but I shall be pleased to hear what you are pleased to give me." He fell into an attitude of profound attention.

Angioletto, having bowed once more, began.

It so happened that Lorenzo de' Medici, that monster of genius, had not long printed his *Caccia col falcone*. Angioletto had it by heart against his need; using it now he could never have made a better choice— as, indeed, he guessed. It was as good as a play to watch Borso's wary eyes at the commencement of this piece, and to see them drop their fence as the declamation went on. Lorenzo begins with a pretty description of the dawn on Tuscan hilltops—

>"Era già rosso tutto l'oriente,
>E le cime de' monti parien d'oro," etc.

Borso, neither approving nor disapproving, kept his head disposed for more. At

> "Quando fui desto da certi rumori
> Di buon sonagli ed allettar di cani"

he began to blink; with the quick direction to the huntsman—

> "Deh, vanne innanzi, presto Capellaio,"

he stifled a smile. But the calling of the hounds by their names broke down his guard. Angioletto shrilled them out in a high, boyish voice—

> "Chiama Tamburo, Pezuolo e Martello,
> La Foglia, la Castagna e la Guerrina,
> Fagiano, Fagianin, Rocca e Capello,
> E Friza, e Biondo, Bamboccio e Rossina,
> Ghiotto, la Torta, Viola e Pestello,
> E Serchio e Fuse e'l mio Buontempo vecchio,
> Zambraco, Buratel, Scaccio e Pennecchio...."

Every muscle of the keen old hunter was now quivering; his eyes were bright, his smile open and that of a child. To the last word of the poem— and it has length— he followed without breath the checks, the false casts, the bickering of the huntsmen, the petty incidents of a breezy morning in the marshes, nodding at every point, missing nothing, cracking his fingers, cheering under his breath, with delight undisguised and interest unalloyed. The moment it was ended he seemed prime for a burst of heedless comment; but he stopped, shut his lips with a snap, and became the inscrutable ruler of a fief of the Empire once more. But Angioletto knew that he had pleased him, for all that he walked off as he had come, without word or sign.

He had pleased every one. Homing to his nest in the Borgo, he caught his little Bellaroba in his arms with a rapture none the less because it had been earned at a stretch. It was long before he could find time and breath to lead her into the garden and have the story out. Olimpia, coming down to look for them in the dusk, found that a seat for two would easily hold one more. It should be added of Angioletto that he suppressed the incident of the Countess Lionella's salute.

At supper there were evidences that, whatever had been Angioletto's fate, all had not gone so well with the Captain of Lances. Not that appetite failed him; indeed, he ate the more for his taciturnity. Yet not repletion made him sigh, for he sighed consumedly before he began and rather less when he had finished, as though the kindlier juices of our nature had got to work to disperse the melancholic. Angioletto rallied him upon his gloom, but to no purpose. The meal was a silent one;

almost the only conversation was that of the minstrel's foot with Bellaroba's under the table.

The truth was, that of conversation the Captain had had enough before supper— a very short colloquy with his Olimpia. In it he was brought to confess that he had seen his patron that morning. "Well?" had been Olimpia's commentary— a shot which raked the Captain fore and aft. Well, he desperately admitted, there was nothing actually arranged: *patienza*! His most noble master had been greatly harassed with affairs— the Duke's approaching visit to Rome, the precise forms which must be observed, the punctilios, the hundred niceties of etiquette; "Ah, *patienza*!" urged the sweating Mosca.

Patience, she saw, was the only wear; but, per Bacco, he should learn it too! She was in a high rage. The Captain was given to know that Ferrara was a great city, with more houses in it than one; in fine, he was shown the door. Supper first was an extreme and contemptuous condescension of Olimpia's, urged by the thought that a fed Mosca might be a more desperate Mosca, while a lean one would be desperate only for a meal.

A true relation of what passed in the Palazzo Guarini may serve to show how just she had been. The Count had received news of his henchman's attendance with a nod, had kept him waiting two hours in the *cortile*, then remembered him and bid him upstairs.

"Well, dog," said the young lord, from his dressing-table, "and why the devil are you so late to report yourself?"

"Ah, Excellence, believe me— " began to stutter the Captain.

"That is exactly what I will not do, my man. Who was that wench at your back yesterday?"

The Captain rubbed his hands. "Excellence, a wench indeed! A golden Venetian— glorious! Dove-eyed, honey-tongued, and very much your lordship's servant, I do assure you."

"You are so completely and at such length a fool, Mosca," said Count Guarini, with a yawn, "and strive so desperately to be rascal in spite of it, that I am almost sorry for you. Tie me these points, my good fellow, get me my sword, and go to the devil with your golden Venetian."

That, believe me, had been all. Therefore Captain Mosca, as he slunk out into the dark after supper in obedience to his inexorable Olimpia, felt that he must be more ingenious than he had supposed. At the same time it is only fair to say that when he had spoken so hopefully of his affair to the lady on the pillion he had believed every word of his own story. A man puts on spectacles to suit his complexion: the Captain's was sanguine.

V

FORTUNE WITH THE DOUBLE BLADE

"Similemente agli splendor mondani
Ordinò general ministra e duca,
Che permutasse a tempo li ben vani,
Di gente in gente, e d'uno in altro sangue."— *Inf.* vii. 77.

Angioletto had cause to believe in that star of his, for it never wavered in the course it held. Borso's court found him much to its taste. The men, however tall, of looks however terrible, bent their height and unbent their scowls to him; he was the pet of all the women; the very Fool, saturnine as he was (with a bite in every jest), had no gibe to put him to the blush withal. He made money, or money's worth, as fast as friends. A gold chain with a peregrine in enamel and jewels came to him by the hands of the Chamberlain; nothing was said, but he knew it was from the Duke. Countess Lionella could not reward him enough— now a jewel, now a gold cup, at one time a purse, at another a crystal phial filled with Jordan water. And so it went, the star waxing ever. He could have maintained the discreet house by Porta Angeli out of his earnings, and he did; but you have to pay for your luck somehow, and it very soon happened that he could not maintain himself in it. He was only too popular. The Count Guarino wanted him at the Palazzo Guarini; the Countess insisted that he should remain in bond at the Schifanoia; the august couple wrangled publicly over his little body.

"What, Madam," cried the Count, "is it not enough that you absent yourself from my house? Must you keep my friends out of it also?"

"He was accredited to me, my lord," said the lady, "to me, therefore, he shall come."

"Good madam," returned Guarini, "I admire your taste as a man, but deplore it as a husband. I think the little poet will do better with me."

"Stuff!" cried the Countess, "I might be his mother."

Said the Count: "Madam, I need not deny it; yet it is very evident that you are not his mother." He spoke with some heat.

Lionella was mightily amused. "Jealousy, my lord?" She arched her fine brows.

"I don't know the word, Madam," he answered her, touched on a raw. Jealousy appeared to him as the most vulgar of the vices.

"Prove that to me!" the Countess pursued him. Guarini made her a bow.

"Perfectly, Contessa," said he. "You shall have your poet, and he shall be my friend." Wherein the Count showed that to be a gentleman it may sometimes be necessary to appear a fool.

The matter was thus settled, and Angioletto ravished from his nest.

His last night at home— *a casa*, as he loved to call it— need not be dwelt upon. Bitter-sweet it was, yet his courage made it more sweet than bitter. Bellaroba was tearful, clung to him, kissed and murmured incoherently because of sobbing. He loved her more than ever for that, but as became a prudent husband, thought to say a word in season.

"My dear," he said in her ear, as he held her close, "you are very young to be a wife, and too young to be properly left alone with such companions as your Olimpia, whom I distrust, and Monna Matura, whom I abhor. But what can I do? I must make our fortunes, and pray to God that your beauty do not mar them. Follow my advice, my injunctions even, and it will not. Keep much at home, go not abroad unattended or uncovered. Your hooded head makes you surpassingly beautiful; you need not fear to be a figure of fun. At the same time it shields most of your sacred person from profane eyes. The great shield of all, however, is to have business before you when you are from house. Go briskly about this— whether it be market, mass, or mischief— and no one will look at you twice. At home it should be the same. There may be visitors; if Monna Olimpia can contrive it, there will be a good many. You may judge of their quality by her anxiety to receive them. Be guarded then, my dear, and go by contraries. They will not find the pattern of the carpet so interesting as you should do. Give them prose for their poetry, vinegar for their sweet wine, bitter herbs when they look to you for cane of sugar. Keep your honeycomb for him who is trying to earn it. Think where I am going, my Bellaroba! To what temptations, blessed Lord! to what askings, to what suggestion of wanton dealing! Remember that in all this I shall have your honour to keep, as you have mine. Say a great many prayers, my little heart, for the welfare of my soul and of yours; lock your door at night; let Monna Matura go with you to mass and confession; and— and— oh! my wife, my little wife, but I love not the leaving of you!" And so these poor children cried on each other's breasts, and so fell to the unspoken tongue of Love's elect. Next morning he went early, leaving her kissed in bed.

He saw her once again, spent a most blissful two hours in her company, before the Countess Lionella took it into her head to shelter from the summer heats in a villa she had above Monselice. Thither Angioletto was forced to go in her train. He found it intolerable, went with a heart of lead; for so cheerful a soul he was what he looked, parched and wan. This lasted a week. Then came a paper, scrawled with brown ink marks, which, after much study, he took to imply—

"MY LOVE ANGILETO, I love you more every day. I cry a good deal for lack of you. I kiss you two hundred times, and will be good and happy,

"Your dutiful BELAROBA."

This revived him amazingly: he went singing about the gardens which hung upon the side of the grey hill, and composed a pastoral comedy to be acted by the Countess's ladies in the Temple grove.

Lionella very openly and without afterthought made love to him. He was a charming little lad, it is true; but quite apart from that, he was the only male creature above servant rank in the household. I describe him so because I cannot bring myself to call him a man; but he was quite man enough for the lady's intent. It is a surprising instance of the tact there was innate in the youth that he checked every undue liberty on the part of his mistress without endangering her self-respect or his own high favour. Perhaps he allowed matters to go a little too far. His were times of artless Art and of franchise— immoral, yet mainly innocent. Children call each other pet names, hold hands, kiss, and no one is hurt. So it was in Ferrara when Borso ruled it. *Præteriere Borsii tempora!* True enough. There were those who saw that tuneful time in the shaping; we, alas! look down on the splintered shards. But we know that if Assyrian balm was ever for the world's chaffer it was in the days of Borso, the good Duke.

Angioletto loved his Bellaroba with all his heart: no debonair Lionella could decoy him to be untrue. But he was debonair himself, of high courage, and mettlesome; and he may have gone a little too far. He was now become her confidant, secretary, bosom friend. Whence came the shock of crisis.

One morning Lionella called for him in a hurry. He found her, an amused frown on her broad brows, pacing the terrace walk, holding an open letter in her hand. The moment he came in sight the Countess ran towards him, drew his arm in hers, and began to speak very fast.

"My dear boy," she said, "I am in a fix. You shall advise me how to act, the more willingly I hope, as you are in a sense the contriver of all the mischief. You know the Count my husband well enough to agree with me that he is a man of gallantry. He has proved it, for it is plain that he would never have left me (to my great content) to go my own gait unless it had been worth his while. I do him perfect justice, I believe. He has never thwarted me, nor frowned, nor raised an eyebrow at an act or motion of mine. Never but once, and that was when I proposed to take you into my service. Don't blush, Angioletto, it is quite true. He then raised, not his eyebrows— at least I think not— but some little objections. I said that I was old enough to be your mother— no, no, that also is true, my dear! He answered, 'No doubt; but it is very evident that you are not his mother.' That again may be true, I suppose? However, the affair ended in great good-humour on both sides, and here you are, as you see! But now the Count sends me this letter, in which he says— let me see— ah! 'Your ladyship will remember my not ungenerous conduct in the matter of the little poet, Angioletto, on whose account you had certain benevolent dispositions to gratify'— neatly turned, is it not? 'I have now to propose to you, turn for turn, a like favour to myself, which is that you shall take into your service a young gentlewoman of Venice, who is but newly come to Ferrara'— What is the matter, Angioletto? You put me out. Where was I? Oh, yes— 'She is respectably bred, very modest, very diligent, very pious, moderately handsome.'— My dear boy, if you want to sit down, by all means say so. We will sit together here.— 'The name she goes by with those who know her is Bellaroba.'— Bellaroba, indeed! Well— 'I am very sure that you will have no reason to regret my excellent choice on your behalf; and it is the more timely because I learn from Fazio that one of your women has fallen sick of the small-pox'— and so on. The Count is occasionally sublime. I like particularly the list of the young lady's qualifications and the reference to his own kindness to myself. Now, what am I to say? I see you are puzzled. Well, I will give you time."

What Angioletto himself was to say is more to the purpose. I think it much to his credit that his first ascertainable emotion after the buffet of assault was one of wildest exultation at the prospect. It shows that he had never for a moment distrusted the meek little partner of his fortunes. Whisps of such doubt did afterwards float across his pretty morning picture, but he put them away at once. Next came worldly wisdom. True Tuscan that he was, his instinct was to decline perilous rapture if waiting might bring it on easy terms. For a long time he weighed instant joy against policy. Finally, as he was more Italian than Tuscan, and more boy than either, he decided to jump the danger. The vision of Bellaroba shy in the rose-garden, of himself crowning her soft hair, bending over her, kissing her upturned face; of the Countess behind one thicket looking for him, and the Count behind another looking for Bellaroba— it was too much to resist!

"Madama," he said, "it is hardly for me to advise in such delicate matters. I should not, by right, dare say what I am about to say upon your invitation. Yet if I were his nobility, Count Guarino Guarini, not the least of my pleasant moments would be that in which I could say, 'I have a noble lady to wife, for she honours me as I have honoured her.'"

That was a very dextrous remark, vastly pleasing to the Countess. She kissed the speaker then and there, wrote her letter hot-head, talked about it all that day, and worked herself into such a fever of curiosity that she cut short her villeggiatura by six weeks, so as the sooner to see the girl who could inspire her with such admirable ideas of her own magnanimity. She even grew quite enthusiastic upon her husband's account, almost sentimental about him. This much the wily Angioletto (who did not study character for nothing) had allowed for in his calculations.

It is by no means certain that the Countess was as wise as her guide. The facts which induced the letter were these. Guarini had chanced upon an early mass at San Cristoforo and Bellaroba kneeling at her prayers. She, all unconscious of any presence but her own and her Saviour's, was looking up to the Mother who had made Him so, dim-eyed, and smiling rather tenderly. Her lips framed petitions for the coming home of Angioletto. She had hooded her head as he commanded, and it became her as he had foreseen. With her added cares of wifely duty this gave a sober look to her untameable childish bloom; she was almost a business-like beauty now. To Guarino the pathetic appealed more nearly; to him she seemed a pretty nun, a wood-bird caged. He never took his eyes off her— she caught him in a soft mood and ravished him. A little saint in bud, he swore; a wholesome, domestic little household goddess, meek and very pure, who would carry home her beauties unaware and oil the tousled heads of half a dozen brothers and sisters. Homeliness is neither Italian word nor virtue; but just as it describes Bellaroba, so an inkling of its charm thrilled the young lord who saw her. Could one cage such a gossamer thing? Fate had done it, why not he? At least he could not lose sight of her. He tracked her to the house under the wall, saw the door scrupulously shut upon her, wandered up and down the street for half an hour, returned a laggard to his palace— and yet had her full in vision. She possessed him until mass-time following: the same things happened. Guarino was hit hard; he took certain steps and got information which tallied with his better instincts. It guided also his subsequent efforts, for obviously the more direct remedies would not meet his case. Therefore, he wrote to the Countess, as you have seen. Her reply delighted him, and the rest was very easy. Borso signed the order of appointment, boggling only at her name. "Buonaroba I know," said he. "What am I to think of Bellaroba, Guarino?"

"Your Grace shall be pleased to think that his daughter has chosen her for her own person," said the Count.

"Hum," said Borso, and signed the parchment.

Then came another scrawl for "my love Angilotto," in which the miraculous news was told.

"Olimpia took it very ill," she wrote, "but the Signor Capitano talked her happier— at least, he stayed a long time. I hope you will think it all for the best. I am very good, and kiss you many times,

"Your BELAROBA."

Olimpia had indeed been very cross, as Captain Mosca would have testified. She had not, at any rate, talked *him* any happier: that he would have upheld with an oath. The experienced man knew the whip of sleet on his bare skin; but this was worse than any winter campaign; it left him dumb and without the little ease which shivering gives you. It had not been a question so much of talking as of keeping his feet. Olimpia, when the news came, had raged like a shrieking wind about the narrow house. "My dearest life! Soul of my soul!" was all the Captain had to fend the blast. It was no time for endearments— Olimpia raved herself still. Tears, floods of them, followed, whereat the Captain melted also and wept. He did foolishly. Demoniac gusts of laughing caught and flung him to the rafters, chill rages froze him where he fell. He lost his little store of wit, sagged like a broken sunflower, and was finally pelted from the door by a storm of Venetian curses, in which all his ancestors, himself, and any descendants he might dare to have, were heavily involved. Bellaroba, trembling in her bed, heard him go with a sinking heart. "Olimpia will come and murder me now," she said to herself.

But Olimpia slept long where she fell, and next morning decided to garner her rage.

VI

ENDS AND MEANS

"Amor che a null' amato amar perdona."

Bellaroba, who pleased the Countess, for the same reasons, no doubt, did not please the Count. It is possible to be too demure, and very little good to have domestic charm if you shut the door upon the amateur. Lionella had never had so much of her lord's society as during the month that followed her return to Ferrara. She did not complain of this; on the contrary, the more the maid held off and the man pursued, the more Lionella was entertained. Angioletto, invited to share her sport, proved dull. She confessed to more than one of her women (including Bellaroba) that if she had not been very much in love with the poet she would have thought him a fool. You see that she made no secret of her weakness. The fact is, she did not consider it a weakness; whereby you have this remarkable position of affairs at the Schifanoia, that Bellaroba was invited to be a student of her husband's amours, and he of hers. Considering the state of their secret hearts this might have led to matter of tragic concern; if they had loved less it would have done so. As it was, they were quite indifferent. Their hours were a series of breathless escapades— romance at fever heat. Stolen meetings before dawn among the dewy rose-bushes, chance touchings, chance kisses, embraces half tasted, and looks often crossed— of such were their days at the Schifanoia. Meantime a coiled ladder watched out the sun from a myrtle thicket, of which and its works came their happy nights. Then, as she lay in his arms, the Maid of Honour vanished in the child who was so lovely because she so loved; she could prattle, in the soft Venetian brogue, of boundless faith in her little lord, of her simple admiration of him and all he did, of her wonder and delight to be loved. She could tell him of what she could do, and of how much she could never do, to please him and pay him honour. And Angioletto would nod gravely at each point that she made, and kiss her now and then very softly to show her that he was perfectly satisfied. So soon as the first swallow twittered in the eaves, or the first pale line of light trembled at the casement, he had to fly. But he waited in the rosery till she came tiptoe out; and then the day's alarms and the day's delight began. Eh! It was a royal month, a honeymoon indeed!

But it could not last— barely saw its round of eight and twenty days. Lionella was a lady born, as it were, in the purple. Command sat lightly on her; she had never been disobeyed. She now grew querulous, exacting, suspicious, moody, sometimes petulant, sometimes beseeching. It gave Angioletto the deuce's own time now and then; but he might yet have weathered the rocks— for his tact was only equalled by his good temper— if the Countess had not precipitated matters. There came a day, and an hour of a day, when she spoke to him. She had spoken before; her ambitions had always been verbal— but now they were literal, all the "t's" were crossed. That was a moment for Angioletto to take with quick breath.

He took it so. Instead of hinting at his duty, or hers, he blundered out the fact that he did not love her.

"Dog," cried the Countess, "do you dare to tell me that?"

"Madama, I do indeed," he answered sadly, for he saw his house about his ears.

Lionella checked herself; she bit her lip, put her hands ostentatiously behind her back.

"You had better leave the house, Master Angioletto," said she drily, "before I go further and see to it."

He bowed himself out. Then he sought his poor Bellaroba, found her in the garden, drew her aside without trouble of a pretext, and told her the whole story.

"My lovely dear," he said, "I am a broken man. There has been a terrible scene with Madama, in which she got so much the worst of it that I was very triumphantly ruined. You behold me decked with the ashes of my scorched prosperity. What is to be done with you? For I must go."

"Oh, Angioletto," cried Bellaroba, trembling and catching at his breast, "won't you— can't you— ruin me too? Then we shall be happy again."

He pressed her to his heart. "Dearest dear," he said, half laughing, half sobbing, "you are quite ruined enough. Stay as you are. I will see you every night What! By the Mass, are you not my wife?"

"Of course I am, Angioletto. But nobody thinks so— not even any priest."

"Eh!" he cried, "but that is all the better. Only you and I and Madonna the Virgin of the Greeks know it. She never blabs secrets, and you dare not, and I can't. So you see it is well arranged."

She loved him most of all in this gay humour, and provoked him to new flights.

"But, you wild boy, how can you see me when you are ruined?" she asked, all her roses in flower at the fun of the thing. "How can you be in the Schifanoia if you are thrust out of it?"

Angioletto, with a mysterious air, kissed her for answer. "Leave that to me, my dear," he said. "Never have another of the maids to sleep with you, and lock your chamber door. Now I must go, because I am kicked out. Good-bye, my bride; I shall see you long before another dawn."

She let him go at last, and turned to her duties with less sighing than you would have supposed, and no tears at all. Her belief in the wisdom, audacity, and decision of her Angioletto was absolute. She had never known him to fail. Yet if she chanced to think of the towering Count Guarini plying her with flowers and sweatmeats, she shivered to remember her citadel naked of all defences. This made her feel homesick for her lover's arms. Like a sensible girl, therefore, she thought of the Count as little as possible; still less of another sinister apparition, that of the obsequious Captain Mosca, craning his lean neck round the corners of her vision, grinning from ear to ear.

Free of the Schifanoia (whose dust he was yet careful to keep upon his shoes for the sake of her it harboured), Angioletto walked briskly down the street, shaping his course for the Borgo. He had been rounding a plan even while he was announcing to Bellaroba that he had it cut and dried; and now he was to execute it. True, it was a little extravagant, depended too much, perhaps, upon other people's estimations of him tallying with his own; but you will have found out by this time that the youth was a realist. Ideas stood for things with him; and, as he said, if he could not make them stand so to his auditory he was no poet. This was a heresy he could not allow even supposititiously. The idea was excellent; the thing, therefore, no less. Therefore he concluded that he should not fail of his plan.

Beyond the Porta Angeli, in Borso's day, was to be found a huddle of tenements— fungus-growth upon the city wall— single-storied, single-roomed affairs, mostly the lodging of artificers in the lesser crafts. Among them all there was but one of two floors, a substantial red-brick little house with a most grandiloquent chimney-stack. And very rightly it was so, for it belonged to the Court chimney-sweep.

On this eventful noon Sor Beppo, the sweep, was sitting on his doorstep in the sun, eating an onion, one of many which reposed in a vinegar bath on his knees. He was quite black, save where a three-days beard lent a gleam of snow to chaps and chin; being toothless, he was an indifferent performer upon the onion. But his hearing was as keen as his eyesight. He caught Angioletto's vivacious heeltaps upon the flags, and peered from burly brows at the smart little gentleman, cloaked, feathered, and gaudy, who looked as suitable to his dusty surroundings as a red poppy to a rubbish heap.

Angioletto, stopping before him, took off his scarlet cap with a flourish.

"Well, young stabbing blade," said Beppo, "and who may you be?"

"Sir," replied the youth, "I am a poet." Beppo rubbed his shooting chin with a noise like the scraping of nutmegs.

"Well," said he, "I'll not deny that it's a trade, and a lawful trade; but for my part I sweep noblemen's chimneys and am proud of it. Shake hands, poet."

They shook hands, with great cordiality on the poet's part.

"Sit down, poet," said Beppo.

Angioletto sat on the doorstep beside him without a word.

"Will you have an onion, my friend?" the old fellow went on to ask.

"Thank you, Sor Beppo, but I have already dined. Let me rather talk to you while you finish your meal."

"It is not so much a meal as a relish," said the sweep. "But talk away— we'll never quarrel over terms."

"I hope not," Angioletto took him up; "because I have done with poetising and have a mind to try your trade."

Beppo, his mouth full of onion, paused in his bite to gape at this dapper page, who, all scarlet and white as he was, talked after such a fashion.

"How'll that be now?" he said. "You've never come all this way to crack a joke?"

"Ah, never in the world, my friend," cried Angioletto. "I am in earnest."

"You may be as earnest as a friar in the pulpit, and yet pretty bad at chimney-work, young master. What do you know of it, pray?"

"Nothing at all," replied Angioletto, as if that helped him.

"Look at that now," cried the triumphant Sor Beppo.

"Pardon me, Master Beppo," said the youth, "you cannot look at it yet, but you very soon shall. Have you a chimney to hand?"

"Ah, I might have that," the old man agreed, with a chuckle which ended as a snort. "There might be a chimney in my house that's not been swept for thirty year, having little time and less inclination to sweep 'em for nothing but glory. But, happen there were such a piece of work, what then?"

Angioletto pointed into the house. "Is that the chimney, Beppo?"

Beppo nodded. "That might be the chimney in question, my gentleman."

With a "By your leave, Sor Beppo," Angioletto stepped delicately into the room. He threw down cloak and cap, unstrapped girdle and hanger, stripped off his doublet, and stood up in shirt and breeches. Beppo watched him, all agape, too breathless to chew. Before he could interfere—

"By the Saints, but he's in!" he cried with arms thrown up. "Eh, master, come you back, come you back!"

"What do you want?" a muffled voice came from the chimney. Beppo sawed the air.

"Don't you play the fool up there, my boy, don't you do it! That's as foul as the grave, that chimney is. I'll have ye on my soul as long as I live, and I can ill afford it, for I've a queasy conscience in my black shell." He seemed to be treading on pins.

He was answered, "We will talk of your conscience and its shell when I come back. Take off my shoes, will you?"

A neat leg was pushed into the fireplace; then another. Beppo did the office, meek as an acolyte. Then he sighed, for the legs drew up the chimney and vanished in dust.

"There goes a lad of spirit to his gloomy end," murmured brokenly the sweep, as he looked at the little red shoes in his hand. "I would not have had that come to pass for twenty gold ducats. But, Lord! who'd 'a thought it of a Court spark, that he should be as good as his word? Not I, used to Courts as a man may be." He fell to scratching his head.

"Hey, hey!" he cried, as there was a prodigious scuffling up the chimney. "Now he strangles, now he strangles!" A shower of soot came down. Beppo flacked about the room; then two heavy objects fell. Beppo crept up. "Mary Virgin, he's killing birds," he said, in an awed whisper, and picked up two owls with wagging heads. The recesses of the chimney were still very lively. "Eh, there he is again," said the old sweep. "What now?" Down came a rat, squeaking for its life, then three in succession, very silent because their necks were wrung. "This is better than a cat any day of the seven," said Sor Beppo. "What a diamond of a poet! He should be crowned with laurel-twigs if I were Duke Borso in all his glory. Being but Beppo the sweep, he shall be free of my mystery the moment he's free of my chimney-stack."

He could await Angioletto's coming now with equal mind. The lad had approved himself. I leave you to judge of the welcome he got when, breathless, scratched, and sable as the night, he showed his white teeth at the door. Beppo, in fact, fell weeping on his neck. By this simple device Angioletto was enabled to keep his word, and Bellaroba to find him black but comely.

VII

THE CAPTAIN'S TREADINGS

While Angioletto and his Bellaroba dwelt in a paradise, none the less glorious for being as sooty as the darkness which veiled it, the estate of Captain Mosca, that hungry swordsman, was most unhappy. Divorced from bed and board, cast off by his mistress, and not yet adopted by his master, the poor man felt dimly about for supports, conscious that his treadings had well-nigh slipped. At such a time the gentle eyes of Bellaroba— nobody's enemy— courted him, like a beam of firelight on a rain-scoured street, with a smiling invitation to share the peace within doors. He hung uneasily about the gateways in these days, cold-elbowed by the lackeys, ignored by the higher sort, unseen by the quality; he burnished the lintels with his shoulder-blades, chewed many straws, counted the flagstones, knew the hours by the signals of his stomach. Then, if by hazard Bellaroba should come dancing by with a "Good morning, Signor Capitano," a "*Come sta?*" or, prettier still, a bright "*Sta bene?*" what wonder if the man of rage humbled himself before the little Maid of Honour? What wonder, again, if she, out of the overflowings of her happiness, should give him an alms?

No wonder at all, but pity there should be; for the Captain played an unworthy part. I suppose his standard was not very high. I know he was hungry; I know that nothing degrades a man so low as degradation— since what he believes himself, that he is; but I find it hard to excuse him for draining Bellaroba of her little secrets. Judas that he was, he took her sop, and then sold her for thirty pieces of silver.

The draining of a well so limpid was the easiest thing in the world. She was too absurdly happy, too triumphant altogether in the successful craft of her brilliant little lord, to be continent. She dealt in semi-transparent mystery with her manipulator from the moment he had won her compassion. Her secret was none from the first, or it was like the secret which a child will tell you, all the louder for being said in your ear.

"My dear little friend," said the smirking Captain, when he had it, "what you tell me there is as wine in my blood. I declare it sets me singing tunes."

"Ah, but he is wonderful, my Angioletto," said she, and her eyes grew larger for the thought of him.

"For a stripling of his inches he beats any cock that ever fought a main," Mosca declared; "blood of Blood, but he does! What and if he did square up to me— do I bear a grudge? Never, upon my body."

"You will not— you would not— ah, tell Olimpia of this, Signor Capitano?" she hazarded. The Captain stroked one eye with the back of his finger. He looked pityingly upon her with the other.

"Ah, my dear soul," he said, sighing, "could you think it of old Mosca?"

Bellaroba hastened to disclaim. "No, no, no, I did not think it, Signor Capitano. But for a minute I had a little fear. Olimpia never loved Angioletto at all, and I don't think she loves me very much— now."

"To be plain with you, my lamb," said the Mosca, "she has no such vasty love for me. I have not set foot within her door since a certain day you may remember."

The girl shivered. "If I remember it! Ah, Madonna delle Grazie, she had a devil that day!"

"She had seven, I'm sure of it," cried the Captain. "So I leave you to judge how much of your story she may worm out of me."

He so beamed upon her, kissed her hands with such a lofty stoop, that she felt ashamed of herself, and begged his pardon.

This brought the Captain to his knees. "By the God who made the Jews," he swore, "I leave not this raw flagstone till you have unsaid those words!"

In the end, after a prodigious fuss, he drifted away down the corridor and left her to go about her business.

But he drifted not very far. He felt himself full of affairs which were as meat and drink to his spirit starved by neglect. It was so great a thing to have a pretext for approaching Count Guarini. That young lord had a way like a keen-edged knife. You might weave a whole vestment about your errand, fold upon fold of ingenious surmise, argument *pro*, argument *con*; Guarino Guarini would dart eyes upon you— slash! he had rent your fabric and discovered you naked underneath, a liar ready for the whip. Nor, to do him justice, did he ever fail to apply it. Truth was, indeed, the only key to Guarino's chamber.

Truth, and timely truth, was what the Captain felt he had at last. With it he braved the supercilious doorkeeper; with it he forced the fellow to lift his intolerable eyelids.

"By the powers of darkness, my friend," he said, "it will be a bad day's work for you if you deny me this time." So he won his admission and faced his master.

"Now, Mosca, your lie," said the Count, with his cold-steel delivery. Mosca did not stumble.

"Master," he said, "I can do you service."

"Do it then," whipped in the Count.

"I can tell your Excellence why he succeeds no better with La Bellaroba."

"Ah!" The Count was suspicious, but interested.

"The little lady has a lover."

"Body of a dog!"

"Body of Angioletto, Excellence."

"Angioletto? That spaniel? How many more laps will he cradle in? Cut his tongue out, my good fellow, and then come to me again."

"Excellence, may I speak?"

"I suppose so. Speak."

The Captain waited no further invitation, but told the whole story from the beginning. Guarino thought upon it for a moment.

"He will come to-night?" he asked.

"Certain, Excellence."

"Then we have him. You have done well, Mosca— it was time, my friend, for you are an expensive hack to keep at grass. Now listen. Take Bellaroba away— command of the Contessa, of course. Take her to the little house in the Borgo. Make all fast, and return here in time for the steeple-jack. When you have him in the trap, run him through the body, raise the devil's uproar, and denounce him to the patrol. Do you understand me?"

"Perfectly, Excellence."

"Take my purse from the table and off with you then."

Captain Mosca bowed to the ground and backed out.

VIII

FIRST MIDNIGHT CONVERSATION

The Borgo of Borso's day was, as you might say, a sucker of the city of the Po, a flowery crop of villas and gardens about the city's root. There was the discreet house which Captain Mosca had once chosen for his Olimpia; there also was that which Guarino Guarini maintained for his (or any) Bellaroba. It is probable that there were many such houses in the Borgo; it was a very pleasant place, heavy scented with lilac and hawthorn in the spring, drowsy all the summer through with rustling leaves and the murmur of innumerable bees. The place was quiet; there was no traffic, no hint of the city bustle; on the other hand there was the notoriety which must always attach to any act done where no others are doing. Time, day-time especially, hangs heavy in the Borgo. One machinates in the face of many green shutters, which are not necessarily dead because they are shut.

This reasoning does not attack the sagacity of Count Guarini, for the only circumstance which could give it force was entirely unknown to him. He did not know that the Borgo held Bellaroba's friend, Olimpia, or that it sheltered under the same roof Olimpia, the Captain's enemy. He knew nothing of Bellaroba's friends and cared nothing for the Captain's enemies. But, as a matter of history, the proceedings of Mosca upon that eventful day were of the greatest possible interest to Signorina Castaneve. Donna Matura, trust her, had not failed to report his first appearance, stork-like, in the Borgo. No subsequent voyage of his into those parts (and he made many) was lost upon Olimpia. Captain Mosca, honest man, made a preposterous accomplice. His rusty cloak, the white of his observant eye, the craning of his neck, the very angle of his sword— cocked up for frolic like a wren's tail— spoke the profuse conspirator. He spent money liberally, seemed to have plenty more, had his finger to his nose with every other word. He brought a troop of underlings; a bevy of young women under his orders turned the little shuttered house out of doors— at every window carpets, curtains, hangings of all sorts, fluttered as if for a triumphal procession. Flowers came in stacks: "H'm!" said Olimpia, "there's a woman in this." A couple of asses brought skins of wine. "That will be wash for the lean hog himself," she added. From that time forth she never left her shutter. To make herself the more sure she gave orders to Donna Matura to close all the shutters alike. Captain Mosca, on one of his returns to the Borgo, looked up at the blind green eyes of his former haven and, chuckling, rubbed his hands. This artless outlet to his feelings was interpreted for what it was worth behind the shutter.

By six of the evening Mosca, seeing Olimpia's house still keep a dead face, threw off the last remnant of his cares and bade himself be merry. "My handsome friend is either asleep or on a journey, it appears," said he to himself. "That, on the whole, is well. I cannot think she would be pleased at the advent of little Bellaroba riding pillion to me. Still less would the honour about to be paid the young lady afford her any gratification. Least of all would her observations on the subject tend to clear the air. No, no. Everything is for the best, it seems, and the world still a tolerable place. Now for my little wood-bird." He paid and dismissed his work-people, then rode off himself to fetch Bellaroba. And Olimpia, from her shutter, watched him go.

There was no trouble on the child's score. The Countess was away; a feigned message from her was enough. Had she been at home and in a good humour, she would have accorded a real one, no doubt; so the deceit was quite harmless. Bellaroba demurred a little that she could not in person warn Angioletto, but the Captain begged her to have no fears. Time pressed; it was evident the Countess's service was urgent. Yet the Captain swore by all that he held sacred— to be sure no great things, but Bellaroba could not know that— to deliver her message to the lad with his own hand. "For," said he, and confirmed it with an oath, "if I don't see him this very night it will be a pity:" words which were afterwards thought to have been prophetic by the curious in such matters. So Bellaroba entrusted him with her scrawl to "My love Angilotto," and the Captain chewed and swallowed it when she was not looking. Then he lifted her to his horse and rode with her into the green-sheltered Borgo, just as it was settling into twilight. And Olimpia, from her shutter, saw them come.

I spare you the picture of her fury: it was not seemly, for all it was very white and still. The sight of a handsome girl shuddering in a cold stare under the grip of an evil spirit can never be pleasant; and where the experienced Donna Matura shrank from what she saw and heard, it becomes not me to tread. Donna Matura was of her country, that cheerful, laughing Midland of the Po, and neither felt the Venetian throb of pleasure nor conceived the excesses of Venetian pain. Extremes touch on the Lagoon. Donna Matura saw her gold-haired mistress white and drawn, saw her witless shaking, saw her tear and rend herself, heard her jerked words of loathing, blasphemy, and obscene defiance— and fairly fled the house. "For," as she said, "if words of man or woman could bring the rafters about our ears, or open a pit to send us lightly whither we all must go who have heard them, those words which Madam Olimpia spat about her must surely do it." So much she confessed to afterwards, but no more; for she stayed nothing more.

Olimpia may have leaned twisting against her wall for about an hour, mouthing insane babble from her blued lips. It was at least quite dark when she came to herself, lit the lamp, wiped the cold beads from her forehead, smoothed and bound her hair. She was not herself, nor looked to be so; she had a face completely colourless, lips like grey mould, and burning black eyes. But her hand was steady; she hardly winked; her breath, which came through her nose, was even, though it whistled rather sharply. Whatever she was about— and she seemed to be acting a part— she did with extraordinary care, down to the changing of her crimson dress for a dark green one. The former had been loose and clinging, made of velvet; the dark green was of cloth, fitted her close, and, as she ascertained by a few gestures, gave free play to her arms. She knocked off her heeled Venetian shoes, whose clatter was familiar to the house, and bound on flat-soled sandals instead. Over her head she had a black lace scarf, on her hands leather gauntlets. Lastly, she took from a press a long, double-edged knife, felt its temper, and stuck it inside her stocking, under the garter. She made a final hasty sweep of the room with her unquiet eyes as she went out of it.

The door of the house she knocked upon was opened by a page, who asked her business.

"Mosca, Captain Mosca, is my business," said she in a whisper.

"The Signor Capitano is occupied, Madonna," replied the boy.

"I know it, I know it," she answered. "But my business is the lady's business also. I must see them both— and at once. Let me pass."

The page vowed and swore by all the company of Heaven that those were her actual words. He was put to the torture and cried in the most heartrending manner; but he held to it, so long as he could hold to anything, that the visitor had said "her business was the other lady's business." What a further application of the question might have brought we cannot tell, since he fainted before it could be tried. "The boy Gasparo appeared to take no further interest in the elucidation of the truth," reported the judges, "and we recommend that he be chastised for contumacy." He was, at any rate, no witness of the scene which followed Olimpia's entry. There was that about her, a subdued haste, a deliberation, a kind of intensity got by rote, which fascinated the youngster and left him staring in the hall.

Olimpia walked across it alone, went straight to a door at the bottom on the right-hand side, turned the handle, and entered. There was a table spread with supper; there was Captain Mosca seated at it eating a peach from his wine-glass; there was Bellaroba, flushed and marred with tears, leaning against the further wall. She gave a little gasp of fear when she saw what the doorway framed; after that she followed Olimpia about the room with the same incurable fascination which the page-boy had felt. Olimpia shut the door as softly as she had opened it, and as softly shot the bolt.

Then it seemed that Mosca felt her presence, for he turned, saw, and jumped up with a cry mingled of fear and rage. It was found out afterwards that he was unarmed. This will explain his alarm. Disastrous honesty! his sword was upstairs in the bed.

There followed a most curious scene. The Captain stood up by the table and dogged Olimpia with his narrow eyes. When she advanced, he backed; when she stopped, he stopped. In this manner, eyeing each other without a blink, they made the round of the table. Bellaroba cowered by the wall; pursued and pursuer brushed against her in turn. She shivered and moaned a little at every touch; but they were too intent upon their game to know that she was there. In the second round, Mosca, who was again close to her, reached out his hand for a knife from the table. Quick as thought Olimpia was at him, reached across and drove her knife through his hand into the wood. Mosca howled, but his fear by now was such that he must be free to run as before, though he maimed himself. He tore his hand away and left Olimpia holding a fixed blade. She wrenched it out and made a pounce. The miserable Mosca turned to Bellaroba. He laid what he had left of hands upon her shoulders; he pulled her from the wall; he set her before him and hugged her close to his breast. Thus he made her back a shield against the long knife, and with her he fenced and held off his enemy for minutes more. Olimpia, horribly busy, scorched the girl's neck with her breath— but she never made to hurt her.

Then came the end. Olimpia made a lunge at his right side. The Captain hugged Bellaroba there. At the next moment the long knife was below his left arm, buried to the hilt, and defender and defence rolled heavily to the floor. Olimpia walked to the table and helped herself to the Captain's Val Pulicella.

· The watch (whom the page had roused after Mosca's first cry) broke in by the window, disentangled Bellaroba, bound the hands of both prisoners behind their backs, and marched them and the boy off to the Castle. Count Guarini, coming in an hour later, found his murdered lieutenant for his only guest.

IX

SECOND MIDNIGHT CONVERSATION

In that same night of mine and countermine Duke Borso, who had broken up the circle early by reason of his toothache, went wandering the long corridors of the Schifanoia under the sting of his scourge. He found his spacious pleasure-house valueless against that particular annoy, but (as always) he was the more whimsical for his affliction. Nothing works your genuine man of humour so nearly as himself. The sight of his own image, puffed and blinking in nightcap, bed-gown, and slippers, when he came upon it in a long mirror, set him chuckling. He paused before the absurd epitome to apostrophise, wagged a finger at it, and got wag for wag. "We might be two drolls in a pantomime!" said he to his double. "Your arm, gossip:" he crooked an elbow. "It seems," he continued, "that we are both sufferers, my poor fellow! Magnificence goes drooping; a swollen estate does not forbid a jowl of the same proportions; and give me leave to tell you, brother, that we have each of us been better dressed in our day. Fie, what a pair of quills below your gown; and what a sorry diadem to stand for two duchies and a marquisate of uncertain age! Duke and my brother, if we were to be spied upon by any of our Court just now, what sort of a reverence should we get, think you? Eh, you rogue, as much as we deserve! I will tell you, good Borso, my own poor opinion of these things. A Duke who cannot be dukely in his shirt, a Pope who is but an afflicted biped between the blankets, is no Duke at all, is a Pope by toleration. There should be some such test at every crowning of our sort. Souse a Bishop in his bath before you let him warm his chair; cry 'Fire!' on the stairs of the Vatican and watch your Pontiff-elect scudding over the Piazza in his sark, before the Conclave sing *Veni Creator*. Judge of your Emperor with a swollen nose, blacken your Dukes in the eye: if they remain Dukes and Emperors you may safely obey them. They are men, Borso, they are men! Yes, you spindle-shanked rascal, you may well wince. Do you ponder how you would stand assay? So do I ponder it, brother, and doubt horribly." He clapped his hand to his face. "Steady now, steady, here comes another bout. Ah, Madonna of the Este— but this is a shrewd twinge! Fare you well, brother Fat-chops. I must walk this devil out of me." He waved a hand to his brother of the looking-glass and slippered away, groaning and sniggering to himself. So he walked and was philosophical till two of the morning. At that hour he was ready to drop with fatigue; but his pains had left him. "I will sleep, by the grace of Heaven," he said. He plumped down in the embrasure of a door, prepared to follow his humour: the door yielded and he with it. "Who am I to outrage a lady's chamber?" he muttered, half asleep. "To be sure she seems to invite me. Let us look at this complaisant sleeper." He went into the room. A glimmering lamp burned before a shrine, enough to show him to a decent four-post bed, empty. "By the great god Pan!" cried Borso, "my luck holds. Courage! I am not a Duke for nothing, then." He shut and bolted the door, slipped into the bed and was asleep in three minutes. It was twenty minutes after two.

At the stroke of three, with a scarcely perceptible rustling, Angioletto slid down the chimney and stepped into the room. He carefully brushed himself with a brush which hung by the hearth. The chimney was by now thoroughly clean, however. He next washed his face and hands, undressed, and crept softly to the bed. Very quietly he inserted himself between the sheets, very softly kissed the shoulder of the sleeper; very soon he was as sound as his bedfellow.

The Duke awoke, as his habit was, with the first light, and saw the curly head on the pillow beside him. He whistled softly to himself.

"Now, by the tears of the Virgin," said he, "how did this lady come in? It would be as well to know it, since plainly I must go out." He sat up in bed, clasped his knees, and frowned a little. "It is clean against the traditions of my house," he ruminated, "but I think I will go. And the sooner the better."

Suiting action to word, he had one foot on the floor when Angioletto, with a long sigh, opened his eyes, turned over, and saw him.

"The devil!" said Duke Borso.

"Madonna," was his second venture, when he had recognised the impropriety of his first, "Madonna, I am this moment about to retire-"

Angioletto, whose eyes had attained their fullest stretch of wonder, opened his mouth— but not to speak. He gaped at the lord of the land.

"Madonna— " Borso began once more. Then the other found his voice—

"Alas, my lord Duke, it is Madonna I thought to find. Where is my wife?"

That was Borso's cue to stare.

"Your wife?" he cried, "your wife! Heaven above us, man, why the devil should your wife be in my bed?"

Angioletto, with the deepest respect always, suffered a smile to play askew about his lips.

"Alas, Magnificence," he said, "if I dared I would ask him, why the devil he should be in my wife's bed?"

It was the youth's way to preface his audacities by the assurance that he dared not utter them. But the retort pleased Borso. His eyes began to twinkle.

"Look ye, young gentleman," said he, suppressing his wish to chuckle, "if this is your wife's bed, I am sorry for you, for I give you my word she has not been in it to-night. But I confess I should like to know why your wife has a bed in my house."

Angioletto nodded gravely.

"I should be the last person to deny your Grace's right to all information. Bellaroba is my dear wife's name, her country is Venice, her duties are to be about Madama Lionella's person. My own duties are to be about hers, so far as I may."

"Fair and softly, my friend," said the Duke, "not so fast, if you please. Do you know that Maids of Honour may not marry without permission, and, in any case, may not be visited by their husbands during their service?"

"Magnificence, she was not married without permission. Or rather, she was married before permission was needed."

"Eh, how may that be now?" said Borso, tucking in his chin. "Did she come here as Signora Qualcosa?"

"She came here as Bellaroba, Magnificence. No one knows of our marriage but your Grace and the Holy Virgin."

"Then you are not married, but should be. That is your meaning— eh?"

"Ah, by Heaven, Magnificence," cried Angioletto, "we are the most married couple in the world!"

"H'm," was all Borso had to say to that. "And who made her of Madama's Court?"

"It was your Grace."

"Oh, of course, of course, man! But why the deuce did I do it?"

"It was at the request of Count Guarino Guarini, Magnificence?"

"Eh, eh! now I recollect. Ah, to be sure! That must be a very agreeable reflection for you at this moment, my friend," he said, with a sly look.

Angioletto took the equivoque with dignity, "I have perfect confidence in my wife, my lord Duke."

Borso shrugged. "Well, it is your affair— not mine," he said. Then he changed his tone. "I think, however, we will come back to what is my affair as well as yours. Be so good as to tell me how you came here."

"I came down the chimney," said Angioletto calmly. "I am by calling a chimney-sweep."

"Upon my word," Borso said, "this is a fine story I am piecing together! How long have you been of that trade, pray?"

Angioletto received this shot with firmness, even dignity. "I was formerly a poet attached to the Court, Magnificence. But when Madama turned me away it became necessary that I should see my young wife; so I became a chimney-sweep for the purpose."

The Duke's mouth twitched too much for his own dignity. He pulled the bedclothes up to his nose, therefore, before he asked—

"Why did Madama turn you away, sir?"

Angioletto, for the first time, was confused. He hung his head.

"I hope your Grace will not insist upon an answer," he replied in a troubled voice.

Borso looked keenly at him for a time. "No, I think I will not," said he. "Are you the lad who sang me the *Caccia col falcone*?"

"The same, my lord Duke."

"I thought so. Now, sir, to come back to this performance of yours, which I suppose is not the first by any means— eh?"

"It appears to be the last, my lord," said Angioletto ruefully.

"I think it is the last," replied the Duke; "for I hope you understand that I can have you clapped into gaol for it."

"Pardon, Magnificence— he can do more. He can have me hanged for it."

"I don't agree with you," said Borso. "If my name were Ferdinand of Arragon, or Sforza, or della Rovere, yes; but being Borso d'Este, no."

"Your Grace puts me to shame," said Angioletto, with feeling. "I am to take it then— "

"You shall take it as you please, my friend," Borso rejoined, with his chin once more upon his clasped knees. "For my part I propose to take *you* and keep you under lock and key for a season— as at present advised."

Angioletto bowed, as well as one may who is sitting up in a very soft bed. His voice was quite meek.

"I shall in all duty obey your Grace's directions, and will leave behind me but one small request, which I am persuaded Borso d'Este will not refuse his prisoner."

"And what is that, my good friend?"

"It is the care for the person and honour of my wife, my lord Duke," answered Angioletto.

This set Borso rubbing his nose. He thought before he spoke again.

"As for your wife's person, my man," said he, "it will be as safe in my dominions as all persons, whatever their ages or conditions. Her honour is another affair. That is neither for me nor my laws, but for herself. And perhaps you will let me add that if to-night is a sample of her course of living, you are putting upon me a rather onerous charge."

"My Lord, my Lord," cried Angioletto here, "I will answer for my wife's honour with my last drop of blood. It is her person I cannot answer for if I am in prison."

"I have told you that I will answer for her person, master poet. I would much rather leave her honour to you and your drops of blood. So you may go to the Castle with a clear mind. To the Castle, moreover, you shall undoubtedly go, if it is only to teach you that the possession of a wife is no passport to other men's chimneys. First, however, I will ask you to do me a small service, which is to go to my bedchamber and send me my gentlemen, my dresser, and my clothes. I am, you perceive, entirely at your mercy. You will follow these persons back to me here, and will then give yourself up as I shall direct."

Angioletto, out of bed by this time, knelt to the Duke's hand.

"I am your Grace's servant," said he. He hastily dressed himself and went about the business he was bidden on.

"Madam the Virgin," said Borso, with a half-laugh, "that is a fine young man! If he had not made so free with my chimneys I would advance him. Advanced he shall be!" he cried out after a while. "Zounds! has not Guarino made free with his wife? Eh, but I fear it." He shook his nightcap at the thought. "A couple of days' reflection in a half light will do the lad no harm. He'll dream of his wife, or compose me some songs. Bellaroba, he called her. I remember the jade— a de- mure, rosy-cheeked little cat, for ever twiddling her fingers or her apron-ends. Those sleek ones are the worst. Poor boy! I'll advance him. He shall be librarian, go secretary to Rome or Florence. I'll have him about my own person. By the Sons of Heaven, but he's as good as gold! Ah, I hear him."

The Duke's gentlemen bowed themselves into the room, followed by the dresser.

"Good morning, my friends," said Borso. "But where is my mes- senger?"

"Magnificence, he is at the door," said the usher.

"Bring him in, Foppa, bring him in," cried the Duke; "we know each other by now."

Angioletto was introduced.

"Master Angioletto," the twinkling old tyrant said, "get you down-stairs to the Captain of the Archers. Say to him as follows: 'Captain, my lord the Duke begs you to conduct me surely to the Castle, and keep me prisoner there during his Grace's pleasure.' Will you oblige me so far?"

"I shall obey you exactly, my lord Duke," said Angioletto, making a reverence.

He went at once and gave himself up. In some quarter of an hour's time he was lodged in the Castle, in a cell upon the level of the moat. Next door to him on either side (though he knew nothing of it) were two women who had been brought in with a page-boy over night upon a charge of murder. Their case, indeed, was one of the first matters which engaged the attention of Duke Borso after mass.

X

ORDEAL BY ROPE

The prison chills made Olimpia shiver, the prison silences made her afraid. The wavering moan of the page-boy, who had been tumbled on to a straw bed after his first bout of the question, drove home the reality of her situation, and made her sick. Olimpia was one of your snug pretty women; she loved to be warmed, coaxed, petted; liked her bed, her fire; liked sweetmeats, and to see people about her go smiling. Mostly, too, she had had her way in these matters, for she was a beautiful creature, smooth and handsome as a Persian cat. Jealousy, on this account, was a new experience; she had never suffered it before, did not realise it now. Besides, it was over; she had killed her faithless lover. But the dark, the cold, the silence, the calm enmity of the dim walls—these were but an intensification of familiar discomforts. She had always been afraid of the dark, often cold, often quelled by quiet, made sullen by indifference. She hated all this, and felt it all, in spite of the glory of the Captain's killing. It seemed more awful now, more unendurable than ever, because— she knew there was no good disguising it— because it stood for something else. Ah, ah! she was in danger. So sure as she thought of this, Olimpia's heart stood still, and then suddenly throbbed as if it must break. It surged up into her throat. Her tongue clove to her palate, she felt the bristling of her flesh, could hear her heart quite loud making double knocks at her side. The page-boy moaned to himself through it all; a rat hidden somewhere bore him company by scratching most diligently at the brickwork. She could not hear anything of Bellaroba— the only familiar thing in this vast black horror. The panic gained upon her till her head swam in it. She could not die! Ah, never, never, never, by Christ on His throne!

The sickening futility of that final word, Never, in the face of the dead certainty announced by the inexorable walls, served to make the wretch's case the more desperate. Panic, chalk-white, staring panic-fear, swallowed her up: the next few hours flew by as minutes, while she was cowering and gibbering in a corner. Before the inevitable you either resign or rave yourself mad— there is no middle course. Bellaroba took the first. Sitting in her cell with her cheek pressed against the wall which (though she knew it not) penned also her Angioletto, she never opened her eyes, nor cried, nor moaned; but where she settled herself at her entry there she was found when they came to hale her to the judgment. She gave no trouble, made no sign; but she let down her hair to cover her bare neck, and if she blushed it was that folks should see her blood-smirched evening finery by the light of day. She was a very decent girl always, and this seemed to her horrible even in a pit of horrors. Olimpia, clinging to life, was driven upon the second course. It took two halberdiers to hold her up.

Borso had before him the deposition of the page-boy and the report of the watch. From the words of the first he suspected that both women were concerned— until he had heard the second. This was to the effect that the Captain's head had been cut off.

"No, no," said Borso to himself, "I am heartily sorry for my young friend the chimney-sweeping poet, but I can't think him a fool. He would never have married a woman who could cut off a man's head. Yet stay! It may be that she floored the Captain and that the other rounded off the job with that gratuitous touch. She— that other— was eating walnuts when the watch came, I gather. She could have cut a dead man's head off, never doubt it. Well, let us see, let us see."

Then it was that he gave the order: "Bring the two women before me."

He did justice ever in the open. A broad green field outside one of the gates served him for court. Two gibbets and an open pit stood for the terror of the law; he himself, on a gilt chair under a canopy, for the majesty of it. The day was bright, breezy, and white-clouded. The poplars twinkled innumerably, the long Este gonfalon flacked and strained in the wind. Spectators with soldiery to hedge them kept a wide square about the plain. From their side the figures in the midst— the red, gold, and white about the pavilion, the steel of the soldiers, the drooping women between them— were about as real as a handful of marionettes. It seemed impossible such puppets could decide issues of life and death. But the red hangman and his machines were grim touches for a puppet-show.

Olimpia Castaneve was brought forward first. She was more composed by now— the air, the sun, the cheerful colours of the court, had warmed her. She stood alone facing Borso. He, at first glance, remembered every shred of her; but he betrayed nothing. There was no one more blankly cool in this world than Borso on the judgment-seat.

"What is your name, mistress?"

"Magnificence, I am well known in Ferrara."

"Your name," thundered the Duke, "by the face of the sky!"

"Olimpia Castaneve."

"Did you cut off the head of the Captain of Lances, who was called Il Mosca?"

Olimpia was looking very handsome, and knew it.

"Magnificence," she said, "my hand is on my heart." It was.

"What the devil has that got to do with it?" asked Borso, looking about him for a reason.

"Serenity, if my heart were guilty, it would burn my hand. If my hand were red, it would soil my heart."

"Pouf!" said Borso, and puckered his face. "Stand back, Castaneve. Now for the little one. How are you called, baggage?"

Bellaroba shivered a very little, and looked solemn.

"Bellaroba, my lord."

"Very pretty; but I must have more."

"There is no more, my lord. I am wife of Angioletto."

"Well, well. I know Master Angioletto, and he me. We'll have him here, I think. Hi, you!" said he, turning to an officer of his guards. "Go and fetch the chimney-sweep."

Ten minutes passed; then Angioletto came up between a detachment of men, unbound. He was not observed to falter throughout his course over the broad field; but his eyes were fever bright and colour noticeably high. Bellaroba did not look up at him; her eyelids fluttered, but she kept her head hung, and as for her blushes they were curtained by her long hair. He, on the contrary, directly he had bent his knee to the Duke, turned to where she stood, and, in face of the whole city, put his arms about her, and found a way to kiss her cheek. The broad ring of onlookers wavered; the twitches played like summer lightning over Borso's face.

"Come here, Angioletto," he said. Angioletto drew near the throne.

"You see now, my friend," the Duke continued in a low voice, "what may happen to one's wife if she keeps not her bed o' nights. A certain Captain Mosca has been stabbed. More than that, his head was attacked when he had ceased to take any interest in it, and cut off. I ask no words from you, no comments, no adjurations, for you are a prejudiced party. Your wife and this other woman between them have done the Captain's business. Mine is to find out how. Stand aside now and listen."

Angioletto started, opened his mouth to speak— but the Duke put up his hand. "Young man," said he sternly, "I am Duke of Ferrara, and you are my prisoner. Be good enough to remember that."

Angioletto hung his head. Borso turned again to Bellaroba, but kept the other in his eye.

"Now, missy, what had you to do with Captain Mosca's headpiece?"

"Nothing, my lord."

"What!" he roared. "Did you not cut it off?"

"No, my lord."

"Why not, girl? He was your enemy, I suppose?"

"I think he was, my lord."

"Think! Do you not know it? What did he want of you?"

"He wanted to make me bad, my lord."

"Ah! So you stabbed him, eh?"

"No, my lord."

"Come now, come now, girl. Look at your frock."

She did look and was silent.

"Well!" Borso continued, after a sharp glance at Angioletto. "Did your husband cut it off?"

"No, my lord, he wasn't there— but— "

"Well— but what?"

"He would have killed him, my lord."

"Oh, the devil he would! Why?"

"Because he loves me, my lord."

"H'm. Well, Miss Bellaroba, where's your hand?"

She held it out. "Here, sir."

"What a little one! Well, put it on your heart. Now, how does it feel?"

"It jumps, my lord."

"Does it burn you, child?"

"No, my lord; it's quite cold."

"Stand down, Bellaroba. Castaneve, come forward."

His face just now was a sight to be seen— crumpled, infinitely prim, crow-footed like an ivied wall; but extraordinarily wise; with that tempered resolve which says, "I know Evil and I know Good, and dare be just to either." He was thinking profoundly; every one could see it. Best of the company before him Angioletto, the little Tuscan, read his thought. His own was, "Unless I fear Justice I need not fear Borso. Dante saw the death of his lady to be just. Courage then!"

"Mistress Castaneve," said Duke Borso, "you declare yourself innocent?"

"Excellency, I do, I do! Ah, Mother of God!" The panic was creeping up Olimpia's legs, to loosen the joints of her knees.

The Judge turned half. "Mistress Bellaroba, you also declare yourself innocent?"

"Yes, my lord," she said.

"Diavolo!" muttered Angioletto, "he is not 'my lord'; he is 'Magnificence.' I must scold her for this afterwards."

"The position of affairs is this," said the Duke, aloud. "One of these prisoners is guilty of the deed, and the guilty one is the liar. Now, I will not put an innocent person to death if I can avoid it; and I will not put these women to the question, because I should wring a confession of guilt from each, and be no more certain than I was before. I may have my own opinion, and may have proved it on various grounds. That again, I do not care to obtrude. I do not see that I can better the precedent set me by a very wise man and patriarch, King Solomon of Zion. Let the women judge each other. My judgment is that the innocent of these two shall hang the guilty."

The bystanders were silent, till one man shivered. The shiver swept lightly through the company like a wind in the reeds, and ran wider and wider till it stirred the farthest edge of the field. All eyes were upon the prisoners. Borso's blinked from below his shaggy brows, young Teofilo Calcagnini's were misty, Angioletto's hard and bright. Bellaroba had been motionless throughout, except when her lips moved to speak; she was motionless now. But Olimpia was panting. The unearthly quiet was only broken by that short sound for ten minutes.

"Bellaroba," then said the Duke, "what say you? You declare that you are innocent. Will you hang the guilty and go free?"

For the first time she looked up, but not at her judge. It was at Angioletto she looked, Angioletto at her.

"No, my lord, I cannot," said Bellaroba in the hush. The wind shivered the reeds again, then fainted down.

"Castaneve," said the dry voice, "what say you? You declare that you are innocent. Will you hang the guilty and go free?"

The drowning Olimpia threw up her hands to clutch at this plank in the sea-swirl. Free! O God! The word turned her.

"Magnificence, I must, I must, I must!" She wailed, and fell a heap to the ground. Bellaroba covered her eyes. Teofilo Calcagnini shook the tears from his. Borso sat on immovably, working his jaws.

It is at this point that the conduct of Angioletto touches the sublime— a position never accorded by posterity to his verse. It proves him, nevertheless, the greater artist to this extent, that he was equally the slave of the Idea, though working in more intractable stuff: himself, namely; his own little heart throbbing in his own young body. Therefore he deserves well of posterity, which finds his verses thin. Said Angioletto: "Yes, Bellaroba is my adorable wife, loved beyond all women, deserving beyond all price. Yet if she killed the Captain she is guilty of death, and the sentence is just whoever perform it. And if, being guiltless, she is hanged by the guilty, the action will glorify her; for it is the price she pays for clean hands."

Then, in the midst of that waiting assembly, he called the girl to him by her name, took her face in both his hands and kissed it very tenderly, smiling all the time through his quick tears.

"My dear little heart," said he, "your husband is proud of you. All that you have done is admirable in this black business. In a very short time I shall see you again. Though it is a higher flight than the Schifanoia chimney, it is quicker done. Trust me, Bellaroba; you know I have never failed you yet."

He could say no more, but took her in his arms and held her there, speechless as he was with inspiration. She, seeming to burn in the fire that consumed him, lay quite still, neither sobbing any more, nor shivering. So they clung together for a little. Then Angioletto lifted up his face from her cheek, and put her gently away from him.

"Let justice be done, Excellency," he called out in his shrill boy's voice, "we have said our say to each other."

Borso spoke.

"Justice shall be done. The innocent has condemned the guilty: let that woman be hanged. We have learned the value of clean hands this day. Mistress Bellaroba, you have a man in ten thousand; Angioletto, my friend, you have what you deserve, a woman in ten million. It is not fair that the worth of you two should be known only to me and the Blessed Virgin; you shall tell it now to a priest. Come along, and let me have the whole story with my breakfast."

Thus Duke Borso did judgment for his good town of Ferrara in times very remote from our own. The Ferrarese used to say that it needs a sound lawyer to know how to break the laws.

THE END

HISTORICAL CONTEXT

During the period this book was originally written, the world was a very different place. The events of the time produced an impact on the authorship, style, and content of this work. In order for you the reader to better appreciate and connect with this book, it is therefore important to have some context on world events during this timeframe. To this end, we have included a detailed events calendar for the 19th century for your reference.

Please give consideration in particular to the era around *1899*, the year in which this work was first published.

Disclaimer: Some scenes throughout history may not be suitable for children, for example, in relation to war or violence. Please use your own discretion before reading this section to your child or allowing your child to read it.

1801 Britain unified Ireland as a single monarchy. Dublin's parliament has been demolished. Ireland's official church will be the Anglican Church. No Catholics are permitted to hold public office.

1802 The British signed the Treaty of Amiens with France.

1804 The Royal College of Surgeons of London was founded.

1805 Napoleon was crowned in Milan. He intended to invade the United Kingdom. A French armada sails north to the Spanish town of Cadiz. Napoleon dispatched French and Spanish ships from Cadiz to attack the British. At Trafalgar, the British defeat Napoleon, foiling his invasion plot. The Lewis and Clark Expedition, led by Meriwether Lewis and William Clark, became the first Americans to cross the west when they reached the Pacific Ocean.

1806 Lewis and Clark find a skeleton of a 105' blue whale near Cannon Beach, Oregon.

1807 The US Congress bans the slave trade within the US and the British Parliament abolishes the slave trade throughout the British Empire with a penalty of £120 per slave introduced for ship captains.

1808 Napoleon intervenes between King Charles IV of Spain and his son Ferdinand and imprisons them both promoting his brother Joseph to the throne of Spain from the Kingdom of Naples. Spaniards despise French troops and Napoleonic meddling. In Spain, a barbaric battle erupts, with Napoleon, as usual, oblivious to human emotions. Portugal becomes a participant in the anti-French uprising. British troops are dispatched to assist the resistance. Napoleon's demise commences.

1809 Sweden relinquishes Finland to Russia as a Grand Duchy. Russians returning from California erected a fort in Honolulu and attempt to establish a settlement on Kauai.

1810 The British frigate HMS Minotaur sinks killing 480 people. The United States annexes West Florida from Spain.

1811 Outside of New Orleans, slave plantations are aware of Haiti's victorious slave revolt (1791-1804). On January 8, between 200 and 500 slaves from a variety of plantations in the New Orleans area band together to revolt against their masters. They murder for the sake of liberty. The slaves were defeated in a musket duel and as a lesson to other slaves, their heads were displayed on pikes.

1812 An earthquake measuring 7.7 on the Richter scale destroys 90% of Caracas, Venezuela, and kills 15,000-20,000 people.

1813 Napoleon's invasion of Russia affected Russia's ability to aid its Orthodox Christian Serbs in their revolt against Ottoman rule. Albanian forces looted Serb towns as the empire swept towards insurgent Serb territories.

1814 Napoleon was exiled to the island of Elba, located off the west coast of Italy, in the Tyrrhenian Sea. During this time, the victorious nations and France agreed to sign another Treaty of Paris. The Congress of Vienna brought together Napoleon's conquerors to forge a stable Europe.

1815 Mount Tambora in the Indonesian Archipelago began a week of eruptions. Its stratospheric detritus reduces solar radiation. September in the Northern Hemisphere is characterized by cloudy days. Crops fail and cattle perish across the majority of the Northern Hemisphere as a result of the famine. Napoleon enters Paris after escaping from Elba and begins a stretch of a 100-day rule.

1816 The Dutch regain Suriname from the French after the defeat of Napoleon.

1817 José de San Martín leads a revolutionary army over the Andes to attack Spanish royalists in Chile. In England, 60,000 people gather in a field to demand universal suffrage. In the US, the New York Stock Exchange is founded.

1820 a gang of revolutionaries in England assassinate government cabinet officials in order to spark an uprising known as the Conspiracy on Cato Street. One of them was a police officer. Others attempted to discredit legislative reform through the plot. The conspirators were convicted, and five were hanged and then beheaded, marking the end of England's decapitations.

1821 Michael Faraday, the son of a blacksmith, defied aristocratic expectations to become a physicist at the Royal Institution. His electromagnetism research lays the groundwork for electric motors and contributes to modern physics' "field theory," which contains the formula $E = MC2$.

1822 French scholar Jean-François Champollion deciphered Egyptian hieroglyphics using the Rosetta Stone.

1823 Austria, Russia, and Prussia dispatched French troops to Spain in order to crush the liberal movement and re-establish Ferdinand VII's authority. Ferdinand launched a vengeance-killing spree against his supporters.

1824 In the United Kingdom, the Royal Society for the Prevention of Cruelty to Animals is founded.

1824 Louis XVIII died and was succeeded by his conservative brother Charles X.

1825 Portugal acknowledges the Independence of Brazil.

1826 Siam and Britain sign a trade and peace treaty. Previous presidents Thomas Jefferson and John Adams both die on the 50th anniversary of the Declaration of Independence, President John Quincy Adams refers to this as "visible and palpable remarks of Divine Favor"

1827 Britain, Russia, and France declare their independence from Austria over the Greek independence struggle, with Russia desiring to protect Orthodox Christians. At Navarino Bay on the western coast of the Peloponnesian Peninsula, a combined British, French, and Russian force sinks an Egyptian and Turkish fleet.

1828 Noah Webster published the first American Dictionary.

1829 Robert Peel introduces the Metropolitan Police Act of 1829 into Parliament to establish a unified police force for London marking the world's 1st modern police force.

1830 US President Andrew Jackson signs the Indian Removal Act, a key law leading to the forced removal of the Cherokee, Chickasaw, Choctaw, Creek, and Seminole tribes out of Georgia and surrounding states, setting the stage for the Cherokee Trail of Tears

1831 On the Italian peninsula, the papal states underwent revolutions. Pope Gregory XVI expresses opposition to all forms of democracy and makes an appeal to Austria. Austrian troops march across the peninsula, crushing uprisings.

1832 The Reform Act is passed by the British Parliament under Charles Grey's leadership, changing the electoral system in England and Wales and increasing the electorate from approximately 500,000 to 813,000 voters.

1833 In Japan, excessive rain causes crop failures and the Tempo famine. (About fifty years prior, Japan suffered a famine.) Prosperity ebbs and flows. Three years later, the famine would kill 300,000 people.

1834 The British government agrees to compensate slave owners under the 1834 Abolition Slavery Act. Numerous slaves were emancipated in Canada. The remaining 781,000 slaves were freed, but no claims for compensation were made.

1835 The United Kingdom and Spain renew their anti-slavery pact. Spanish slavers suspected of being involved in human trafficking were to be brought before mixed commissions in Sierra Leone and Havana. The US national debt is $0 for the first and only time in history.

1836 During the Battle of the Alamo 1,500-3,000 Mexican soldiers overwhelm the Texan supporters, killing 182-257 Texans including William Travis, Jim Bowie, and Davy Crockett

1837 Canada gives its black citizens the right to vote. New York City banks fail, and unemployment reaches record levels resulting in the causing panic.1838 Cells were a point of contention for scientists in

1838 Cell theory is on the verge of becoming the fundamental unit of life. A devastating fire destroys half of Charleston

1839 The Edict of Toleration, issued by King Kamehameha III of Hawaii, allows Roman Catholics on the islands to freely practice their religion.

1840 In his book *Chemistry in Its Application to Agriculture and Physiology*, Justus Liebig discussed agriculture and physiology. This will transform agriculture and pave the way for further industrialization advances.

1841 Naval cannons began firing non-explosive cannonballs. A French time-delay system enabled the safe discharge of explosive shells by high-powered flat-trajectory cannons. They will be available to all three fleets by the end of the decade. The US Supreme Court rules that the kidnapped slaves from the Spanish schooner the Amistad are free.

1842 John Francis makes an attempt to assassinate Queen Victoria.

1844 Australia's "Protection of Children Act" permitted Church missionaries to abduct indigenous children in order to "civilize."

1845 Mold can survive due to the increased speed with which potatoes are transported from the Americas to Europe. Crop failures were reported across Europe, including Ireland, as a result of the mold.

1846 A conflict begins over the disputed border of Texas, prompting the Mexican–American War.

1847 The manuscripts of Emily Brontë's "Wuthering Heights" and Anne Brontë's "Agnes Grey" were sent to the publisher T.C. Newby and were published later that same year.

1848 Niagara Falls stops running for 30 hours due to an ice obstruction.

1849 Abraham Lincoln applies for a patent (and is the only US president to do so) for a device to lift a boat over shoals and impediments.

1850 The Taiping Rebellion was commanded by Hong Xiuquan, an ethnic Hakka (a Han subgroup) and the self-proclaimed brother of Jesus Christ.

1851 Thousands of prospectors, including Chinese and Californians, sought gold in Australia. Tent cities with a population of 40,000 people popped up. The long-reviled Window Tax is abolished in the United Kingdom.

1852 Louis-Napoleon (the nephew of Napoleon Bonaparte) consolidates conservative support and dissolves parliament. A coup is put down and a dictatorship is established. He is elected by peasants and religious believers.

1853 US President Franklin Pierce signs the Gadsden Purchase, acquiring 29,670 square miles (76,800 square km) from Mexico for $10 million (now southern Arizona and New Mexico.)

1854 Great Britain and France declare war on Russia, intensifying the Crimean War.

1855 An earthquake, a tsunami, and a fire wreaked havoc on the majority of Edo (Tokyo).

1856 The Russian Empire, the Ottoman Empire, Great Britain, France and the Kingdom of Sardinia sign the Treaty of Paris which brings the Crimean War to an end.

1857 Gustave Flaubert's *Madame Bovary* is partially published in France. It's about an unfaithful woman who becomes embroiled in a scandal. Flaubert must file a lawsuit in order to have his complete work published.

1858 Pencils with an attached eraser are patented. Minnesota is admitted as the 32nd US state.

1859 In October 1859, John Brown led a raid on the federal armory at Harpers Ferry, Virginia (today West Virginia), aiming to start a slave liberation movement. Brown was tried for treason against the Commonwealth of Virginia for the murder of five men, as well as inciting a slave insurrection. He was found guilty of all charges and was hanged on December 2, 1859, he was the first person executed for treason in the history of the United States.

Charles Darwin sat on his *Origin of Species* for 21 years and finally made it public.

According to British scientist John Tyndall, CO2 and water vapor trap heat in the atmosphere. And he said changing gas concentrations may cause climate change.

1860 In America, George Crum invented the potato chip. He started a restaurant with a basket of potato chips on each table.

1861 Abraham Lincoln is inaugurated as the 16th President of the United States. On April 12, 1861, Confederate troops fired on Fort Sumter in South Carolina's Charleston Harbor and less than 34 hours later, Union forces surrendered, marking the beginning of the Civil War.

1862 Victor Hugo's historical masterpiece *Les Misérables* is published. It's about the 1830 Paris uprising against King Charles X. The ten-part series was a great seller in Europe and North America. Crowds at bookstores were quelled by cops.

1863 Abraham Lincoln issues the Emancipation Proclamation to free slaves in US confederate states.

1864 Ulysses S. Grant is appointed commander of the Union Army. General Ulysses S. Grant's Union Army at Potomac attacks Robert E. Lee's Confederates at Rappahannock River.

1865 President Abraham Lincoln is assassinated.

1866 A lone Russian student attempts to kill Tsar Alexander II. The state turns against all pupils. A new education minister tightens regulations on institutions.

1867 The US purchases Alaska from Russia for $7,200,000, about 2 cents an acre.

1868 The U.S. Constitution's 14th Amendment is ratified stating: All persons born or naturalized in the United States and subject to the jurisdiction thereof, are citizens of the United States and of the State wherein they reside. No State shall make or enforce any law which shall abridge the privileges or immunities of citizens of the United States; nor shall any State deprive any person of life, liberty, or property, without due process of law; nor deny to any person within its jurisdiction the equal protection of the laws.

1869 The National Woman Suffrage Association originates in New York, founded by Susan B. Anthony and Elizabeth Cady Stanton.

1870 The 15th Amendment to the US constitution is adopted, guaranteeing the right to vote regardless of race.

1871 Journalist Henry Morton Stanley begins his famed expedition to Africa.

1872 Jesse James' gang robs a bank of $1,500 in Columbia, Kentucky. Yellowstone becomes the world's 1st national park.

1873 Japan's envoy to Europe and America returns optimistic about Japan's development. The Meiji administration removes Confucianism as the official state philosophy.

1874 Britain establishes a colony 62 miles deep and 250 miles broad in what is now Ghana. During combat, a British commander ordered his soldiers to wear brown jackets and khaki pants instead of the typical red coats.

The U.S. government had assured the Sioux that the Black Hills would be theirs forever.

1876 Conservatives took power in former Confederate states and were operating "redeemed" governments. These regimes were designing sophisticated vote boxes, literacy exams, and poll charges to limit black voting.

1877 The U.S. economy was in a slump, and worker unrest swept the country. Three million males, or around 27% of working-age men, were unemployed. San Francisco is enraged by affluent Chinese hiring. Denis Kearney, a prominent orator, is chanting "The Chinese must leave."

1878 The British, angry with Russia's southerly advance, sing "We don't want to war, but by jingo if we do, we've got the ships, the soldiers, and the money!"

1879 Frank W. Woolworth founded the first American five and dime stores with the idea of purchasing items directly from the source and setting the items at fixed prices. The idea of fixed prices eliminated the need to haggle.

1880 After many unsuccessful assassination attempts, radicals fail again, blowing up the tsar's dining room, killing eleven and injuring 56. The tsar was late. Many members of the radical group "Will of the People" were arrested, nearly destroying it.

1881 On July 2, 1881, a dissatisfied aspirant shoots President James Garfield. Doctors keep poking their fingers into the gunshot wound, creating an infection. Garfield dies 9/19.

1882 Alexander III blames Jews for Christ's death. Jew-hatred spreads over Russia's dominion.

1884 With 2,500 women and children, sick, and injured, the British army oversees the Egyptian evacuation from Khartoum. Muhammad Ahmad's troop encircles.

1885 King Leopold II of Belgium establishes the Congo as a personal colonial possession. The Berlin Conference gives Congo to Belgium and Nigeria to Great Britain.

1886 After a four-year hunt, American forces capture Geronimo.

1887 Anne Sullivan starts teaching 6 year old blind-deaf Helen Keller. The Yellow River or Huáng Hé floods in China, killing between 900,000 and 2 million people, becoming one of the deadliest natural disasters in history.

1890 Idaho became the 43rd state. Wyoming gains statehood despite allowing women to vote. Wyoming joins the union.

1891 The Social Democratic Party of Germany advocates for an eight-hour workday, a ban on child labor under the age of 14, government regulation of working conditions, the repeal of laws restricting the right to assemble, secret ballot voting for judges, an end to laws that disadvantage women, a graduated income and property tax, free medical care, a people's militia for defense, and secularization.

1892 Ellis Island opens as a US immigration inspection station becoming the gateway to the US for more than 12 million people.

1893 New Zealand becomes the first country to give all women the right to vote.

1894 Alexander III died at the age of forty-nine, leaving twenty-six-year-old Nicholas as Emperor of Russia. At the coronation festivities, a stampede caused the deaths of nearly 1,400 people.

1895 Oscar Wilde's play the "Ideal Husband" premieres in London.

1896 A tsunami strikes a Shinto festival on beach at Sanriku, Japan killing 27,000, injuring 9,000 and destroying 13,000 homes.

1897 Wademar Haffkine, a Ukranian bacteriologist, performs the first human trial for a vaccine for the plague on himself during the Bombay epidemic.

1898 Spain declares war after rejecting the US ultimatum to withdraw from Cuba sparking the Spanish-American War.

1899 Cuba is liberated from Spanish rule by the US and American occupation continues until 1902.

1900 The Boxer Rebellion began as an uprising against foreigners that occurred in China about 1900. It was started by peasants but was eventually supported by the government. The Boxers were a Chinese secret society that embarked on a violent campaign to drive all foreigners from China. Several countries sent troops to halt the attacks. The U.S., Japan, and Europe sent troops to China to rescue civilians and put down the Boxer Rebellion. Angry troops march across Beijing, assaulting anyone they believe to be Boxers and end up harming and looting innocent Chinese.

A billion people in 1800 are now 1.7 billion in 1900.

This concludes the historical context.

Thank you for your interest in our publications. Please don't forget to check out our other books and leave a review if you enjoyed this book.